"Final word: Christian fiction with a powerful kick."   —Afro.com

Praise for *Lady Jasmine*

"She's back! Jasmine has wrecked havoc in three VCM novels, including *Too Little, Too Late*. In *Lady Jasmine* the schemer everyone loves to loathe breaks several commandments by the third chapter."   —*Essence*

"Jasmine is the kind of character who doesn't sit comfortably on a page. She's the kind who jumps inside a reader's head, runs around, and stirs up trouble—the kind who stays with the reader long after the last page is turned."   —*The Huntsville Times* (Alabama)

Praise for *Too Little, Too Late*

"[In this book] there are so many hidden messages about love, life, faith, and forgiveness. Murray's vividness of faith is inspirational."
        —*The Clarion-Ledger* (Jackson, Mississippi)

"An excellent entry in the Jasmine Larson Bush Christian Lit saga; perhaps the best so far . . . Fans will appreciate this fine tale. . . . A well-written, intense drama."   —*Midwest Book Review*

Praise for *The Ex Files*

"The engrossing transitions the women go through make compelling reading. . . . Murray's vivid portrait of how faith can move mountains and heal relationships should inspire."   —*Publishers Weekly*

"Reminds you of things that women will do if their hearts are broken. . . . Once you pick this book up, you will not put it down."
        —UrbanReviews.com

Praise for *A Sin and a Shame*

"Riveting, emotionally charged, and spiritually deep . . . What is admirable is the author's ability to hold the reader in suspense until the very last paragraph of the novel! *A Sin and a Shame* is a must read. . . . Truly a story to be enjoyed and pondered upon!" —RomanceInColor.com

"*A Sin and a Shame* is Victoria Christopher Murray at her best. . . . A page-turner that I couldn't put down as I was too eager to see what scandalous thing Jasmine would do next. And to watch Jasmine's spiritual growth was a testament to Victoria's talents. An engrossing tale of how God's grace covers us all. I absolutely loved this book!"

—ReShonda Tate Billingsley, *Essence* bestselling author
of *I Know I've Been Changed*

Also by Victoria Christopher Murray

Never Say Never

Victoria Christopher Murray

A TOUCHSTONE BOOK
Published by Simon & Schuster
New York London Toronto Sydney New Delhi

Touchstone
A Division of Simon & Schuster, Inc.
1230 Avenue of the Americas
New York, NY 10020

TOUCHSTONE and colophon are registered trademarks of Simon & Schuster, Inc.

Designed by Aline C. Pace

Manufactured in the United States of America

ISBN 978-1-62490-432-5

Never Say Never

The beginning . . .

I never meant to fall in love with my best friend's husband.

I mean, who does that? Truly, that is the plotline of some dying soap opera or supermarket romance novel. This kind of thing never happens in real life. Women aren't that scandalous.

At least that's what I thought—until it happened to me.

It wasn't like I planned it, though I know that's no excuse. All I can say is that what happened to me was about situations and circumstances; it was the wrong man at the right time.

That's how it is sometimes, you know? Sometimes, Mars aligns with Venus, the stars set in the sky in a certain formation, the cow jumps over the moon, and *bam!* You're in the middle of your best friend's marriage.

I don't mean to sound like I'm making light of this whole situation. Because trust me, this was a sad state of affairs where people were hurt and hearts were broken. Even now, just remembering it all makes me sick, but not in the way you think. I'm sick with love. I have never loved a man the way I loved him.

I know that there are women—and men—who are ready to condemn me to death row, but the thing is, many of those who sit in judgment of me would've done the exact same thing, in the exact same way, if they'd been in the exact same place.

But you know what? There really isn't any way to convince you; I need to show you, tell you every detail. Then, after you know how it went down, you can decide: would you or wouldn't you?

So, this is my story . . . well, not mine alone. This is the story of Emily Harrington-Taylor and Miriam Williams. And this is how it all began . . .

Miriam Williams

We were just three best friends doing what we always did. Three best friends having our monthly get-together on the second Tuesday of the month—lunch at Roscoe's Chicken 'N Waffles.

We'd been doing this for twelve years, since we graduated from USC. But today, we'd changed it up a bit. Today, instead of driving over to Hollywood and meeting at the Roscoe's on Gower, we decided to check out the new one closer to my home, the one on Manchester.

Maybe that was a sign. Maybe if we'd kept everything the same, the world wouldn't have changed. Maybe if we'd been in Hollywood, Michellelee wouldn't have gotten that call just as I was stuffing that first sugary bite of a waffle into my mouth.

We'd been talking and laughing—or rather Michellelee and Emily had been doing all the talking, and as usual, I was just laughing.

Then Michellelee's BlackBerry vibrated on the table.

I glanced at Emily and we rolled our eyes together. There was hardly a time when our celebrity friend wasn't called away from one of our lunches. That's just how it was for one of the most recognizable faces in Los Angeles. As the evening anchor for KABC, Michellelee, who had combined her first name, Michelle, with her last name, Lee, and was now known by just one name, had one of the top ten news jobs in the country, even though we were just a little more than a decade out of school.

"You know she's going to have to rush out of here," Emily said to me.

I nodded, but then frowned when I looked back at Michellelee. Our friend wasn't talking, she was just listening, which was the first sign that something was wrong. My heart was pounding already. Today was Tuesday, September 11, and for the last ten years, on this date, I was always on edge.

"Okay, I'm on my way," she said. "I'll call from the car."

She clicked off the phone, and when she looked at me and Emily, I swear, there were tears in her eyes.

"There's been a fire . . ."

Emily and I both sat up straight.

Michellelee said, "At that new charter school on Western."

"That would be Chauncey's firehouse," I breathed.

"Jamal's there today, too," Emily said, as if she needed to remind me that her husband worked with mine.

I hardly recognized Emily's voice, so different from the glee that was inside her a few minutes ago.

Emily asked Michellelee, "What else did they tell you?"

Michellelee shook her head. "No names. But more than twenty children were taken to the hospital." Then her eyes moved between me and Emily. "And three firefighters were rushed to the hospital as well."

"Oh, no," I moaned, and Emily took my hand.

"Don't go there," Michellelee said, moving straight into her elder role. She was the oldest of the three of us, even if only by nineteen days. "This doesn't mean that any are your husbands. Let's not start worrying."

"I've got to get over there." Emily said what I was thinking.

Michellelee nodded. "We'll take one car; I'll drive." She scooted her chair away from the table and marched toward the hostess stand to pay the bill.

It took me and Emily a couple of seconds to follow, as if our brains were just a little behind. Finally, we jumped up and grabbed our purses and sweaters, leaving our half-eaten dishes right there on the table.

Now, sitting in the backseat of Michellelee's Mercedes, I could feel every bump on Manchester as we sped down the boulevard. My eyes were closed, but I didn't need to see Michellelee. I could imagine her—her camera-ready, perfectly plucked and arched eyebrows were probably knitted together, causing deep lines in her forehead.

Then there was Emily. I couldn't picture her expression, though I'm sure it was a lot like mine, a face frozen with fear. Every few seconds, I heard Emily sigh right before she said, "I can't reach Jamal." I stopped counting after she said that for the fifth time.

I wasn't even going to try to call my husband. It would be futile, especially if they were in the midst of a fire. Cell phones never left the firehouse.

But even when Chauncey was at work I didn't call. I never called because if I ever started, I'd never stop. I'd call every fifteen minutes for my own peace. So he called me. Like he'd just done a little over an hour ago, as I was pulling into Roscoe's parking lot to have lunch with my girls. He'd called just to tell me that he loved me.

It sounded like command central in the front of the car, with Emily and Michellelee doing what they did best: taking control. So

I did what I knew: I took my cares to God. I prayed like my life depended on it. Because it did. There was no way I'd survive if anything happened to Chauncey.

I didn't pray for my husband alone; I prayed for Jamal, too, because if anything happened to him, my heart would still be broken. Jamal was Chauncey's best friend, but he was dear to me also. I'd known him almost as long as I'd known Chauncey; I couldn't imagine our lives—and definitely not Emily's life—without him.

So I kept my eyes closed and my lips moving like I'd done so often over the years. My husband was living the firefighter's life that he'd dreamed of as a child, but his dreams were my nightmares. The way he earned his living had me on my knees every time he walked out the door. The daily stress was so much that I'd once asked myself if I should've married him. I had started thinking that maybe it would've been better if I'd never fully loved him than to love him with everything I had . . . and lose him one day.

But my bone-deep love for Chauncey trumped my fears, and really, I'm glad about it. Because truly, it would've been impossible to walk away from that man and it would've been a travesty to miss out on all these years of love.

For a moment, I let those years flash like cards through my mind. From the time I first saw Chauncey when he was a counselor in my Upward Bound program, to the birth of each of our three sons, to when he kissed me good-bye this morning and every second in between.

The memories made me tremble. The memories made me pray.

But then, in an instant, something washed over me. A calm that was so complete. It was almost as if Chauncey was there, wrapping his arms around me. I reveled in that space, knowing for sure that my prayers had been answered. After some seconds ticked by, I breathed. It was clear: Chauncey was fine.

But my heart still pounded, now for Jamal. I didn't have that same peace about my best friend's husband, and that made me sick.

I shook my head. Why was I allowing all of this into my mind? There were fifteen firefighters on duty at any one time. Plus, for a fire like this, other stations would be called in. The firefighters who were hurt didn't even have to be from Fire Station 32.

So I turned my focus back to God. I went back into prayer, crying out in my soul. I started praying for Jamal especially, but also for everyone who'd been at that school.

It felt like I'd only been praying for a minute when the car slowed down and I opened my eyes.

"Okay." Michellelee eased to a stop in front of Centinela Hospital. "I'm gonna park, but you two get in there."

I wasn't sure Emily had heard a word that Michellelee said, because she was out and just about through the front door of the hospital before the car was in park. I jumped out and rushed behind Emily, though it was impossible for me to keep up with my friend's long strides. I'd expected her longer-than-shoulder-length hair to be flying behind her, Sarah-Jessica-Parker-*Sex-and-the-City* style. But she'd twisted her curly hair into a bun and I hadn't even noticed when she'd done that.

"We're here about the fire at the school," Emily said to the woman at the information desk. "Has the room been set up?"

Emily spoke as someone who'd been through this kind of tragedy. Of course, she had. As a child-life psychologist, she was always in schools, and hospitals, and community centers helping children navigate through adversity.

Even with her slight Southern drawl, her words and her tone were professional, but I could hear the tremor in her voice. The woman didn't notice it; she wouldn't, it was so slight. But I heard the shaking, sure that I would sound worse if I'd been able to speak.

"Are you one of the family members?" the woman asked.

Emily said, "I'm a child psychologist," as if those words alone were enough to give her a pass.

She was right. The woman nodded and pointed toward the elevators. "On the second floor." She peered at us with sad eyes. "Room two-eleven."

As we marched toward the elevator banks, Emily explained, "Whenever something like this happens, the hospitals set up a room." She pressed the elevator button over and over as if that would make it come faster. "It gives the hospital administrators a central place." When the doors opened, we rushed inside and Emily continued, "Now, when we get up there, we'll probably see some of the parents of the children and maybe even family members of the firemen."

I nodded and breathed, relieved. It sounded as if Emily didn't think Jamal or Chauncey was one of the injured. Maybe God had told her what He'd told me. Maybe both of our husbands were fine. And if that was the case, then I didn't need to be here; I wanted to go home.

But I didn't say that to Emily as we rode in the elevator, and then, once again, I was running behind her, taking four steps to her two as we strode down the hall. By the time we found the room, I was huffing and puffing.

She pushed the door open and I heard the collective intake of air. Every man, every woman, held their breath as the door opened wider. All eyes were on Emily as if they expected her to say something.

It was the way she looked; on the one hand, with her long blonde hair and sea-blue eyes, Emily was the walking definition of what America called beautiful. But her manner and authority were beyond that. She stood, back straight, shoulders squared, eyes wide open and direct. She carried herself as if she knew everything.

Emily held up her hand in a little wave, letting everyone know that she was just one of them.

I wasn't sure if anyone in the room noticed me, but that was the way it always was when I was with Emily and Michellelee. At five two, I was at least seven inches shorter than both of them. By nature, I just didn't stand out.

Not that I wanted to stand out today, especially not in this small room, with about two dozen blue chairs pressed against the stark, hospital-white walls. There were two more rows of chairs in the center.

My eyes searched for a familiar face; I expected to see at least one of the many firemen's wives that I'd met over the years. But through the sea of black and white and Hispanic faces, I saw no one that I knew.

"Has anyone been in here to talk to you?" Emily whispered to an African American couple who sat by the door, holding hands.

The man glanced up and nodded. "Just to tell us they were getting the identities of the children who'd been hurt and then the ones who . . ." He stopped right there, and shook his head. "None of us know anything."

I got that feeling again; I wanted to go home. I wanted to wait for Chauncey there. Tonight, he'd fill me in. It would be late when he got home, but I would wait up and then he'd tell me all that had happened. We'd grieve together. At home. Together. Away from all of this. Together.

"Emily, I'm going to go—" But before she could even turn to face me, the door swung open, and now we were just like everyone else. We inhaled and focused on the three men who entered, all wearing hospital scrubs.

"We're looking for the parents of Claudia Baldwin, Kim Thomas . . ."

Each time a name was called, someone leaped from their seat and the air thickened with grief.

The family members were escorted out, but before the doctor who had been calling names could turn away, the man sitting by the door jumped up. "What about our daughter? LaTrisha Miller?"

"We'll be back in a few minutes," the doctor said in a voice that I was sure was meant to be compassionate, but sounded curt, sounded tired. "We'll let everyone know as soon as we can."

That was not enough for Emily. She marched behind the doctor into the hallway, and I was right with her. Stopping him, she said, "Excuse me; I'm Doctor Harrington-Taylor and I'm here to check on my husband. He's a firefighter and I don't know if he's here for sure, but I think he was at the school."

"Oh," the doctor said, looking from Emily to me. "Were you called?"

And then there was a wail. A screech, really, that was so sharp, it sliced my heart.

All three of us turned our eyes toward the sound that came from behind a closed door marked "Quiet Room."

It took a few seconds for Emily to compose herself and get back to her business. "No, we weren't called," she said. "We heard . . . about the fire." She paused and turned to me before adding, "Our husbands were probably at the school. My husband is Jamal Taylor and hers is Chauncey Williams."

The doctor repeated their names and nodded. "I'll see what I can find out, Doctor Harrington," and then he rushed away.

That's exactly what I wanted to do, rush away and go home. My eyes were on the door of the Quiet Room as I said, "Listen, Emily. I'm going to—"

"Emily! Miriam!"

We both turned as Michellelee hurried toward us. "I went to the school, but Cynthia was already set up," she said, referring to another reporter from her station. "So I told them that I would see what was happening over here." She looked at Emily and then at me. "Have you heard anything?"

Only Emily responded. "Nothing yet. What did you find out?"

It was the way that Michellelee lowered her eyes and shook her head that made me want to cover my ears.

"All I know is that there were a lot of casualties."

I did everything I could to keep my eyes away from Emily. I didn't want her to see what I was thinking; I was so afraid for her husband.

"Okay," Emily said, her drawl more pronounced, showing me just how scared she really was. "That's horrible, but it doesn't mean that it's Jamal or Chauncey." She nodded as if that motion was helping her to stay composed.

I knew that I needed to stay right here, at the hospital with Emily. But more than needing to be here, I needed to go home. I had to get myself together so that I could be strong for Emily if it came to her needing me. I wouldn't be able to be strong if I stayed here in front of this Quiet Room.

"Listen." The word squeaked out of me. "I'm going to—"

"Emily!"

The three of us swung around, at first standing there in shock. Jamal ran toward us, but we were still frozen; at least, Michellelee and I were.

Emily shrieked and then made a mad dash for Jamal, although that's not really how it felt to me. This was playing out like one of those Hallmark commercials where the lovers race toward each other in slow motion.

I watched my best friend wrap her arms around her husband before Jamal swept her from the floor and into his arms.

"Oh, my God," Emily said. "Thank God."

Finally, I found my legs and rushed over to Jamal. "I'm so glad you're all right," I said.

It must've been the sound of my voice that made him open his eyes. Slowly. Emily slid down his body and Jamal faced me. The tears in his eyes made me frown.

"What's wrong?" I asked. "Were you hurt?"

"Are one of you Mrs. Williams?" someone asked over my shoulder. "The wife of Chauncey Williams."

But before I had a chance to turn around, Jamal whispered my name. "Miriam."

It was the way he said it that stopped me cold. "What?"

"Miriam," he said again, this time shaking his head, this time releasing a single tear from the corner of his eye.

My heart started pounding before my brain connected to what was happening.

"Mrs. Williams."

This time, I turned to face the voice. "Yes," I whispered.

"I'm Doctor Adams. Would you mind coming with me, please?"

"Where?" It was hard for me to speak through lips that were suddenly too dry.

"Over here." The doctor pointed across the hall. To the Quiet Room.

I shook my head. "I'm not going in there." Turning back to Jamal, I said, "Please. Please. Where's Chauncey?"

His eyes drooped with sadness as he shook his head again.

"Is Chauncey back at the fire station?" I cried.

"Mrs. Williams."

The doctor called my name at the same time Jamal said, "Miriam. I am so, so sorry."

I felt Michellelee's arm go around me. I heard Emily's sob as she took my hand.

But it wasn't until the doctor began, "Mrs. Williams, I'm sorry to have to tell you this but . . ." that I understood.

"No!" I heard a scream so sharp that I knew it couldn't have come from me, even though it rang in my ears. "No." I released my pain again.

Jamal stepped to me. "Miriam, I'm so sorry. But Chauncey . . . he died."

That was when my world ended. Because just like I said, if Chauncey was gone, then I'd have to go, too. So right there, I let it go. My whole world stopped. I just let it all fade to black.

2

Emily Harrington-Taylor

The bedroom was almost midnight dark, even though the sun still shone outside. But I'd closed the mini-blinds and drawn the drapes, wanting to give Miriam complete rest since I wasn't sure when she'd sleep again. I was pretty sure the only reason she was sleeping now was because of total shock. My hope was that she wouldn't wake up for days so that she wouldn't have to face this.

I shifted in the worn, oversized chair, keeping my eyes on my best friend. Well, I couldn't exactly see her, at least not well. But my eyes had adjusted to the darkness and I could make out her form on the bed. For just a moment, I closed my eyes, trying again to pray, but the burning behind my lids from unshed tears made me open them quickly.

Still, I whispered, "Thank you, God," and like before, guilt struck me like lightning.

How could I thank God for saving Jamal when Chauncey was gone?

I moaned, then covered my lips. But then I realized that the sound hadn't come from me. Another moan; I jumped up and in three strides I was standing at the edge of the bed.

"Miriam," I whispered, just in case she was still asleep.

Slowly she rolled over and I turned on the nightstand lamp. As

I sat on the edge of the bed, I could see the confusion in Miriam's reddened eyes.

"Em?" Then she glanced over her shoulder. "Where's Chauncey?"

At first I paused, not quite sure of what to say. But before I had to figure it out, I saw the memory of the tragedy flood Miriam's eyes and her tears flowed right away.

"Oh, God!" she sobbed. "I was hoping this had just been a nightmare."

"I know," was the only thing I could think to say.

"Em, how am I supposed to do this? To live without Chauncey? What are the boys and I going to do?"

Too many questions, and no answers. So, I did the only thing I could. I pulled Miriam into my arms and held her as she cried. And I cried with her.

The door to her bedroom opened and over Miriam's shoulder, I saw Michellelee tiptoeing in. But once she saw me holding Miriam, she rushed over, jumped onto the bed, and wrapped her arms around both of us.

Michellelee and I were a human ball of protection around Miriam, a wall of Ralph Lauren pants and St. John's skirts, but even though we held her as tightly as we could, it wasn't enough. I knew it wasn't enough because it wouldn't have been enough for me. Nothing would be enough if I were to ever lose Jamal.

After a while, Miriam inhaled a deep breath and Michellelee and I pulled back. But not too much, because if she started crying again, I wanted to be right there.

"This doesn't even feel real," Miriam said.

"I know." Michellelee reached for Miriam's hand. "It doesn't feel real to me either."

I took Miriam's other hand, but said nothing. Not that I had to; we were all so close that most of the time, no words were needed.

"Oh, God!" Miriam said suddenly and swung her legs over the side of the bed.

"What's wrong?" Michellelee and I spoke at the same time.

"I've got to get the boys."

"Jamal went to get them, remember?" I said.

Her brows bunched together, and then she nodded. "I guess I forgot. I'm a bit confused."

If it had been me, I would've been a lot more than confused. I ran my hand over Miriam's hair, which had been smoothed back into a bun, exposing the patch of white hair along the left side of her forehead.

"What am I going to tell them?" Miriam whispered, and her tone let me know that new tears weren't far away.

"Don't worry," I said. "We're going to help you. Jamal and I."

"And me," Michellelee piped in.

Miriam nodded. "Okay." She paused. "But I still don't know what we're going to say. Especially to Junior. He was Chauncey's shadow, you know." She sobbed. "He wanted to grow up to be just like his dad."

I leaned forward to let Miriam fall against me once again.

Michellelee said, "Miriam, please don't cry," even though tears were streaking down her cheeks. "We're here. Remember, we're the Red, White, and Blue," she added, referring to the name some guy had given us at a frat party our sophomore year. The guy was drunk and the name had stuck.

Miriam sniffed and looked from me to Michellelee. "We've been through a lot together."

"We have," I said.

Miriam said, "I've known you guys half my life. And you've always been there for me."

"Just like you've always been there for us," I said.

"Well . . . not always." Miriam looked down and away from me.

"That was a long time ago," I said, knowing exactly what Miriam was talking about. The thing that almost made me quit our friendship. When she had lost her mind when I told her that I was interested in Jamal.

But even though we'd come close to turning from friends to enemies, we'd worked through it, exactly the way women who were meant to be best friends for life were supposed to.

"Yeah, and we've had a lot more ups than downs," Michellelee said, wanting to shift the conversation away from bad memories.

"Yes," I said. "We graduated together."

"And started our careers together," Michellelee added.

"Or in my case," Miriam said, "started my family." She shook her head. "You guys were always there."

"That's what sisters are for," Michellelee and I said together.

After a moment of silence, I said, "We've done everything together, so we're not going to leave you now, Miriam. You can count on us."

There was a quick knock on the door and Jamal stepped in. I breathed deeply, with relief, wondering if I would do that every time I saw my husband. Though I always knew Jamal's job put him in daily danger, that was never my concern. I'd decided long ago that there were only two things I could do about my husband's job: I could worry or I could pray. I wasn't going to waste my time doing both. So I'd chosen prayer, believing that involving God was far better for my soul and my sanity. Once that decision was made, every day I would send up a prayer of protection when Jamal left home and then give a prayer of thanksgiving when he returned twenty-four hours later.

But now, seeing Jamal, and experiencing that deep feeling of relief, made me wonder if my heart had changed. Would I now be filled with fear?

"Hey," Jamal said, looking at me with a slight smile, like he was glad to see me, too. He hugged me, though our embrace lasted for only a second. Then he squeezed Michellelee's hand before he knelt in front of Miriam. "The boys are here," he said softly.

Miriam asked, "Did you tell them?"

There was a bit of hope in Miriam's voice. As if she hoped Jamal had already delivered the news.

"No." He shook his head. "I thought you'd want to do that." Then he rephrased his words. "I thought you should be the one . . . to tell them."

Miriam nodded. "But . . . I don't know how . . ."

Before she could finish, Jamal took her hands in his. "We're here, we'll tell them together."

"You'll stay?"

The hope, the doubt, the fear, the pain that was all wrapped together in those two words broke my heart into a million little pieces.

"Of course," Jamal said, then he glanced over his shoulder at me and I nodded.

"Thank you," she said. "I couldn't do this by myself."

"Don't worry," Jamal said. "It'll be—" He stopped short of saying it would be fine, then added, "We're all here for you." Jamal rose to his feet. "I'm going to get back out there. The boys think I picked them up because their dad had to work an extra shift."

"Okay. I need a minute to make sure that I don't bust out crying the moment I see them."

"Take your time." Jamal moved toward the door.

"I'm going with you," Michellelee said. "I'll see if the boys want a snack or something."

"That's a good idea," Miriam said. "Thanks."

"Right after that, though, I have to leave. I have to get to the studio." Her apology was inside her tone. "Is that okay?"

"Of course," Miriam said. "You have to go to work. Life goes on . . . right?"

Michellelee hugged her.

"Are you going to be reporting on the fire?" Miriam asked.

She nodded. "It's the lead story. But I'll come right back here after I get off." Michellelee rubbed Miriam's back for an extra moment, then hugged me before she followed Jamal out of the bedroom.

I waited until the door was closed before I told Miriam, "You can do this. And it's okay if you cry."

"I have to be strong for the boys. They're going to be devastated."

"I know. But like Jamal said, he and I and Michellelee will be here for you and the boys. And you know, our pastor will be here, and Chauncey's family, and so many other people who love you and the boys."

Miriam's brown eyes were glassy, but even behind her tears, I saw her relief. As if she was just beginning to understand that she was not alone. "Okay. I can do this."

I reached for her hand and helped her stand. She swayed just a bit, as if she wasn't standing on solid ground. I tightened my grasp. "I got you," I whispered.

"Thank you." Then after taking just two steps, she turned and hugged me, wrapping her arms around my waist since I was so much taller than she was. "I love you, Em," she said.

Okay, that was it. I wasn't going to make it. All I wanted to do was sit right there in the middle of the bedroom and bawl like a baby. But I blinked rapidly, to keep back my tears and hold back my grief. "I love you, too, Miriam. Jamal and I love you and the boys. And we're here with you. Forever."

"Forever," she whispered as she stepped away from our embrace.

"Forever," I repeated, and then added, "No matter what."

When the edges of Miriam's lips twitched into the smallest of smiles, I told her, "I promise." Then, I took her hand and led her out of the bedroom.

3

MIRIAM

When people looked at Emily, Michellelee, and me, no one ever said that I was the prettiest; that was a toss-up between Emily and Michellelee. Or that I was the smartest, another toss-up that probably didn't include me. I'm not putting myself down, I'm just being honest. I know my weaknesses, but I also know my strengths. And one of my strengths, one thing that I could do better than Emily and Michellelee: I could act my butt off.

I'd been part of the Black Thespians at USC and always received resounding ovations at the end of my performances. Whether I was Lady Macbeth during our summer Shakespeare festivals or Dorothy in our own rendition of *The Wiz*, I was respected by the audiences and by my peers.

So many told me that I should take my dreams and my skills to Hollywood, though I never took them seriously. I mean, yeah, I was talented enough, but Hollywood had little to do with talent. It was all about how you looked. Not only am I African American, I am a short, stocky black girl who is a realist. There was no place for me in that superficial industry and I wasn't about to go on auditions and get my feelings hurt.

But today, at this moment, I was using every bit of the talent I had as I faced my sons.

"Mom, where were you?" my youngest son, Stevie, said as I stepped into the kitchen.

"Uncle Jamal told you she was taking a nap," Mikey, my middle child, answered before I could say a word.

Stevie glared at his brother before he turned to me. "You were sleeping in the middle of the day?"

"That's what a nap is, dummy!"

I was just about to scold Mikey, but Jamal jumped in.

"Hey, Mikey, you're the big bro, remember? Remember what I told you? You don't want to talk to your brother like that."

Mikey poked out his bottom lip and even though he sat at the table all the way across the room, I could see his long lashes as he lowered his eyes. The kind of eyelashes that women paid for. Eyelashes just like his father's.

A sob rose up in me, but I held it back as I took in all of my sons. My two youngest boys sat at the kitchen table with their schoolbooks and an opened package of graham crackers in front of them, while Junior (who hadn't looked up yet) sat at one of the barstools at the counter.

The scene unfolded like just another ordinary end-of-school day. This was what it would look like when Chauncey picked up the boys and then sat with them as they did their homework.

It wasn't until I saw Jamal staring at me that I realized that my bottom lip was trembling. I sucked it between my teeth, but I couldn't stop the rest of my body from shaking.

"Uh, boys," Jamal said, though his eyes stayed on me. "Can you come with me and your mom into the living room?"

I hadn't even thought about where I was going to tell them this news. The living room was definitely better than the kitchen.

"Can I finish my homework?" Stevie asked. "'Cause last year, I got all A's and Mikey didn't."

"That's 'cause you were only in the second grade. Everybody gets A's in the second grade!"

"Boys!" I said, then reached out my hand toward them. "We'll get to your homework in a little bit. Come on; I want to talk to you."

My three sons stood and marched toward me, the youngest, Stevie, to the oldest, Junior, looking almost like triplets. I had been pregnant for three years in a row, as if once Chauncey and I started having children, we just couldn't stop. And it had been fine with me. Junior had been born in March 2002; Mikey, the following March; and finally, Stevie, the March after that. I would've kept going; it was Chauncey who thought three was enough. Now, I wished that I'd had ten more of his children.

It wasn't until I turned around and bumped into Emily that I remembered that she was there.

She hugged Stevie, then Mikey, as they came out of the kitchen, but when Junior walked out, he stopped and took a long look at Emily, then Jamal, then me.

"What's wrong?" he asked. "I can tell something happened."

To be honest, I was kinda surprised it took Junior that long to figure it out. My ten-year-old was supersensitive, so intuitive—just like his father.

I only had a second to decide the best response. "Yes," I said, "something did happen." In that instant, I imagined Chauncey kissing me this morning as he walked through the front door and I had to take a breath to keep the shaking out of my voice.

"Is it Dad?" Junior asked.

I looked down and away and moved toward the sofa. I didn't want to say anything until the three of them were sitting down. "Come in here, Junior," I said in my no-nonsense tone.

He did as I asked, and just seconds later, we were all in place. I don't know how the seating got arranged: I was on the couch next to Jamal, and Stevie was next to me. Mikey and Junior sat right across from us on the love seat. And Emily stood behind them.

"Mom," Junior said. This time, he was the one with the no-nonsense tone. "What's going on?"

There was no need to prolong this. "You're right, Junior. It's your dad."

I watched my son swallow hard and the tears shot instantly to my eyes. "There was a fire today."

"Did Dad get hurt?" Junior asked before I could get out any more.

I nodded.

"Did he die?"

I lowered my head and sobbed.

Jamal answered for me. "Yes, Junior." Then he looked at Mikey and Stevie. "I am so sorry. But your father died in the fire today."

"Daddy died?" Mikey cried, and Stevie joined him.

I held my youngest in my arms and motioned for Mikey and Junior to join me. Only Mikey leaped over to me.

"Why did Daddy have to die, Mommy?" Stevie asked, as he cried.

"I don't know, baby."

As I held my two sons, I stared at my oldest still sitting across from me, not moving, not crying. It didn't even seem like he was breathing.

Jamal said, "Are you all right, Junior?"

My son asked, "Did you go to the fire, too, Uncle Jamal?"

"Yes."

"Were you there when Daddy died?"

Jamal nodded. "I wasn't in the exact room. Your dad went in to try to save some of the kids who were trapped in the back of the building. He got them out, but he didn't make it. I was in another part of the school, but when they told me your dad was in there, I tried to go back in to help him."

"But you couldn't save him?"

"No," Jamal said, and as I held my sons, I could hear the emotion in Jamal's voice. "I wanted to, but it was too late. Your dad is a hero, Junior. He didn't want to leave you, but he had to help those kids, you know."

I watched as my son let seconds go by, then moved his head up and down. His eyes were filled with water when he stood and took small steps toward me and his brothers. Still holding my two sons as best I could, I reached for my eldest. Junior knelt down, laid his head in my lap, and finally sobbed.

I felt Jamal's arms around me and my sons. Across the room, tears streamed down Emily's face. She took a step toward us, then stopped and backed away as if she didn't want to intrude. I closed my eyes and cried some more, and settled into the little bit of comfort that I felt being close to my three sons.

✦

Jamal and Emily had stayed so long that I almost invited them to spend the night. But they'd left, and now it was just me and my sons, the way it would be from now on.

I stared at my children lying every which way in my bed. Thank God it was a king-size or else I wouldn't fit in. I tried to remember the last time any of my boys had slept with me—letting the children in our bed was against Chauncey's religion.

"The marital bed is for the folks who are married."

He'd always laugh when he said it, but my husband meant it.

I agreed with him, I always did. But tonight I wanted my sons with me, and I had a feeling that tonight Chauncey would approve.

Slipping under the covers, I reached toward the lamp, then pulled my hand back and rested my head on my pillow. I wasn't afraid of the dark; it was just that I felt closer to Chauncey in the light. But when I closed my eyes, I saw nothing but darkness anyway.

The tears were coming, I could feel them. But then, a peace, a calm, and a memory . . .

July 2, 1993

I WAS DEEP into this book. Everybody had been talking about this novel, and I'd finally gotten my hands on a copy from the library. I'd just started, but I couldn't believe how Bernadine's husband had left her . . . for a white woman! I read a page, then turned. Read a page, then turned, never looking up. Reading was what I loved to do. Inside the pages of a novel, I didn't have to think about my life.

But then I was interrupted, and I wasn't happy about it.

"Hey!"

It took me a moment to force my eyes away from Savannah, Bernadine, Robin, and Gloria. When I looked up, I was staring into the light brown eyes of a guy I'd never seen before.

"Didn't you hear us calling you?" he asked.

"I didn't hear anyone calling me," I said, wanting this guy to leave me alone so that I could get back to *Waiting to Exhale.*

"Well, I've been calling you," he said, like he couldn't believe that I hadn't heard him.

"And what did you call me? Hey?" I asked, trying not to twist my neck since I was really trying to act more sophisticated, like Sondra and Denise on *The Cosby Show.* They never twisted their necks, not even when they got angry.

I wanted to be like them, but it was hard 'cause when I didn't like what someone was saying, my neck got to rolling. And right now, I could feel a roll comin' on.

I continued, "I don't answer to 'Hey!'"

The boy's grin was wide, though I had no idea why he was smiling at me. I wasn't hardly smiling at him.

"Okay," he said, nodding. "You got me. So your name's not Hey." He put one leg up on the picnic table bench and then leaned against it like he was cool or something. "Why don't you tell me your name so the next time I call you, I'll call you in a proper kind of way."

"Why would I tell you my name? Who are you?"

"Oh, I'm sorry. I'm Chauncey. Chauncey Williams. I'm one of the new counselors here at the camp this year."

"A counselor?" I asked, kinda surprised. He looked like he was my age. "How are you a counselor?"

"Well, I've been a part of the Upward Bound program for a couple of years, and this summer they said I could work here."

"They let *you* be a counselor *here?*"

"Why you gotta say it like that?" He laughed. "But to answer your question, yes, ma'am."

I frowned. "Why you calling me ma'am?"

"I'm just being polite."

"You don't have to be polite to a teenager."

"Yeah, I do. Everyone should be polite to everyone else. That's the way my mama raised me."

As soon as he said that, I looked away. Whenever someone told me about their mother, I got this little pinch in my stomach that made me sad all over.

He said, "So, now that I've told you my name"—I looked back up at the boy—"and I've told you why I'm here, are you going to tell me your name so that we can be friends?"

I was sure there was a lot of doubt in my eyes. I didn't have friends and I wasn't interested in making friends. To me, friendship and trust went together, and I didn't trust anyone. How could I? I could never trust my parents, not that I ever knew them. But how could I trust anyone who could just give away a baby and then never come to see if she was okay?

How could I trust anyone after I had lived with dozens of families who'd taken me into their homes, but never into their hearts.

And finally, I certainly couldn't have any trust in my heart after Mr. Barnes, my guidance counselor, who was the first person who ever believed in me. He told me I was smart and that I was going to be somebody someday. He was the first person I ever thought of as a friend. But now he was in jail for the things he'd done to me and some of the other girls last year when I was in ninth grade.

So having friends and trusting people didn't work for me. Being by myself was the safest way.

"So, are you going to tell me your name?" Chauncey asked again.

"Miriam," I said.

"Miriam. That's a pretty name for a pretty girl."

I had to blink. Several times. Pretty? No one had ever said there was anything pretty about me. Not my name, which wasn't pretty like the other girls' in my school: Monique, Nicole, and Sheree. Now, those were some pretty names.

And as far as *me* being pretty, this guy had to be kidding. No one ever thought the chunky girl with the white streak in her hair was pretty. Kids used to bully me all the time, calling me Skunk. So, what was this guy's game?

"Well, Miriam." He said my name and then paused. "You need to go on into the clubhouse. They're serving lunch."

"I'm not hungry."

"You gotta eat."

"Maybe you didn't hear me," I said, rolling my neck. "I'm not hungry."

"Awww, come on, what're you trying to do? Get me fired on my first day?"

It didn't look like this boy was ever going to leave me alone. With a sigh, I slammed the book shut, swung my legs over the bench, then stomped across the grass toward the clubhouse.

But as I marched away, Chauncey called out, "I hope we get to see each other again, Ms. Miriam."

I didn't turn around, and for some reason, that made him laugh.

"Oh, you gonna play hard to get, huh?"

Hard to get? I just kept on walking.

"Well," he was yelling now 'cause I was kinda far away from him, "I'm gonna be here all summer. And I promise you that by the end, you and me, we're gonna be friends."

Still, I didn't look back, but for some reason, that last thing he said made me smile. Something I hadn't done in a long, long time . . .

✦

CHAUNCEY HAD MADE me smile on that day and so many days after that. No matter what was going on in our lives, he could bring me joy. With a hug, or a kiss, phone call, or an e-mail, every part of me was happy, always.

And now, as I lay there in our bed, I knew for sure that there was no way I'd ever smile again.

That thought, and knowing that my Chauncey was gone . . . made me cry all over again.

4

Emily

I couldn't tell you who started it. I don't know if it was me or Jamal. All I know is that right after I eased my car next to his in the underground parking garage of our building and jumped out, I was in his arms and our lips were locked.

How we made it across the garage, to the elevator, and then up to our condo, I would never know. All I know is that our lips never parted. We were like teenagers, kissing with abandon, not caring where we were or who saw us. Not that I expected to be seen. It was after two in the morning. We didn't leave Miriam and the children until all the boys were asleep. Junior had tried to fight it, but finally, even he gave in to the emotional exhaustion that came from hours of tears. When we left, only Miriam was awake, and really, I didn't want to leave her. I wanted to stay all night, but she wouldn't let me.

"Go home with your husband," she'd whispered when Jamal had gone into the kitchen to make sure that all the pizza we'd ordered, but had not eaten, had been put away. "He's hurting, too," Miriam told me. "He knew Chauncey way longer than I did and today, Jamal lost his brother. He needs to go home to cry and you need to be with him."

I valued the opinion of my best friend, especially when it came to marriage. Miriam was an Olympic-gold-medal wife, as far as I was concerned. Not once in all the years that I'd known them had I not seen a smile on Chauncey's face.

"You're right," I said to her.

But tears seemed to be far from my husband's mind. The moment we stepped into our condo, our clothes took off on a trajectory all their own. By the time we hit the bedroom door, we were naked. By the time we hit the sheets, we were connected. And by the time the clock had ticked off five minutes, we'd gone to heaven and returned.

Then, we did it again, slower this time. Tenderly, gently, though I could feel Jamal's pain in every kiss, in every caress. I could hear his pain in every moan and every call of my name. His heart was crying as tears fell from my eyes.

Now, we lay still. Jamal was on his back with my head resting on his chest. I waited until I heard the smooth, solid rhythm of his sleep-breathing and then I slowly lifted my head. He shifted, then settled down, and I positioned my elbow so that I could rest my chin on my hand and just stare at my husband.

Only the moon that was slowly bowing to morning illuminated our bedroom, but it was enough to see Jamal. And the beautiful black of his skin. I held my arm out, and now Jamal looked even richer against the paleness of my Caucasian genes.

This was one of the many things that I loved about me and Jamal. We were total opposites who fit perfectly together. I knew that from the moment I saw him, though it took us years to get to the same point . . .

✦

January 26, 1998

I did NOT have sexual relations with that woman, Monica Lewinsky . . .

"Oh, my God, he's lying," I shouted at the TV as I scooted to the edge of the couch.

"So what?" Michellelee said. "I knew what he was when I voted for him."

I stared down at my roommate, stretched out on the floor with a bunch of magazines in front of her. Michellelee had been my suite mate for a year and a half now, along with Miriam, and in that short time, the three of us, each only a child, had grown to be as close as sisters. But not once had we ever talked about who she—the only one of us who'd had her birthday in time to register—had voted for.

"You actually voted for Bill Clinton?" I drawled. I had been trying to keep the twang out of my voice now that I was in LA. But I couldn't help it. When I got upset, the inner Mississippi came out of me.

Michellelee sat up and crossed her legs, yoga-style. "Uh . . . yeah. Who else was I going to vote for? Bob Dole?"

"Of course. He was going to reduce taxes, and reduce government. The federal government is getting too big."

"That's what all you Republicans say. The government is your enemy, until you need a friend."

That was a smart retort, a line I'd never heard before, but I still had to stand up for the man my daddy had campaigned for. "Did you know Bob Dole has two Purple Hearts?"

Michellelee glanced up with a look that told me she thought my words were silly. "That Purple Heart qualifies him to be president as much as being black qualifies Bill Clinton."

I fell back onto the couch. "Why do black people always say that Bill Clinton is black? It makes no sense."

Michellelee shrugged. "'Cause he is. We gotta claim him 'cause, trust me, he's the closest we'll ever get to having a black president."

"Well, then, you go right ahead and claim him, because I don't want him. Just wait. You'll see what's going to happen." I wagged my finger at Michellelee. "He had sex with Monica and the truth will all come out. Then Hillary will leave him and next will come his impeachment. And then"—I jumped up from the couch and flicked my wrist as if I was shooting a basketball—"Bob Dole will be president!"

Michellelee laughed. "No, you fool. Al Gore will be president."

Before I could tell Michellelee that I'd move to Canada and play college ball there if Al Gore were ever to become the president, the door to our townhouse busted wide open. "Guess what?" Miriam came in huffing and puffing like she was going to blow our house down.

"What?" Michellelee and I said together.

"I got you a date, my boyfriend's best friend. You're going with me to the Upward Bound Awards program tonight."

Michellelee and I stared at her for a moment and then Michellelee turned to me with a pointed finger. "She must be talking to you."

Now, Michellelee knew that wasn't true because in all the time I'd known Miriam, she'd never once tried to set me up.

"You know who I'm talking to." Miriam set her hands on her wide hips and spoke in that mother-scolding voice that she used.

"First of all, I do not need you to find me a man. I mean, look at me." Michellelee stopped for a moment, then twirled like the ballerina on the music box that my parents bought me the first time they took me to Paris. "Out of the three of us, who's beauty personified?"

Michellelee's question was a rhetorical one that made Miriam and me roll our eyes, though I couldn't really be mad at Michellelee. She always said those kinds of things, but not out of conceit. She was simply stating a fact, and my parents had taught me never to be mad at the truth.

Michellelee continued, "So, I don't need your help 'cause I have no problem pulling dudes." She flopped down on the sofa next to me and picked up one of the magazines she'd been flipping through earlier.

Miriam whined, "But you never pull the right one."

"Says who?"

I leaned back and closed my eyes. I'd heard this track before. My best friends would go back and forth—Miriam would tell Michellelee about some guy she thought was perfect for Michellelee, and Michellelee would tell Miriam to mind her business. They would keep at it until Miriam stomped away, because that's how it was going to end. Miriam would be mad and Michellelee would shrug her off.

Helping Michellelee find the right man seemed so important to Miriam. I guessed it had something to do with the way she was raised. From the moment we met, she'd made it known that she wanted a husband and a family more than she wanted even her college degree. It seemed to me that she was going to get her wish; her boyfriend, Chauncey, was the only guy I knew who wanted to get married as much as Miriam did. So, I guessed, Miriam wanted the same thing for her friends—well, at least that's what she wanted for Michellelee.

Of course, she probably wanted the same for me, though she never did anything to try to help me. Maybe it was because she thought life was different for white girls. Or maybe she thought life was just different for me.

Actually, she had a point. While I was still in my mother's womb, she and my daddy had already planned for my wedding day. According to their dreams, I was going to marry Waldorf Astoria the Fourth.

That was not his real name; that was just what I called Clarkson Wells, the son of my father's medical business partner and best friend.

"This time, I'm not trying to set you up." Miriam's voice broke through my reverie. "You'll be doing Chauncey a favor. His best friend in the whole world just came home."

"Where's he been? Prison?" Michellelee smirked.

"No, that would be *your* last boyfriend. By the way, is Pookie out yet?"

I couldn't help it, I had to laugh.

"His name is Luke," Michellelee said, as if she was more insulted by what Miriam had called him than by what Miriam was saying about him. "Not Pookie, and he wasn't in prison. He just had to take care of some outstanding warrants."

"Whatever!" Miriam said. "Look, Chauncey's friend just got back from Mississippi."

My eyes popped open. "Mississippi?"

"Not your part of Mississippi, Emily."

What was that supposed to mean?

"He's been in Mississippi taking care of his grandmother," Miriam explained. "She died two weeks ago, and he's finally back home. Chauncey wants to cheer him up and he thought you two would have fun together."

"Oh, great. Just what I need, some guy crying on my shoulder all night about his dead grandmother." Michellelee shook her head. "Not interested."

"Please, Michellelee! I'm not asking you to marry Jamal. Just do this double date with me tonight and if you don't like him, fine. I will never ever ask you to go out with another guy again in my life."

Michellelee closed the magazine and laid it flat on her lap. "So you're saying that if I do this tonight, you'll forever give up trying to hook me up?"

Miriam laid her hand across her chest like she was saying the Pledge of Allegiance. "I give you my word."

"If I were you, I'd get this in writing," I said.

Miriam glared at me, but when Michellelee said, "Okay, I'll go," Miriam clapped her hands with glee.

"But"—Michellelee stopped Miriam's celebration with that one word—"I'll only go if Emily goes, too."

"What?" I snapped my head toward her so fast I was sure that I'd have whiplash in the morning.

"If I don't like this guy, I'll have someone to talk to."

"No, thank you," I said.

"Come on," Michellelee said. "It'll be like a triple date, only you'll be alone." She laughed.

I tossed the pillow at her. "I refuse to be anyone's fifth wheel. Plus, I already have plans. I'm going to sit here and wait for KCAL Breaking News and the announcement that Bill Clinton *did* have sex with that woman."

"Michellelee," Miriam said, ignoring me and glancing at her watch, "we have to be ready in like an hour and a half."

"So not only do I have to go on this date, but I have to look like a star in ninety minutes?"

"Yeah, but if anyone can do it, you can."

The obvious sucking up worked. Michellelee grinned. "Okay. I'll find something fabulous to wear."

While Michellelee strolled up the stairs to her room, Miriam rushed into hers, which was right off the living room, and I didn't move from the couch. Instead, I turned from channel to channel, watching and waiting for the news to come about the president. Just a bit more than an hour later, a knock on our door interrupted my viewing. I was annoyed; I didn't feel like entertaining Chauncey and his friend until Miriam and Michellelee were ready, but I had to be the good roommate.

Then, I opened the door, took one look outside, and stood straight at attention.

"Hey, Emily," Chauncey said.

"Hello." But I wasn't looking at him. My glance went straight over his shoulder and I took in the most beautiful vision.

Now, one thing you must know—I wasn't one of those white girls who chased black men. Not that I was prejudiced; I just came from a long line of Mississippi Harringtons who preferred the pre–Civil War days. In my family, everyone stayed with their own kind. My grandmother had even told me that was biblical, and certainly, I was going to follow the Bible.

But my grandmother had never seen a man who looked like this. This guy was hot!

"So . . . you gonna let us in?"

"Oh, I'm sorry." I could feel the heat rise on my cheeks. I stepped aside, but I never took my eyes off Chauncey's friend. Miriam had told us his name, hadn't she?

My eyes followed every step he took as he strolled past me. While Chauncey had on a fake leather coat over his suit, his friend wore a tailored overcoat that was buttoned up but still left a peek of his white-with-black-pinstripe shirt and black diamond patterned tie. My mother had taught me to love a well-dressed man.

As I motioned for them to sit down, Chauncey finally introduced me. "This is my boy, Jamal."

Jamal!

"Nice to meet you," I said, holding out my hand. Now, my friends often teased me about my proper Southern ways. But I wasn't so uncool that I shook people's hands. Right now, though, I had an ulterior motive—I wanted to touch him.

Then he opened his mouth. "Nice to meet you, too."

I had to hold on to the chair so that I wouldn't swoon! He

sounded just like Barry White, whom Michellelee blasted from the stereo.

"So, I guess the girls aren't ready." Chauncey opened his coat and sat down on the chair. Which left only the couch for Jamal.

"No," I said. "But I'll go check on Miriam."

"You don't have to," Chauncey said. "I'm sure she's just about ready."

"I don't mind." Moving quickly, I grinned at Jamal, then pushed open Miriam's door without even knocking. Closing the door behind me, I whispered, "I'm going with you."

"What?" she said louder than I wanted her to. "And why are you whispering?"

"Chauncey and Jamal are right out there and I don't want them to hear us, but I'm going with you."

"So Michellelee talked you into it, huh?"

"Yes," I said, thinking that was a good excuse. "But I need thirty minutes to get ready."

She shook her head. "I have to be there for photos, so if you're not ready in fifteen, we're outta here."

I leaped out of her bedroom, grinned again at Jamal, then took the steps two at a time to my bedroom, which was next door to Michellelee's. I don't think I'd ever moved so quickly, and before fifteen minutes had passed, I was back downstairs before either Michellelee or Miriam.

"So, you're going, too?" Chauncey asked, looking a little confused.

"Um . . . yes. Miriam didn't tell you?" Even though I was talking to Chauncey, I was looking at Jamal. "I love to support the Upward Bound program. It's such a good cause." Then, without giving either one of them a chance to answer, I slipped down onto the couch next to Jamal. "Were you with Upward Bound, too?"

"No." He shook his head.

Not Upward Bound? That was how Miriam and Chauncey had met; I thought Jamal had been part of that program, too. Well, I'd just have to find another way to connect. But before I could switch subjects, Michellelee sauntered down the stairs at the same time that Miriam came out of her room.

Since I wasn't supposed to be a part of this little party, I sauntered off to the side as the introductions were made. I watched Michellelee as she looked Jamal up and down, but her smile was steady.

"We'd better get moving." Miriam opened the door to the front closet, where we all kept our coats.

Chauncey led the way and Miriam followed him, but before Michellelee could step out of the door with Jamal, I called her back. When Jamal looked back over his shoulder, I said, "I forgot something and I need Michellelee."

Michellelee frowned as I pulled her back into the townhouse. "What's up?"

Michellelee and Miriam were like sisters to me, so what was most important was my relationship with Michellelee. If she was into Jamal, then I would back away. But if she was not . . .

"What do you think?"

"Of what?"

"Of him? Do you like him?"

"Jamal?" She shrugged. "He's okay; I'm just not into that kind of guy."

"You're not into the tall, dark, and handsome kind?"

She waved her hand. "He's fine, but in such an obvious sort of way. I like my men with a little more of an edge." Then she paused. "Wait a minute . . . why're you asking me? Are you interested?" she said like she couldn't believe it.

I nodded.

"He's black," she said.

"I noticed."

"And you're blonde."

"I have been all my life and the carpet matches the curtains."

"Ewww!" Michellelee said. "You're nasty." But then she grinned. "Well, go for it, girl."

"Are you sure? I mean, I don't want to start anything . . ."

"Oh, really? You don't?" Michellelee took two steps back, then looked me up and down the way she'd just done Jamal. "That must be why you just painted on that dress, 'cause you don't wanna start anything." She shook her head. "But I ain't mad at you. Go get yours."

Michellelee was right. I was wearing a Tadashi design that hugged every part of my six two frame. I didn't have the hips that Michellelee swayed, or the behind that Miriam rocked. But I had boobs. And my girls were on full display in this dress with the V neckline that almost went all the way down to my navel.

"Okay," I told Michellelee. "I'm going for him."

When we stepped outside, the car horn blared and we knew it was Miriam. She was standing outside of Chauncey's twelve-year-old Jeep when we rushed up.

"Come on," she said, "we've got to get going. You get in the middle." She directed Michellelee to the backseat, where Jamal was sitting.

Before Michellelee could move, I slid in. "I'll sit in the middle." I made sure not to look at Miriam because I knew she was giving me one of those looks that could take my life away.

But there was nothing that Miriam could do. By the time she slipped into the front seat next to Chauncey, I was secure in my place. By the time we got to the Hollywood Palladium, Jamal and I were chatting as the friends that I hoped we'd be.

"So you agree with me about Bill Clinton," I said as Jamal helped me out of the Jeep. We'd been talking about politics all the way over.

"Yeah. I mean, don't get me wrong. He was my man before; I even did some work on his campaign. But with what's going down now . . ."

I grinned and turned to Michellelee with triumph all over my face. She just rolled her eyes. She'd been right. Jamal wasn't her type. He had political sense.

But the deal was sealed when we walked into the Palladium and Jamal helped me into my seat.

"By the way, how tall are you?" he asked. "About six two?"

"Good guess."

He nodded. "So, do you model?"

I sighed, wishing I had a hundred dollars for each time I'd been asked that question. Why in the world did people think every tall white girl was a model? It had to be the same disease that made everyone think every tall black guy was a basketball player. And since I was almost eye to eye with him in my three-inch heels, I was sure he'd had that question a lot in his life. So I decided to just give him a pass and answer.

"No modeling, but my height does come in handy. I play basketball."

He frowned. "With USC?" When I nodded, he held up his hand. "Wait a minute. You're *that* Emily Harrington?" he asked, sounding amazed. I had been a highly recruited player from high school, so I wasn't surprised that Jamal knew me—at least by name.

"Yes, how many Emily Harringtons did you think there were?"

We laughed together.

"Aren't you from Mississippi?" he asked.

"I am. And you just got back from there, right?"

The smile that he'd been wearing faded quickly and I was so sorry I'd asked.

"Yeah. I had to take care of some family business."

Wanting to get back to the happy place where we'd been, I

changed subjects. "Do you play any sports?" I asked, getting danger-
ously close to that stereotypical question.

But it worked because his grin came back quickly. "Yup. Basketball."

"You're kidding."

"I played at Crenshaw."

"Crenshaw High? They have an amazing reputation."

"Yup."

"So," I began, "you didn't want to play at the college level?"

His smile went away again. "I was accepted to UCLA, but just
a couple of days after graduation, I had to leave for Mississippi. You
know, for my grandmother."

Well, since this topic wasn't going to go away, I decided to use it.
"Where does . . . did your grandmother live in Mississippi?"

"In Natchez. Do you know where that is?"

I nodded. "Natchez is about ninety miles south of Jackson."

"Which is where you're from," he said, more like a statement, but
I answered like he was asking a question.

"Correct."

Though there were others at the table and a whole program that
went on from the stage, Jamal and I kept talking, keeping our conversation to a whisper. I found out that he'd just enrolled at West
Los Angeles College, the same college where Chauncey was, as a
second-year student studying to become an EMT. He told me that
their lifelong dream was to become firemen.

We talked about school, sports, a little bit about our pasts and
our hopes for our future. By the time Jamal helped me out of my
chair when the program was over and we walked back to the car,
we were officially friends, the first accomplishment of my mission.
When we got back to the townhouse, Jamal walked me and Michellelee to the door while Miriam stayed in the car with Chauncey.

At the door, Michellelee said, "Good night, Jamal," without even making eye contact with him as she spoke.

But once she stepped inside, I lingered outside with him. "It was great meeting you."

"You, too. You're kinda refreshing."

I didn't know what he meant by that; it sounded positive, but I was certainly aiming for something more than refreshing. "So . . . I hope to see you soon."

"Oh, yeah. Definitely."

Definitely! That was a great word. "Okay, I'll see you later."

He stood right there until I stepped inside; I leaned against the closed door, but I wasn't able to stay in that moment for long.

"You're really feeling him!"

My eyes snapped open. I'd forgotten that I wasn't alone. "Yes." I nodded at Michellelee. "I really like him," I said as I fell onto the sofa. "Not only is he hot, he's smart, and cool, and interesting, and . . ."

She held up her hand like she didn't want to hear my litany, which was too bad because I could've gone on and on and on.

She said, "I get it, and he seems like he's into you, too."

"He's going to call me." Then I sat up straight. "Oh no. I didn't give him my number."

Michellelee laughed. "Don't worry. He knows where to find you."

I settled back down. She was right. He was Chauncey's best friend. He was probably asking for my number right now . . .

✦

I blinked THREE times and came back to the present, though the memories stayed with me. When I closed the door that night, little did I know that Jamal and I were a long road and many years away from our bliss.

But we'd found each other, felt each other, and I'd always been convinced that anything that God put together could never be taken apart. So once we married, though I was aware of the danger of Jamal's career, it had never been a concern. We would last forever.

Of course, I knew no one lived forever. I just never thought death would separate us. Instead, I preferred to think that Jesus would come back and lift me and Jamal up at the same time.

Today, though, had proved that I couldn't hide from reality.

That's why I didn't want to take my eyes off Jamal. Not that I had ever taken my eyes off him. From the first time I saw him, I knew that, physically, he had all the gifts. He looked just like that actor that my girls loved so much. Idris Elba. Yes, Jamal was Idris Elba before there was even an Idris Elba. He was sexy and soulful. In the way he walked, in the way he talked.

But right now, I wasn't thinking about the brightness of his eyes or the fullness of his lips. I didn't care about the sharp angle of his jaw or the cleft in his chin. Tonight, I just celebrated the rise and fall of his chest.

Jamal parted his lips and released a small moan, though he stayed asleep. Then, as if he knew I was there, he lifted his arm and I lay back against his chest, now feeling the rhythm of his heart.

I was exhausted, but I refused to close my eyes. I wanted to dance to the beat of Jamal's heart. I wanted to twirl to every one of his inhales and swirl to each of his exhales. I wanted to celebrate because I now realized the preciousness of this gift in my bed. Lying with her husband was something that Miriam would never do again.

The thought of that made new tears flow. I had to save Miriam from as much pain as I could. I had to make sure that she would get through, and know that every day, in every way, Jamal and I would be there for her.

Always!

5

MIRIAM

I couldn't believe my eyes had opened.

My wish, even in my unconsciousness, was that I would sleep straight through to eternity, but when I twisted my head to the side, I saw the reasons why I'd awakened.

My boys were next to me, a tangled mess of limbs that made me wonder how in the world they had slept. My lips tried to curl into a smile, but then a jolt sprang from my heart, reminding my lips that there was nothing to smile about.

I pushed myself up, then wobbled a bit as I stood. My body was drowning in a sea of exhaustion, though I couldn't figure out why. I hadn't done a thing but cry. I guess grief made one weary.

My cell phone chirped and I grabbed it from the nightstand. The message icon indicated that I had twelve messages, which surprised me. I hadn't heard the alerts before.

I clicked on the icon, but only read the last message:

Our plane lands at noon. I've rented a car. Mama Cee said to tell you she loves you and the boys, and I do, too.

Again, my lips tried to smile, but couldn't. Still, I felt relief as I read the text from my brother-in-law, Charlie, once again.

I tucked my phone into the pocket of my sweatpants, not bothering to check the other messages. I never received many—just Emily, Michellelee . . . and Chauncey called me on the regular. But my voice mail was probably filled now with condolences and I just wasn't up to hearing everyone else's sadness.

I tiptoed across the room, though I didn't need to. My children could sleep through an earthquake. But still I treaded softly, mostly out of habit. It was my way of not disturbing Chauncey on those days when he needed extra rest.

I never wanted to wake him, then. I would pay a billion dollars to wake him now.

Closing the door behind me, I stood in the hall wondering what I was supposed to do next. What did a woman do on her first day without her husband? Was I supposed to walk differently? Talk differently? What was I supposed to eat? What was I supposed to drink? What was I supposed to say? What was I supposed to think?

The ringing telephone stopped me from just standing there, and when I pulled out my cell, my lips tried to smile once again.

"Hey, Miriam," Emily said the moment I answered. "Did I wake you?"

"No, I kinda slept off and on, but I just got up."

"I didn't want to call too early, but I couldn't wait any longer. I had to check on you and the boys."

I took a couple of steps away from the bedroom. "They're still asleep." I didn't add that I wanted them to sleep for days so they wouldn't have to deal with this reality. Or maybe it was that I didn't want to deal with their reality.

Last night, I didn't think it was possible to hurt more, but with each tear that my sons shed, another piece of my heart was torn away. All I wanted to do was kiss my sons and make them feel better. But while kisses healed boo-boos, they did nothing for broken hearts.

"So, how are you, honey?"

Surely that was a rhetorical question. Or maybe it wasn't. Maybe my best friend wanted to know that I wanted to die right now. Maybe she wanted to know that if I didn't have children, I would already have taken a Costco-size bottle of sleeping pills and joined Chauncey in paradise.

Then Emily quickly spoke, as if she read my mind through the phone. "We're on our way, Miriam. We were just waiting for you to get up."

"No, you don't have to come over," I said before I added the lie, "I'm fine, and I know you guys have things to do."

"The only thing we have to do is be there and do what we've always done for one another."

I glanced at the clock and it was barely seven. They had left only a few hours ago, but there was no talking Emily out of her plan. Once she made a decision, she never changed it.

"We'll see you in a little while," she said. "Love you."

"Mean it," I said, ending the call the way we always did. I hung up and breathed, relieved.

The truth was, I wanted Emily and Jamal there. I needed them to help me fill in the blanks until Mama Cee and Charlie arrived.

I tiptoed back into the bedroom. All I wanted to do was crawl into the bed and pull the covers over my and my children's heads. But I had to be the grown-up here.

I grabbed fresh underwear from my dresser drawer, then went into the bathroom. Slipping out of the sweatpants and shirt that I'd changed into last night, I took a quick shower, then went about my regimen as if life hadn't changed. Brushed my teeth, twisted my hair into a bun, then slipped into my bra and panties. I glanced at the sweatpants that I'd just left on the floor, and after a moment, picked them up and jumped right back into them. The best anyone was going to get out of me today was clean underwear.

Before I left the bathroom, I glanced at myself in the mirror. Yesterday, I would've said that this was the best I could do as a mommy. Today, this was the best I could do as a widow.

A widow.

That word stopped me cold. I was really a widow, really a woman who'd lost the love of her life.

Thank God the doorbell rang before that thought settled too much in my mind. I scurried from the bathroom, rushed to the front of the house, and then I took a deep breath before I pulled open the door.

I tried my best to lighten my voice. "I need to give you guys a key, huh?" This time, my heart allowed my smile to remain for a few seconds.

Emily smiled back as she hugged me, then she passed me to Jamal and he did the same. Jamal held me a little longer, as if he knew that I needed to feel the strength of a man's arms around me.

"How are you?" Emily asked.

Then, I have no idea what happened. The dam broke and tears gushed out.

"Oh, Miriam," Emily said as she put her arms around me again and led me to the sofa.

"I'm sorry," I said, and tucked my sobs back inside. "I don't know what happened. I've been doing so well."

"You don't have to do well, honey. You don't have to hold anything in."

Emily and I sat, and Jamal stood in front of us, shifting from one foot to the other. For the first time, I really looked at him and saw the reddened rims of his eyes.

He said, "Uh . . . are the boys asleep?"

I nodded. "They're still in my bedroom and I didn't want to wake them up."

Jamal's eyes moved between me and Emily. He finally settled on Emily when he said, "I'm gonna go check on them," before he left us alone.

I shook my head. "Em, how am I going to do this?"

"It's going to be hard. And I can't say that I know how you feel, but I do know that you're going to be able to do it. With your friends, with your family . . . and, most of all, with God."

With God. I hadn't thought about God at all. Not since He let me down.

"Not sure how much God's going to help me."

Emily reared her head back. "Miriam!" she said, as if my words were blasphemous.

I knew that was a shocker. Emily had started going to church with me when we were in college and we'd both been members of Hope Chapel ever since, so those words had to sound like craziness from my mouth to her ears.

"Why would you say that?" Emily questioned.

I recalled the moment when God had let me down. "When we were in the car with Michellelee rushing to the hospital, God told me that Chauncey was all right."

"He did?"

I nodded. "I felt such peace. The only one I was worried about was"—I paused, giving myself time to lower my eyes—"I was only worried about Jamal. And so, I prayed and prayed for him."

Emily squeezed my hand. "Thank you for praying for my husband."

"I prayed for both of them," I said. "But God lied about Chauncey. Chauncey wasn't fine."

"Well," Emily paused and pondered her next words. "Maybe

God did say that because really, Miriam, what can be finer than being with God? And that's where Chauncey is, so he *is* fine."

I wondered if what Emily said was true. When I felt that peace, was that the exact moment when . . . I shuddered and ran my hands up and down my arms, trying to warm my suddenly chilled skin.

"You cold?"

"No."

"Okay." A beat. "You know God didn't let you down, right? You know He's here and He's going to stay."

I shrugged. "Whatever. He can be wherever He wants to be. He just doesn't have to worry about hearing from me, because I don't have anything to say to Him."

"You can't stop praying."

I shook my head, but then Jamal saved me from having to disappoint Emily any further when he came back into the living room. "The boys are still sleeping."

"That's good. And I hope they stay that way until my mother-in-law gets here. She'll cuddle and coddle them . . ." Another smile came to my face as I thought about my mother-in-law with my sons. But like the rest of my smiles, this one didn't last long. Looking up, I said, "Jamal, I need to start making"—I paused for a second—"the arrangements . . . and I don't know who I should talk to."

Jamal lowered himself onto the ottoman in front of us and while Emily held my hand, he said, "Are you sure you want to do this now?"

I nodded. "It's not like waiting is going to change anything."

"Okay," Jamal said before giving a quick glance to his wife.

"Plus, I don't know how long Mama Cee will be able to stay in Los Angeles," I said. "I want to do everything so that she can get back quickly."

"I'm sure she's not thinking about leaving you anytime soon," Emily said.

"Well, whether she stays or goes is fine," I said. "I'm still ready to get started." Looking at Jamal, I added, "So—"

Emily's ringing cell stopped Jamal from speaking, and as she answered it, then stood and took a few steps away from us, Jamal took my hands in his. "How are you doing?" he whispered.

I studied him a little longer this time, and his eyes were glazed with the sadness of the thousand tears he'd probably shed. But also in his eyes I saw the love that he'd felt for his best friend. Though best friend would never completely define Jamal and Chauncey's connection. Theirs was a brotherhood that was thicker than blood. Finally, I responded, "I'm doing about as good as you."

When he squeezed my hands and nodded, I knew that he understood and I wasn't alone. We shared seconds of silence as he held my hands and waited for his wife.

Finally, Emily came back. "I don't know why I hadn't thought of this," she said. "That was the school board. They need me to come and speak to the children."

I don't know why I hadn't thought of it either. Dr. Emily Harrington-Taylor was one of the best child psychologists and life coaches in the country. Even though she had a private practice, she was usually one of the first called in for any kind of tragedy or trauma that involved children.

Jamal asked, "Where are they meeting?"

"They've gathered the parents and children at First Baptist of Inglewood."

"For classes?"

"No, for a session to discuss what happened, to let the parents know next steps, and to bring the children together to grieve. It's actually a good idea, but honey"—Emily eased back down to the couch and turned to me—"I hate to leave you."

"Oh, no. Go, Em. You have to go. You're the best and you have to help those children."

"What about you?"

"I'll stay," Jamal said. "I'll help Miriam start the arrangements and take care of the boys when they wake up."

I watched Emily's shoulders slack with relief, as if she didn't feel like she was abandoning me altogether. "Thank you, sweetheart." Then, to me, she added, "I'll get back here as soon as I can."

I shook my head. "Don't worry about me. I'll be surrounded in a few hours. My mother-in-law, my brother-in-law, and your husband." I tried to smile again. "Seems to me, I'm in good hands."

Emily stood and grabbed her purse. "That you are." She kissed her husband, a soulful kiss that made me turn away. I couldn't watch that kind of kiss that I would never have again. "Bye, babe. I'll call you." Then she hugged me.

The three of us walked to the front door together and then Jamal and I stood side by side as Emily stepped outside. "Wait!" Facing us, she said, "What about the car? We came in mine, remember?"

"Someone will drive me home." He added, "Don't worry, you go talk to the kids."

She smiled. "I will. And you take care of Miriam."

6

Emily

Slipping into the car, I glanced back at Miriam and Jamal standing at the door, and for a moment, that picture of them startled me. They stood the way Miriam and Chauncey always did whenever Jamal and I were leaving their home, side by side and waving as we drove away.

I didn't think it was possible, but my heart ached even more now. I would never see Miriam and Chauncey like that again, and my eyes filled up. I waited until I rounded the curve of the street and was out of their sight before I eased my car to a stop.

Except for the moment when I'd heard that Chauncey had died, I'd fought to keep my tears inside. But now I leaned my head against the steering wheel and let them flow. I wasn't crying just for Chauncey and the others who'd died. My tears were also for the ones left behind. Especially Miriam, who had loved Chauncey just about her whole life. It was impossible to imagine what Miriam would be like without him. Would she ever laugh again, have fun again, or even love again?

And what about their children? After eight years of marriage, Jamal and I were still childless. That had never been a big deal for us. Testing showed we were fine, so Jamal and I believed if we were supposed to have children, we would. But in the meantime, Junior, Mikey, and Stevie filled our lives with joy, and thinking of them without their father made me sob harder.

There was so much pain. That was the problem with grief. It left physical and mental devastation in its path.

This was going to be the most difficult time of Miriam's life, but I was going to be there with whatever my best friend needed.

My best friend.

At least the thought of that brought a smile to my face. Because while we loved each other dearly from just about the moment we met, we had that one little hiccup where, I swear, I came close to tossing our friendship aside. And it was all because of Jamal . . .

✦

February 2, 1998

I knocked just one time and then barged into Miriam's bedroom. She was pretending that she was asleep, but I knew that she wasn't. So I bounced on her bed.

Miriam didn't think I could see her, but through the reflection in her mirror, I could tell she was squeezing her eyes tighter as she snuggled into her pillow.

Okay, I knew my suite mate was not an early riser on a good day, and certainly not on a Saturday. But after eight wasn't early, right? Plus, I had waited a week and I needed to talk now.

I whispered. "Are you awake?"

"No!"

"Yes, you are!" When she didn't move, I added, "Come on, I need to talk."

With a sigh, Miriam finally rolled over and pushed herself up. She pressed her back against the headboard, crossed her arms, and glared at me. "This had better be good. And by good, I mean something like Oprah announced she's running for president, or you've just won the lottery. Anything else could get you cut for waking me this early."

I laughed because that was a good one. I didn't think Oprah was a Republican, but I'd vote for her. But even though I laughed, Miriam didn't. "Okay, okay," I said. "You're going to love what I have to say." I paused, wanting to build up the moment. "Give me Jamal's telephone number."

"What?"

"If you don't have it, get it from Chauncey."

"I have it," Miriam said, "but why . . ."

I didn't even let her finish. "Because!" Then I grinned.

She stared at me for just a second more, then she scooted back down in the bed and pulled the covers all the way up and over her head.

"Miriam!" I snatched that blanket away, knowing that she'd be freezing in that little baby-doll nightie she had on.

"Didn't you hear what I said?" she asked.

"You didn't say anything."

"Well, let me give you another hint." She grabbed the blanket from me and covered up again.

For a moment, I just stood there, incredulous. "Why won't you give me his number?"

Miriam didn't say a word, but she knew me better than that. Did she really think I was going to walk away just because she didn't feel like talking?

"Miriam!" I kept calling her name until she tossed back the blanket and sat up again.

She crossed her arms again and poked out her lips. "Emily"—
she said my name slowly— "I introduced Jamal to Michellelee. I
wanted the two of them to get together."

"They didn't like each other," I said. "You saw them together.
They didn't say a word after hello."

"That's 'cause you were doing all the talking."

"No. Jamal and I were talking together. Look, if I thought for a
moment that Michellelee was into him, I wouldn't be asking for his
number."

"I'm surprised that you're asking for his number anyway."

"Why?"

She threw up her hands as if I was aggravating her. "Jamal? Really? You're trying to tell me that *you're* interested in Jamal?"

"Yes," I said with a frown. "Why wouldn't I be? He's really cute,
really smart, loves basketball, hates Clinton, and he's an overall great
guy. Oh, and he's Chauncey's best friend, so can you imagine the fun
we'll have? Best friends with best friends?"

"You forgot one thing." She paused. "He's . . . black."

I blinked a couple of times, because that was not what I'd expected. "And your point is?"

"He's black, Emily!"

"What is it with you guys?" I asked. "Michellelee said the same
thing, that Jamal is black. As if I couldn't see that for myself."

"Well, if we both told you—"

"I know what color he is. But I also know that he's really cool
and I want to get to know him."

"What about your boyfriend?"

"Boyfriend?" She must've known something that I didn't because
I didn't have a boyfriend, not even a casual one.

Miriam said, "You know, Waldorf Astoria."

"Clarkson's not my boyfriend."

"He calls you all the time."

"He calls me from Mississippi, so what? He's the guy that my parents want me to marry, but I haven't been interested in him since kindergarten, and you know that."

"Maybe you need to give him another try. He might make a good husband."

"Husband? I'm not looking for a husband!" I shouted. "I don't want to marry Clarkson or Jamal. I'm just trying to talk to him."

The way Miriam tucked her chin to her chest and folded her arms tighter let me know that she was buckling down. She was not about to be moved. "I don't think you should talk or do anything with Jamal."

Even though we'd been going back and forth for a couple of minutes, I couldn't get my best friend's words to compute in my mind. Slowly, I sat down on her bed. "Really?" I whispered. "You don't think I'm good enough to see Jamal?"

"It's not that." She loosened her arms and softened her voice. "Okay, let me give it to you real, let me give it to you straight. Have you ever read the book or seen the movie *Waiting to Exhale?*"

"No," I said, wondering what in the heck a movie had to do with our conversation.

"Well, you should see it. 'Cause this brother leaves his wife . . . for a white woman."

At first, I pressed my lips together. "And?"

"And? It was awful and terrible and I hated reading and watching every second of that."

"Wait a minute." I paused. "Is Jamal married?"

"No!" she said, as if I'd asked the stupidest question.

"Then what does this have to do with—"

"Look," Miriam said, not letting me finish. "There aren't enough brothers out there. Do you know the ratio of black men to black women?"

I shook my head.

"Well, neither do I, but that's not the point. Whatever the ratio is," Miriam said, "the fact is, there are not enough black men to go around. So many sistahs don't have a man, and will never have a man because our men are either in prison or are batting for the other team, or"—she paused, as if she was going in for the big finish—"they're hooking up with white women."

I couldn't even get the word out of my mouth, but finally it came. "Wow!" I stood up and moved toward her bedroom door, but I couldn't leave like this. When I turned around, the heat of my anger was already flashing beneath my skin. "So, you're saying that you're going to help the cause by keeping me away from Jamal?"

She hesitated, and spoke even softer this time. "Something like that."

"Because I'm white."

I felt like I'd hit a three-pointer with those three words, because Miriam slid down in the bed a little. Maybe I made her feel bad, and that was good, because my feelings were so hurt. But I didn't make her feel bad enough, because after a few seconds, she nodded.

All I could do was shake my head. "I thought we were friends."

"Don't go there, Em. You know we are."

"No, we're not. If we were, then all you would want is for me to be happy."

"Come on, Em. I do want that. But we also said we would always be honest with one another, right?"

That was the truth. That was our promise. "Yes. Honesty." I turned back to the door. "Thanks for being honest," I told her, barely glancing over my shoulder.

"Emily!"

I grabbed the door, swung it open, and then slammed it shut. "Emily!"

I heard her calling me until I got up to my room. Then I slammed my door for good measure.

If anyone had ever told me I'd have this conversation with the woman I thought of as my sister, I would've called them a liar . . .

✦

JAMAL'S REACTION HAD been even more unbelievable than Miriam's. I'd gotten his number, thanks to Michellelee and her budding investigative reporter skills. But when I called Jamal, his response had been much the same as Miriam's.

"Uh, Emily, I think you're cool and everything, but . . ." He didn't even have to finish. After talking to Miriam, I knew what he meant. But he went on anyway. "I'm not trying to hurt your feelings or anything, but I'm not into—"

"White girls," I had finished for him and then slammed down the phone.

I smiled a little now as I remembered the way I had called him and Miriam every single name listed in the Book of Curses. I had paced in my room, ranting to myself about how it wasn't just white people who were prejudiced. I'd made a commitment that day that I would never have anything to do with Jamal.

But God had different plans. Me and Jamal, Miriam and Chauncey. The four of us had grown into a happy family.

Now, though, we were three, and I prayed that we would be able to find a new happiness among us. But we'd need help with that.

I put my car back into drive and once I reached the traffic light, I pressed the button on the console to activate the Bluetooth feature.

"Call Pastor Ford," I said.

Three seconds passed, then the ringing of the phone. Five rings and I was just about to hang up when my pastor answered.

"Good morning!" Pastor Ford's groggy voice came through the car speakers.

I glanced at the clock on the dashboard and cursed inside. I was so unfocused, I hadn't even remembered the time; it wasn't even eight o'clock.

"Pastor, this is Emily; did I wake you?" And before she could respond, I added, "I'm so sorry to be calling this early."

"No, no, it's all right. I was just up late last night. So much going on."

"I know." I sniffed back my emotions and said, "I should've called you last night, but . . ." Another breath. "Pastor, Chauncey Williams died."

"Oh no!" she exclaimed. "In the fire?"

"Yes."

"I was going to call you and Miriam this morning to make sure everyone was all right. Yesterday was crazy. Quite a few of our children went to that school; so many were hurt and we lost one."

"Oh," I groaned.

"Yeah, I know. I was with the Millers all last night; they lost one of their six-year-old twins and it was all that I could do to comfort them." There was silence and I could imagine the pastor shaking her head. "Now, Chauncey. How're Miriam and the boys?"

"I'm worried about her, Pastor. I talked to her this morning and she's really upset with God." I repeated the conversation Miriam and I'd had. "She won't even pray," I said, finishing up. "And that scares me."

The slight chuckle from Pastor Ford sounded more bitter than sweet; still it surprised me. "You don't have to worry. Miriam has enough in her, believe me. She's been praying to God for so long, she might stop, but her heart won't."

I shook my head even though my pastor couldn't see me. "I'm just afraid because now is when she needs Him the most."

"You're right about that, but just because she's mad doesn't mean God's going to turn His back on her. We might do that to people when we get mad at them, but He doesn't do that to us.

"She's all right, Emily, and it's okay that she's upset. She serves a big God and she has big expectations, so right now, it's understandable. But there are two things I know: she'll get over it and God is fine with it."

"Okay," I said, feeling just a bit better.

"I need to get over there," Pastor said. "Are you there now?"

"No, I'm on my way to First Baptist. Some of the parents are bringing their children over for some counseling. I was called in to help."

"Good. So, who's with Miriam? Her mother-in-law?"

"Not yet. She's on her way; right now, only Jamal is there."

My pastor paused for so long that I called out her name to make sure that the call hadn't disconnected.

Finally Pastor said, "So, how's Jamal? I know how close he and Chauncey were."

I sighed. "He's doing well. We've both shed quite a few tears."

"I know you're concerned about Miriam, but make sure you take care of him, too."

"Oh, I definitely will, Pastor."

"And just keep praying around Miriam. Soon, she'll open up her mouth, too. I'll give her a call now and I'll see you over there later."

"Thanks, Pastor."

I clicked off the phone, but then hit the call button again.

"Call Red," I said into the speaker.

I could barely understand Michellelee when she mumbled, "Hey, girl."

"You just getting up?"

"Yeah, a long, long night. Are you with Miriam?"

"I was, but I just left. I was called in by the school district."

"Girl, there's so much tragedy behind that fire. Chauncey and nine kids."

"Wow! I didn't know it was that many."

"Yeah, and now they're pretty sure it was arson."

"Are you kidding?"

"Yup, and because it was September 11, Homeland Security is all up on it."

"I cannot believe this. Well, I just spoke to Pastor and she's on her way over to Miriam's."

Michellelee groaned. "I cry every time I think about her."

"I just had my own breakdown; I couldn't even drive. But we're gonna make it. All we have to do is stay close to Miriam. Between you, me, and Jamal, we're going to have to keep her covered twenty-four-seven. Are you in?"

"You know I am. What do you want me to do?"

I smiled, though I wasn't surprised. This was just how the three of us were with one another.

We were the Red, White, and Blue, and would get through this tragedy together.

7

Emily

There was no other way to say it: I was just sad.

And this was only the first day. As I sped from the church, I prayed that the crying that was still in my ears would fade. The entire sanctuary of First Baptist had been filled with parents and teachers . . . and the children, who were still traumatized and would be suffering for a long time. All of those children had been in the building when the fire started. More than half had been rushed out when the smoke alarms first sounded, but the fire had been aggressive. Dozens had been trapped, and those children had had to experience the abject fear that came with being on the edge of death. They'd seen the flames, inhaled the smoke, felt the smothering heat, and some may even have seen their classmates die.

I'd explained to the parents that this was going to be a long road to recovery, and though I'd given them tips about not leaving their children alone, and letting them sleep with the lights on, I wasn't sure how I was going to handle all of this trauma and tragedy. The city had called in only three psychologists. But three were not enough with this devastation.

Turning my car onto the freeway, I accelerated, so glad that I was heading toward home. But even though I was three miles away from the church, I could still hear the wailing in my ears. Especially the cries of LaTonya Miller.

I'd shed so many tears since yesterday morning, it was a wonder that I had any left. But I had plenty now, for LaTonya, the six-year-old who lost her identical twin sister. That gorgeous, precious little girl still pierced my heart.

"Mommy and Daddy said LaTrisha died!"

She kept saying that over and over, though I was convinced that she didn't have a complete understanding of what that meant. Or maybe, because she was a twin, she did. I was concerned about all the children, but especially about LaTonya. I suspected that the closeness she and her sister shared, a relationship that had been established before they were born, could bring a ton of other issues. It was these unknown issues that truly concerned me. It was why that little girl had already captured my heart.

I was grateful that LaTonya was with both of her parents, and even though the Millers were grieving the death of one daughter, they were willing to do whatever they had to do to help the child who was still with them. The Millers, though only in their twenties, seemed to be parents who understood their love would save their child.

The Millers were parents who were so different from mine.

I glanced at my cell phone, hesitated, then pressed the Bluetooth before I could change my mind.

"Call Mom," I said into the speaker quickly.

As the phone rang, I held my breath, praying that the call would be answered. It rang, and rang, and rang. Just when I was sure that my mother would let my call go to voice mail once again, I heard her voice.

"Emily?"

"Yes, Mom."

"Call me at home. He's not here."

"Okay, I'm going to call you right back. Please pick up."

"I will, honey."

I clicked off and then commanded the hands-free unit to call her at home. As she waited for her house phone to ring, I imagined my mother deleting my call from her cell, erasing the evidence that she'd spoken to me.

When my mother picked up on the first ring, I was happy and sad at the same time. Happy to speak to her, sad that I could count the number of times that I had in the last year.

"How are you, sweetheart?"

Those words resonated through the car and then wrapped around me like my mother's arms, making me feel loved and safe for a moment.

"I'm . . . okay."

"What's the matter?"

It had to be her mother's intuition, another sign that we were still connected, that she still loved me.

I answered, "It's Miriam . . . her husband died."

She hesitated for a moment. "Miriam?"

"My best friend." I sighed inside.

"Oh my! What happened?"

"He died in a fire."

"Oh, goodness. That's so sad. How is she?"

I let a beat or two pass, wondering if my mother would backtrack and ask about Jamal, since I had mentioned that it was a fire. Then I said, "She's not good."

My mother tsked and moved on. "Well, I'll say a prayer for her."

I attributed my mother not asking about my husband to her not remembering that Jamal was a firefighter, too.

"Anyway," I began, deciding to move on as well. "I've been called in to work with the children who were in school at the time."

"The fire was at a school? Oh, my goodness."

"It's been pretty tough, and so I just wanted . . . I just needed to speak to you. To hear your voice."

"I'm glad you called, sweetheart, because you have to be strong. For the children. They need you, and they're lucky, because you're one of the best."

"Thanks for saying that, Mom. Anyway, how are you?"

"We're doing well here. You know, I'm still very involved with DAR," my mother said.

That made me smile. My mother had been one of the key women in the Mississippi chapter of the Daughters of the American Revolution since I could remember. When I was a little girl, I loved to go with her to the auxiliary meetings. She didn't let me go often, but I lived for the afternoons when I could be with all of those women, wearing their Sunday best, sitting around drinking tea and eating crumpets and tea cakes. It felt so grown-up to me. I always thought I was going to be just like those women, with their demure ways and Southern sensibilities.

But I was so wrong. Maybe it was because I was too much of a tomboy. Or maybe it was because I'd soon grown to be so tall. Or maybe it was because once I was a teenager, I didn't care much about the ways of the women who were lineal bloodline descendants of someone who fought in the American Revolution. I cared more about the present than I did the past.

"This year," my mother continued, "I'm working with the scholarship committee and the literacy outreach program that we just started."

"That sounds so good, Mom. I wish I were there— we could work on that together."

There was a moment of silence as both of us reflected on my words. We both knew that I wouldn't be there with her. Probably never again.

After a moment, I asked the question that I knew would make both of our hearts break. "How's Dad?" My question wasn't perfunctory. I truly wanted to know.

"He's playing golf," she said, as if I'd asked an ordinary question about an ordinary father.

"Mom . . . do you think . . . if I called him—"

She didn't even let me finish, and I could almost see my mother, sitting in the Victorian-decorated parlor (they never called it a living room) of the six-thousand-square-foot home that I'd grown up in, shaking her head.

My mother answered my question with her own. "Are you still with Jamal?"

"Mom, you say that as if we're just dating. We're married."

"That is exactly why your father won't speak to you," she said in a tone that sounded like she was scolding me.

"You don't approve of my marriage and you speak to me. Even when you know Dad's going to be mad if he finds out, you still do it. Why can't he love me the way you do?" I cried.

My mother sighed. "It's different for me," she said. "Your father's heart is truly broken. He doesn't understand it and in a way, he blames himself."

"This is so ridiculous. He's blaming himself like I went out and became a stripper or something."

"And that may have been easier for him to accept!"

Why did I keep doing this to myself? Every time I called, I went there. And every time I went there, I got my feelings hurt.

"Emily," my mother said, her voice much softer this time. "Your father will never accept your marriage. If you want him to forgive you, you know what you have to do. Until then—"

"I'm not forgiven and I'm disowned," I said, finishing for her. "Can you at least tell him that I called, and that I asked about him?"

"I'll see. I don't like getting your father upset."

That meant my mother would never say a word. It was the way she was raised—she was old-school Southern. She lived to please her husband. That was her job and she'd done it well. Growing up, I never once saw my parents disagree in any way about anything. Because my mother always went along.

That's what she was doing now, agreeing with her husband, even though he was wrong.

"Okay," I finally said. "Well . . ." I didn't want to hang up, but there was nothing else to say. I wanted to add something like, "I'll see you at Thanksgiving," or "I can't wait till Christmas." But I hadn't celebrated a single holiday with my parents in the eight years since Jamal had put the ring on my finger.

"You be well, sweetheart."

"I will." Then I hung up, wondering why I had made that call. I felt worse than before.

My heart yearned for the old days. The days when I was Daddy's girl, and Mother's princess. The days when I woke up every morning knowing that I was special, knowing that my mother was proud, and I was the apple of my daddy's eye. I longed for the days when I knew both of my parents loved me in all ways and would love me always . . .

◆

May 12, 2000

"This is Absolutely ridiculous," I said as I came down the stairs, stepping carefully as the graduation gown billowed around my ankles. The smell of white roses had assaulted me from the moment I walked out of my bedroom.

"I already told her that it smelled like a funeral parlor up in here," Michellelee said, even though she didn't look up from the notepad on her lap.

I figured that was Michellelee's salutatorian speech. She hadn't parted with that pad from the moment she learned that she'd been selected to speak.

"I would prefer to say that it smells like a flower shop," I said, sitting down next to Michellelee.

Miriam looked over her shoulder, smirked, then went back to smelling one of the bouquets of white roses. "Don't hate 'cause I'm so loved," she said. "My boo did the dang thing, didn't he? I mean, one hundred flowers? How many did you guys get?" She stopped for a moment. "Oh, wait. Y'all didn't get any."

She laughed, and I laughed with her.

What Chauncey had done for Miriam was definitely special, but that's how it'd been the four years I'd known him. Every day, Chauncey made sure Miriam knew that she was loved. And that made Chauncey an amazing man to me. He loved the ground that Miriam waddled on, and she deserved it. All the love she'd missed in her childhood, she had now. There was nothing more wonderful than that.

When the bell rang, Miriam tore her nose away from the flowers and dashed to the door. "My boo!" she shouted.

I looked at Michellelee, she looked at me, and we both rolled our eyes. True love was so special, I guessed.

"Miriam, it's just supposed to be the three of us this morning," I said.

"I guess Chauncey couldn't stay away." She swung the door open. "Boo," she began, but then her voice faded.

"Emily!" my mother drawled as she sailed into our townhouse with her arms open wide. She didn't say a word to Miriam, who still stood at the door, holding it for my father, who had a big old camera in his hand.

I jumped up from the sofa. "Mom, Daddy. I thought you guys were meeting us at the campus. You have to get over there because it's going to be hard to get seats." That had been my excuse to keep my parents away. I loved my parents dearly, but sometimes they could be a bit over the top. I added, "There're going to be over thirty thousand people there."

"We don't have to worry about seats," my mother said. "Your father talked to Michael this morning."

"Michael?" I asked, having no idea who she was talking about.

"Michael Eisner," she said in a tone like I should've known. "Didn't you know he's one of the commencement speakers?"

"One of the commencement speakers, yes, one of your friends, no."

"Of course I know him, Daughter," my father piped in, calling me by the not-so-original nickname he'd given me when I was born. "He's a member of Delta Upsilon, too, and we've gotten together a few times over the years. I talked to him last night and now we're in the reserved section."

See what I mean? Whose parents did that?

My father added, "Though with as much money as I paid this school over these years, I should've been sitting on the stage."

My parents laughed, but my father meant what he said.

"I think you should still get over there as early as you can. The lines are going to be outrageous."

"Now, why would we go over there when we can be here?" my mother said. "We want to spend some time with you, Emily."

"That's right, Daughter," my father said. "Last night you ran off right after dinner."

"Sorry about that, but we really wanted to get to that party," I said.

My mother waved her hand. "We forgive you. All I want to do today is focus on your graduation." She took both of my hands in hers. "I am so proud of you."

"Thanks, Mom."

"Yes, Doctor Harrington. We are very proud," my dad said before he kissed my cheek.

"I'm not a doctor yet, Daddy."

"But you will be very soon," my mother said. "Proudly following in your father's footsteps."

I grinned, pleased that my parents were happy. I wasn't following in the exact footsteps of my father; he was a pediatric heart surgeon. But with my PhD in psychology that I'd get in the next four years, at least I'd be in the "Doctor" club. That was good enough for my parents.

My father said, "The only thing that would've made me happier is . . ."

Before he could finish, my friends piped in, "If you had gone to Ole Miss!" And then they giggled.

My parents filled up any room they entered, so for these last few minutes, I'd forgotten that Miriam and Michellelee were there. Now, I was horrified. I couldn't believe my friends were making fun of my father like that. It was true that he had said those exact words at least one hundred times last night when my parents had taken us all out to dinner. But to repeat his words back to him this way; my friends didn't know who they were messing with.

It was the mood of the day that saved Miriam and Michellelee. The only thing my mother did was turn her head slightly and say, "Oh, hello, ladies," as if she was just noticing them. Even though Miriam was the one who had opened the door, and even though my mother had almost been standing on Michellelee's feet, she truly hadn't seen my friends.

My parents! I had to love them and I believed they really did try. But they lived in such a secluded community. Not just in terms of where our home was, but in terms of where their minds were. My parents came from old money. Both of them. Generations of doctors on my father's side and federal judges on my mother's side. My parents only dealt with people in their class and of their color.

"Anyway," I said quickly, trying to divert the attention away from my girlfriends. "Miriam, Michellelee, and I were going to stay here and take some pictures before we headed over to the campus."

"No time for pictures," my father said, waving the hand that held his camera.

I glanced at my friends and apologized with my eyes.

My father continued, "There is something we have to show you before we go over to the school."

"What?"

My mother said, "Don't ask any questions, just come with me." She took my hand and led me toward the door.

As I passed Miriam, I shrugged. From the stories I'd told them, and after finally meeting my parents last night, my friends surely understood. When my parents were around, it was all about Dr. and Mrs. Harrington.

"I'll be right back," I said as I followed my mother.

Not that I expected Miriam and Michellelee to stay behind. My friends were way too nosy for that. I didn't have to turn around to know that both of them were right behind me.

I took two steps out of the townhouse and screamed. Well, I

didn't scream. I opened my mouth to scream, but I didn't have the chance. Miriam and Michellelee screamed for me.

There it was—my dream car. The car I was absolutely sure my parents would buy for me four years from now, when I received my PhD. But it was here now. A red Porsche 911. Sitting in front of our townhouse. With a white bow on the grille.

A bunch of people stood around the car, gazing at it in awe.

"Oh, my God," Michellelee said. "It's red! That must mean it's mine."

Those words made me find my voice. "I don't think so." Turning to my parents, I could barely breathe. "It's mine?"

"It's yours, sweetheart," my mother said.

"Yes, it's yours, Daughter," my father added.

"Thank you," I said, squeezing them both as tightly as I could.

"I had wanted to get you two of these," my father said, "but your mother stopped me." When he laughed and my mother didn't, I knew he was telling the truth.

Turning to Miriam and Michellelee, I clapped my hands and squealed. And my girls joined in with me.

"We've got to go for a ride!" Miriam exclaimed.

"But it only has two seats," I said.

"That's okay, we'll stuff Miriam in the back."

Any other time, Miriam would've been pissed at Michellelee. But now she nodded as if that was a good idea.

I turned to my parents. "Can we?"

My father dangled the keys and I jumped up and down.

"Thank you, Daddy. I love you so much."

"And I love you, Daughter. In all ways and for always," he said before he snapped the first photo . . .

❖

IN ALL WAYS and for always. Those were words my father had said to me every day of my life. In the morning when Nellie (the woman who helped raise me) got me up, dressed, and to the table for breakfast, my conversation with my father was always the same.

"Good morning, Daddy."

He would lean over so that I could kiss his cheek. "Morning, Daughter." Then he would wait until I climbed into my chair before adding, "Do you know how much I love you?"

Even though I knew what he was going to say, I asked, "How much?"

"In all ways and for always."

And at night, after I said my prayers, whenever my father was home, he would come in and say the same thing before he tucked me into bed. It was our little game. A game that told me how much I was loved and how I would always be.

But those days were so far away. I no longer had that car, just like I no longer had my father's love. I had to sell the car for funds when my parents took their support away. And I'd have to walk away from Jamal if I wanted my father in my life again.

That was never going to happen. I'd never leave Jamal, because he loved me in a way that I thought my father did, but actually didn't. Jamal really did love me in all ways and for always. No matter what I did, no matter what mistakes I made, no matter what, Jamal would be there. Just like I would be there for him—in all ways and for always.

At least that was one promise of love that I would always be able to depend on.

8

Miriam

t was a dream and I knew it, but I wanted to stay in my semicon-
scious state for as long as I could. As long as my eyes were closed,
I was with Chauncey. At least, that's the way it felt. Like Chauncey
was right here and we could travel back in time together. Back to a
day that I would always remember . . .

✦

June 9, 2000

It wasn't supposed to be this way in Los Angeles. Not this month.
This was supposed to be June Gloom, when the marine layer made
the days cloudy and cool. But the weatherman didn't get the memo,
because my first week as a full-time working girl had greeted me with
record-breaking, ninety-plus-degree temperatures.

It had been hard, trudging from my studio apartment in my thir-
teen-year-old, beat-up, rusting Toyota that I'd copped a week after
graduation. Every morning, I left my place on La Cienega, cool and

collected, but was a hot mess by the time I drove up to Beverly Hills to my management training job at the Beverly Hilton.

It wasn't the most glamorous job for a USC graduate with a BFA in theater arts, but you know what, I had a job. And it wasn't like I'd gone to college to build a career, like Emily and Michellelee. They were pursuing their dreams and I was going after mine. I wanted to be a wife and mother. That was the desire that God had put on my heart and I was never going to apologize.

Until Chauncey decided to make me his wife, though, I had to work, which was proving more difficult than I'd thought. Not that the training program was all that mentally challenging. But physically, it was a beast. This first week, they'd had me on my feet behind the front desk for the entire eight hours every day.

Now all I wanted to do was get home and celebrate my first weekend, my first days off.

The back of my blouse was sticking to the pleather seat and I was so glad to get out of this broke-down car. But it was even hotter outside and I had no idea where I was going to find the energy to climb up to my third-floor apartment.

By the time I got to the second landing, I was too pooped to go on; I had to take a break.

"I really need to lose at least twenty pounds," I whispered.

"What?" A voice came from above. "Are you talking to yourself?"

Looking up, I grinned. Peeking over the railing was my boo. "What're you doing here?" I was able to move a bit faster, knowing that at the top was my reward.

"I came to see you," Chauncey said. "To make sure you made it through your first week okay."

When I got to the last step, I was breathing like I needed a ventilator, but Chauncey pulled me up and into his arms, making me forget just how tired and funky I was. To anyone passing by, Chauncey and I, with our round bodies, probably looked like overstuffed teddy bears. I didn't care. I just loved this man.

But then I remembered how hot I was and I pushed Chauncey away. "Ewww . . . I'm stinky and sweaty." I wiggled from his embrace. "Let me get inside and freshen up."

"Girl, you don't have to freshen a thing for me. I even love your funky behind."

I sucked my teeth as Chauncey followed me into the apartment. "I thought you were working today."

"Nope. I wanted to make sure that I'd be here when my baby came home." He started singing, "My baby can bring home the bacon and then fry it up in the pan."

I laughed. "I haven't brought home any bacon yet. I don't get my first paycheck for another two weeks."

"Oh, okay. So you're cool? Got enough money?"

I nodded and almost asked this man to marry me right then, 'cause I loved the way he loved me. I turned the floor fan to high, then unbuttoned my blouse and moaned with pleasure when the cool air caressed me. If Chauncey hadn't been standing right there, I would've stripped down to nothing. But even though Chauncey and I had been intimate since my eighteenth birthday, I wasn't crazy about standing in broad daylight butt-naked in front of anyone, not even my man.

"Baby, why don't you come over here and let me take care of you." Taking my hand, he led me to my pullout sofa. "Just lean back"—he gently pushed me down on the couch—"I'm gonna make you feel good."

By the time Chauncey lifted my legs up and slipped my pumps from my feet, my eyes were closed. Then he pushed and pressed his fingers against the arch of my foot and I almost screamed out loud. He kept up that pleasure on my right foot and then shifted to my left. And I swear, I was just floating on air.

For minutes, and minutes, and minutes he kept on and on and on, and the weight of this week eased from my shoulders (and my feet).

"This . . . feels . . . so . . . good."

"Ssshhhh . . ."

So, I did what my boo said and just focused on the bliss. When I felt Chauncey set my feet back on the couch, like he was done, I wanted to cry. I missed that good feeling already. But then he took my right hand, something he'd never done before, and he massaged the tips of each of my fingers before he made his way down to the center of my hand. When he squeezed that spot between my thumb and forefinger, I did cry out.

Chauncey chuckled, but I didn't care how crazy I sounded. I wanted him to do it again. Then he took my left hand and did the same thing, making me scream out once more. I was drifting in ecstasy; but then I felt something cold against my finger.

My eyes popped open, and even though Chauncey had loosened me so much that I felt like a noodle, my eyes were clear enough to see that he had put a ring on my finger.

My eyes didn't leave that silver band that hugged the fourth finger on my left hand until I heard Chauncey's voice. I turned, and there was my boo on bended knee.

"Baby, would you do me the honor of—"

"Yes," I screamed, wrapping my arms around his neck, and making him tumble backward. He pulled me down, I fell on top of him, and we rolled across the floor laughing.

"Oh, my God!" I kept saying over and over. "Of course I will marry you. I cannot wait to marry you. Let's get married right now." I was still giggling because I knew we looked crazy, but I meant every word I said.

He laughed with me. "Now, that's funny."

"I'm not kidding," I said. "If I could, I would marry you today. Right now."

"But what about that wonderful wedding you've been dreaming of since you were a little girl?"

"It was never like that for me, you know that, Chauncey. I never dreamed about a wedding. The only thing I've ever wanted you've already given to me." I held out my hand and stared at the ring. "I just wanted the right man to love me."

Chauncey's eyes began to glisten, like my words had touched his heart. He was on top of me and when he lowered his head to kiss me, it was a fact, I was truly loved. When he leaned back, he asked, "Do you mean that, baby? Do you really want to get married without a big wedding?"

"I really mean it." I held his face between my hands and made him look me square in my eyes. "I want to be your wife now."

He nodded and then pulled me up from the floor. "My mother is going to kill me, but let's do this. Let's make this happen."

"Really?" I squealed. "Tonight?"

He shook his head. "We can't do it tonight because of licenses and stuff like that, but let's figure this out. And maybe by next week at this time you can be Mrs. Miriam Williams."

When I squeezed my arms around his neck, my plan was to never, ever let this man go, and I never would have if God hadn't taken Chauncey away from me . . .

✦

WITH THAT THOUGHT, I let my eyes open slowly, leaving Chauncey behind in my dreams. I stretched my arm in front of me and looked at my hand, the same way I'd done that day.

I'd been wearing the same ring, this thin band with just a chip of a diamond, for the last twelve years. I'd never upgraded, as I often heard women at the PTA and Pop Warner football talk about doing with their rings. Upgrade to what? Nothing would ever be as special as this ring. This ring that Chauncey had purchased with just the little bit of money that he'd saved from his first job as an EMT. Yes, this ring was far from the biggest diamond I'd ever seen, but it had been given to me by the biggest heart I'd ever known.

So how was my heart supposed to keep beating without that kind of love?

It had been three days since I lost him, and really, the fact that I was still breathing was a wonder to me. I was functioning, and there was only one reason why I was able to go on—Jamal.

Through it all, Jamal had been by my side. First, on Wednesday, he sat next to me and Mama Cee at the funeral home as we chose Chauncey's casket, picked out the program, selected the flowers, and discussed how many police escorts we'd need.

Then yesterday, he was there again, explaining all the legal papers and filling out the insurance forms. He made every call, mailed every claim; there was nothing I had to do. Even last night as the house filled with family, friends, church members, and Chauncey's fellow firefighters, Jamal stood next to me, meeting and greeting because I found it too hard to speak. He was there, even though Emily had to work. He was there, so I didn't feel so alone.

But it was last night, when Pastor Ford asked all of us to pray, that I was truly grateful for Jamal. Even though I didn't think there was any point in praying, I had joined the circle, bowed my head, and listened to Pastor pray. It was hard to stand there, though, as emotions rose up in me. All I wanted to do was scream out and demand answers from God. But right when I parted my lips, a hand closed around mine. I didn't have to open my eyes to know it was Jamal. I could feel his strength and that kept me calm.

Jamal was wonderful, but he was not Chauncey. And the first tears of the day rolled down my cheek.

The knock on my bedroom door relieved me from my thoughts and when my mother-in-law peeked in, I wiped my tears away.

"I'm just checking on you before Charlie and I get going," Mama Cee said.

"Get going? What time is it?" I glanced at the clock. "Oh, my God. I have to get the boys." I made my move, but my mother-in-law held up her hand.

"Stay in bed. The boys are good, I made them breakfast."

"Why didn't they wake me up?"

"We told them not to," Mama Cee said, as she sat on the edge of the bed.

I leaned back against the headboard. "I can't believe I slept this late."

"Eight-thirty is not late." Mama Cee chuckled. "And you need to rest so that you can be strong for your sons."

"Mama Cee, I can't imagine that I'll ever be strong again."

She patted my hand. "I know it seems impossible right now. The days look dark and the nights are even more bleary. But I can promise you, as a woman who lost the love of her life all those years ago, you do make it through. One day, you'll think about Chauncey and you'll smile before you cry."

I blinked, but that didn't stop my tears. "Here you are comforting me, and I should be doing that for you."

"Just being here with you and the boys gives me comfort."

"I know, but I have to remember that you're hurting, too."

She nodded. "A mother is never supposed to bury her child. But I just hold on to the Lord and boldly demand that He hold on to me."

Her words made me fold my arms across my chest.

"Go back to sleep," Mama Cee said. "Charlie's going to drop

me off at Leah's," she added, referring to the beauty salon where she'd been going for almost thirty years before she moved to Arizona. Every time she came to LA, Mama Cee went to the shop, since she claimed that no one in Arizona could get her hair right. "And then," Mama Cee continued, "Charlie is going to stop by to see a couple of his friends. Will you and the boys be all right?"

"Definitely. By the time you get back, the house will probably be filled with folks."

"Okay. I have my cell if you need me," she said before she stepped out of the bedroom.

No matter what Mama Cee said, I needed to get up and at least check on my sons. But I needed just a few more moments. Because here, in bed, was where I felt closest to Chauncey.

I reached for the pillow where he'd laid his head just four days ago and rubbed my hand across the case. Then I pulled it as close to my chest as I possibly could, and squeezed.

"Chauncey," I whispered. "Chauncey, Chauncey, Chauncey."

◆

WHEN THE DOORBELL rang, I moaned. Even though it was almost noon, I hadn't even been out of bed for an hour and I wasn't ready for company. At least I was dressed, if you could call my jeans and T-shirt being dressed.

But when I opened the door, I was grateful once again.

"I should've known it was you." I stepped aside so that Jamal could come in. "You don't have to check on me every day."

He wrapped me in his arms, giving me that morning hug that had helped me through the last three days. "Well, I'm not here for you," he said, stepping back. My frown made him chuckle. "I told the boys last night that I would take them out this afternoon."

"Really? They didn't say anything to me."

"I just kinda figured they needed a break. They haven't been out-side since . . . you know. So, I'm going to take them out to lunch."

"Jamal, thank you!" I turned toward the stairs. "They're up in Mikey and Steve's room just watching TV and playing video games. I'll get them."

Jamal called over my shoulder, "No, let me get them ready."

I moved away from the steps, then watched as Jamal trotted up the stairs to the room that the boys had been sharing since my mother-in-law and brother-in-law arrived. Minutes later, the boys bolted down the stairs with Jamal behind them.

I kissed them all good-bye, hugged Jamal, then stood at the door and waved at my sons until Jamal's car was out of sight. When I turned around and closed the door, there was nothing but silence.

Last night the house had been filled with so many people, chat-ting, and laughing, and eating the food that overflowed. Everyone had been here to support me, but in truth, it all just irked me. Be-cause while they continued to live, my life had stopped. But no one seemed to get that, and after a while, all I wanted was to be left alone.

But now I was by myself and this didn't feel so good either.

I wandered into the living room and stopped in front of the fire-place, taking in the pictorial history that revealed just how happy my twelve years with Chauncey Williams had been. I studied the photo we'd taken after our Friday afternoon, city hall wedding, exactly one week after Chauncey had proposed.

Emily and Michellelee stood by my side and Jamal stood beside Chauncey. Thinking about the hope I had that day brought new tears and I bit my lip, trying to hold them back. I was so tired of crying.

I moved over to the photo at the other end of the mantel—the picture where I sat in a high-backed chair that looked like a throne, with all of my men holding court. The last family picture we'd taken three months ago. The final picture.

No matter how much I tried, a tear rolled down my cheek.

In the middle of all the pictures on the mantel was a stone that Chauncey had picked up on our two-night honeymoon in Santa Barbara. It was right outside the cottage that we never left once we arrived that Friday night. And then, on Sunday, when it was time to go home, Chauncey picked up this stone, saying he had to take a piece of our honeymoon with him.

When we got back to his apartment, he had painted the words: *As for me and my wife, we shall serve the Lord* on the rock.

Those memories really had my tears flowing now. But still, I rolled the stone over and stared at my sons' names, which Chauncey had painted on the rock when each was born.

"It wasn't supposed to be like this, Chauncey," I said, returning the stone to its place. "We were supposed to be together, forever."

A breeze brushed over me and I stopped. I shivered, but not because I was cold. There wasn't a single window open in the house, so where had that come from?

My eyes darted from one corner of the room to the other. Then I turned back to the pictures on the mantel and stared into the still eyes of my husband. Could that have been Chauncey?

I stood listening to the silence and waiting to feel that breeze again. But after about a minute, I said, "What am I doing?"

Was I going crazy? Was I always going to be waiting for some sign of Chauncey?

When the telephone rang, I sighed with relief. I didn't care who was on the other end. Talking to someone who'd dialed the wrong number was better than being alone like this.

But it wasn't a stranger.

"Hey, Miriam!" Emily sang through the receiver the moment I picked up. "How are you?"

"I'm good," I said, perching on the arm of the sofa.

"I'm just checking on you. I wish to God I could be there with you."

"I know, but I'm good."

"I want to be with Steve, Mikey, and Junior, too."

"There'll be time for that. You have to do your job right now."

Emily sighed. "There was so much loss, Miriam. So much tragedy."

"It's so sad." I shook my head.

When I didn't say anything for a few seconds, Emily spoke up. "Miriam?"

It took a moment for me to swallow the boulder that had expanded in my throat. "Yeah," I squeaked.

"Oh, sweetie."

"I just don't know how I'm going to do it, Em. The funeral's in a couple of days and I don't know how I'm going to say good-bye to Chauncey."

"You're going to do it, and we'll be with you. We're going to help you through this week, next week, next month, next year, whenever you need us."

"I know," I sniffed, "and I can't thank you enough. You and Jamal have been great."

"Well, I haven't done anything, but I'm really glad that Jamal has been able to sub for me. By the way, is he there? I wanna just say hello; I left so early this morning he was still asleep."

"No, he took the boys out for lunch."

"Oh, good. Where was he taking them?"

"Probably to that four-star restaurant we used to depend on in college . . . McDonald's."

We shared a small laugh.

"Listen, I'm on my way to the Children's Hospital, but I'm gonna try to get to you tonight."

"Don't worry about me, Em. I promise you, I'm good."

"I know you are. I was just thinking that maybe I could come over and we could read the Bible together like we used to."

I wasn't even going to lie to her. That wasn't going to happen. So all I said was, "I know you gotta go, so love you!"

She sighed. "Mean it."

Slowly, I hung up the phone, and for the first time since Jamal had left with the boys, calm covered me. Since the day we met, Emily had been a blessing. And now, both she and Jamal were the balm for my grief.

Even though it had been fourteen years, I still carried a sliver of regret for the way I'd handled Emily when she'd told me that she was interested in Jamal. I was so wrong, but my opinion didn't matter. Nothing and no one was going to keep Emily and Jamal apart. It took some time, but just like Emily had been trying to tell everyone, she and Jamal were perfect together, just like Chauncey and I had been.

At least my friends would have their happy ending. At least that was my hope—that Emily and Jamal would grow old together and get to do all those things that I'd never get to do with Chauncey.

I stood up. People would be coming by soon, so I couldn't sit here, reflecting. I needed to get moving.

I waited for just a moment, though, wanting to feel that breeze again. But when I felt nothing, I ambled into the bedroom. Jamal and the boys had been gone for almost an hour and I couldn't wait for them to get back.

No matter what I thought last night, I now knew the truth. I didn't want to be by myself.

I just couldn't do it.

9

MIRIAM

My mother-in-law kissed me on the cheek and then held my face between her hands. "You're going to be fine," she said before she hugged me and then climbed the stairs as if her sixty-year-old bones ached.

I watched until she disappeared into the darkness of the second-floor hallway, then I turned back to the living room. When I faced Jamal I said, "Tomorrow. The funeral's really tomorrow, isn't it?"

When my shoulders started to heave, Jamal rushed from where he'd been sitting and put his arms around me.

Even though I tried not to, I sobbed. "I can't say good-bye to him, Jamal."

"I know," he said, as we sat together. "I know."

"Good-bye, I don't think I can say it." I couldn't stop shaking my head. "Good-bye is final."

He nodded slowly and squeezed my hands as if he understood. "I know this may sound a bit crazy"—he lowered his eyes—"but I don't think we're really saying good-bye." A pause. "Because I can feel him." Now he looked at me. "It's crazy, I know, but I can feel Chauncey. Like he's still here."

Before he even finished talking, I was trembling. "Oh my God!" I shouted, startling Jamal. "I know exactly what you're saying because I feel Chauncey, too."

"No, I mean, I really feel him, Miriam. Yesterday, when I was driving over here, I felt like he was right there, riding shotgun."

"I'm telling you, that's exactly how I feel. On Friday, when you took the boys to lunch, that happened to me. Right here in the living room. And then, over the weekend, I've felt him everywhere. Sometimes in the kitchen, sometimes in the bedroom. And I can hear him, too. I can hear him saying . . ."

We spoke together, "Everything's going to be all right."

Silence followed our words and we stared at each other.

"Do you think," I began in a whisper, "do you think that Chauncey is really here?" I let my eyes wander around the living room.

Jamal nodded. "I can't support it scripturally, but I know what's in my heart. Somehow, he's here, and that's why we won't really be saying good-bye."

Fresh tears came to my eyes, but not because I was sad. I was so grateful to have someone taking this journey with me. It made sense that Jamal understood. He loved Chauncey the way I had. We didn't have a blood connection, we had a deeper connection, on a soul level. Chauncey was my soulmate. Chauncey was Jamal's soul brother. And we were the only two people on earth who loved him that way.

Realizing that made me reach for Jamal and wrap my arms around him. When he held me back, I closed my eyes. And he must've closed his, too, because he should've seen Charlie before we heard his cough.

It was more of a clearing of his throat, but it was enough to make Jamal and me jump back and away from each other. We'd been sitting together in the center of the sofa, but now we were on opposite ends.

"Uh," Charlie said when I looked up.

I felt like a teenager who'd been caught.

"Uh," Charlie said again. It wasn't much of a word, but at least he was saying something, because Jamal and I were mute.

Then Jamal sprang up from the sofa. "I'm going to get out of here." He grabbed his jacket. "Is there anything you need before I leave?"

"Nah, big bro," Charlie said, calling Jamal by the name he'd called him since childhood. "We're good. And you've been here all day, so just go on home."

Jamal nodded and barely looked at me when he said good night. Still sitting on the sofa, I watched Charlie walk Jamal to the door.

"Tell Emily I said hello," Charlie said, a bit loudly.

When my brother-in-law came back into the living room, he asked, "Are you all right?"

"I'm good." I nodded. "Finally, I think I'm really good."

Charlie peered at me as if he was waiting for more, but I didn't have another word or ounce of energy to give to him. All I did was give him a good-night hug and then go into my bedroom. It didn't take me long to lie down and close my eyes. And for the first time since I lost my husband, I slept straight through to morning.

But now that I was awake, neither the comfort of Jamal's words nor the comfort of his arms around me last night had followed me into this morning. All I felt now was dread.

I peeked up at the clock. Even though it was just after six, there was no time to wallow in grief. I had to get myself and the boys ready for our ten o'clock good-bye.

I inched over to the edge of the bed, thinking the next time I laid my head down, Chauncey would really be gone forever. Reaching across the bed, I did what I'd been doing every day—I grabbed Chauncey's pillow, held it to my chest, and inhaled, imagining that I could smell him. I squeezed, imagining that I could feel his strength.

Then, I spoke to the pillow and imagined he could hear the words of love I had for him.

After a moment, I set Chauncey's pillow back on his side of the bed and then slipped into my bathrobe before stepping out of my room.

The aroma of brewing coffee embraced me even though the house was still just-a-bit-after-dawn quiet. I stopped in the kitchen, poured myself a cup, then peeked into the backyard before I pushed the sliding door open and stepped outside.

I rested my cup on the patio table before I wrapped my arms around my mother-in-law. "Good morning."

"Mornin' baby." As I sat next to her, she asked, "Did you rest well?"

I nodded as I sipped. "It was my best night so far, but now that it's morning, now that it's today . . ."

"You're gonna make it, baby. We all are." She patted the worn leather cover of the Bible on the table in front of her. "That's one of the promises of God. He promises to turn our mourning into dancing."

I took another sip, sure that I would never dance again.

"Yes," Chauncey's mother continued, "the Lord really does feel our pain and He's shedding a tear or two for us."

My mother-in-law gave me a sideways glance. I knew what she was thinking. Usually when she got to doing her little preaching, I was her Amen corner. Whenever she sang about how good God had been to her, I was her background singer, adding my praises, too.

But even though God had brought me so far, it felt like it had all been for nothing. He'd taken away the greatest treasure that He'd ever given to me. So, what was the point of all the other good things?

My mother-in-law opened her mouth in a perfectly shaped O, but before she could speak, Charlie slid open the patio door.

"You finished reading your Bible, Mama Cee?" he asked.

It took her a moment to unlock her eyes from me, but she nodded as she faced her son. "Been finished for a while now. Just sitting here, talkin' about how in the midst, God is still good."

Charlie paused for a moment, as if he was waiting for me. When I said nothing, he piped in with "Amen."

I guessed he was going to play my position and I almost smiled.

Charlie slipped into the chair on the other side of me and then asked his mother, "Did you talk to Miriam yet?"

My eyes moved back and forth between them. "About what?"

To Charlie, Mama Cee said, "I haven't had the chance." To me, she said, "Charlie suggested something last night and I don't know why I didn't think of it." She rested her hand over mine. "We want you and the boys to come live with us."

"What?"

"Yeah," Charlie said from the other side, making me feel as if I was surrounded by this idea. "It's going to be a lot with the boys, and we can help."

I shook my head. "Arizona? I don't know. It's hard for me to imagine my life past tomorrow."

"I know," Mama Cee said softly, in that voice that always made me want to lay my head on her chest. "But we're your family and I want you close so that I can take care of you the way my son would want."

In the last week, I'd had lots of reasons to cry, and my mother-in-law had just added another one. She'd given me lots of these tear-jerking, heartwarming moments over the years.

But I just couldn't cry anymore, so I sighed deeply. "Can I think about this?"

"Of course. We just wanted you to know this is an option."

"A good option," Charlie added.

Mama Cee said, "An option we want to happen."

Reaching across the table, I took my mother-in-law's hand and then my brother-in-law's, too. "I'm so grateful for you."

"So, you'll really think about it?" my mother-in-law asked.

"Definitely; there's a lot to consider, though. Especially how it will be for the boys."

"The Lord will lead you." She patted my hand, and turned her gaze back to the rising sun.

We sat in the silence of the budding morning, and finally Charlie said, "You want me to get the boys up?"

"No," I said softly, "I'll do that."

This was it. It was time. My legs were as heavy as my heart when I pushed my chair back. I took small steps, as if somehow slowing down could stop the inevitable.

As I stepped into the house, the doorbell rang and I released a deep breath. Today was going to be hard, but now that I heard that bell, I could do it. I rushed to the door, then fumbled with the locks, not releasing them fast enough. I was already smiling when I swung the door open, but then my smile faded right away.

"Oh."

"Oh? That must be Swahili for 'I'm so glad to see my best friend.'" Michellelee dumped the garment bag she was carrying onto the settee by the door, then hugged me. I still had the door open and I peeked outside, searching for another car. But only Michellelee's Mercedes and Charlie's rental car were in front of my house.

"Who were you expecting?" Michellelee asked.

I shut the door. "No one in particular. I mean, everyone has been stopping by. Anyway, Mama Cee made some coffee. Want a cup?"

"Definitely. And then"—she hooked her arm through mine—"I'm here to help you with whatever you need."

"Thanks, but there's something I've gotta tell you."

"What?"

I opened my mouth to tell Michellelee about Mama Cee, Charlie, and Arizona. But then I took one last glance at the front door and in an instant decided to keep that news to myself.

At least for now.

"What do you have to tell me?" Michellelee asked.

"Only that I love you."

"Awww . . . mean it," she said as she gathered me into a hug.

10

Emily

S team still filled the shower, even though it had been at least a minute since I'd stepped out. I wiped the mirror, making a small circle so that I could see my reflection.

I'd hoped that fifteen minutes under all of that steam would have been refreshing, but exhaustion was still written all over my face.

Talk about difficult times. I'd had five twelve-hour workdays in a row, each filled with nothing but sorrow. I'd even missed church yesterday because there were so many survivors to see. The countless siblings and classmates and friends left behind. There wasn't any kind of training that taught me how to keep my emotions in check under these circumstances. It was impossible, and so often, I just lost it.

I wrapped myself inside the oversized towel and wished that today wasn't today. Because if it had been a different day, I would've crawled back into bed and slept until my bones told me it was okay to rise. But today was the day and as exhausted as I was, I had to be strong for two people I loved so much: Miriam and Jamal.

When I opened the bathroom door, the sun was just beginning to make its debut, so the light in the room was dim. But I could see my husband clearly, sitting on the edge of our bed, wearing nothing but a pair of white briefs, a shocking and beautiful contrast to his skin. His head was down, his eyes were closed, and the tips of his fingers were pressed together, forming a steeple. He was a gorgeous sight: the perfection of his calves, his muscular thighs, his biceps that bulged.

But what was most attractive to me was seeing my husband in prayer. I wanted to join him, but I didn't need to be next to him to do that. Even standing this far across the bedroom, I could hear his silent plea to God, I could feel his words. That's just how we were— connected. It had always been that way. I knew it first, but it didn't take long for Jamal to get the same clarity that I had about us . . .

✦

April 18, 2001

I'd kind of coasted through the undergraduate program at USC, but this graduate program at UCLA was much more serious. I'd made it through the first semester with a decent enough 3.4 GPA. But I wanted to go for the gusto to finish my first year.

That's why I'd been up until just a little before dawn studying. Not that my professor would care that I was exhausted. Professor Gaylord, like the other teachers in the Psych department, was very strict and serious. The moment the clock struck nine, he was locking that door.

Glancing at the clock once again, I saw I would make it, if I got going now. I gathered my leather backpack and dashed out of the tiny apartment my parents had rented for me right across from the campus. But the moment I stepped outside, my cell phone rang.

Cell phones were really cool, but calls always came through at the most inopportune times. I started not to answer but curiosity grabbed ahold of me. I had to make it to class on time, but certainly I could talk and run at the same time.

"Hello," I said, breaking into a trot.

"Emily?"

I recognized the voice right away and it stopped me cold—well, maybe it didn't totally stop me, but it slowed me down. Even though I knew who was on the other end, I spoke as if I didn't. "Yes, this is Emily Harrington."

"Uh, Emily. This is Jamal."

"Jamal?"

"Yes, Jamal Taylor, Chauncey's friend."

I let a couple of moments pass as if I was trying to connect the dots, even though I was sure that Jamal knew I was pretending. It was true that he and I weren't friends, but we'd seen each other numerous times since he'd brushed me off three years ago. It was hard to stay out of each other's path when our best friends were dating and then had finally married. But it didn't matter the occasion: whenever I saw Jamal, I was aloof. He barely got a hello out of me and never a good-bye.

But now, here he was, on the other end of my phone.

"Oh, Jamal," I said. "I didn't recognize your voice."

"That's cool. It's not like you hear me all the time. How're you?"

"Good. What can I do for you?" I asked, keeping my words and my tone formal.

"If you have a moment, I want to talk to you about Miriam and Chauncey. You know their first anniversary is coming up in about two months."

I waited a beat. "I know that. And . . ." I said, keeping my cool facade, though I was heating up just at the sound of his voice.

"Well, I wanted to do something special for them."

"Like?" I wasn't giving him an inch.

He proceeded. "I was thinking about doing something like a destination party. Having a first-anniversary celebration in Maui for them."

I couldn't help it. I stopped moving. Maui! Now, that was special. "Wow!" I said.

"Yeah," he said, sounding as if he was pleased to get a positive word out of me. "I was hoping we could get a bunch of their friends to gather their pennies and go down there for a long weekend or something. I was going to pay for Miriam and Chauncey. You know, their airfare and hotel."

"Wow!" I said again, hating myself for being impressed.

"So, that's the idea," he said, "but I need someone to help me work it out, and that's why I'm calling."

Oh, okay, was I really supposed to believe that? I was sure he really did need help, but this felt like a ruse to spend time with me. I knew it! I'd always known it: Jamal liked me.

Then he said, "I called Michellelee, but she told me that she was going to be in Indiana covering the upcoming McVeigh execution."

And with just those few words, he'd blown up my world. I just needed to stop thinking that there would ever be anything between me and Jamal and just help him out for Miriam's sake.

"So, what do you need from me?" I asked, speeding up my steps.

"Help with the planning. I need a partner to make sure that I do it right and don't forget anything."

"Sure, I'll help."

"Great, great. Well then, let's get together. Maybe we could go out to dinner."

Going out to dinner was one of the things I wanted to do with him from the moment he walked through our door. But I said, "Dinner would be difficult. My schedule is quite full. How about we just meet for coffee?"

"Okay."

Did I detect a tinge of disappointment in his voice?

He said, "Do you have any time today or tomorrow?"

"No," I said bluntly, even though my schedule, except for studying, was completely open. "I'm busy, so let's do Saturday morning."

"I was hoping to meet with you sooner."

"Sorry, but like I said—"

"You're busy," he finished for me.

"Yes, so let's do Saturday," I said, feeling like, finally, I had some control. "At Magic's Starbucks. The new one in Ladera." That was right around the corner from Miriam's and I could hook up with her afterward.

"That'll work. You wanna meet around nine?"

"Let's make it ten," I said.

He laughed as if he was onto my game. "Okay, ten it is. Thanks, Emily."

When I hung up the phone, I was mad at myself on so many levels. I was mad because I'd thought that he had called me, Emily Harrington, because he wanted to talk to me, Emily Harrington. And then I was mad because I even cared.

But at least I made it to my class on time, though I really could have done without the lecture. It was hard to concentrate with Jamal Taylor on my mind.

He stayed on my mind for the next two days. And he was really on my mind when I woke up on Saturday morning at five o'clock trying to decide what I was going to wear five hours later.

By eight, I was sick of myself, as I marched back and forth from my closet to my bed. "I'm just going to have coffee. This is no big deal."

But the fact that half of my closet was thrown across my bed and shoes and boots were tossed everywhere let me know that something my daddy always told me was true: a fool could never fool himself.

Finally, I made a choice, but only because it was nine-fifteen and I refused to be late. I put on my rhinestone-studded jeans with the matching jacket, and I strutted up to Starbucks with nothing but confidence. That is, until I saw him sitting under one of the green umbrellas outside.

But I kept my stride as if he had no effect on me, and when he stood to greet me, I congratulated myself on still breathing.

"Hey," he said in that voice. He reached out and held me in an awkward hug, and I quickly slipped away. "So, you wanna go in and get a drink?"

"That's why I suggested Starbucks." I started walking toward the door, not even waiting for him.

He was quick, though, and right behind me. I had no doubt his eyes were on me. Too bad there wasn't much to see from behind. Now, if he was in front and walking backward, I would've given him quite a show.

We gave our orders to the barista: a chai tea latte for me, and the bold pick of the day for him. Straight, no chaser, no cream, no sugar—nothing but black coffee.

Once we had our drinks in hand, he said, "It's kinda nice. Let's sit outside."

"Let's sit in here," I responded, and led the way. Sitting at the table, I pulled out my PalmPilot and got right to business. "I'm going to take some notes."

"Wait a minute, Emily." He reached across the table, touched my hand, and the electricity shot straight from my fingers down to my toes. He said, "I've wanted to apologize to you for a while now, but you never gave me much of a chance."

At least he'd noticed that he'd been ignored.

"That's why I called Michellelee first," he said. "'Cause I had images of you hanging up on me, and I would've deserved it. But can I have a moment to explain?"

I leaned back in my chair, crossed my arms. That was my signal that he could go on.

"When we met, I really liked you and I thought we were going to be great friends. But then you called and were talking about dinner and going out, and I didn't see you that way."

"Why not? We talked for what, two, three hours? You liked me, I liked you. So what was it?" I put my finger to my head as if I was thinking for a moment. "Oh, yeah," I said, as if I'd just remembered. "I was an ineligible player, all because I was . . ."

I stopped so that he could finish, but all he did was lower his eyes.

"That's what I'm sorry about. Because I should've never said that. I should've just told you that I wanted to be friends and not said anything else."

"You're right about that."

"I really *wanted* to be friends. You were so cool. You're still cool."

"How do you know that? I could have cooled off."

"You haven't." He grinned. "Plus, I keep up with what's going on with you through Miriam and Chauncey."

"Oh really? Why?" I hoped my tone sounded like I was just curious and really didn't care. But inside, my heart was doing some kind of thumpity-thump-thump thing.

"Because I wanted to know what was going on with you and I was mad at myself for missing out on a good friendship. So I apologize for the way it went down and I really hope that we can be friends."

I shrugged. "Let's just see what happens," I said, knowing full well that when I got back to my apartment, I'd be dancing all night.

For the next couple of hours we talked and planned, forgetting that I was Emily, the white girl, and he was Jamal, the black guy. We were just Emily and Jamal, friends of Miriam and Chauncey, planning the surprise party of the century.

"Now about the expenses," I said. "I can help out, and I'm sure Michellelee will want to help as well."

"No, I got this. My grandmother left me some money back when she passed and I've been waiting for the right time to spend a little bit of it. This is it."

Awww. I was trying my best not to look at him with puppy-dog eyes, but I was sure that, the way I was adoring him, he was soon going to be calling me Rover.

"Now, you guys," he began, "y'all are gonna have to pay your own way. I ain't that special."

"Oh, don't worry. I'm gonna pay my way. Because if a guy were to pay for a trip like this for me, he would definitely want something that he definitely wouldn't get."

He laughed. "I knew I liked you."

"I knew you liked me, too."

We sat back and laughed together . . .

✦

THAT WAS THE moment that broke the ice, that opened the door, that encouraged me to pursue this man once again. And thank God I did, because in Maui, our world changed.

Those memories always made me smile. But not today.

My eyes were still on my husband as he stayed in his prayer-ful stance. Then, without opening his eyes or lifting his head, Jamal reached out his hand toward me and I rushed through the fog of sadness that was so heavy in our bedroom. When I sat on the bed, he wrapped his arms around me and I held him as if I was trying to blend us into one.

Finally, he kissed my forehead. "You look tired." His fingertips trailed along the side of my face.

"You do, too. What time did you get in last night?" I asked.

He looked away for a moment. "It wasn't that late. I waited until everyone had left and Chauncey's mom had gone to bed. And then, I left Miriam . . . and Charlie." He turned back to me. "I didn't want to wake you when I got home. I know how hard you've been working."

I nodded. "How's Miriam?"

He shrugged. "She's hanging in there for the boys and for Mama Cee and Charlie."

"I just hope she really understands . . ."

Jamal pressed his forefinger against my lips. "She does."

I released a sigh of relief. "She keeps telling me that she doesn't know what she would've done without you."

"Well, Charlie's been there, too."

"Yeah, but you're closer to Miriam and the boys. I know Charlie is their uncle, but Junior, Mikey, and Stevie are used to having you around." I took a breath. "So, everything is ready?"

He nodded. "The only thing left is . . . to say good-bye."

There it was again, that burn behind my eyes. "Well, I got up be-cause I knew you'd want to get there early." I stood, but Jamal pulled me back down onto the bed.

"No."

"No?"

"I've been there every day. I've helped with everything. Now they need some time together as a family."

"They consider you family, Jamal. I'm sure they want you there this morning."

"We'll meet them at the church." He pulled me close to him again. "All I want is to spend some time with you."

He kissed me, a gentle kiss. And even as the towel around me loosened and fell away, all Jamal did was kiss me. There was nothing sexual behind our connection. This was a kiss that was pure love.

Pulling me down onto the bed, he covered us both with the duvet. "I just want you to hold me," Jamal said.

I squeezed him as tightly as I could.

We rested in the silence, and even though sadness was still thick in the air, I found comfort in Jamal's arms.

After a few minutes, he said, "I can feel him, Emily."

I stayed quiet, wanting just to listen. If there was one contention in our marriage, it was that sometimes Jamal felt as if I was analyzing him. So I was always careful, but especially now, in this moment.

I didn't say anything until Jamal repeated his words, and then I only said, "I know."

More silence before he asked, "Do you feel him?"

As much as I wanted to tell Jamal that I did, we never lied to each other. Not even about the little things. "No," I said. "I don't, but I know you do. I think you're going to feel him for a long time."

When Jamal nodded, I snuggled even closer.

He said, "I've been fine till now. But now that the day is here . . . I don't know if I can do it."

I released a quiet sigh. Jamal's words were so similar to Miriam's. It hadn't occurred to me before, but my husband and my best friend were sharing the same pain, and I was even more grateful they had each other.

"It's going to be hard, but what I know is that you can do it," I finally said, wanting to encourage him. "Sweetheart, you're the strongest man I know. It's one of the reasons why I love you so much."

He squeezed me and we stayed there, lying in the bed, holding each other. Until it was time to get up and get ready for Chauncey's funeral.

11

Miriam

I was in an ocean of black.

For the last seven days, that phrase had been nothing more than a metaphor for my life. But today, it was real.

My home was filled with people wearing black. Black dresses, black suits, black shoes, black boots. Even the firefighters who'd come from all around the city wore their formal black uniforms.

The only one who wasn't in black was me. Today, I wore yellow. A plain sleeveless dress that was a bright yellow. A shocking yellow. A sunshine yellow. What I wore was *my* metaphor for what Chauncey meant to me.

Maybe it was my dress that kept people away. Maybe my dress was why I was in the midst of all of this chatter and clatter, and yet, I sat alone. I was in the center of my couch, staring at the guests who'd come to my home for the repast. The mourners were mingling among themselves, and had forgotten about the guest of honor.

I folded my hands deeper into my lap, feeling so alone in the middle of this crowd. Was it that everyone felt they'd already said everything they had to say to me? Or was it that now that Chauncey was settled in his final resting place in Inglewood Park Cemetery, there was nothing more to say?

My eyes moved slowly through the room. Sprinkled among the acquaintances were the people I really knew. Pastor Ford and Mama Cee sat in the chairs across from me talking, about God, no doubt. And then Charlie and one of his and Chauncey's high school buddies weren't too far away. Next, I caught a glimpse of Emily and Michellelee standing by the door. Their heads were so close together, like they were planning their getaway. Well, if that was their plan, I wanted to go with them.

Then my eyes settled on the one person I really wanted to talk to.

I wanted to jump up and run over to Jamal. But that would've been too obvious. So, instead, I stood slowly, smoothed out my dress, then strolled past the people who filled my home. I plastered a smile on my face as the comments came.

"Chauncey's in a better place."

"Everything happens for a reason."

"The Lord's not gonna give you more than you can handle."

"We're here for you, you won't be alone."

With each cliché, all I did was nod and keep moving. When I was right under the dining room arch, I paused, watching Jamal as he stood at the table, directing people as they came in to sample the dozens of dishes that had been prepared for the post-funeral meal. Jamal moved with ease, as if this was his home.

Then he looked up. And when he saw me, he moved, I moved, and we kinda met in the middle. "Hey," he said, pulling me closer with his smile, "how're you holding up?"

"I'm good," I said. And after a pause, I added, "This morning was hard, but not as hard as I thought it would be."

"I know what you mean," Jamal said as he put a couple of chunks of cheese and crackers on a small paper plate and handed it to me.

I didn't want a thing to eat, but I took the plate, thinking that this was exactly what Chauncey would do.

He said, "When I woke up this morning, I wasn't sure I was going to make it."

"Really?" I tilted my head. "Last night, you encouraged me."

He shrugged. "I was only being strong for you. I had to make sure you made it through today."

If I had been talking to God, I would've praised Him for giving me such a caring friend, a loving friend. "Thanks, but you don't have to be strong around me." Gently, I rested my hand on his arm. "We're going through the same thing. We miss Chauncey in the same way. It's different for us than it is for other people."

He shook his head. "I don't think so. Look around this house," he said, gesturing with his hand. "There are a whole lotta people grieving Chauncey."

"I know," I whispered, then took a step closer so that I wouldn't be overheard. "But it's different for you and me. Everyone here either knew Chauncey by blood or by acquaintance. But you and I knew Chauncey on a different level, on a soul level."

He tilted his head as if he was pondering my words.

I said, "And so, it makes sense that we go through this together. Because we get it, we understand each other's pain."

He nodded.

"I'm just saying," I kept on, "that I'm glad I have you. And I hope you know that you have me, too."

He smiled just a little. "I know that."

"Okay, so, let's make a promise right now. We don't have to be strong, we just have to be here for each other, 'cause in the coming weeks, I'm gonna need a soft place to land."

He cocked his head a bit to the side. "A soft place to land." A beat. "I like that."

I nodded. "You're that soft place for me."

"Good. 'Cause I really want to help you and the boys through this."

"There is something that you can do to help me."

"Whatever you need," he said.

"Well, when this is all over"—I laid the untouched cheese and crackers back on the table—"I really want to get together to talk about Chauncey. Some of the things only you can tell me."

"I'm sure you know everything. No one knew him like you and his mother."

"Yeah, but there are things that only you know. I'm talking about when you and Chauncey were growing up. I want to know everything, because now . . ." I stopped for a moment. My tears were trying to make a comeback. "I have to pass on as much as I can to the boys. Especially Stevie. I don't want him to forget his dad."

"Okay," he said gently, as if he'd sensed that I'd almost had a breakdown. "We can do that this week. I can come over here, or maybe we can go to lunch."

"Getting out would be great."

He nodded. "I'll check with Emily and see what her schedule's like."

"Emily . . . okay, yeah." I didn't know why I felt a bit annoyed when he mentioned Emily. I mean, she was the one who was my friend. It was because of her that Jamal was even here with me so much.

But then Jamal made me forget about his wife when he did what I'd been craving. He gave me the medicine that he'd been giving me all week. He pulled me into his arms and held me. I closed my eyes and soaked in the strength of him, the feel of his muscles, the love inside his embrace.

The sounds of the repast faded and it was as if we were alone.

He gave me no tired clichés, or false words of hope—he just held me like he was hurting, too. Like he understood me because my pain was the same as his. He held me as if we were just two sad souls finding comfort in each other.

I would've held him like that for hours. But I couldn't, so I opened my eyes. And looked straight into the bright blue eyes of Emily.

12

Emily

"E mily."

I heard someone calling my name, but they sounded far away, like they were calling me from another country.

"Emily."

It was as if my ears were clogged. Like four of my senses had taken leave of me and only my sense of sight was working.

"Emily!"

I shook my head and blinked at the same time.

"Emily! Are you okay?"

I turned around so that I could face Pastor Ford. But I also turned around so that I wouldn't have to see what I just saw.

"I'm sorry, Pastor. Did you say something?"

"Yes." My pastor's eyes were thin slits as she studied me. "Are you okay?"

"Yes," I said, shaking my head, hoping to completely rid the image that had sandblasted itself into my mind. But the image alone wasn't the problem. It was my thoughts that played like a soundtrack alongside what I'd seen. Thoughts that explained why Miriam was in Jamal's arms. Thoughts that weren't good.

"Are you sure?" my pastor asked me again.

"I am." I sighed as if exhaustion was the reason for my distraction. "It's just been a long day."

Pastor Ford nodded; I knew she'd accept that excuse. "It's been more than a long day; it's been a long week." When Pastor Ford sighed, too, I heard her exhaustion.

She'd officiated at three of the funerals, and that had to take quite an emotional toll.

Pastor asked, "How's Miriam really doing?" She looked over my shoulder. "I've been talking to her, but only a sister-friend knows for sure."

The image of Miriam and Jamal rushed right back so fast and so hard that I swayed just a bit. This time, I blinked rapidly to dispose of it. "I think she's okay. I haven't had a chance to spend a lot of time with her because of work."

Was that it? I asked myself. Was that why she was holding on to my husband that way?

"I've spoken to her a few times," Pastor said. "I try to call to pray with her since she's not doing too much of that herself right now."

Maybe that was it. Maybe she was mad at God and so she was holding on to Jamal.

Then Pastor Ford asked me about my husband. "Is Jamal doing okay?"

Another flash.

"He's doing well, too," I said.

"Really?" My pastor sounded like she didn't believe me.

"I mean, it's been hard on him. But my husband's strong and he'll get through this."

Pastor Ford's eyes narrowed once again. "Just make sure that you're taking care of Jamal. Sometimes a man doesn't want to be strong. Sometimes a man just wants to be human."

I nodded. "I'm hoping my schedule will ease up a bit. That fire . . . there are so many victims."

"I know." Pastor's voice was softer this time and she reached for my hand. "Before I asked about Jamal and Miriam, I should've asked about you. I know working with those kids is tough. I know how connected you've been to those children and their families."

I nodded. "It's exactly the same as it is for you. All I want to do is help, and take away just a little bit of their pain. But it's hard."

Before I could say anything else, I felt a hand on my shoulder. Then, "Excuse me, Pastor."

I stiffened a bit at Miriam's voice and when I spun toward her, I wondered if my expression was telling a story. I searched her face for her story, but all that was there was what I'd seen all week, grief and deep sorrow.

Miriam spoke to our pastor, not to me, "Would you mind if I took Emily away for a moment?"

"No, go ahead." Pastor Ford waved her hand. "I have to leave in a little while, but if I miss you, I'll give you a call tonight."

When Pastor stepped away, Miriam spoke as if she hadn't had her arms wrapped around my husband just a few minutes ago. "Come back here with me."

I didn't want to go anywhere with her. I wanted to stand right there, confront her, ask her what was going on. But this was a funeral and I couldn't turn it into a fight.

So with my lips pressed together and my arms stiffly by my side, I marched behind Miriam with my eyes wide open. I was looking for signs, trying to see if there was anything to explain what I'd seen and the thoughts I had.

Miriam didn't say a word until she opened the door to her bedroom and we stepped inside. I was shocked to see Michellelee already in there, sitting back on the lounger, flipping through a magazine.

"Oh, you found her," Michellelee said, tossing the magazine aside.

I stepped into the bedroom, crossed my arms, and sat down on the bed. "So, you wanted to talk to me?" I glanced at Michellelee. "To us?" I wondered if she was going to give me an explanation for why she was all over my husband that way.

Miriam didn't say a word as she walked across the room to the dresser. I watched as she opened her top drawer, then pulled out two boxes. Her head was still down as she faced me and Michellelee.

"After what happened to Chauncey, I decided that I had to make sure that everyone I love knows how I feel. So"—she looked up— "these are for you."

She handed us the boxes. Michellelee grabbed hers right away, but it took me a moment. This was the opposite of what I expected, but after a couple of seconds, I took my box from her hand.

"Oh my goodness!" Michellelee exclaimed before I'd even removed the top off mine.

But once I did, I held up the same silver link bracelet that Michellelee had in her hands. It was the same bracelet that Miriam had on, and I'd admired it when I first saw her at church this morning. The only difference was, a single red heart dangled from Michellelee's, the heart on mine was blue, and Miriam's, of course, was white.

The Red, White, and Blue.

After all these years, we still referred to ourselves that way. The name had stuck with us when some drunk guy during our sophomore year had yelled out at a party that the three of us were the American flag.

"Yeah, you're red," he told Michellelee, who was decked out in her best Delta Sigma Theta paraphernalia.

Then, he made a big deal of looking down his nose and calling me the blue-blooded basketball player.

I'd actually laughed at that, but when he turned to Miriam, I'd held my breath. Michellelee and I knew the stories of how Miriam had been teased and bullied because of her birthmark, the white streak in her hair. If that guy had said anything mean, he was gonna have to fight two angry women, because Michellelee and I would defend Miriam until the end.

But when he said, "And you, Miss White, your hair is cool," I breathed and laughed again.

From then on, around campus, we were known as the Red, White, and Blue. And we loved it because that sealed our bond even more. But this symbolism of our friendship was the best.

"I'm . . . I'm . . ." I turned the heavy links over in my hand. "I don't even have the words."

Miriam said, "Well, I do. I wanted you guys to know how much I love you. And how much I appreciate all that you've done for me. Not just since Chauncey passed away, but for half my life. You are, and will always be, my sisters."

Michellelee and I sat there, stunned at this sentiment.

"Here!" Michellelee stood up and held out her wrist to Miriam. "Help me put this on."

As Michellelee held out her left arm, she used her right hand to fan her tears away. "This is just so beautiful," she sniffed, once Miriam had finished.

Then my best friend turned to me. "You need help?"

I nodded, because it was too hard to speak. As Miriam looped the bracelet around my wrist and hooked it, I blinked back my tears of guilt. How dumb was it for me to think anything about Miriam hugging Jamal?

When my bracelet was secure, Miriam said to me, "I really have to thank you, Em, for how much you've helped me this week."

"I . . . I haven't even . . . really been here."

"But you have, you kinda sent your surrogate." She smiled. "And I appreciate that. I was just thanking Jamal for everything, too. I didn't buy him anything, though." She laughed a little. "But I let him know that I would've never made it without him and you." She paused. "And you, too, Michellelee."

So that's what their hug was all about. Really, I should have known. We all hugged each other. All the time. It had to be pure exhaustion that had me seeing and thinking something that wasn't even there.

I stood and hugged Miriam. I held her the way she'd held Jamal in the dining room. Totally innocently. And as I held her, I closed my eyes and asked God to forgive me for my thoughts.

"We are best friends," Miriam said when she pulled back.

"Yes. And we'll be that way forever."

She kissed me on my cheek. "Love you."

"Mean it," I said.

Then Michellelee linked her arms through both of ours. "And I love you—mean it, too, guys." She kissed both our cheeks and then, arm in arm, the three of us walked out of the bedroom.

13

MIRIAM

This was life after death.

An empty house. Though it wasn't really empty. Every bedroom was filled with my three sons and Mama Cee and Charlie, who had stayed even though Chauncey's funeral had been days ago.

But without Chauncey, this was an empty space. Or maybe it was just that my heart wasn't really beating.

"What are you doing now?"

I held up the mop. "I just cleaned the bathroom," I told my mother-in-law.

She frowned. "Didn't you do that yesterday?"

I shoved the mop into the corner. "Did I?" I shrugged. "There've been so many people coming in and out of this house over the past week, I just want to get everything back in place."

My mother-in-law grabbed a bottle of water from the refrigerator, then sat at the table. "Why don't you sit with me for a couple of minutes?"

"I will, Mama Cee. I'm gonna start dinner first."

"I was thinking that Charlie should take us out tonight. You've been doing nothing but cleaning and cooking and washing," she said, her voice thick with concern. "You deserve a break."

I laid the pan on the stove, then reached into the refrigerator for the pork chops that I'd thawed out last night. "Charlie doesn't have to do that." I didn't want to go anywhere. I wanted to cook and clean and wash and talk and laugh as if life was the same. Because as long as I moved, I didn't feel.

I said, "And anyway, you know these restaurants out here charge so much money."

"I wasn't talking about anyplace fancy. I just want to get you out of the house."

"I already started cooking, Mama Cee. Maybe next time."

"Okay," she said. "Maybe tomorrow."

As I rinsed the pork chops, I could feel my mother-in-law's eyes on me like a laser. There was no reason for her to worry. As long as I was cooking, and cleaning, and washing.

Then the phone rang and I dropped the meat and grabbed the receiver, grateful for another distraction.

"Hey, Miriam. What's going on?"

This daily call was my only reason to smile. "Nothing. How are you and Em doing?"

"We're good. Emily's at work."

"I can't believe the hours she's putting in, but she did call me this morning and asked me what I wanted to do about the boys."

"She told me that she wanted them to speak to someone. One of her colleagues, since she's too close Junior and 'em. I told her that was a good idea."

"I want to talk to them about it first," I said. "To see if it's even necessary."

"Okay, if you want, I can talk to them with you."

I smiled. "That would be great. The boys are still home. They're not going back to school till Monday."

"That's probably best."

"I thought so. I know it'll end up being almost two weeks that they'll be out, but I want to make sure they're okay before I let them go, you know?"

"You're doing the right thing."

"And they're spending time with Mama Cee and Charlie," I added.

"Now, that's a good thing."

I wanted to tell him that it would be good for the boys to spend time with him, too, but I didn't want to impose on Jamal that way. He'd been with me every day before the funeral and now that it was over, I didn't expect him to give me his time like that.

"So . . . otherwise, you're good?" he asked.

I took a quick look over my shoulder and my mother-in-law was still sitting there, sipping her water, and now listening to my conversation. "Yeah," I said, even though I wanted to say so much more. I wanted to tell him that even though the pomp and circumstance of laying Chauncey to rest was over, I still cried every night. I wanted to tell him that I still ached with grief that was breaking my bones. I wanted to tell him that I was scared that I would feel this way for the rest of my life.

But with Mama Cee so close, I couldn't tell the truth. All I could do was add, "I'm really good."

"Oh. Okay," he said, sounding surprised.

I could tell he expected more. "What about you?" I asked.

He paused. "I'm trying to hang in there."

It was clear that today wasn't a good day for Jamal, and I wanted to reach out and hold him the way he'd been holding me, the way I missed so much, since I hadn't seen him since the day of the funeral.

"I'm so sorry," was all I could say, though, because of Mama Cee.

Several silent seconds passed between us, as if Jamal was waiting for me to open up to him the way he'd just done to me.

Finally, he said, "Well, I was just checking on you."

I swallowed the hard lump in my throat. I wanted him to stay on the phone. I wanted to keep talking. I wanted to help him and I wanted him to help me.

But instead I said, "Thanks." Then I spoke quickly. "Tell Em I'll give her a call tomorrow."

"Yeah. Okay."

I clicked off without saying any more, not even a good-bye.

"Is Jamal all right?"

I took a moment before I turned around. "Yeah, he's just missing Chauncey, you know?"

Mama Cee nodded slowly. "Those two were so close. As close as Charlie and Chauncey." She paused. "Those were *my* three sons," she added softly.

Taking a seat at the table next to her, I placed my hands over Mama Cee's. She was such a strong woman, so spiritually centered, that sometimes I forgot that she had lost her son.

"Mama Cee, we're going to be all right."

She squeezed my hand. "Have you given any more thought to coming home with me and Charlie?"

"Were you talking about me and the boys moving down there *now?*"

She nodded. "I can't imagine you here"—she paused as her eyes roamed around the kitchen—"by yourself. Without Chauncey."

"Well, I haven't had any time to think about it," I said. "I certainly wasn't thinking about moving this soon."

"Why not?"

"The boys have school . . . and everything."

"I have a news flash." She paused. "We have schools in Phoenix."

I smiled. "I know. It's just that I'm not sure it'll be good for the boys to have this much change in their lives."

"What's good for the boys is to be around people who love them. Now, I know you as their mama love them with all your heart. But why not have a couple more hearts helping you out?"

I gave myself time to think about her words. Truly, I wanted what was best for my sons. There was no way to know what the impact of losing their father would be. So maybe Mama Cee was right.

Still, for some reason, I wanted to slow this down. "You may be right. So, over Christmas . . ."

Mama Cee frowned. "Christmas? Why wait till then?"

"I'm thinking that at Christmas, I won't have to take the boys out of school. As it is, they've already missed over a week. So, if I wait till the holidays, I can spend more time down there, look around, consider some places to live, check out job opportunities . . . you know, all that stuff."

Mama Cee shook her head, and her shoulders rose slowly as she stiffened. "I really think you need to do this before Christmas."

Her tone had changed, and now there was an urgency to her words.

"There's just something in my spirit, baby. I want you and the boys with me."

I waited a second before I said, "Do you know how much I love you?"

She softened and her shoulders slacked. "Probably not as much I love you," she kidded.

I smiled. "You know what?" I paused, wanting to be sure of what I was about to say. "We'll do it."

"Really?"

I nodded. "The boys and I will move."

When my mother-in-law clapped, I held up my hands, trying to temper her excitement. "Now, I'm not sure how soon. I really don't want to rush it . . . for the boys."

"Okay." She pushed herself up. "Let me go tell Charlie. He's going to be so excited."

I swear, it looked like my mother-in-law was cha-chaing out of the kitchen.

I laughed. And then I sighed. Well, decision made—it looked like the boys and I were on our way to Arizona.

14

Emily

I pressed the button for the penthouse and then leaned back as the elevator ascended. Closing my eyes, I took a deep breath, trying to rejuvenate my body.

But it didn't help. It wasn't just the physicality of the fourteen-hour days that made me so weary. It was the emotionality of the sessions that wrung every ounce of energy from me.

Especially today.

Especially LaTonya Miller.

For ten days now, I'd been working with LaTonya, and just yesterday, I was sure that we'd had our first breakthrough. LaTonya had told me that she wasn't going to cry anymore. Of course, I knew that wasn't true, but it was an indication that she was beginning to heal.

At least, that's what I thought.

But the call this afternoon from her parents had stopped me dead in the middle of planning for another session, and I'd driven like I was flying a 747.

At their home, which was right off Crenshaw, Mr. Miller had met me at the door with tears in his eyes while his wife sobbed quietly on their living room sofa.

"Doctor Harrington," he said, shortening my name as many of the parents of my clients did.

That was all that he needed to say. In his tone, I heard his desperate cry for me to save his child.

I asked, "Where is she?"

"In her bedroom."

There was no need for the Millers to lead me back through the long hallway. I'd been to their home three times already.

I paused at her bedroom door for a moment, studying the six-year-old who sat in the middle of one of the twin beds with her legs crossed. She'd created a fort around her tiny body—six stuffed animals surrounded her: two bears, two dogs, two elephants were her protection.

In LaTonya's lap was the framed picture of her sister, the one her parents said she slept with, then carried with her throughout the day. I'd told her parents that the picture was fine, but I wasn't quite sure how to handle this new crisis.

"Hey, LaTonya," I said softly, not wanting to startle her.

She didn't look up; her eyes were steady on the photograph.

I approached her bed slowly, then pushed aside one of the elephants so that I could sit down. I rested on the edge of the bed, with my eyes on the girl, who still hadn't looked up at me. From the moment I'd met LaTonya the day after the fire, I felt like our hearts were connected. It had startled me at first, when I saw her that day, sitting on the pew in the church between her grieving parents. I stared at her for a long time—she looked just like the little girl in my dreams, just like the little girl I imagined that Jamal and I would have one day.

"How are you?"

Finally, LaTonya raised her head, and her brown eyes were wide circles as she looked at me. "Are you mad at me, too?"

"No." I spoke and shook my head at the same time so that she would be sure. "I'm not mad at you at all."

"Mommy and Daddy are mad."

"No," I said again. "They're not mad."

"Mommy was crying."

"She's sad because of what you did."

She lowered her head again. "I'm sorry," she said softly. "I was just trying to start the fire so that I could die and go to heaven, too."

Even though her parents had told me how Mrs. Miller had found LaTonya in the kitchen, standing on a chair, with a newspaper rolled up and aimed at the flame on the stove, I still wasn't prepared to hear the confession from this little girl.

She said, "I don't want LaTrisha to be in heaven by herself."

"She's not by herself. Remember we talked about this. Remember she's with Jesus?"

She nodded. "That's what Pastor Ford said, too."

"Pastor Ford is right."

"And Mama said that LaTrisha is with Grandpa, too."

I nodded because I could feel my emotions rising inside of me. I said, "So, see? LaTrisha's not by herself."

"But suppose Jesus doesn't know her, and He won't play with her?"

I couldn't remember another time when words made me want to laugh and cry at the same time. "You don't have to worry about that. Jesus knows LaTrisha really well."

"He does? When did He meet her?"

"A long, long time ago."

"Before we were one year old?"

"Yes," I said, needing to keep this really simple. "Before then."

"So, do you think He's playing with her?"

"I don't know how it really works in heaven, but I know that everyone who's there is very happy and excited to be there."

"If LaTrisha's happy, she wants me to be happy, too. 'Cause I'm not happy since she died."

There was a boulder growing in my throat. "She's going to want you to be there, but she doesn't want you to come for a long, long time. Because there's something else that she wants you to do."

"What?"

"Since she's with Jesus and since she's happy, LaTrisha wants you to stay here with your mom and dad and take care of them so you will all be happy."

The little girl didn't move. Her eyes were filled with wonder, as if she was listening to a fairy tale.

I continued, "LaTrisha wants you to stay here because she doesn't want your mom and dad to be by themselves. Because if you go with LaTrisha, who will take care of them?"

"Nobody." She thought for a moment and tears filled her eyes. "Then they'll be sad."

I nodded. "And you don't want them to be sad, do you?"

She shook her head. Then suddenly she jumped up and wrapped her arms around my neck. "I'm sorry, Doctor H.," she said. "I'm sorry."

I hugged her back. "I know you are, sweetie. So, now you have to make me a promise."

She leaned back and stared into my eyes.

I said, "You have to promise that you won't do anything like that again."

"I promise," she whispered.

"And you should go and tell your parents, okay?"

"Okay." Slowly, she slid off the bed and moved toward her bedroom door. But right before she stepped into the hallway, she returned and took three of the animals from her bed and placed them in the middle of her sister's bed. Then she left the room.

I sat still for a moment, then pasted a smile on my face so that I could go and hear LaTonya's brave declaration to her parents.

Our conversation had been simple, though I knew that turning LaTonya around wasn't going to be easy. She was a young child who didn't understand the concept of death, yet she now had to be counseled just as anyone who had thoughts of suicide. That meant she would be on my schedule four days a week, added to a calendar that was already bursting at the seams.

The elevator doors parted and I felt like falling to my knees and crawling to our apartment. But I made it standing upright. When I stepped inside, I called out to Jamal, even though the condo was completely dark, completely silent.

I dumped my briefcase by the door, shrugged off my jacket, kicked off my shoes, then grabbed my iPad from my bag. Even though I usually went into our second bedroom, which was our office slash library, and worked until midnight, I wasn't going to do that tonight. My plan was to jump into bed, check a few e-mails, and then hang out with my husband.

But when I walked into our bedroom, the lights were already off, and Jamal was already in bed, snoring softly.

I stood at the door for a few minutes and sighed. For the last few nights, since Chauncey's funeral, this is where I'd found my husband, even though normally he never went to bed before midnight. But from the moment we'd come home from the repast on Tuesday, this was where Jamal seemed to spend all of his time. He was just sleeping and hardly talking.

I walked to my side of the bed, flicked on the nightstand lamp, then turned, to see if the soft light woke him up.

He didn't move.

Gently, I put the iPad on the bed, then strode into my closet. It didn't take me more than a minute to strip, replace my suit with my favorite USC T-shirt, then climb into bed with my husband.

In the past, Jamal would feel my presence and wake up. But not tonight.

I leaned against the headboard and opened my iPad, but I didn't even hit the e-mail icon. Instead, my eyes stayed on my husband.

Jamal had always been so sociable, so active. But now, even when I called him during the day, he was in bed. Trying to sleep away his days and his nights. Of course, this was grief, but grief was a spirit that gripped people and kept them wallowing in sorrow. One of the first lessons in Psych 101: the longer a person stayed depressed, the longer it would take them to come out of that state. It had only been a few days, but I wanted Jamal to get up, get out, and get moving.

Work wasn't the answer; he hadn't even been released to return to the fire station, which honestly was fine with me. I wasn't sure if I ever wanted him to return to work. But I had to find something for him to do. Some way for him to begin to make the climb back to his normal life.

Putting my iPad aside, I rolled over until my body was pressed against his and I kissed his neck. Soft, butterfly kisses that I continued until I felt him stir. When he rolled over and faced me, his eyes were already open.

For a long moment we just lay there on our sides, face-to-face, staring.

Finally, I whispered, "Hi."

"Hi. You just getting home?"

I nodded. "It was a long day, but I couldn't wait to see you."

That brought a smile to his face, though he didn't say anything.

"What did you do today?" I asked.

"Not much."

Although I was sure that I already knew the answer, I asked, "Did you go out?"

"No."

"Oh . . . I was thinking that maybe you would have gone over to Miriam's. To check on her and the boys."

"No, they're all right. Mama Cee and Charlie are still here, so they don't need me."

Of course that wasn't true, but it wouldn't do any good to tell Jamal that. He already knew it. We needed to talk, though I hesitated because I didn't want to be his therapist. I just wanted to be his wife. But right now, I wasn't sure if there was a difference. "Jamal . . ."

He shook his head, already knowing where I was going. "I don't want you to be my psychologist, Emily," he said, like he always did.

"I promise that's not what I'm doing, but you can't keep your grief inside. You need to talk, just talk. And I promise I won't say anything."

He hesitated, and after a few seconds, he began, "I can't explain it, but it feels like I'm drowning in grief. It's making me feel crazy."

"You're not crazy. You're normal." My words were just instinct. Truly, I had meant to keep quiet like I promised.

He continued, "Besides you, there're only two other people in the world that I have truly loved. My grandmother and Chauncey." He paused. "And now they're both gone."

He sounded so sad, and all I wanted to do was hold him. But if I did that, he would stop talking, and he needed to get this out.

After a deep sigh, he said, "I should be getting over this . . ."

"It's only been a little more than a week," I said. "Trust me, there's no expiration date on grief. But you're going to get through this," I said, wanting to encourage him. "Your strength is one of the things that I admire about you."

"You say that all the time."

"Because it's true."

"I don't feel that way right now."

"I know. But you know, one of the things that you can do, one of the things that may help, is if you get up and get out. Do some things you like. Go running on the beach, go hang out with some of the guys. Any of those things will help you take your mind off Chauncey, even for just a little while."

This time, there was no hesitation. "I don't know if I want my mind to be taken away." He reached for me and pulled me close. "I don't want to talk about it anymore."

"All right," I said, feeling as if we'd made some progress, even though I wanted more.

But for now, I just lay in his arms, glad that he'd opened up a little and praying that tomorrow he'd give me a little bit more.

15

Miriam

My telephone hadn't stopped ringing.

First, the call had come from Emily, early this morning as she drove to her office. The next one was from Michelle-lee, as she sat in the back of the town car that took her to the television station each day. Then Pastor Ford, a few members of Hope Chapel, and even some of Chauncey's firefighter brothers.

So many calls, but really, it was just one conversation. The calls were so similar, I could have recorded my voice and then just pressed Play without any of them noticing.

"Hey, Miriam; I was just calling to check on you. How are you?"

"I'm good."

"And the boys?"

"They're good, too."

At this point, everyone sighed as if they were relieved that they now had permission to carry on with their day and their business. Now they wouldn't have to worry about being part of some rescue mission to save me and my sons.

"Well, just know that I'm praying for you," the calls continued.

"I know that. Thank you."

"Of course, and you know it will get even better with time."

Emily had added that she would call me later, Michellelee had said that she was going to stop by after work, and Pastor told me that I could call her at any time if I ever needed anything.

Then everyone hung up. And though they may have felt better, not one of them knew my truth.

People probably would have been upset to know that I'd stopped telling them what I was thinking or how I was feeling. They were all tired of hearing it anyway. Of course, no one ever said that, but I could tell that's how they felt. Their weariness showed in the ways their eyes kind of wandered when they were standing in front of me, or in the pauses I heard on the phone, which let me know they were multitasking and hardly listening.

It was okay, though. I thought about the number of times I'd had to listen to a grieving spouse, or son or daughter. Listening to someone who had immersed himself in sorrow was a heavy burden for everyone who was around. I got that now. So since the funeral, I kept my cares to myself . . . and Jamal.

I tossed the *Essence* that I'd been flipping through aside, then wandered over to the living room window. The sun shone brightly, as if it were proud to be hanging high in the sky on this autumn Friday. I peeked up the street, then turned and looked as far down the street as I could. There was no sign of my sons, though I didn't really expect to see them.

I'd been so grateful when Charlie had gathered the boys and taken them all out bike riding about an hour ago. The boys seemed grateful, too, since they hadn't been out of the house that much. Now, even they were ready to go back to school.

Turning toward the sofa, I stared at the phone, willing it to ring. But then, I wondered, why was I waiting for Jamal to call? Couldn't I call him?

I grabbed the telephone, but when I picked it up, someone was already on the line.

"Hello?"

"Hey, Miriam."

"Jamal!" I exclaimed. "I was just calling you."

"Really?"

"Yeah, I wanted to check on you," I said. "For once."

"Well, that's why I was calling you. What's going on?"

"Nothing much. Charlie took the boys out and Mama Cee is resting, so I was just sitting here and thinking about you." I paused. That was not exactly what I meant, so I rephrased, "I mean, I was wondering how you were doing."

"I knew what you meant, 'cause I've been thinking about you. How're you feeling?"

I sighed as I sat on the sofa and tucked my feet beneath me. "It's been ten days, and I can't believe this, but my heart hurts more now than when I first found out. All I ever do is cry."

"I know," he said. "I think it's the shock. It's wearing off and reality is setting in."

"Not that I expected to be over it. I mean, I'm sure it will take years, but I really want to start feeling better. Little by little, I just want to see some sunshine, you know?"

"I know."

"Well, everyone says it'll get better." I shrugged.

"Emily thinks that getting out might help. Maybe you need to get out, too. Maybe we can get out of the house together."

I swung my legs off the couch. "That would be great. I've been staying close to home 'cause it feels safer here. I never know when I'm going to break down."

"I just haven't had the energy to go out."

"Energy isn't my problem. I've been doing so much cooking

and cleaning and anything I could find to keep my mind off Chauncey."

"Maybe I should've tried that. I've been trying to sleep it away. So, this just proves that Em is right."

"Of course she is. Your wife is brilliant," I said, and we laughed together.

"Then good. Let's go out tomorrow. I'm hoping that Emily won't be working and the three of us can do lunch."

"Okay, I'll check with Mama Cee and Charlie to make sure they'll be able to watch the boys."

"Cool. How much longer are they going to be here?"

"I don't know, but not much longer. I worry about Mama Cee and her asthma." I stopped. This was the point where I could tell Jamal about my move to Arizona, though something inside of me wanted to keep that to myself. So I just said, "I love having them here, but I have to make sure that Mama Cee's health is okay."

"Well, I'll make sure to see them before they head out. So . . . Em or I will call you back to confirm tomorrow."

"Okay!" I hung up the phone feeling just a little bit of hope that some kind of relief from all this grief was on the way.

I glanced up and was surprised to see Mama Cee standing just a few feet from me. "I thought you were still resting."

"I was. Sounds like you're going out," she said, still standing in place.

"Yeah. That was Jamal. He and Emily want to take me out to lunch."

Mama Cee nodded before she walked toward her favorite chair. She settled into the cushions. "You need to get out a little bit and I think the three of you can help each other."

"That's what I'm thinking. Jamal knows how I feel, and Emily's been working so hard I'm glad to be able to spend some time with her."

"Well, don't worry about the boys. Charlie was saying something about taking them to Magic Mountain tomorrow."

"The boys will love that. But what about you, Mama Cee? I can't see you getting on any roller coasters." I laughed.

She waved her hands. "That's for you young ones. I don't mind going to the park, though. I'll just take my book, sit, and read while Charlie fools around with the boys. It'll be fun. And it'll give us time to spend with the boys since we have to head home next week."

"I figured Charlie would have to get back to work soon." I stood and walked toward the foyer. "I'm going to get dinner started."

But before I could step away, Mama Cee said, "Have you told the boys about moving to Arizona?"

I took a moment before I faced her. "No, not yet. I want to work everything out in my mind first. But don't worry, Mama Cee. We're moving there. You can count on it."

She nodded slowly, but didn't speak at first. Instead, her eyes stayed on me as if she was trying to see something that I wasn't saying.

What was wrong?

Then suddenly my mother-in-law turned away. She faced the window and her voice was just a whisper when she said, "I hope so, baby. I really, really hope so."

16

Emily

My toothbrush was in my hand when Jamal entered the bathroom, then eased up behind me. He wrapped his arms around my waist, and I grinned as we both stared at our reflection in the bathroom mirror. I was only wrapped in a black towel; he wore nothing but his white boxer briefs. Through the mirror, I did what I always did when we stood this way; I marveled at the beauty of our contrasts.

"Good morning," I said.

He responded by pressing his lips against my neck, and then his tongue did small swirls on my skin, sending shivers and memories through me. I closed my eyes, taking in and enjoying each sensation. And then I wondered . . . when was the last time we'd made love?

Seconds passed in my mind—had the last time been the night of the fire?

My eyes snapped open. Impossible!

But when I thought about it some more, it was true. We'd both been so wrapped up. Me, in my work. Him, in his grief. Now, eleven days had passed. For many, that would be no time at all. But for

Jamal and me, making love was our way of life. It's just what we did . . . we ate, we slept, we worked, we smashed.

This was going to have to be fixed. I missed my husband, but not only that, connecting on that level was always therapeutic. Of course, it would be a stress reliever for me, and it would help Jamal's pain. That theory wasn't something that I'd learned in undergrad, grad, or when I'd received my doctorate. That theory wasn't in any textbook, nor was it part of any study. That theory was what I knew in my gut: sex was great relief from grief.

So, I needed to get on my job. Tonight. No, this afternoon. As soon as we came back from lunch, I would toss my husband on the bed and have my way with him. Over and over again.

When Jamal leaned back, a smile was on his face. "Good morning." He finally spoke his first words to me. "Do you know how long it's been since we've shared this bathroom in the morning?"

"I know, babe."

When he stepped toward the shower, he said, "I'm just glad you didn't have to work today."

"I have the whole weekend," I said, then rinsed out my mouth. "I'm so glad to have this little break."

"Yeah, you've been worried about me, but you need to take care of yourself, too," he said.

Turning around, I leaned against the edge of the sink and watched my husband through the clear shower doors. He loved cool showers, so the bathroom never steamed up with him the way it did with me. At this moment, I was grateful for that, and as he lathered up with the soap, I had the chance to appreciate every inch of his excellence.

If we weren't going to lunch with Miriam—

I said, "Don't worry, babe. I'm going to take care of myself and take care of you, too."

For a moment, he stopped what he was doing and grinned. "Watch out now. Don't start none, won't be none."

"Oh, I'm gonna be starting something. As soon as we get back home."

He laughed, then went back to soaping up.

I said, "I'm really glad we're taking Miriam out."

Jamal replied, "I was hoping to get a chance to see the boys, too, but Mama Cee and Charlie are taking them to Magic Mountain."

"That's cool. I want to spend some time with them, too, since they're going back to school on Monday."

His back was to me now, but I still kept my eyes on my husband. This was the first time I'd heard more happiness than sadness in his voice. Maybe the talk we had helped. And if talking could do this much, what would sexing do?

If I didn't stop thinking about sex, we'd never make it to lunch. Turning away, I rushed into our bedroom. I needed to be dressed before my husband got out of the shower.

Less than forty-five minutes later, we were in Jamal's car, heading down La Brea toward Inglewood. As he drove, we didn't say a word, at least not out loud. Jamal drove with one hand, and with the other, he held mine. Every few minutes, he squeezed, letting me know how much he loved me. Every time, I squeezed back. I didn't even have to look at him. We knew what we meant to each other.

He didn't let go of me until he stopped the car in front of Chauncey and Miriam's house; that's how I still thought of it. One day, I'd see it as just Miriam's home. But not yet. I guess that was my own grief, my own way of holding on for a little longer.

I hopped out of the car and knocked on the front door.

"Hey, honey," I said the moment Miriam opened it. I hugged her tightly. "I feel like I haven't seen you in forever."

"It's great to see you," she said with an enthusiasm that I hadn't heard in the almost two weeks since Chauncey had been gone.

I stepped back to get a better look at my friend. This was as good as I'd heard Miriam sound, and this was certainly as good as she'd looked. She was wearing an outfit that I'd never seen before— a long, T-strap sundress with all the colors of fall. Her low-heeled gold sandals were the perfect accent, along with her hoop earrings, which were such a change from the little pearls she always wore.

Who was this girl?

"You look terrific."

"Do I?" she asked, smoothing back her hair, which was still in her signature bun.

"Yeah, you really do. So, you're ready to go?"

She nodded and I put my arm around her shoulders after she locked the door. Then we moved toward the car, almost skipping like schoolgirls.

I had no idea what was helping Miriam to ease out of her grief, but whatever it was, I wanted to grab some and squeeze it into a bottle, so that I could use it as needed: a little for Jamal, a little for Miriam, when necessary.

Jamal stood, holding the car doors open for both of us. "Check out Ms. Miriam," I said.

As he reached out to hug her, my cell phone rang. Before I even looked down at the screen, I knew it was trouble. I held up a finger. "I have to take this."

Jamal nodded as I moved a few steps away.

"Doctor Harrington!"

The urgency in Mr. Miller's voice brought tears to my eyes. "Mr. Miller! What's wrong?"

"We're at Children's Hospital. It's . . . it's . . . LaTonya. Please, can you come?"

"Of course. I'm on my way." I was already moving as I clicked off my phone. To Jamal, I said, "It's LaTonya."

I didn't share many details of my clients with my husband; patient/client confidentiality was serious to me. But I'd told him that LaTonya was having a particularly difficult time.

He nodded. "Okay."

I took two steps toward his car, then stopped. "I don't have my car."

"Take mine, of course." He glanced at Miriam. "Don't worry about us. We'll take Miriam's car, right?"

"Definitely. I'll drop you home," she said.

"Okay. I'm so sorry." I kissed Jamal, then slid behind the wheel.

LaTonya was in the hospital . . . what had she done?

As I slowly backed out of the driveway, I had one of those sinking feelings in the pit of my stomach.

This was not going to be a good day.

17

Miriam

Jamal and I watched Emily speed away.

"It's horrible what Emily has to deal with," I whispered. "I'm so grateful my boys are doing well. At least as well as can be expected."

"Death is tough for adults. I can't imagine what it's like for a child who can't fully grasp the finality of it."

"That's the part that's hard. Mama Cee, Charlie, and I talked to the boys last night. About how they felt, about missing their dad."

He turned to face me. "Really?"

I nodded. "I know you wanted to be here when we did that, but it just kinda happened."

"So how did it go?"

"I'm not sure how much Stevie really grasps the whole concept. And even Mikey goes back and forth. I was most concerned about Junior, but he seems to be coping. He's been trying to step in a lot with his brothers. I think he feels like he's the man of the house now."

That made Jamal smile. "He's a good kid."

"And I want him to remember that. I don't want this to change his life in that way. I don't want him to grow up before he's supposed to."

"You're a good mom for recognizing that."

"I'm gonna keep my eyes on him, on all my boys. I just hope they'll be all right."

"Well, you know if they need to talk to anyone, one of Emily's colleagues will be glad to step in."

I nodded. "You guys will be the first ones I call if I see any signs. I don't want anyone speeding down the road one day because Junior, Mikey, or Stevie are in trouble."

Jamal said, "Well, I guess it's just you and me. For lunch. Is that okay with you?"

"Of course. I just have to go back inside to get my car keys."

When I turned, Jamal followed me up the driveway and to the front door. I had no idea why my hand shook as I put the key in the lock.

It must've been the call that Emily received.

Once we were inside, I said to Jamal, "The keys are in my bedroom." I left him standing by the front door, then walked into the bedroom and grabbed the keys from the dresser. I stood in front of the mirror for an extra couple of moments. My hands were still shaking slightly. What in the world had me so jittery?

It had to be Emily.

Back in the living room, I was surprised to see that Jamal had settled on the couch. He looked so easy, so at home, that whatever had me shaking faded quickly. I said, "You know what? Do you want to just stay here? We can order in for lunch."

He grinned. "I was thinking the same thing. Since it's just us, it'll be easier this way."

"Yeah." Then I waved him over. "Come on. In the kitchen we have every menu for every restaurant within fifty miles."

"All right then," he said as he followed me. We checked out the Chinese, Thai, American, Italian, Indian menus, but after ten minutes of no decision, I finally said to Jamal, "You know what we should do?"

Then together we said, "Order pizza!"

We laughed as I picked up the phone and dialed the number. We ordered a cheese pizza and some wings, and then I set the table as if we were having a four-course dinner. By the time I poured a glass of lemonade and Jamal grabbed a beer from the fridge, our lunch had arrived.

Now Jamal took over, paying the delivery guy, then filling our plates with pizza and drumettes. Once we sat down, he prayed over our food and we settled into our meal.

After taking my first bite, I released a moan. "This is good."

"What? The pizza?"

"No. The fact that I don't feel like I'm in the depths of hell at this moment. I mean, my heart never stops hurting, but this is the first day I can say I'm feeling a little better."

Jamal nodded. "I feel you. This is the first morning I woke up feeling halfway good, too. Made me hopeful."

"Me, too!"

Jamal blew out a long breath. "I'm feeling all of this emotion and grief, and Chauncey and I were just friends."

I shook my head. "You don't believe that. You were closer than brothers. Everybody knew that."

Jamal nodded. "Mama Cee always quoted that scripture to us. Proverbs 18:24. And she was right, because we were like brothers five minutes after we met."

The thought of that made me smile. "Friends since you were nine." I stated the fact that Chauncey had told me many times.

"Yup," he said, chomping on a chicken wing. "The fourth grade. It was the cap that Chauncey was wearing that started it."

"The cap?"

"Yeah, snapbacks, those athletic hats that everyone wears now. They were just getting big back then. And back in the day, they used to be blank and we would have our own letters pressed on. Whatever we wanted.

"Anyway, the first day of school, Chauncey shows up wearing this snapback with 'Billie Jean Is Not My Lover' on the front."

"Really?" I said, a bit shocked by that. "The Michael Jackson song?"

"Yup!"

"You know that's hilarious, right? I can't believe Mama Cee let him walk out the house wearing that."

"She didn't. I found out that he'd bought the hat and kept it hidden when he was home. He didn't break it out until he was far away from Mama Cee." Jamal laughed. "You know Mama Cee didn't play that."

"You guys became friends because of a hat? Chauncey never told me that."

"Yup. I mean, here was this little chubby kid . . . and you know how he walked. Even back then, he had that strut, that kinda pimp stroll that even though he was only nine, made him look like he was grown. I was impressed."

I laughed, imagining Chauncey walking through the elementary school halls.

"We became friends right then. Bonding over MJ. Because both of us were Michael Jackson connoisseurs."

"Big fans, huh?"

"Fans?" Jamal sucked his teeth. "Dude, Chauncey and I were the MJ tag team. Chauncey knew all the words, and I had all the dance moves down."

I had to cover my mouth to keep my laughter inside.

"I'm telling you," Jamal kept on, "I could do Michael Jackson better than Michael Jackson could do himself."

"Are you serious?" I looked at him sideways, still giggling.

"Oh, yeah! I could moonwalk. I could spin. I could stop dead on my toes."

I held up my hands as if I'd heard enough.

"Oh, really? You want me to lay some of this on you?" Jamal didn't wait for me to answer. He put down his pizza, stood up, slid to the center of the room, then did a moonwalk that could have rivaled Michael Jackson.

I clapped and cheered. "I cannot believe you. All these years I've known you and I've never seen you do that. You've been holding out on me."

"Well, you know," he said, popping his collar. "I'm just sayin', you better recognize."

Now I was buckled over with laughter as Jamal pimp-strutted back to the table. I laughed so hard that I cried. The first tears in weeks that hadn't come from sorrow.

"Now, you and Chauncey," Jamal said, "I remember the day he met you."

"Really?"

He nodded. "He told me he met this girl at camp who was all over him."

I stretched my eyes wide open. "Get out of here! He didn't really say that, did he?"

Jamal cracked up. "You should see the look on your face. But yup, that's what he said. No worries, though. I knew he wasn't telling the truth."

"I can't believe he told you that. When he came up to me, I didn't like him at all."

"The way he was bragging, I figured it had gone down something like that."

I laughed. "But it didn't take long for that to change. Chauncey was so cocky, but in a good way. I really liked that about him. Because he wasn't the finest or the fittest, but that didn't matter. He was the kindest, and the gentlest . . ."

"And the most courageous," Jamal said in a low voice.

His smile was gone; the mood had shifted. "You're thinking about your grandmother."

He nodded.

I'd heard the story dozens of times, though never from Chauncey. My husband never spoke about when their friendship changed, but I had a feeling that Jamal needed to talk about it, and today, I needed to hear it.

Gently placing my hand over his, I gave him permission to go on.

"We were twelve, Miriam. Just twelve years old." He shook his head as if he had a hard time believing twenty years had passed. "And we found my grandmother on the living room floor."

Every time I heard that, my mind imagined the scene. The two of them, Chauncey a little bit chunky, already at, or pretty close to, his adult height of five foot five. And Jamal, the total opposite, taller than the boys his age, which was the reason why he was the star center of their middle school basketball team. I could see the two of them together, talking, laughing, then walking into that apartment.

"Chauncey was the hero that day on so many levels. Because I didn't even want to go to my house. I wanted to go over to his 'cause Mama Cee always had snacks waiting for us. My grandmother couldn't afford those afternoon treats."

When he paused, I knew he needed help. So I said, "But it was Chauncey's idea 'cause he hadn't seen your grandmother in a while, right?"

Again, Jamal nodded. "I was actually kinda mad at him 'cause the only time I got to eat a Twinkie was at his house. But that's just how he was; he wanted to see my grandmother." He shook his head. "When I put my key in the door, and we took two steps into that apartment . . ."

Jamal had described this scene to me before: the two of them standing in the entry, his grandmother in the living room, fallen on her back, her legs sprawled wide.

"I yelled out for my grandmother, but I couldn't move," Jamal continued the story. "I was so scared that she was dead. But Chauncey went right into action. He just dumped his backpack, dropped to his knees, pressed his ear to her chest, then shouted for me to call nine-one-one. I still didn't move until he started screaming at me to make the call 'cause he couldn't do everything." He lowered his lids as if the memory was heavy. "I was finally able to get to the phone, and the whole time I watched Chauncey blow air into my grandmother, then pump her chest. He did that over and over, never stopping.

"And all I did was talk to the nine-one-one operator and cry." Again, he shook his head. "Chauncey saved more than my grandmother's life. He saved me. I don't know what I would've done if she'd died when she went into that diabetic coma. I would've lost the only person I'd loved and the only one who'd loved me."

I squeezed Jamal's hand.

"We'd always been close, but Chauncey became my brother for real that day. I'm talking about after what he did, I loved him from my heart!" With his fist, he beat his chest. "From then on, I would've done anything for him. That's what you have to know, Miriam, that I would've done anything I could to save Chauncey at that school. Anything. I would've given up my life . . ."

"Don't say that! I know you did everything. And Chauncey wouldn't have wanted you to give up anything for him. He would've said it happened the way it was supposed to, it happened for a reason."

He twisted his lips, doubting my words. "I can't think of any good reason for Chauncey to die."

I had to agree with that. "Neither can I, but Chauncey wouldn't want you sitting here wondering why it was him and not you."

He gave me a long sideways glance.

I said, "I know that's what you're thinking."

"Are you a mind reader or something?" he asked with half a smile.

"No, I just know you. And I know my husband would've wanted you to forget about the way he died, and just remember the way he lived."

"You're right about that. Not many men, especially ones in their thirties, can truly be called great men."

I nodded. "For me, the biggest things about Chauncey were the little things. The things he did that meant so much. Like how he had my coffee on my nightstand every morning. Or how he filled my car with gas every Sunday. Or how he literally tucked me into bed every night. Just little things that made a big difference. Those little things that let me know how much he loved me."

"He loved you for sure. That man had a smile on his face every day from the moment he met you."

I sighed. "I knew my life would always be okay as long as Chauncey was with me." I stopped for a moment. "That's what I worry about the most with Junior, Mikey, and Stevie. Will their lives be okay without their father? I mean, I'm a single mom now, raising three boys. I worry about what it's going to be like for them."

Jamal laid his hand on top of mine. "I know it's going to be tough, but I promise you, Miriam, I'll be here for you and for them."

I lowered my head because it felt like the sad tears were trying to make a comeback, though I fought hard to keep them away.

Jamal said, "You won't be going through this alone."

So many people had said that over the last week and a half, but Jamal was the only one I believed. "Thank you."

My tears betrayed me, and I didn't even realize that until Jamal softly caressed my cheek with his thumb. Then he took my hands and pulled me up. When he wrapped his arms around me, I sobbed. I missed my husband so much, but I was thankful right now for the strength of Jamal. The strength of his arms, the strength of his embrace, the strength of his presence.

"Thank you," I said again, as I started to pull back.

But then.

I don't know what happened.

I tried to step away, but Jamal wouldn't let me go. Or maybe it was that I wouldn't free him.

We stared at each other and stayed that way, as if we couldn't break apart.

That was when his lips began a slow descent toward mine. Or maybe it was the other way around. Maybe I was the one reaching up to him.

But in a moment, we were kissing. A kiss that did not stop. A forever kiss that I didn't want to end. At first it was just flesh against flesh, but then he opened the door, parted his lips, and I invited myself in. Our tongues met, and danced a slow grind.

We stopped, but it was only because we needed to breathe. Jamal nuzzled his face inside my neck and I leaned back, receiving him, reveling in him.

"Jamal!" I breathed his name. "Jamal."

Our lips connected once again as we backed away from the kitchen toward the living room. I tried to push him away, but he wouldn't budge. Or maybe it was that I was pulling him. I don't know.

My eyes were closed as we entered the living room, and seconds later we were on the sofa, the weight of his body all over me. I welcomed him in every way, needing to be close to a man like this once again.

In one swoop, my dress was over my head. Next, my bra and panties were gone. Jamal broke away for just a short time, and in seconds he thrilled me with his chiseled fineness. I knew he worked out just about every day, but I had never seen a man like this—at least, never this close, never this personal.

His perfection made me remember my own imperfections, and right away I wanted to cover up. Here we were in the middle of the day, in the middle of the living room, with the bright light of noon shining through. There was no darkness to hide me.

But the width of my hips, the crinkles on my thighs, the double fold on my stomach didn't seem to matter to Jamal when he laid his body back on top of mine and our lips met once again.

I moaned, savoring the time that moved so slow, yet we traveled at the speed of sound. We spent no time getting to know each other, and I didn't care. I didn't want any of that. I just wanted a little bit of my sorrow to be taken away.

Was it a second, was it a minute, was it an hour . . . I don't know. But the angels at the gate of ecstasy welcomed me in.

I shuddered.

And shuddered.

Then still, I shuddered.

Slowly, my eyes fluttered open, but Jamal stayed right on top of me. I understood. He hadn't left me with enough energy to breathe, so he probably couldn't move.

All I wanted to do was freeze this moment, stay here forever so that I could remember. But I also wanted to stay here forever because I was afraid of what would happen next. What were we going to do? How were we going to look at each other?

Jamal shifted first, slowly rising off of me, and when he looked down, our eyes locked. Now it was our stares that were frozen in time, and I wondered if my eyes were filled with the same shock that stared back at me.

We said nothing as he stood, grabbed his pants from the floor, and stepped into them. While he dressed, I turned away and slipped into my sundress as quickly as I could, this time sans underwear. I had to move quickly before Jamal saw my body and remembered that I wasn't Emily.

Oh God!

Emily!

My best friend!

Emily!

"Miriam."

I squeezed my eyes together, then slowly turned until I faced him. I opened my mouth to speak, but Jamal spoke at the same time.

"I don't know what to say," we said together.

We couldn't help but smile at that.

Jamal held up his hands. "I usually let ladies go first, but I have to say this." He took a short step toward me. "I'm so sorry, Miriam. I'm . . ."

I reached out, needing to stop him. "No, Jamal, no! Don't be. I'm not sorry . . ." I paused, hating myself for speaking that truth.

He blinked, then squinted as if he was trying to get my words to compute.

"I mean, I'm sorry, but . . . but . . . it just happened. It wasn't like we planned this."

"Right, right."

"And we weren't trying to hurt anyone."

"No, no."

"So, I don't think there's anything to really be sorry about. We were just two friends who needed each other in that moment."

He nodded, but said nothing. And I just stood there. What was I supposed to do now?

"So," I said. I had to swallow before I could continue. "I guess I should get the keys and take you home."

I felt like I was frying under the glare of his stare, but then, finally, he shook his head. "I don't want to go." He asked, "What time is it?"

Taking a quick glance at the clock on the mantel, I said, "It's just a little before two."

He nodded and I watched his Adam's apple rise, then fall. "What time will Mama Cee and Charlie be back with the boys?"

I kept my eyes on his. "They won't be back until tonight. Probably late."

He nodded again, then reached his hand toward me. I looked at his arm hanging in the air before I slid my hand into his. He pulled me closer and held my hand tighter.

Then, without another word, he led me into my bedroom.

18

Emily

In all my years of practice, I had never had to face this.

I was trying to save a child's life. A child who had tried to commit suicide twice.

"Doctor Harrington, do you think she's going to be all right? We're not going to lose our baby, are we?"

As I'd been doing from the moment I arrived at the hospital, I reassured the Millers. "LaTonya is going to be fine," I said to Mr. Miller and his wife, who was sitting right beside him.

Mr. Miller shook his head as if my assurances weren't enough. "I just hope she didn't stab herself too deeply."

I tried not to cringe, but it was difficult not to, with the image of what LaTonya had done fresh in my mind. Mr. Miller had told me the moment I rushed into the emergency waiting room.

"LaTonya stabbed herself with scissors. She said she was trying to get all the blood out of her body so she could go to heaven."

My whole body had started to shake then, and still shook now. How was I supposed to handle a child wanting to commit suicide, who didn't even understand death? There had been only one lecture on this subject in school—there were so few cases on record, certainly not enough for any case studies.

Mr. Miller asked, "What's taking them so long?"

"Well, you know she needed stitches," I said, giving him another fact that he already knew. "It won't be too much longer."

Mr. Miller nodded, then stood, though he didn't move too far away from his wife. "I don't know why LaTonya keeps doing this. I don't know why we can't get her to understand."

I'd been at the hospital for an hour and I'd repeated myself countless times. But I would tell the Millers whatever they needed to hear to keep them calm, to keep them collected for their daughter. "You know she's not really trying to kill herself. She's just trying to be with LaTrisha."

"What's the difference?" Mr. Miller asked me again.

"Intent. We know she doesn't understand the concept of death, so she certainly doesn't understand suicide."

"I can't understand any of this. She's just six years old."

"That's the point. She's six and she's grieving. And she's grieving her twin. They had a psychological and physical connection that we may never understand. So, she doesn't really know what she's doing. She's just trying to get to her sister."

Those were my professional answers. But on the heart level, the soul level, I was at as much of a loss as the Millers. I'd thought talking to LaTonya and helping her work through this would be enough. My plan was to engage her on a regular basis, the way I did with any of my clients. We were going to talk, read, draw, everything to pull out her feelings and help her to understand.

Now it looked like she'd need twenty-four-hour care, at least for a couple of days. The thought of her being institutionalized and away from her parents frightened me on so many levels. But right now, that was the only way to save her life.

I watched Mr. Miller reach for his wife's hand and squeeze it, and I wished that Jamal was sitting here next to me. I'd never doubted my skills, but I'd never been in this situation. Right now, I needed Jamal to tell me that I could do this.

"Mr. Miller, Mrs. Miller." Dr. Caster, a pediatrician I'd worked with before, came into the room and the three of us stood as he entered.

Mrs. Miller said, "My baby. Is she going to be all right?"

The doctor nodded. "She just had flesh wounds. Thank God, she wasn't strong enough to cause too much damage."

I exhaled at that news.

He said, "But we're going to keep her here."

"Keep her?" Mr. Miller asked as he looked at his wife. He seemed to hold her hand tighter. "For how long?"

The doctor took a quick look at me, then turned back to the Millers. "We're not sure yet. She's resting now and with the sedative we gave her, she'll probably sleep for most of the day. But we're going to keep her for observation." With another quick look in my direction, the doctor added, "It'll just be for a couple of days."

"I'm not leaving my baby here. If she's staying, so am I," her mother said.

"Of course. I can take you to LaTonya now." Then the doctor said to me, "Doctor Harrington, would you mind waiting? I'd like to speak with you."

I nodded, then said good-bye to the Millers before the doctor led them away. I sank into my chair, knowing what Dr. Caster wanted to talk about. Dr. Caster and I would have to place LaTonya on a seventy-two-hour hold.

I'd never had to do this before. I didn't want to do it now.

After I met with Dr. Caster, I wanted to consult other psychologists before I came up with a plan. But before any of that, I needed my husband.

I wondered if Jamal and Miriam were still at lunch. It was just a bit after two. Pulling my cell from my purse, I pressed Jamal's number and after four rings, I sighed. "Hey, babe," I whispered to his voice mail, "just checking in. I'm still at the hospital, but I'll be leaving here in a couple of minutes. I was going to try to catch up with you and Miriam. Where are you? Call me back."

Then I clicked the icon for my contacts and hit Miriam's number, but her cell went straight to her voice mail. "Hey, Miriam. Where are you guys? Call me."

I thought about calling Miriam's house, but if they'd been there, they would've heard their cell phones. They had to be in some loud, crowded restaurant.

Well, it was probably for the best. I wasn't up to going out now. I just wanted to be with Jamal. And have him hold me, and love me, and assure me that this was going to be all right.

I leaned back, letting my head rest against the wall. My job was to put LaTonya's heart back together. And I would do that, but right now, all I wanted to do was go home.

✦

I felt his touch on my shoulder, I heard his whisper in my ear, "Emily."

I crawled toward consciousness and my eyes slowly opened. "Jamal." My voice was filled with sleep, and with the tips of my fingers, I massaged my eyelids. I felt like I'd been asleep for hours, and the dim light that came through the living room windows told me I was right. When I'd lain down on the sofa, the day had been bright. But now the sun had almost fully taken its place beyond the horizon.

I said, "I must've fallen asleep," as I focused my eyes on my husband crouching in front of me.

"You must've been really tired to do that," he said.

"I was exhausted." My thoughts went back to this afternoon. How I'd signed the paper to commit a six-year-old to a seventy-two-hour hold. How the doctor had said that she'd be kept right there in her room since Children's Hospital didn't have a psychiatric ward. And how her mother had sobbed hysterically, and her father kept asking, "Why, why, why?"

I raised my arms above my head to stretch and get away from those thoughts. At least for a little while. "You're just getting home?" I asked, as I took a look at my watch. It was almost seven. Without waiting for him to answer, I added, "You were out to lunch with Miriam all this time?"

"Uh . . . yeah," he said.

"I tried to call you, and Miriam. But you didn't answer."

"Uh . . . yeah."

"I figured you were in a noisy restaurant or something."

Still kneeling in front of me, Jamal lowered his eyes. "That's probably what happened. We were . . . out. And we . . . talked. You know . . . about Chauncey."

"Was it good . . . to talk?"

He shook his head slightly. "It was hard. It was really, really difficult."

His voice was so low and so sad, and now I was sorry I hadn't been there with him, for him. "I wish I could've gone with you, babe."

"Oh, no," he said. "You had to work. LaTonya is blessed to have you."

It was his voice, his words, his expression, that made me want to throw my arms around him and pull him close. I needed to hold him and have him hold me. But just as swiftly as I made that move,

Jamal gently grabbed my wrists and pressed my hands down before I could embrace him.

I tilted my head, then looked down to my lap, where he still held my hands.

He explained, "When you got that call today, I knew it was serious, and I just want to make sure that you're okay."

This was why I loved this man. It was clear he hadn't had the best of days, but he was more concerned about me. "I'm okay. And I knew I would be better as soon as I came home to you."

He nodded and pushed himself up from the floor. The leather couch squished when he sat next to me. "So, is there anything special that you want to do?" he asked, though his eyes were on the window.

Just how tough had their afternoon been? Just him and Miriam. Doing all of that talking. I put my hand on his arm. "No, I just want to stay home. I just want to be with you." When he faced me, there were tears in his eyes, and I scooted over to be closer to him. Resting my head on his shoulder, I said, "I know you're sad, but tonight, let's just focus on each other. And how blessed we are. And how we'll make it through anything as long as we have each other."

I felt him nod.

We sat together as the clock on the wall ticked seconds away. After a while, I said, "I promise you, time is going to make it better."

"Yeah," he whispered.

Lifting my head, I asked, "So, do you want me to order in for dinner?"

"You can get something; I'm not hungry." Then he stood. "I'm going to take a shower."

"A shower?" I frowned. But maybe that's what we both needed. "You know what?" I said as I stood up. "I'm going to join you."

He spoke quickly, "No, no. I just need . . . I just need . . ." He put his hands up to his head. "Babe, I just need a little while alone. To get over, get rid of . . . the talk . . . all the talk about Chauncey."

"Oh . . . kay." But he was already walking away from me, and I studied him. His head was down, his shoulders were slumped, and I realized the mistake I'd made by leaving Jamal and Miriam alone. Now the hope that he'd had this morning was gone. I wondered if Miriam was feeling the same way. Probably. The two of them had talked and talked and talked themselves right back into their grief.

Well, I'd just have to pull Jamal back. At least to the point where he was this morning. We'd start tonight. We'd relax, watch our favorite movie, and then we'd have dessert, which for me meant making love all night long.

That's the therapy Jamal needed, and I couldn't wait to give it to him.

19

MIRIAM

hardly closed my eyes last night. Not because I couldn't sleep, I just didn't want to. If I'd slept, I might have woken up and discovered that my day had been a dream.

Finally, at just a little before five this morning, the weight of exhaustion had forced my eyes closed. But now I was awake once again and I couldn't help but smile. It hadn't been a dream.

I'd made love to Jamal Taylor.

Rolling over, I stared for a moment at the pillow on the other side of the bed. Then I reached out and smoothed my hand across the pillow where . . . Jamal had laid his head. I didn't know how I felt about all of this. Honestly, I was still in that state called shock.

The first time, anyone could understand. It wasn't our fault; it had started with a tear, a hug, a kiss, and then we were on the couch. Some people might say that was accidental.

But then Jamal had guided me into my bedroom. And the accident turned into a purpose. By then, we were both in our right minds.

And inside my bedroom, it was magic. From the way Jamal kissed me, gently this time, to the way he slipped the straps of my dress from my shoulders. Then, as I hurried over to the bed to hide under the covers, he had undressed and met me on the sheets.

When we made love again, Jamal had taken me to the moon. And afterward, I'd felt like I was floating among the stars when we just lay together.

I'd been sure that Jamal was going to roll over, start convulsing when he realized I wasn't his wife, and then jump out of bed and into his clothes, all the while making plans to move himself and Emily out of Los Angeles so that he would never have to see me again.

But he had stayed. And held me. And talked to me.

"I hope you know that I didn't mean for this to happen," he whispered, even though we were alone in my home.

"I know," I said, and then held my breath, waiting for him to tell me all of his regrets.

"I guess it's just that you're so easy to talk to." I exhaled and he kept on, "You're so easy to be with right now."

"I know what you mean," I said. "I try speaking to other people, but I don't feel like they really hear me."

"And if they did, they wouldn't understand."

"Or they expect me to just move on, and I'm not ready to do that yet."

I felt him nod. "I know we have to move on . . ." He stopped.

And I finished, "But I'd like to stay here for just a little while longer." When I said that, I closed my eyes, not quite sure what I meant. Was I talking about staying in the memory of Chauncey? Or was I talking about staying here in bed with Jamal?

I didn't have to explain myself, though. All Jamal did was pull me a little closer. For minute after minute, Jamal just held me. He held me as if he'd held me before. He held me like he'd hold me again.

But as every good thing always does, our time came to an end when he picked up his watch from the nightstand. He kissed the top of my head and then rolled from the bed.

When I moved to get up, Jamal shook his head.

"I'm taking you home," I said, thinking that he'd forgotten about his car.

"I'm going to take a cab."

"You don't have to do that," I said.

"Yes, I do." He paused. "Just let me go like this."

It felt like he was saying more than good-bye; it felt like he was saying never again. My lips trembled, but I sucked my bottom one between my teeth. I didn't deserve to feel bad about this because clearly, this was the right thing to do.

At least I didn't hurt as much as I had when the day began.

That was how it ended. With just a soft kiss on my forehead and then he was gone.

Just a little more than twelve hours had passed and I'd hardly gotten out of this bed. I'd sat up to hug the boys when they'd rushed into my bedroom to tell me about Magic Mountain. Mama Cee had followed them, and I told her I had a headache. She herded the boys away, told me to call her if I needed anything, and left me alone to press Play on my mind's video over and over again. I kept thinking about how Jamal and I lain together, talked together, grieved together.

I tucked the memories into a corner of my mind, promising myself that I would leave them there. I pushed myself up. I only had two hours to get the boys ready for church.

Church!

Not that I wanted to go, but Mama Cee wasn't going to miss church two Sundays in a row. Then my thoughts went straight to Jamal, and I wondered if he and Emily would be at Hope Chapel.

"Stop it, Miriam," I whispered as I closed my eyes and shook my head, trying to cross those thoughts out of my mind.

Of course they were going to be in church. Weren't they always? They were going to be everywhere. Jamal and Emily were part of my church family, Chauncey's work family, not to mention that Emily was my sister.

Emily! Emily! Emily!

I squeezed my eyes shut and groaned. How could I have done that to my best friend?

I took a breath. It wasn't going to help a thing to beat myself up. I couldn't take it back and I wasn't fool enough to believe that when Jamal made love to me, it was the same as when he made love to Emily.

It meant nothing to him.

So . . . why did it feel like everything to me?

I jumped off the bed. Maybe if I got moving I could stop acting like some lovesick teenager. Inside the bathroom, I leaned into the bathtub and turned on the water full blast. As I waited for the water to warm, I shrugged my bathrobe from my shoulders and then glanced in the mirror.

But then I quickly turned away. I couldn't even look at myself.

I blinked rapidly to fight the tears, but when I stepped into the shower, I released them, letting my emotions mix with the water. I sobbed because my heart really did hurt. I was so sorry for what I'd done.

At least the beginning was the end. I would do everything I could to put what happened out of my head, and out of my heart. I had to, since I was sure this would never happen again.

20

Emily

My head was bowed and my eyes were closed, but my ears were not hearing the prayer that Deacon Brown was shouting through the sanctuary. Instead, my mind was on my husband. As the deacon went on and on about the grace of God in our lives, my thoughts were somewhere else.

Last night had been a shocker!

While Jamal had showered, I'd stayed in the front of the condo, ordering my salad, then I watched TV as I waited for my dinner to be delivered and for Jamal to join me. About forty minutes later, my food showed up, but Jamal hadn't. When I went into our bedroom in search of my husband, I found him. In bed. Asleep. And it was barely eight o'clock.

For a couple of moments, I stood at the door, just watching, just waiting for him to jump up and say, "April Fool's," though we were in the middle of September. But Jamal didn't move. Not even when I sat down on the edge of the bed, not so softly, hoping to wake him.

But even though he hadn't told me he was going to bed, and even though I'd wanted to spend some time with him, I wasn't mad. Yes, I needed my husband, but it was just as clear that right now, he needed me. Jamal had fallen back into the abyss.

All I could do was return to the living room, sit on the sofa, tuck my feet beneath me, turn on the TV, and watch a rerun of our favorite movie, *Love Story*, all by myself.

My mind, though, was on my husband the whole time.

Then, this morning, another shocker!

I'd been awakened with a bit of hope—Jamal's kisses all over my shoulders, on my neck, on my head.

I rolled over to return his affection, but with a gentle touch, Jamal pushed me down and slid on top of me.

"Babe," I giggled, until he pressed his lips against mine. It was such a soft kiss, such a Jamal kiss. When he raised his head, I said, "This is exactly what I'd wanted to do last night. But you fell asleep on me." Playfully, I pouted. "Do you know how long it's been since we made love?"

"I'm trying to fix that now," he said with another kiss.

I waited until we broke apart before I said, "But we don't have time."

Still, he lowered his head again, his lips aimed for mine.

"We're gonna be late for church," I said. "And you know how Pastor wants us in the front row, especially since now you'll be leading the Men's Prayer Circle."

He sighed and rolled onto his back. "I'm not going to church."

"What?"

"I don't feel well."

Wait a minute. Wasn't this the man who'd just tried to make love to me? "What's wrong?" I placed my hand on his forehead.

"It's not a cold or anything. I just don't feel well."

I stared at Jamal. This wasn't the first time we'd missed church, though we hardly did because we were part of Pastor's Leadership

Council. He knew Pastor depended on us. So, if he was staying home, something was up and it wasn't good.

I paused for a moment, trying to decide the best way to approach this. "Jamal," I began.

But he shook his head before I could say anything. "Emily, no. We just did this two days ago. I know you think I should get out of the house. I know you think I'm strong. I know you think I'll get through this." His eyes were focused on the ceiling.

"No, hear me out," I said, gently touching his arm. "You're right about all of that, but there's one other thing I know will help." I took a breath, knowing I'd need fortitude for this hard sell.

I said, "You need someone to talk to. Everyone who is grieving does, there's no way around that. Someone who can hear you and help pull you through."

He was silent, which was better than him telling me no. So I continued, "I'm your wife, not your therapist. But I can set up an appointment with one of my colleagues."

Jamal sucked in air.

I said, "You only have to go once and see. If it doesn't work for you, don't go back."

More silence.

"I just know from my heart that getting out of the house is good, and talking with someone will make that better."

He didn't look at me when he said, "Give me some room. Give me some time."

"Okay, okay," I said, doing everything to keep my voice and tone soft. "But can I say one more thing about this?"

He hesitated again, then nodded.

"The reason why I'm called in to work at the beginning of any tragedy is because we know grief is physically, emotionally, and mentally painful, and the recovery process is slow. But the thing is, you have to begin the process immediately. It doesn't mean that you will recover right away, just that you've taken the steps." I paused, but he didn't respond. "Grief plants roots, Jamal. And once the roots are planted, it's hard to dig them up. You have to dig deeper and dig longer."

The way he blinked, I could tell he was considering my words.

I finished with, "I don't want to rush you through the process. I just want you to begin. I know it feels like I'm bugging you, but it's just that I want to do everything I can to help you."

Turning his head, he caressed my cheek with his fingertips. "I'll think about it."

"That's all I'm asking," I said. "I love you."

"I love you, too, Emily. I really do."

"I've never doubted that. I've never doubted you."

He lowered his eyes.

I said, "So . . . what about church?"

He shook his head.

Church was where my husband needed to be, but there wasn't any room for another lecture.

"Okay, then, I'll play hooky with you. Let's go out to breakfast."

"No, Em. I'm cool here. You go."

"I'm not going without you."

"Go!" Then he rolled away from me. Discussion over.

I lay still, staring at him, trying to decide. Maybe it was best that I go, since it didn't look like I'd be doing much if I stayed home. Maybe in church I'd hear a word I could bring back to Jamal.

And in church I could definitely pray. There was nothing like corporate prayer.

So that's what I'd done. I'd showered, blow-dried my hair, did my makeup, dressed . . . and the whole time, Jamal stayed in bed. When I went over to him to kiss him good-bye, he was asleep once again.

"Amen!"

That shout brought me out of my thoughts, and I lifted my head like the other parishioners now that Deacon Brown had finished. Turning, I did another quick scan of the sanctuary. Miriam and Chauncey always sat next to me and Jamal, and Michellelee sat right behind us.

Well, Michellelee was in place, but Miriam wasn't. Now I wished that I'd called her this morning.

When I heard Pastor Ford say, "Everyone, turn in your Bibles . . ." I twisted and faced the front of the church. Maybe Miriam was here, but didn't think she should sit in the front anymore. Or maybe she'd chosen Jamal's method of coping and she was still in bed.

The church filled with the rustling of Bible pages and I did the same, though I found the scripture that the pastor had directed us to, Deuteronomy 28:47, on my iPad.

Pastor Ford said, "With all that's been going on in our community and right here in this church since the fire, I want to talk about the importance of guarding your heart. Especially during times of trouble, when you feel less joy and more sorrow, it's important not to let the devil get ahold of your emotions."

I nodded like everyone else in the sanctuary.

"Now, looking at those scriptures"—she lowered her eyes—"I can sum it up in a couple of words: if you do not serve God with joyfulness and gladness of heart for all that you have *already* received, you will be open to attacks from the enemy and that's whom you will serve." The pastor looked up and slammed her hand against the podium. "Hello, somebody!"

Murmurs of agreement rose through the congregation.

"Let me explain how this applies to us right now." Pastor Ford picked up her Bible and strutted in front of the altar. Holding the holy book above her head, she said, "If you love the Lord and are serving Him, you are aware of your abundant blessings. Blessings that are spiritual, financial, emotional, physical—it would take years to go through your life and write down every blessing you've received.

"But then something happens: you lose your job, you get divorced, or a devastating fire causes you to lose someone you love. What we tend to do is focus on this singular incident. But does that make sense? Does that wipe out everything that we know and all that we've experienced from God?"

"No!" the parishioners shouted.

Pastor Ford returned to the podium. "Now, I'm not saying that as Christians we will never find ourselves angry at God, or questioning God. We have big expectations for our Big God. But don't get it twisted, keep all of that in check. Don't go over the cliff with it, because whatever makes you bitter will keep you from getting better."

"Amen!"

"Through Christ, you can crawl out of grief, you can flourish. But it won't happen in the middle of your mumbling and grumbling and complaining. Thriving can only happen in the midst of joy. Understand what I'm saying: happiness and sadness are about circumstances. But joy, that's your inner celebration. When all around you seems to be crumbling, you can have joy. Because you know whom you serve, and you know what He's done, and you know what He's doing and what He will do again."

"Amen!" folks shouted.

"Oh, hear what I'm saying," Pastor Ford sang. "Amp up your joy. Because the world didn't give it to you, so how can you let the world and circumstances and losing a job and divorce and even death take that away!"

People were on their feet cheering, and it took a moment for the sanctuary to quiet enough to hear the rest of Pastor's message. She went on to challenge us to find joy in our lives every day, to seek God so that He could remind us of the blessings we had. And to keep a gratitude journal so that we'd have someplace to go, we'd have words to review, if our pain ever got so deep that we couldn't remember.

By the end of the sermon, we were all on our feet, shouting with praise. And, in the midst of it, I lowered my head and sent up a silent prayer for Jamal. I prayed that this message would reach his heart through me.

I was so encouraged by the time I held up my hands for the benediction. But when I stepped into the aisle once Pastor dismissed us, my thoughts rushed back to Miriam.

"You're looking for her, too?" Michellelee said, moving from her seat and standing next to me.

I nodded. "Did you talk to her?"

"I talked to her yesterday morning before you guys were meeting for lunch, but I didn't call her this morning. I just thought she'd be here." Michellelee shrugged. "I'll check on her later, 'cause I've got to get to the station."

"On a Sunday?"

"I'm not working. I just want to see if there's anything new about the arsonist. No one's called, but I can get a lot more information there."

"I'm still hoping it was some sort of accident, because the thought of one person doing this . . ." I shook my head as my eyes continued to scan the crowd.

Then I spotted Miriam, on the other side, all the way in the back. "There she is!" I pointed for Michellelee's benefit.

We pushed our way through the congregation, even as some tried to stop Michellelee to chat. Members of Hope Chapel loved seeing the news star of Southern California every Sunday.

By the time we got to the back of the church, Miriam and Mama Cee were almost at the door.

"Miriam!" Michellelee and I called out at the same time.

At first, only Mama Cee paused. But then she pulled Miriam's sleeve, and she turned around, too.

"Oh, hey, Emily," Miriam said, without a bit of enthusiasm.

"You were going to leave without saying anything?" Michellelee asked as she hugged her.

"I didn't know you guys were here."

"Uh . . . yeah," Michellelee said. "Where else would we be?"

"Good morning," I said to Mama Cee, hugging her.

"Good morning, baby."

Turning to Miriam, I said, "So, how are you?"

She shrugged as if that was a good enough answer.

"Where's Charlie?" I asked.

"He went to round up the boys," Mama Cee explained. Then she turned to Miriam. "I'm going to go to the ladies' room; I'll be right back."

"You want me to go with you?" Miriam asked.

"Not unless you have to pee, too," Mama Cee said.

Michellelee and I laughed.

Michellelee said, "Mama Cee, I don't have to pee, but I'm gonna walk with you 'cause I'm parked on that side of the church and I have to get out of here." She turned to Miriam. "I'll call you later." Then she pointed to me. "You, too."

I waited until Mama Cee and Michellelee were a little bit away before I asked Miriam, "Why were you sitting back here?"

"Well, we were a little late. And with Mama Cee and Charlie with me . . . you know."

Her tone was so flat, nothing at all like my friend I'd seen just twenty-four hours ago. "I'm sure Pastor Ford still wants you sitting up front."

She lowered her eyes. "It really doesn't matter. Her message is the same no matter where you sit, right?"

"Right." I grinned and grabbed her hand. "And today was a good message." I waited to see if Miriam would agree, and when she didn't, I wondered if she was still mad at God. But maybe she wasn't—she was in church. "When I didn't see you, I thought you'd stayed home."

Miriam shrugged. "Mama Cee said I needed to be here."

"She's right." I sighed. "I wish she'd talk to Jamal."

Miriam asked, "Where . . . is . . . he?"

"He didn't want to come, can you believe it?" Miriam looked away as I continued, "Listen, I wanted to ask you about what happened yesterday?"

"Yesterday?" she said, still not looking at me.

"Yes, did anything happen when you guys went to lunch?"

"Lunch?"

I frowned. Why was she parroting me? "Yes, you and Jamal went to lunch, right?"

"Right."

"So, was everything okay?"

"Okay?"

I tilted my head and spoke a little slower. "Yes, was it okay, because Jamal came home a little down. Like something had happened."

This time, she didn't repeat what I said, but she paused so long, I wondered if she was going to answer me at all. Finally, she said, "I don't know what could've happened. We just . . . talked," she said softly.

"About Chauncey?"

She nodded.

I sighed. "I think that really affected Jamal, really bothered him."

Now her bright eyes became teary ones. "I'm really sorry, Emily."

"Oh honey." I hugged her. "I'm not blaming you. It's really good that you and Jamal have each other to talk to. You need each other. I just wanted to make sure that's all it was."

She shook her head. "That's all. We just talked."

"Okay, I'm back!"

Miriam and I turned as Mama Cee walked up the aisle, and for the first time, I noticed the church had cleared out.

Miriam rushed to her mother-in-law's side. "Here, let me help you."

Mama Cee glared at Miriam as if she was trying to figure out what her daughter-in-law was doing.

I said, "Well, I parked on the other side of the building, too."

"Okay, baby." Mama Cee gave me a hug. "Charlie and I are leaving Tuesday, so I hope we get a chance to see you."

"I hope so." Then I took Miriam's hand and squeezed it. "I'll call you later. And don't forget, if you need me, I'm there. Sisters!"

She blinked rapidly, as if she was trying to keep tears away.

I said, "Love you."

"Mean it," Miriam said, so softly I could hardly hear her.

I stood in place as Miriam helped Mama Cee down the church steps, and my heart ached for my friend. Just like Jamal's, her pain was palpable, and it killed me. I was a psychologist. I was supposed to be able to help them. But I felt just as helpless with Miriam as I felt with Jamal.

I turned toward the side exit door, but then stopped. Maybe there was something I could do. Pivoting, I moved down the center aisle and at the front of the church, I paused for a minute before I lowered myself to my knees.

The church was empty when I knelt down on the padded cushions, preparing to pray for Jamal and Miriam.

Empty, except for me and the Lord. And as long as He was there, no one and nothing else mattered.

21

MIRIAM

Either I was having a major heart attack or telling lies to my best friend was the best cardio workout ever. Because for the last half hour, my heart had pounded like I'd done ten one-hundred-yard sprints, which would've been quite a feat for me.

I didn't know what I'd been thinking, but I wasn't prepared to see Emily. When I spotted her pressing through the crowd in my direction, all I wanted to do was pick up Mama Cee and run like hell. But since that wasn't going to happen, I acted like I hadn't heard her calling. The only problem was, I hadn't let Mama Cee in on my deception.

All I could do was stand there, remember to breathe in, breathe out, and pretend that I hadn't just slept with my best friend's husband.

But then Emily started questioning me about Jamal, and it was only because of my theatrical training that I was still able to stand on my wobbling legs and not sound like a babbling idiot. Or maybe I did sound like a fool, I didn't know. All I remembered was talking and trying not to look into her eyes.

Now, as I sat behind Charlie, who was driving my van, I kept checking out the cars behind us, and when anyone pulled up beside us, I held my breath. I wanted to tell Charlie to put the pedal to the metal so that we could get far away from Emily. I was sure she was lurking somewhere, having figured it out. She would catch us at some red light, jump out of her car, and scream for the whole world to hear that I was a liar and a cheat and no friend of hers.

"You okay, Miriam?" Charlie asked as he peered at me through the rearview mirror.

"Yeah," I said, trying to settle down. "I'm good."

His eyes held mine. "So, I was thinking we'd go out to brunch."

"Sounds good." I was so surprised that my voice was steady while my heart was trying to break out of my chest. "Uh . . . I wanna go home and change first, though. Get out of this dress."

Charlie shrugged. "Okay." Then, he glanced at his mother in the front passenger seat. "You okay with that?"

"Yeah." Mama Cee nodded. "I'll change, too."

"Yay," the boys cheered, always excited about going out.

I had never been so happy that my home was close to the church. I needed to get someplace where I could be alone, quick. When Charlie pulled the van into the driveway, I jumped out before he'd even shifted into park. And I was at the front door and in the house before anyone else was out of the van.

Behind the closed door of my bedroom, I finally exhaled.

I slumped onto my bed, wondering why I was such a mess. Of course I was going to see Emily in church. I was going to see her all the time. Everywhere. And that meant I would come face-to-face with Jamal, too.

Jamal!

Now that I'd seen Emily, I could admit that I had really wanted to see Jamal. That had been my hope as I dressed this morning, as I got the boys ready, as we drove to church. I had wanted to see Jamal. Period!

But he hadn't shown up; was that because of me? Was his plan to stay away from church forever? Was his plan to stay away from me?

That couldn't happen. I needed Jamal to know that he didn't need to change his life, his routine, or his schedule, just to avoid me. He needed to understand that I understood. What happened with us was nothing more than one moment in time.

I needed to talk to him, to tell him, to let him know that it was all right—that I was all right. But when could I talk to him? And how? It wasn't like I could go over to Emily and Jamal's condo and talk to him with Emily standing right there. I could call him, but would he answer?

The knock on my bedroom door interrupted my questions.

Mama Cee called out, "Baby, you ready?"

I jumped up from the bed and dashed into my closet. "Almost," I said. "Give me ten more minutes."

"Okay. We're all waiting."

I stripped from my dress, then slipped into a long jean skirt and a T-shirt. In the ten minutes that I'd promised, we were back in the van. Just about thirty minutes after that, we were seated at one of the large circular booths at the Grand Lux in Beverly Hills.

I was in the middle, with my sons on one side and Mama Cee and Charlie on the other.

The waiter, whom I'd watched running around and serving several tables, still greeted us with a smile. "Can I take your drink orders?"

It was a déjà-vu moment that made me freeze. I'd been here before. Not at the Grand Lux, but I'd been in this moment. Me, the boys, and Chauncey. Doing what we often did after church, sitting in a restaurant and enjoying our Sunday afternoon.

Just two weeks ago.

I glanced at my sons, ready to address their distress. But they wore only smiles as they chatted with their uncle. There were no signs of any kind of flashback.

Resilient. That's what they were. I wasn't naive enough to believe that they were not affected. I knew my sons were still hurting. It was just that they'd found a way to live through it, live in spite of it. They were good examples for me.

After my sons all shouted that they wanted orange juice, Mama Cee, Charlie, and I gave the waiter our requests for coffee.

As soon as the waiter stepped away, the boys were back to their chatter.

"Uncle Charlie, can you come with me to my first Boy Scout meeting?" Mikey asked.

Even though Charlie glanced at me, he asked Mikey, "When is it?"

"Next Saturday. Right, Mom?"

I nodded while Charlie shook his head.

He said, "I wish I could, Mikey." Then after a deep breath, he added, "Boys, your grandmother and I have to go home."

"You're leaving?" Stevie asked.

"You won't be able to go with me?" Mikey moaned.

"When are you going back home?" Junior piped in.

Charlie held up his hands, trying to stop the questions, but my sons continued. Together, they said, "I don't want you to go."

It was another one of those break-your-heart moments.

So I jumped in. "Boys, I have something to tell you." Their eyes left their uncle and the three turned to me. "What would you say . . . what would you think about seeing your uncle and grandmother every day?"

Mikey and Stevie tilted their heads and frowned.

Junior turned to his uncle. "You guys are moving here?"

If it wasn't for my mother-in-law's health, that would've been a brilliant idea. Because the truth was, I wasn't sure if I wanted to move. But I said, "No, not them moving here. What do you think about maybe us moving there?"

My words seemed to shock my sons for a couple of seconds.

Then Mikey said, "You mean, like living there with Grammama Cee and Uncle Charlie? All the time?"

I nodded. "Yeah, what would you think?"

After a moment, Mikey said, "That would be so cool."

"Yeah, cool," Stevie mimicked his brother.

Now Mama Cee, Charlie, and I turned our attention to Junior. He was the hard sale. All of my sons had lived their whole lives in Los Angeles and had grown up in that one house. Obviously, at ten, Junior's friendships were more solid than his brothers'.

"So what do you think, honey?" I asked him.

Junior looked down for a moment, then shrugged. "I love hanging out with Uncle Charlie, but what about my friends?"

"We wouldn't be moving right now. And we'd have a few more talks about it, so that we can figure this whole thing out."

Charlie piped in, "I know you have lots of friends here, so we'll make sure you come back and see them." Then he added, "And you've already made some friends in Arizona. Every time you guys come to visit, you make new friends, right?"

"Yeah!" Mikey and Stevie said, and Junior nodded.

To reassure Junior, I repeated, "But it's not completely decided. I'm only going to do this if you want to do it, okay?"

He nodded.

"We're going to make this decision together as a family."

"Just like Dad used to say, right?" Mikey said.

I nodded, and it must've been the tears that came straight to my eyes that made Charlie jump in.

He said, "And I'm not leaving until Tuesday, so we have two

more days of fun!" My younger boys cheered, and even Junior smiled.

My brother-in-law added, "I'm gonna take you to school in the morning."

"Who, us?" Stevie said. "'Cause Junior goes to a different school."

"I know," Charlie said. "So, I was thinking about taking you boys to school"—he paused—"and then heading over to your school, Junior. Aren't you trying out for the basketball team tomorrow?"

"Yeah," he said, his eyes wide. "How did you know?"

Charlie shrugged. "I've got uncle superpowers. I know everything!"

I was the only one at the table who didn't laugh. That's because Charlie had given me an idea.

It took a couple of waiters to bring all of our food, and our table filled with waffles and chicken and eggs and grits. Charlie blessed the food, then the forks hit the plates.

The air filled with my sons' chatter and Mama Cee and Charlie listened as if the children were giving sermons. But my mind had left the table; my thoughts were on a plan that was beginning to take shape.

Now I knew what to do.

It was a bit deceitful, but it would serve my purpose.

I just had to figure out what I would say when I called Emily.

22

Emily

My eyes popped open, and now I knew exactly what I was going to do to save my husband.

I looked over at Jamal, still sleeping, which is what he'd done all day yesterday after I'd come home from church. That was when I knew I had to do something major. Something that would shake Jamal up and get him to remember the man he was just weeks ago, before Chauncey's passing.

Last night, when I'd laid my head down, I had no idea what I was going to do. But then I dreamed of a special time and a wonderful place ...

✦

May 15, 2001

Jamal and I fell into quite a routine. With only eight weeks to plan the destination anniversary celebration for Miriam and Chauncey, Jamal decided that we should meet twice a week, every Wednesday evening and Saturday morning.

And with every meeting, I discovered that I really liked Jamal. I mean, I really liked him. Not only physically—I liked him to his core.

Every time we met, we discovered something else we had in common. Like how we cheered for the same teams: basketball—the Lakers; football—the Cowboys; baseball—the Yankees. Our favorite TV channels—CNN and ESPN. Our favorite food—Thai. Even down to the pieces of chicken—both of us would only eat dark meat.

The only thing—we were at different ends of the spectrum politically. After the Clinton fiasco had blown over, Jamal had reverted back to his Democratic ways. But even with that, we had great discussions. We debated last year's presidential outcome. I felt the Supreme Court had made the right decision; he believed that George W. Bush had stolen the election.

Jamal was wrong, but at least we could discuss it. With him, there wasn't a subject off limits.

Our sessions became the highlight of my week, and I knew he was beginning to be into me, too. I could tell that he was beginning to like me by the way he touched my hand when we were talking, or the way he wiped crumbs from my mouth with the tip of his finger after we ate, or the way he brushed my hair from my eyes when my curls fell onto my face. Then there were times when I looked up and caught him staring at me.

I knew Jamal would be calling me for a reason beyond these meetings soon.

Then I began to wonder, what was I waiting for? I was a woman of the new millennium. Why should I sit and wait?

So, four weeks after we'd started meeting, I decided to do it. On the Friday night before I was going to make my move, I called Michellelee, who was still at work at the KCAL TV studios, where she'd snagged her first job in television.

"Girl, you're still feeling that guy?" she asked.

"Well, we've been spending a lot of time together, you know, planning for Miriam and Chauncey."

"You don't have to explain it to me. Go for it," she told me. "If you're still liking Jamal after all this time, there must be something to it."

By the time I sat at Starbucks waiting for Jamal the next morning, I was ready.

When he walked in, hugged me, and then slid into the chair across from me, he asked, "What's got you all happy?"

"What do you mean?"

"You're grinning like you just won the lottery. Oh wait, you're rich. That wouldn't matter to you." He laughed.

"First of all, I'm not rich. My parents are, and they've always made it clear to me that they were rich and I wasn't. And trust me, money always matters to rich people."

"I hear that. So, what's up? Did you ace an exam or something?"

My plan had been to wait until we finished our business, but since he was giving me the opening . . . "Well, I wanted to talk to you—"

Then his cell phone rang.

He held up one finger, stopping me, before he answered. He must've recognized the voice right away, because now he was the one with a huge smile. The kind of grin that spread his lips so wide his cheeks had to hurt.

"Hey, you!" he said.

Hey, you? Then he stood up from the table without saying anything to me, and stepped outside like he didn't want me anywhere near his conversation.

For a moment, all I could do was stare at the door that he'd just walked through. But after that, I thanked God that call had come in.

Jamal was seeing someone and I didn't even know it. If I'd told him that I was into him, he would've hurt my feelings . . . again.

Well actually, my feelings were already hurt, but this time, he didn't know it. When he slipped back into his seat, my smile was long gone.

"So," he said as if we hadn't missed a beat, "you wanted to talk to me?"

"Uh . . . yeah . . . I was going to tell you . . . something . . . we can do . . . why don't we have Miriam and Chauncey . . . maybe renew their vows?"

He nodded slowly. "That's a great idea. You're brilliant."

He was right about that. I was brilliant, since I'd *just* come up with that idea. But when it came to Jamal, I was a fool! I was pining after a man who was just not into me. Maybe I was too tall, too skinny, though I had a feeling I was just too white. Whatever it was, there would never again be a time when I looked at Jamal as any more than a friend.

For hours after I left Jamal, I still felt bad. There were other guys who were interested in me, but no one had touched me the way Jamal had, and I knew that on some level he liked me a lot. So could something as shallow as race be what was stopping him?

I was deep into my self-analysis when my cell phone rang. If I wasn't so sure that it was my mom or dad calling, I wouldn't have answered. But knowing that it was them, because they called every Saturday night, made me reach for the phone. I needed a little "in all ways and for always" love right about now.

"Emily?" the man said after I'd picked up and said hello. "This is Clarkson," he said with a tinge of "Surprise!" in his voice.

"Hey," I said, groaning inside. "How are you?"

"I'm good. I'm in LA and would love to see you."

The last thing I wanted to do was meet up with Waldorf Astoria. Not only because I didn't have the time, but I didn't feel like being bored out of my gourd as he went on and on about the daily nothings of his life as an executive in some pharmaceutical company.

But then I had a thought. "How long are you here?"

"A week. Until next Saturday."

"What about meeting on Wednesday, in the evening. Say about nine?"

Clarkson agreed and I gave him the directions that would bring him from the Beverly Hills Hotel over to the Starbucks in Ladera. When I said good-bye, I settled back on my bed.

This was childish on so many levels. First, I was using Clarkson, and second, Jamal didn't even care. But since he already had a woman, I wanted to make sure Jamal knew I had a man.

Then on Tuesday, the night before I was to do the grand reveal of my "boyfriend," Jamal called.

"Hey, just wanted to make sure we were still on for tomorrow."

"Yes," I said, wondering why he was really calling. He'd never done a confirmation call before.

"Okay, 'cause there's something I want to talk to you about."

"About the trip?"

"Actually, it's personal. I want to get your thoughts on something."

"Well, I'll be there." I almost added, "I can't wait."

The next evening, Jamal and I arrived at Starbucks at the same time, and I was a little surprised when he got straight to business. Not that I cared. My thoughts were more on Clarkson than on anything personal Jamal wanted to share. About an hour later, Clarkson walked in, a bit early, but for me, he was right on time.

"Oh, excuse me," I said to Jamal, stopping him in the middle of a sentence. I jumped up and waved wildly. Clarkson saw me and I grinned as he took long strides toward me. "Hi!" I said when he finally stood in front of me. I wrapped my arms around his neck. "You look good," I said. "Really good."

On cue, Jamal cleared his throat. "Oh." I pretended that I'd forgotten about him. "Clarkson, this is Jamal. And, Jamal, this is my dear, dear, dearest friend in the world." Then I winked, as if I was kidding about the word "friend."

Jamal stood and as he shook Clarkson's hand, I grabbed my purse.

"So, are we finished here?" I asked Jamal, though my arm was already hooked through Clarkson's as we walked away.

I sauntered out of Starbucks satisfied, but sad. It was officially over with Jamal before it had even begun.

At our Saturday meeting, we were back to business, both of us a bit aloof at first. But the next week we were back to our jovial selves, and gone was the sexual tension that I'd always felt between us. We were more like brother and sister now.

So, we worked and worked and the countdown began. A week, then a day, and finally, we were heading to Maui . . .

✦

NEXT TO ME, Jamal stirred, interrupting my memories. He rolled to his side, but his eyes were still closed. Scooting down onto the bed, I lay on my side and shifted until my eyes were in line with his closed ones.

I whispered, "We're going on a trip."

My words made Jamal stir a little bit more, then his eyes fluttered open.

I repeated, "We're going on a trip."

He frowned, looking as if he wasn't sure if he was awake. After a while, he asked, "Where are we going?"

I let a couple of beats go by. "Maui."

It took a moment, but then his eyes brightened and his lips spread into a slow smile. Leaning over, I kissed him and took him with me on my journey down memory lane . . .

◆

June 2001

I COULDN'T STOP laughing at Miriam and Chauncey as they settled into their first-class seats across the aisle from us.

"I can't believe this!" Miriam said, rocking back and forth.

"Hold on, baby!" Chauncey said. He took a magazine from the seat pocket and fanned his wife. "Don't faint," he kidded her. Then he stopped. "Wait, maybe you should. Go ahead, faint, and I'll give you mouth-to-mouth resuscitation."

I shook my head and pushed my seat back, ready to relax.

"We did it," Jamal whispered in my ear.

I nodded. "At least the first part. Let's see how the rest of the weekend goes."

"It's going to be fabulous," he said. "'Cause we make a great team."

All I did was smile, because I wasn't going anywhere near that road. I'd learned my lesson—we'd always be a great *brother and sister* team.

For five hours, we ate and drank and chatted like the old friends we were. We were the only four flying into Hawaii today. Jamal had planned it so that Miriam and Chauncey would have a night to themselves before the others arrived, and he and I could finalize all preparations.

Midway through the flight, I changed seats with Chauncey and right away my best friend hugged me. "I love you so much, Em, for doing this for us."

"This is just what we do. You and me. Blue and White. And wait until Red joins us tomorrow!"

"So, you and Jamal really did all of this together?"

I nodded.

She glanced across the aisle at Chauncey and Jamal, and I prayed that she wasn't going to give me that lecture she'd given me three years ago about how black and white didn't mix.

Just as I was getting ready to open my mouth and tell her to save it, she whispered, "I'm sorry for the way I reacted about you and Jamal."

It took me a couple of moments to digest her words. "You waited three years to tell me this?"

"Well, when you never mentioned it again, neither did I because I knew that I'd hurt your feelings and I didn't want to do that again. But now that I've had time—"

"Three years," I repeated, wanting to make sure my friend realized how ridiculous this was.

"Okay, you and Jamal do make a cute couple. I've finally seen the light."

With my hands, I waved away her words. "Take that light right back to the dark. I'm not interested in him like that anymore."

"Really?" she said as if she didn't believe me. "But you look so good together."

"Trust me, nothing's there. Plus, he has a girlfriend."

Miriam frowned. "No, he doesn't."

"Yes. He does."

"Uh . . . he's Chauncey's best friend and if he was with someone I would know."

"Well, obviously he's been keeping something from you." I

shrugged. "And anyway, it doesn't matter. I got over Jamal a long time ago."

"Okay," Miriam said, leaning back in her chair. "I guess I just want you to have what Chauncey and I have." She sighed. "Em, I love that man so much. And right now, I'm gonna take a nap so that when we land and get to that hotel room, me and Chauncey—"

I held up my hand. "I love you, White, but please."

We laughed and then both of us closed our eyes. I didn't say another word until Jamal gently shook my shoulder, letting me know that we had arrived.

We were the first to get off and, with our carry-on luggage, went straight to the curb outside, where two members of the staff of the Grand Wailea Hotel met us.

"Aloha," the woman said as she placed white-orchid-and rose leis over each of us. "Welcome to Hawaii."

"Oh, it's on now," Chauncey said. "I'm in Hawaii and I just got laid?" He wrapped his arm around Miriam's waist. "Baby, this won't be the last time I'm laid today, will it?"

Miriam giggled and I shook my head. I could imagine Miriam and Chauncey fifty years from now acting just like this.

The hotel driver opened the doors of the limousine and Chauncey helped Miriam in before Jamal held my hand as I slid inside. Through the tinted windows, I could already see the beauty of this Hawaiian island as we sped by the rising slopes of Haleakala in the distance. Even with all of my travels, nothing had prepared me for the beauty of this tropical wonderland, filled with lush foliage of such vividness that the plants and flowers didn't even look real.

Within minutes, we were at the hotel, and I knew right away why many referred to it as the Hawaiian Disneyland. This Polynesian hideaway was expansive and its elegance took my breath away, from the marble statues in the lobby to the tropical flowers that caressed every single one of my senses. But the best feature was the open side of the hotel, which offered a view of the magnificence of the Pacific Ocean.

As Jamal and Chauncey checked us in, Miriam and I sipped the Hawaiian punch that we'd been given and stood in awe of the sight before us.

"This is so beautiful," she said. "Who chose this place? You or Jamal?"

"Me."

"How did you know about it? From your parents?"

"Nope! When I read that it was a Waldorf Astoria Resort, I figured . . ." I shrugged, grinned, and then Miriam and I laughed out loud.

"What's so funny?" Chauncey and Jamal asked together as they came over to us with the keys.

Miriam and I looked at each other again and giggled.

Chauncey and Jamal just shrugged.

Jamal said, "Well anyway, Chauncey and Miriam are on the fourth floor in the bridal suite."

Miriam clapped her hands. "This is freakin' amazing!"

"And here's your key," he said, handing me the card. "Everyone else is on the third floor. So, let's escort them to their room."

I nodded, but then Chauncey cut in.

"Nah, nah," he said. "We don't need no help, bro. You told me that we were getting here before everyone else so that my bride and I could have some time alone. And that's what I want, to be alone with this beautiful woman."

Chauncey laughed, and I sighed. Every time he spoke about Miriam, his words belonged in a Hallmark card.

We rolled our bags onto the elevator and for a minute,

Chauncey and Miriam forgot that they weren't alone. When the elevator stopped on the third floor, Jamal joked, "You sure y'all don't need no help?"

Chauncey broke his embrace with Miriam for just a moment. "Do I *look* like I need any help?" We all laughed. Chauncey added, "And don't be calling my room for nothing. We'll be fine, they got room service here, right?"

Jamal told him yes, right as the elevator doors closed. I would have said good-bye, but neither one of them would have heard me. I stood watching the elevator door close on my friends. This was not the way I'd imagined our first day on the island. I'd actually thought that the four of us would hang out, walk around the resort, go to dinner, and just have fun. But that was my idea of a great night, not Miriam and Chauncey's.

It wasn't until I heard Jamal clear his throat behind me that I turned around.

"Well," I said, grabbing the handle of my suitcase, "I guess I'll go to my room . . ."

"If you're up to it, there's something I'd like to do."

"What?" I asked, squinting a little.

He grinned. "It's a surprise. Just go to your room, get settled, and then change. Did you bring any workout clothes?"

"Yes, I brought a bathing suit. That's about all the working out I plan on doing."

He laughed. "I'm sure you got a pair of shorts in that bag, and a T-shirt and some sneakers?"

"Please don't tell me we're going to do push-ups on the beach."

"That's a thought, but no. Just get changed."

"Okay." I headed to my room, with a promise to call Jamal in about ten minutes. But it took me longer than that. The view from the room distracted me. What I'd seen from the lobby was nothing compared to the ocean vista outside my window. What I really wanted to do was sit in here and wait for the sun to set on the water.

But I was curious about Jamal's plans. So I changed into a pair of navy shorts and a white T-shirt, then called him. Within a couple of minutes, he was standing in front of my room, in his own workout gear.

My eyes wandered to his bare legs and his well-defined calves.

"So what are we going to do?" I asked, needing something else to focus on besides the parts of his body that were uncovered.

"Be patient," he said, taking my hand.

All the way down in the elevator, I tried to get Jamal to tell me where we were going. He didn't give up his secret, though. Not when we walked through the lobby, or when we trudged by the pool. But then we walked on the hard part of the sand for just a few feet, and I saw it.

"You're kidding!" I exclaimed. "A basketball court? On the beach?"

"Yup." He jogged onto the moveable hardwood floor and grabbed the basketball that was beneath the hoop. Then he bounce-passed it to me.

"I can't believe this. How cool." I held the ball between both my hands. "I wonder why no one is out here playing?"

"You have to reserve it, and I reserved this weeks ago. For you and me. So what do you say? You up for a game?"

I hadn't held a ball in my hands like this since I graduated a year and a half ago. But when my fingertips caressed that rubber, and I massaged the familiar stitching, it all came back to me.

"You sure you want some of this?" I asked, reverting to some of the trash talk that I'd learned during my four years on the USC team. I threw the ball, sending it flying into his chest.

He caught it with two hands. "Ask me that question again."

The heat rose beneath my skin, but I did my best to pretend that I missed that double entendre. "So, what's the game?"

"Let's just warm up. Take a few shots, and then see if you're really up to playing me."

"Pass me the ball," I said.

"As soon as you miss, I get it." He tossed me the ball.

"Who says I'm going to miss?" Then, from right where I stood about ten feet from the basket, I took that jump shot, which had been my signature in school. And even though it had been a year and a half, it was nothing but net.

"Dang, girl."

Jamal bounced the ball back to me and I took another shot. Same result. Then another shot and another score.

"Okay," Jamal said when he caught the ball under the hoop. "Move to the other side 'cause I can't believe you can shoot like that from everywhere."

I laughed. "Have you forgotten?" I grabbed the ball from him. "I'm Emily Harrington."

Swoosh!

"All-American."

Swoosh!

"And if I wasn't trying to be a doctor, I would've been a top pick in the WNBA."

Swoosh!

Jamal laughed. "Okay, I get it. So, am I going to get a turn?"

I passed him the ball. "Yes, but only because my parents raised me to share."

He dribbled the ball a few times, then crisscrossed it between his legs. "So, do you like what you see?" he asked, then took his shot. Like mine, it was all net. When I stared at him, he added, "I'm talking about the hotel. Do you like it?"

"I love it," I said, then told him about the view from my window. "I almost called and canceled on you. I wanted to stand there and watch the sun set."

"We're gonna get a pretty cool view of that from right here," he said as he moved to post up again.

This time, I planned to play defense. He bounced the ball twice, then faked to his right, moved to his left, and made the easy layup. I caught the ball and passed it back to him.

"Good point."

"Thanks." Then he added, "If you really like it here, you should think about coming back." He dribbled the ball four times, and then said, "With Clarkson."

"Clarkson?"

As soon as he said Clarkson's name, he dodged around me and scored. It was easy enough. His words had left me flat-footed.

"Yeah, Clarkson," he said, bringing the ball back into play. "I'm surprised you didn't bring him with you. I mean, you guys seem like you're really close."

There wasn't any point in keeping that facade up. We were friends now, and one day the truth would come out anyway. "We're just family friends," I said, telling the truth and reaching for the ball. "Our parents are best friends who had hopes for a merger among their children."

Jamal laughed. "Oh, okay."

I dribbled the ball as I said, "So, what about your girlfriend?" This time, he was the one caught by surprise, and with just three long strides, I dipped around him for my own easy layup.

"Girlfriend?"

I nodded. "You never talk about her."

"Who are you talking about?"

"Your girlfriend."

His forehead creased with wrinkles.

"One Saturday while you were with me at Starbucks, you got a call."

I stopped and he said, "And?"

Really? Was he really going to act like he didn't know what I was talking about? Holding on to the ball, I said, "You got a call from her, and it was so important, you had to take it outside."

He squinted, and while he was trying to figure it out, I bounced the ball twice and scored another easy point.

"So, you remember now?" I asked when I came back to the center of the court.

"Yeah." He nodded.

"Why don't you talk about her? I was thinking that since you and I are friends, you can at least tell me her name."

He held up his hand to block my shot, but his best defense was his words. "Her name is Mom," he said, right as I flicked my wrist and then watched the ball fly over the backboard.

"Mom?" I stood there, thinking that Mom better be short for something like Momtina or Momvella or else I was going to feel like a fool.

Jamal ran after the ball, then dribbled it back to me. "That call. That was my mother. She lives in Jamaica and we don't talk much."

"Really? You've never mentioned your mother."

He shrugged. "We were never close," he said, bouncing the ball between his legs. "I was raised by my father's mother, though I didn't know my dad all that well either. Drugs, prison, you know the story."

No, I didn't know the story, but I didn't say anything.

He explained, at least part of it. "My mother was on summer vacation, visiting relatives, when she met my father. She was only sixteen, got pregnant, stayed here long enough to have me, then gave me to my dad before she returned to Jamaica."

"Wow."

He shrugged. "My dad gave me to his mom, and that was the best thing that ever happened to me."

Told by anyone else, this would have sounded like a tragic story of a child not wanted. But coming from Jamal, it almost sounded like a fairy tale.

"So, there are two things you should know," he said, before he took a shot and missed. "My grandmother was wonderful, and I don't have a girlfriend."

"Well, for that, you get three free throws."

He laughed as he twirled the ball in his hands. "Now that we've verified that we're both free agents—"

"I just thought you had a girlfriend because it's hard for me to believe you're not seeing anyone."

"That's what I say about you."

"But you're . . . hot. Can I just say that?"

He smiled. "And that's what I say about you."

"And you're smart," I added.

"So are you."

"And you know a little about everything."

"That's what I say about you."

"Okay," I said, taking the ball from his hands. "I guess that's your way of saying you don't want to talk about it."

"I am talking about it. I'm telling you the truth."

I asked, "So, why aren't you in a relationship?"

He shrugged, then changed the subject. "You wanna go for a walk? We can go right down there"—he pointed—"sit on those rocks and watch the sun set."

"Sure." I guessed he felt his relationship status was none of my business, and I had to respect that.

Jamal tossed the ball back onto the court, leaving it where we found it. When we stepped on the sand, I kicked off my tennis shoes and socks, then let my toes sink into the beach. I moaned with pleasure.

As we walked, I soaked in all the music of paradise, the soft crash of the evening surf, the chatter of other guests, and the laughter of children. There was nothing but happiness in this place, and I inhaled.

At the rocks, Jamal held my hand as we climbed to the highest point, then we sat side by side in our front-row seats, enjoying the show as the sun slowly descended. Neither one of us said a word as the horizon brightened into a multitude of oranges. Every hue of orange that God had ever made fused together in the sky, and a few times, I had to remind myself to breathe.

It became all the more wonderful when Jamal took my hand. I didn't read too much into that, though. Certainly, the majesty of the moment made him want to connect with someone, anyone.

But then he took his hand away and with the tips of his fingers he turned my head toward his.

He hesitated for just a moment. "So, you're not involved with anyone?" His voice was thick, but at least he could speak. All I could do was shake my head.

He said, "And I'm not involved with anyone, okay?"

This time, I nodded.

Jamal leaned in and let his lips touch mine. Tentatively, at first. But then he pressed against me as if he'd always belonged there.

His kiss was so soft, so gentle, yet it reached down into my soul. It was the kiss I'd been waiting for. And now that his lips had met mine, the wait had been so worth it.

When he finally leaned back, our eyes connected and stayed that way, as if we couldn't break away. Then, together, we smiled in sync, maybe even already in love.

The sun was gone, the day had ended, and this was our beginning . . .

✦

JUST A FEW seconds had passed, maybe a minute. But as I grinned at my husband lying next me to me in bed, I knew he remembered every moment of that first day in Maui, just as I had.

"So, do you think it's a good idea?" I asked him.

"To go to Maui again with you? Are you kidding?" He kissed my forehead. "I wish we could go tomorrow."

"I wish that, too," I said, knowing for sure that my idea to get him away would help him with his grief. "Let's start making plans. I'll be ready to go in a couple of weeks."

"I'll get right on it," he said before he kissed me again.

Rolling away from him, I stopped right before I stood up. "Oh, I almost forgot. Miriam called last night."

He blinked. "Is she okay?"

"Yes. She was calling about Junior." I told him what Miriam had told me when she called, about Junior's basketball tryouts and how she wanted Jamal to be there with his godson. Jamal's eyes got even brighter than when we were talking about Maui. It was as if Miriam's call gave him a purpose. If he could be there for Junior, he wouldn't have to think about missing Chauncey.

"I would love to do that," Jamal said, sitting up. "I'm surprised she didn't ask Charlie."

"I didn't ask her about him, but I'm not surprised. She really wanted you."

He frowned.

"I mean, you're Junior's godfather."

"Oh, yeah, yeah. I knew that's what you meant."

"So, basketball with Junior today and Maui with me in a few weeks. Your life is grand," I kidded, and then kissed his cheek. But before I could get up, Jamal wrapped his arm around my waist, pulling me back. He pressed himself against me and I could feel the heat of his hard desire.

As much as I wanted this man, I couldn't. "Ah, babe. I've got to get to Children's Hospital for LaTonya and I'm already late."

He rolled away from me.

"I'm sorry," I said.

"No, no, I understand."

I knew he was telling the truth; Jamal always understood. But still, this didn't feel good to me, so I knew it didn't feel good to him. We hadn't made love in two weeks.

I shifted in the bed until I was on top of him. "I promise, I promise, I will do my best to get home at a decent hour and even if you're asleep, I'm gonna wake you up and rock your world."

He smiled.

"Did I say, I promise?"

Now he laughed and I kissed him again before I jumped from the bed. I had a long day ahead, but I was looking forward to it. I would be focused on LaTonya during the day, but tonight my mind, my body, and my soul would belong to the man I loved.

23

MIRIAM

I cannot figure out how I let you talk me into this," Mama Cee fussed from the passenger side of the car. "Getting my hair done twice in a week."

I didn't turn to the left, I didn't turn to the right. I kept my eyes on the road, knowing that if I looked at my mother-in-law she might see the truth. She might see all the lies that I'd told. "It's not twice in a week, Mama Cee. You got your hair done *last* week."

"Well, whenever, I don't need to be going back so soon."

"This is a good idea," I said, knowing that I had to keep persuading her. It had been hard enough to get her to this point.

Yesterday, when we returned home from brunch, I'd immediately set my plan into motion. Getting the kids out of the house—check, since they were going back to school. Getting Charlie out of the house—another check, since he was going to take the boys to school and hang around for Junior's tryouts.

The only person left was Mama Cee and she was going to be the most difficult. There was a good chance she would want to stay in her bedroom and rest. But I didn't want Mama Cee to overhear what I had to say to Jamal.

So I'd come up with this plan: send her to the beauty shop. That would keep her away from home for hours.

I'd called Leah, told her that this had to be her idea, and since we'd been friends for years, she went along with my plan. It had been easier with Mama Cee last night, but now that she'd slept on it, I was afraid she was going to change her mind.

"You're leaving tomorrow, Mama Cee, and who knows when you'll come back. At least now you'll be leaving with a good, deep condition."

"Umph. I can put my own conditioner in. I don't need to be paying all of this money."

"I promise, Mama Cee, you'll be happy you did this."

She folded her arms across her chest. "I'm not going to be happy writing this extra check."

"I told you I was paying for this."

"I don't want you paying for me."

"This is my treat." I pushed my foot down a bit on the pedal. I needed to get to the shop quick!

"But you have to be careful with money now."

"Mama Cee, Leah is hardly charging me anything," I lied. I was paying her triple her normal price for slipping Mama Cee in on a Monday. "And I already told you I'm good. The boys and I are going to be good for a long time because your son took care of us."

"That's because I raised him right. But that doesn't mean that I want you wasting that insurance money on me."

I was glad that I was at a red light because now, even though I didn't want her looking into my eyes, I had to face her. "Mama Cee, nothing I do for you is a waste. After all you've done for me, I could never do enough for you."

"All I've ever done is love you," my mother-in-law said.

"You and Chauncey. When no one else did."

"I don't care about anyone else. This is just me and you. And you never have to worry about doing anything for me, you hear?" Before I could respond, she added, "Wait! There is something I want from you."

"Anything," I said, as I took my foot off the brake and cruised down La Brea.

She let a couple of beats go by. "I want you to be happy. Even without Chauncey, I want you to find a way to be happy."

This was why I loved this woman. All I wanted to do was take her back home and spend the next twenty-four hours before she left for Phoenix just loving on her. And I would do that—right after I took care of my business with Jamal.

"So, can you do that for me?"

"I'm trying, Mama Cee." I edged the car to the curb in front of the hair salon. "Here we are." I held my breath, knowing there was a fifty-fifty shot that Mama Cee would just tell me to turn around and take her home.

But then she gathered her cane and purse and I exhaled.

"Just call me when Leah's almost done."

"All right, baby." Mama Cee eased out, and I kept the car in park until she stepped through the door. She turned around to wave, and I waved back, before I tore out of there like I was being chased.

The first part of my mission was accomplished.

I should've felt better about this than I did, but it was hard to feel good when I'd lied to people I loved, people who trusted me.

Especially Emily.

But I'd only lied so that I could put everything back together. My friendship with Emily was broken. She didn't know it, but I had to fix this before she could ever find out.

Leah's shop was only ten minutes from my home. I swerved around cars, took chances zooming through changing lights, and made that left turn onto my block in just a little over five minutes. I released a long breath when I saw that my driveway was clear. I hit the remote for the garage, drove inside, and parked the van next to Chauncey's car, then closed the garage door behind me. Grabbing my purse, I dashed inside and had just a couple of minutes to catch my breath before the doorbell rang.

I breathed deeply, then went to the door, opening it wearing a frown. "Oh, my goodness. Jamal!"

"Uh, yeah, you look like you weren't expecting me," he said, taking tentative steps into my home. "Emily said you wanted me to take Junior to school, then go to his basketball tryouts with him."

"Yes, I did, I called you, but I forgot to call you back and tell you that Charlie's plans changed and he went with Junior. I'm so sorry. I . . ." I paused when my voice started to tremble. "I'm really . . . really . . . really . . ." Before I could get another word of my lie out, I burst into tears.

"Miriam!" Jamal exclaimed. His face was creased with his concern. "What's wrong?"

"I'm sorry, but I can't do this, I can't—"

"What are you talking about?"

"I lied. I lied to everyone so that you would come over and I could talk to you."

"About Junior?"

"No, Charlie went with him and I knew he was going to do that when I talked to Emily last night," I sobbed. "I just wanted you to come over and I was afraid if I asked you, you would say no. 'Cause everything has changed and I don't want anything to change."

Jamal held up one hand, and with his other he led me into the living room. When we sat on the sofa, he said, "Now tell me again, slower this time." He paused and, with the back of his hand, wiped away my tears.

When he touched me, I remembered everything that I was trying so hard to forget.

"Now," he said softly, "are you ready to start over?"

I nodded and took a moment before I said, "I'm sorry, I shouldn't have lied to you." His touch had calmed me. "I wanted to talk to you about what happened between us and how I talked to Emily yesterday in church."

"You talked to Emily?" he asked, with wide eyes.

"No, no, not about us. In church, she asked about our . . . lunch. She wanted to know if everything was okay because she was worried about you. She said you were home in bed and I felt so bad. I knew it was because of me. And I wanted to apologize for that."

"I didn't stay home because of you. There's no reason for you to apologize."

This time, he was the one who wasn't telling the truth. There were a million reasons to apologize. But I continued, "I also wanted to make sure that we had our stories straight." I paused. "Our stories straight, oh, God!" I lowered my head and covered my face with my hands. "That means that I'm going to have to keep lying, oh, God!"

"Miriam, Miriam." He called my name softly. "This is going to be all right. *We're* going to be all right."

I hid my face in my hands for a few moments longer, then sat up straight, though I didn't feel any stronger. But my voice was steadier. "Jamal, I don't want to lose you as a friend. Even before Chauncey passed away you meant the world to me. So I don't want what happened to change us. Please."

Jamal shook his head.

"If I lost you now, it would be like . . . it would be like . . ." My chin hit my chest and I had to fight to hold the tears.

"Miriam, you're not going to lose me. Nothing's going to change. We're still friends. We'll always be friends."

The softness of his voice, the tenderness of his words, made me sob, even though I didn't want to.

He pulled me into his arms and I cried into his chest, not quite sure why I couldn't stop these tears. Maybe it was because I was grateful. Maybe it was because I still had his friendship and that meant that my heart would go on beating.

I worked hard to pull myself together and finally, I looked up. I wanted to thank him, but then his lips were right there and . . .

Just like the other day, I don't know if I kissed him or he kissed me. But we were together again.

This time, it was better. Because it was familiar and somehow, some way, it felt right.

Gently, Jamal pushed me back onto the sofa, but then he paused for just a moment. "Are we alone?" he asked, his voice sounding huskier, sexier.

It was a strange time to ask, because even if the house had been filled with people, I would've lied. I would've said anything to keep this feeling going.

"Yes." I hardly recognized my voice. I pulled him back toward me and kissed him like my life depended on it. This time, I was the one who broke away, rolled off the couch, and led him into my bedroom. I was the one who tore his clothes off while I slipped out of mine. And I was the one who pulled him down on top of me as if I was sex-starved. I was the one out of my mind.

We didn't last long; I guess Jamal was as hungry as I was, and not long after we started, we lay side by side, breathing heavily. I rested my head on Jamal's chest and he held me as if I belonged there.

I let many silent minutes go by and then I asked, "What—"

Before I said another word, Jamal finished for me, "—are we doing?"

Then, together, we said, "I don't know."

I said, "But, Jamal—"

"Sssshhh." He hugged me closer to him. "We don't have to figure this out. Not right now."

I nodded and just let him hold me. I said, "Can I say one thing?"

"You can say anything."

"When I'm with you, I feel so good. I'm sorry, God help me, but I do. When I'm with you, I don't feel like only half of my heart is beating."

Even though he didn't say anything, I wasn't sorry for what I'd said. My words were probably going to scare him, but I had to let him know how I felt.

He rocked my world when he said, "You make me feel good, too, Miriam."

At that point, if the heavens had opened and angels started singing, I wouldn't have been surprised.

Jamal kissed the top of my head, rolled out of the bed, and asked if he could take a quick shower. As he did, I waited in bed, dreaming with my eyes open.

Once he'd showered and dressed, he moved toward me. And just like on Saturday, he leaned down and kissed my forehead. Then he left without saying another word.

But this time, I didn't cry. This time, I wasn't heartbroken.

Because unlike Saturday, this time, I knew Jamal would be back.

24

Emily

There had never been any doubt in my mind, but I knew it now for sure—I had the best husband in the world. Even though I hadn't been home in twenty-four hours and even though I couldn't give Jamal an estimated time of arrival now, he only had one concern.

"How are you?" he asked. "Did you get any sleep last night?"

"A little," I said, only because I didn't want to worry him. The truth was that my eyes hadn't closed since I'd been in bed with him yesterday morning. I'd stayed up through the night because LaTonya had been awake. Without the sedatives that Dr. Caster had been giving her, she hadn't slept. Instead, she talked about her sister. And when she wasn't talking, she was crying. And when she wasn't crying, she was screaming.

I'd tried to calm her throughout the night, but she hadn't settled down until an hour ago.

"I miss you, babe," Jamal said.

"I know. But as soon as I talk to Doctor Caster, I'll be home. And as soon as I can, we'll be on that plane to Maui. So, how's Junior? Did he make the basketball team?"

"Uh . . . well . . . I didn't go with him. It turned out that Charlie was able to take him."

"Oh," I said, a bit surprised. "Why didn't you just go with Charlie?"

"I got there a little late—you know, Monday traffic."

"Well, I hope he made the team because I'd love to go to his games."

"Yeah, and I'm going to make sure that I hang out with the boys now that Mama Cee and Charlie are leaving."

"That's right! Today." I moaned. "I should be fired as a friend."

"Don't say that."

"No, I really feel bad about not seeing Miriam. Hell, I haven't spent enough time with you."

"Em, stop being so hard on yourself. It's not like you're hanging out. You're working."

"Doctor Harrington-Taylor." I turned around and faced Dr. Caster. I held up one finger, silently asking him to give me a moment.

He nodded, but didn't move away.

"Honey, I have to go, but I'll call you in a couple of hours, okay?"

"Okay, and Emily?"

"Yeah?"

"I love you, babe. I love you so much."

He hung up before I could tell him the same.

"Sorry to interrupt your call," Dr. Caster said. "Can we talk?"

I nodded and followed him down two long hallways before we stepped into a sparse, white-walled office. I sat in the single chair that was on the other side of a desk that could've been purchased at IKEA.

Without any formalities, the doctor said, "It's been seventy-two hours." There was so much more to his statement. Really, he was asking what I was going to do with LaTonya now.

I shook my head. "Seventy-two hours and I don't have any idea where we should go from here."

"Well, as you know," he said, "a person cannot be released from the hold until they agree not to try suicide again."

"That's the rule for adults, but how do we handle a six-year-old?"

He nodded as if he felt my pain. "We know she still has these tendencies. She may not understand what she's doing, but she still wants to do it and I have to fill out this report. All I can say is that she's still talking about killing herself," the doctor told me.

"She doesn't say that." I had to protect LaTonya because in this case, words really mattered. Everything was going to be put in her file. "She says that she wants to go to heaven," I said, wanting the doctor to be clear.

He replied, "If those are the words you want me to use—"

"So once you write this report, what will this mean? Are we actually going to put her into some kind of institution? Some kind of psychiatric hospital?"

The doctor didn't answer me; at least he didn't respond with words.

"I can't see that." I stood and paced. "An institution with a whole bunch of other kids, who will be older than her, which won't help. I know for a fact I can help her. But I have to reach her on her level. I need a little more time."

"Well, I have to write this report today, and all I can say today is that she still has these tendencies if she's not restrained."

"So, we're just going to commit her?" Before he answered, I said, "Wait, I have an idea." Slowly, I sat back down, trying to formulate at least half a plan in my head. "I know what I'm about to ask isn't normally done, but what about if we kept her here?"

The doctor was already shaking his head. "I don't have the staff to take care of her. There's no psych unit here."

"No, what I'm saying is that you keep her in her room and I'll stay with her."

He shook his head slightly, but I went on to explain.

"If you can have her admitted, I'll stay with her twenty-four-seven. The nurses can come in to check her wounds, but I'll be there as her counselor. And with me watching her constantly, she'll receive the same kind of care as she would in an institution."

Again, he shook his head. "You can't stay with her all day and all night. Who will relieve you?"

"I haven't thought this all the way through, but I can make this happen. I have colleagues who can give me a couple of hours, but for the most part, it will be me. I'm willing to make this sacrifice for that little girl and I'm telling you it'll work."

"I don't know," the doctor said, his voice full of doubt. "This is highly irregular."

"What's irregular is having a six-year-old trying to get to heaven and we're about to commit her. There's nothing normal about this, so I say drastic situations call for drastic measures."

At least he wasn't shaking his head anymore, so I decided to go for the slam dunk.

"Think about the alternative, Doctor. Think about taking this child, who has already lost her sister, away from her home, her parents, especially her mother. We're supposed to help our patients, but sending LaTonya away won't be helping her at all."

I could see in his eyes that I had scored.

"Okay," he said, nodding and holding up his hand as if he couldn't take another word from me. "I'll do it. I'll give you a week."

"Thank you, Doctor," I said, stopping myself from jumping up and doing a dance.

"But," he cautioned, "just a week. After that, we're going to need the room, we're going to need the nurses, we're going to need to fill out the paperwork and send her wherever she needs to go."

"I understand."

"And, like you said, Doctor, you or another doctor will have to be with her at all times."

"I'm going to go home for a couple of hours now, but then when I come back, it'll be all worked out," I said, standing up. I wanted to get out of his office before he had second thoughts. "She'll be completely under my care."

"That's good enough for me." He shook my hand. "Good luck, Doctor."

I resisted telling him that luck had nothing to do with this. I was going to work like this was up to me, then pray like it was up to God. That combination always worked for me. "Thank you so much," I told him before I rushed from his office.

The thoughts were swirling in my head as I made my way down the hall. I had to explain this to the Millers, I had to explain this to Jamal, and I had to figure this out in my own mind.

Peeking into LaTonya's room, I was glad to see that she was still asleep. Her parents were at the side of her bed, holding hands, of course. I had to do this as much for them as for LaTonya. This young couple would never survive losing both of their children so tragically.

I watched them until Mr. Miller looked up. I motioned for him and his wife to join me in the hallway. Mrs. Miller hesitated, but I held up one finger, letting her know she wouldn't be away from her daughter too long.

As soon as they came out, I said, "We're going to keep LaTonya here for a few more days."

"Really?" Mr. Miller said. "I thought you said that she'd only be here seventy-two hours."

"That's what we'd hoped, but we're concerned that she still wants to hurt herself."

"But she hasn't tried anything," Mrs. Miller said.

Those were the words of a grieving mother. Yes, LaTonya hadn't tried anything, but she'd been restrained most of the time.

I didn't address Mrs. Miller's words. I just said, "Since we can't release her to go home, I've arranged for the hospital to let her stay here. And I will stay with her." Before Mrs. Miller could protest, I added, "You'll be here with her, too."

The Millers looked at each other and nodded, then Mr. Miller turned back to me. "We just want our daughter to get well, and we know that you'll help her."

"I'm going to try."

"Thank you, Doctor Harrington," Mr. Miller said, and his wife nodded as well.

"No problem." I stopped short of saying I was just doing my job. Because even though I was, this was my mission as well. "I'm going home to freshen up and take care of a few things. I'll see you in a couple of hours."

I waited until they were inside LaTonya's room before I turned around and walked down the long hall toward the elevator. I wasn't looking forward to telling Jamal, even though I knew he'd understand. But it already felt like I'd been away from home twenty-four-seven since the fire. Now I had to tell him I'd be away for the next seven days.

For the first time in my marriage, I felt like I was making a choice between my career and my husband, though that's not what I wanted to do. To me, Jamal would always come first. It was just that in this case, with this little girl, this had to be done. There was a life to be saved.

By the time I slid into my car, I knew that I was doing the right thing. I was using the gift that God had given me to help someone who couldn't help herself. What could be more important than that?

Jamal would understand that, and for at least the one hundredth time in the last twenty-four hours, I thanked God for the man He'd given me.

25

MIRIAM

t wasn't anything we planned, nothing we'd discussed, but Jamal and I fell into a routine. Though it had only been a week since the first time we'd been together, I felt like I'd been living a lifetime of wonderful days with this man.

It had been much easier for us since Mama Cee and Charlie left. In the mornings, I made sure that Junior got on his school bus, I dropped Mikey and Stevie off at their school, and then I came home and pretended I wasn't walking by the front window every ten minutes to check to see if that white Chrysler was there.

Sometime between eleven and noon, Jamal would pull up to the curb, honk once, and I would pull my car out of the garage so he could pull his inside.

While I always pretended that I hadn't been waiting for Jamal, he always pretended that he was just stopping by. He came with his own pretense: bearing papers that needed to be signed or photos of Chauncey he was sure I'd never seen. He always came with something that allowed us both to fake it, though he always came with condoms, too. So we both knew what was going to happen.

And it happened. Every day. We made love.

Never in a million years did I imagine that I would be cheating with anyone, let alone Jamal Taylor. And with everything that I believed, I should have felt horrible about what I was doing.

But I didn't. Because I needed Jamal right now. He was helping me rebuild my heart so that I could breathe again, live again.

Being with Jamal wasn't just about sex. We talked. We laughed. With him, it was safe to cry. And through it all, he held me. He held me the way I'd never been held in my past, he held me the way Chauncey had held me in the present, and he held me, letting me know that I could have a wonderful life ahead.

Before Jamal, I'd been surrounded by nothing but darkness. Now, every day, there was a bit more light.

And Jamal brought light to my sons, too. In the afternoon, he'd pick up Mikey and Stevie, and by the time Junior came home, Jamal was already in the kitchen, helping the boys with their homework. Afterward, they'd play video games, watch TV, or we would just all hang around and talk. And the best part: most of the time, Jamal stayed for dinner.

Moving to Arizona was far from our minds now. We had a wonderful family right here.

With the boys, we lived as families lived. And Jamal and I loved as lovers did. Each day was better, and this morning had been the best.

I'd met him at the garage door, but the moment he stepped inside, he was all over me. He kissed me and ripped open my blouse like he was a hungry teenager. We giggled as he kicked off his shoes, then I tore away his shirt. Our clothes left a trail of lust as we staggered to the bedroom. By the time we got there, I was naked. A few seconds later, I made sure that Jamal was naked, too.

Like always, I was floating by the time we finished, and there was no one in the world happier than me. It felt good not to have the pretense this time. Jamal had come here for me, I had been here for him.

After lying still for a while, he said, "Wait here a second, I have something to show you."

He jumped from the bed and, without any modesty, traipsed across the bedroom, butt-naked. Watching him made me sigh and pull the sheet up over myself even more. He never made me feel like he noticed the cottage cheese on my thighs or the fact that my behind truly needed its own zip code.

I ran my hand over the pillow where he'd just laid his head. Closing my eyes, I pressed my nose against the case, soaking in the scent that he'd left behind. He'd been gone for just seconds and I missed him already.

"You haven't seen any of these," Jamal said, jumping back into the bed.

I sat up and leaned against him as he opened yet another album with plastic-protected photos of him and Chauncey.

"This is proof of what I was telling you," he said proudly. "Proof that we were the kings of the King of Pop's fan club."

As he flipped deliberately through each picture, sharing all the whens, wheres, and whys, I let my mind wander.

I asked myself, what is this?

The first time Jamal and I had sex, I'd been sure that it was just one moment in time. Then one time became two, three, and four moments. And now being with him was beginning to feel . . . permanent. I was beginning to feel . . . important to him because he was spending more time with me than he was spending with his wife.

Whenever I thought of Emily, my gut twisted.

The only good thing was that I hadn't heard from her since this had become . . . become what? An affair? I'd expected to be ducking and dodging her calls, but she hadn't reached out to me at all.

I didn't dare ask Jamal about Emily, not wanting to bring up her name. Because then I'd have to talk about what the hell I was doing to the woman I still loved like a sister. And talking about her could remind Jamal that I was not Emily.

So I took the low road, not mentioning her and glad that I hadn't heard from her. Glad that she was probably deep into a case, helping a child who couldn't help herself. That thought made my heart twist with my gut. Emily was saving children while I was screwing her husband.

God forgive me, but I just wanted Jamal for a little while. He wasn't my husband, and one day, I'd have to give him back.

"You can keep this one," Jamal said, nudging my attention back to him.

I looked down at the photo of Chauncey and Jamal, dressed like miniature firemen.

"Awww . . . when did you take that?"

He leaned back. "Have you been listening? This was the first Halloween after we decided we were going to become firefighters. We were determined and getting these costumes was proof."

"So cool to know what you wanted to be when you were young, and then to grow up and actually do it. To live your passion . . ."

My blinking eyes were signals that I was thinking about how Chauncey's passion had killed him. Jamal closed the photo album, tossed it aside, then wrapped his arms around me.

"Are you okay?" he whispered.

"Yeah." Looking up at him, I said, "I am."

There was so much more I wanted to say. Like how my heart was changing because of him. But I couldn't say that. So I tore my gaze away and scooted to the other side of the bed.

"I'm going to get some orange juice," I said, because I couldn't think of anything else to do. "Do you want a glass?"

"Nah, I'm cool."

I wrapped myself in the sheet and then traipsed into the living room, stepping over our clothes along the way. In the kitchen, I quickly poured a glass, but right when I walked past the front door, I saw a shadow and then the doorbell rang.

"Miriam!" Michellelee shouted. "Miriam, girl, open the door."

I froze right where I was.

"Miriam!"

There were a couple of reasons why I couldn't just stand there. First, my car was in the driveway, and in that instant, I thanked God that it was my car and not Jamal's. And, secondly, she'd seen me, or at least the outline of me through the door's side glass panels, which were covered with only sheer curtains.

"Miriam! I know you're right there. Come on!"

That proved it; she had seen me. Quickly, I devised a plan. Wrapping the sheet a little tighter, I opened the door, but only slightly.

I coughed. "Hey, Michellelee, I'm not . . ."

But she blew up my plan, pushing past me and barging into my home.

"I rushed over to tell you," she said, sounding out of breath. "They caught the arsonist. Someone's been arrested for setting fire to the school."

Every single thought I had flew right out of my mind with this news. "Oh, my God!" My hand was shaking as I set my orange juice on the table by the door. "So, it *was* arson?"

"Yup! I told you."

"Who was it?" I asked, as if I would know someone who would do something so heinous.

She shook her head. "Some crazy man who said he was getting back at the president because he wasn't born in this country and was using the Social Security number of a dead man in Virginia."

"What?"

"You can't make this stuff up."

"Oh, my God," I said, sitting on the settee by the door. "I can't believe this." Then I looked up at Michellelee and saw that her eyebrows were knitted so close together she had a unibrow.

I gasped as my eyes followed her gaze. She was staring at the trail of clothing that led to the bedroom.

She said nothing at first, but then she whispered, "Is there somebody here?"

Now, I could've lied. I could've told her that those clothes belonged to the boys. But she would never have believed it. Especially since Jamal's size 13 sneakers were on top of the pile.

"Yes." I stood up, grabbed her hand, and pulled her back toward the door. "But . . . but . . . but, it's just that . . ."

"Oh, no, girl!" Michellelee leaned back on one leg, put her hand on her hip, and gazed at me as if she was impressed. "Honey, I'm happy for you. Get your freak on."

I groaned because there was nothing freaky about this.

"This is good, Miriam." She put her hand on my arm. "This is really a good thing."

"Well, I just . . ." I paused. There was no way to explain this. Taking a quick look back at the bedroom, I said, "You should go."

"Okay, yeah," she whispered. "I understand, you don't want to introduce him to me yet." Then she yelled out, "But one day, he's gonna have to meet your sister-friends!"

She laughed and I stood as still as a rock. She hugged me before she strutted out of the door. I rushed to close it behind her, but before I could, Michellelee turned around. "Well, if you have time after freakin' your man, check out the news this evening. It's breaking news now, but I'm going to review the whole story live at five." She reached for my hand and squeezed it. "I'm so happy they caught this nut, but I'm also happy for you, Miriam. Go on with your life." With another squeeze, she was finally gone and I was able to close the door.

I leaned against it, really just wanting to die.

Jamal had heard it all, I was sure of that. Slowly, I returned to the bedroom, and I'd half expected him to be dressed and ready to go. But then I remembered that most of his clothes were on the floor, the evidence in the living room.

He sat on the edge of the bed. "Does she know it was me?"

I shook my head.

"Okay, then." He breathed. "I'd better go."

"Jamal, please . . ."

It must've been the fear in my voice that made him say, "It'll be all right."

Still, I wanted to protest. I wanted to ask him about the boys; they'd be expecting him today, tomorrow, and the next day.

But then he said, "I just need to go right now," and I exhaled as he hurried into the bathroom to shower.

We'd been in our own world until Michellelee busted in. And now that she had committed this home invasion, would our lives change?

I was so afraid that it would all be different now.

26

Emily

I t had been four days. Four solid days of talking and crying and reading and crying and drawing and crying. And, finally, there was a breakthrough. Finally, LaTonya was talking more about her mom and dad than she was talking about her sister. For the last twenty-four hours, she hadn't said a word about wanting to go to heaven.

What was going on with LaTonya felt good, but I wasn't really sure how to measure success with such a young child.

I was hopeful, but I didn't know.

I did feel, though, that LaTonya was making enough progress that after four days, I could go home. At least for a couple of hours.

I needed a bear-size hug and so much more from my husband.

As I steered the car out of the parking lot, I thought about calling Jamal. I'd spoken to him this morning, but that was before Dr. Caster agreed that I could take a couple of hours without one of my colleagues being there.

I picked up the phone, then tossed it back. Surprising him would be so much better.

I'd only driven a block away from the hospital when my cell phone rang, and before I looked down, I prayed that it wasn't Dr. Caster.

I glanced at the screen and smiled. "Hey, Red," I said to Michelle-lee.

"Doctor Harrington-Taylor, where have you been? I've been calling and calling. Calling your cell, calling you at home. I was about to use my contacts at LAPD and send out the blue cavalry."

"I'm sorry. I haven't been able to talk on my cell. I've been staying at Children's Hospital for a few days."

"Oh." Michellelee toned her voice down. "Related to the fire?"

"Yes," I said. "It's starting to look good, though. But you didn't catch Jamal when you called my apartment? He could have told you I was working."

"I called a couple of times, but only got your voice mail. Did he go back to work?"

"No, not yet."

"Well, I only called in the mornings before I went into the studio because Craig's been in town. But anyway, I was calling to see what you thought of the news."

"What? I haven't seen CNN in days."

"Nothing to do with politics, dear." Then Michellelee filled me in about the alleged arsonist's arrest.

"You kept saying that it was arson, but I just could not believe that someone would do this. Set fire to a school?" I shook my head. "That man has all that blood on his hands."

"Can you imagine what the trial is going to be like?"

"A zoo, I'm sure." I was still shaking my head, still unable to fathom how one person could be responsible for so much devastation.

"But I didn't call to bring you down. I was calling to tell you that we should have a girls' night out to celebrate."

"Celebrate?" I frowned.

"Yeah, catching that scum. We should take Miriam out."

"Michellelee, celebrate is not exactly the word I'd use. I know

Miriam will be happy in some ways, but it's going to be sad, too. It's only going to remind her about Chauncey."

"Blue, let me school you about White. Yeah, she loved her husband, but she has already gotten her groove on. I just left her house five minutes ago; she's already seeing someone."

"No, she's not!"

"Yes, she is! I wouldn't have believed it if I hadn't seen it."

"You met him?"

"No, but his clothes were all over the floor. Leading straight to her bedroom."

"What!"

"Girl, she was wrapped in a sheet and must've forgotten about the clothes because when I peeped them, that brown-skinned girl turned Delta red! I'm telling you."

"Wow!" I said.

"It was a wow for me, too, but you know what? I'm not mad at her. She's doing exactly what Chauncey would want, so we should take her out to celebrate that."

"Wow!"

"You said that already."

"No, I mean, we are talking about Miriam. She's the shy, solid one. Who's the man?"

"I told you—"

"I know you didn't meet him. I'm just thinking out loud. Well, I guess if she's moved on like that, then I'm glad for her."

"So, when should we get together?"

"Well, I'll be working with this client until Tuesday, and when I get back to the office, I'll have to catch up with my other files. But I can do it at the end of next week."

"Sounds like a plan. I miss my girls."

"I know. That fire wreaked havoc on everyone. With you covering the story and me with my clients."

"And Miriam getting her groove back."

Michellelee laughed, but I didn't.

I was happy for Miriam, I really was. But something just didn't feel right. First of all, the only person Miriam had loved in her life was Chauncey. There was no way she'd be out searching for someone else so soon. And even if she was ready to move on, Miriam wasn't the type to just go out and pick up someone, so she had to be seeing someone she knew. And if it was someone she knew, was it someone she'd been involved with before?

No! See, this was the problem with this psychology degree I had. I was always looking for the "something else" and overanalyzing everything. Why couldn't this just be what it was?

Michellelee hung up with promises to call me over the weekend, but when I put the phone down, I still couldn't get Miriam out of my mind. My best friend had had one boyfriend, one love, one marriage. Not that I didn't want to be happy for her . . .

But when I turned my car into my apartment building, by the time I got to the elevator, I was shaking with excitement. This was downright carnal. All that occupied my thoughts now was sex with my husband.

I was moving so fast, I fumbled my keys, then busted through the door.

"Jamal!" I screamed, hoping that I didn't give my husband a heart attack. Then I waited by the door, expecting him to come charging out of the bedroom.

But there was nothing. Either I had shocked him so much his heart had stopped, or he wasn't home.

I dropped my bag by the door. "Jamal," I called again, this time sounding like I had some sense.

I searched every room of our condo and discovered how much my husband had missed me. The duvet on our bed was sprawled on the floor, the cap was off the toothpaste and still on the counter, the toilet seat was up in both bathrooms, and there were more dishes and glasses in the sink than in the cabinets. And I'd only been gone for four days.

Jamal needed me. I just wished he was home, because I needed him.

Talk about disappointment. But in a way, I was glad, too. At least Jamal wasn't in bed, sleeping through his depression.

During our calls over the past few days, I couldn't really tell how Jamal was feeling. He was so concerned about me, and never wanted to talk about himself. But him being out right now was a good sign. It was a bit after three; hopefully, he was taking a jog on the beach.

Just as I picked up the phone to call his cell, I heard his key in the door.

I sprinted into the living room and Jamal had barely stepped over the threshold before I jumped into his arms, pushing him backward, almost making him fall.

"Whoa!" he said, his voice full of shock.

But I hardly let him breathe. I planted kisses over every inch of his face, holding on to him tightly, not caring that I hadn't had a decent shower since I'd left.

"Oh, my God, babe," he said, catching his breath. "You're home."

"Yes, and I missed you!"

"I missed you, too, but I didn't know you were coming home today."

"I was trying to surprise you." Finally, I stepped away, giving him some room. "But I was the one who got surprised. You were out, huh?"

"Uh . . . yeah."

"I figured you were out on the beach."

"Uh . . . yeah."

"That's a great thing." I led him to the couch. When we sat, I couldn't keep my hands off him.

"I've been worried about you, Em." He cupped my face between his hands and looked at me with love. "You're tired."

"I am, but things are getting better."

"So, LaTonya, she's good?"

"Almost," I said. "But tell me about you, tell me what you've been doing."

He looked away as if he didn't want to talk about it. But then he faced me and hit me with the bombshell. "I had lunch with Donald."

My heart sank just a little when he mentioned his fire chief's name. "Yeah?"

The fear must've been in my voice. "Yeah, we met at the Lobster House, but you don't have to worry. I'm not going back . . ."

I exhaled.

"Yet," he added. Then he paused. "You knew that I was going to go back, right?"

I nodded.

"I love what I do."

"I know."

"Just like you love what you do."

I smiled.

"And, I promise you, I'll be safe."

"I know," I said again, and forced myself not to say what I was thinking—that Chauncey had probably made this same promise to Miriam the morning he died. "I knew you'd be going back. Life goes on."

"Yes, it does."

"I guess I wasn't ready to start thinking about that—life moving on. Not with you and not with Miriam."

Jamal frowned. "What . . . what do you mean?"

"Michellelee just told me that Miriam is seeing somebody. Can you believe it?"

The way Jamal's Adam's apple crawled up, then down his throat, I could tell that he wasn't ready for this news either. "Really?"

"Yeah, Michellelee doesn't know who the mystery man is, but their relationship has progressed to . . . being intimate."

He stared at me for a moment, then just nodded. This was nothing like the excitement Michellelee had. But I understood. As close as he was to Chauncey, it had to be hard for him to think about another man coming in and taking his best friend's place.

"But let's not talk about Miriam or anyone else. I only have a few hours before I have to go back."

"Oh . . . so, you're not home? I mean, for good?"

I shook my head. "I wish, but I really want to keep LaTonya in therapy for the full seven days. I'll be home Tuesday, but I do have a couple of hours now." I leaned in so close there was barely space for air between us. "I want to do something special."

"Okay," he said. He looked down at his hands. "Something special like what?"

"Something special like spend a couple of hours in bed with you," I whispered in his ear.

I waited to see what my normally oversexed-couldn't-get-enough man would say. But when he didn't give me anything, I said, "But first, I have to take a shower."

"All right. I'll be waiting right here for you."

I stood as seductively as I could in my jogging suit that I'd worn twice since I'd been away. Taking his hand, I tried to pull him up. "Instead of waiting, why not join me?"

He shook his head. "Uh, I just took a shower. I was on the beach, and I came back a little while ago, and I took a shower, and then went back out and then came back."

Why was he talking in circles? I held up my hand. "Okay, okay. You don't have to convince me you took a shower. I can smell it on you."

"What?"

I laughed out loud. "Don't look so horrified. It's just that you smell like my soap. You know, that perfumed soap that you hate. You must be out of your Irish Spring." I shook my head. "You really did miss me, didn't you?"

He just nodded.

I kissed his forehead. "I'm going to make this quick!" Inside the stall, I turned the knob just a few notches away from the right, wanting to get the water as hot as I could take it.

The steam was already rising when I stepped inside, and then I leaned against the marble wall. This was just another reason to be grateful for being home. First, seeing my husband, and now being able to take a shower where I had more than enough room to turn around rather than the small stalls in the nurses' lounge.

I let the water's heat soothe me, relax me, almost render me unconscious. Really, I could have lain down and just let the water caress me, but before I was really ready, I turned it off. I needed whatever energy I had for Jamal.

The towel rack that had been stacked with towels just days ago was down to just one. I grabbed it, but didn't bother to dry off; there was no need.

The towel was barely around me when I rushed out of the bathroom. I was ready to jump right on my husband, but Jamal was just sitting on the edge of the bed, fully clothed.

I let the towel fall away, and Jamal stared as if I was a vision. This was the reason I still worked out. I wanted my husband to look at me like that for the rest of our lives.

"Why do you still have on all of those clothes?"

Slowly, he stood. "Babe."

I didn't like the way he said that. "What?"

"I . . . I have to go."

It was my turn to stare at him. Where in the world did my husband want to go instead of being with me?

He said, "I just got a call from Donald. He wants me to come down to the station."

"Why?" I dipped down, picked up the towel, and wrapped myself up.

"There are some papers I need to sign about the fire. Someone is at the firehouse, I guess from the police investigative team, and they want to talk to the men who were there."

"They want to do that now? The fire was weeks ago."

"I know . . . uh, yeah . . . but, I got the call."

"Oh . . . kay," I said, peering at him, trying to figure out what he wasn't saying.

"If there was anything I could do, you know . . ."

I held up my hand. "I know." Of course I understood. Jamal had put up with far more with my career. With a sigh, I bounced down onto our bed. "So, how long do you think you'll be?"

He shrugged. "I don't know, a couple of hours."

A couple of hours was all I had. I didn't want to pout, but I couldn't help it. Jamal took my hand, lifted me up, and wrapped me in his arms as if I was his gift.

"I'd rather be here with you," he whispered.

I let him hold me for a few more moments before I said, "I know." I stepped back so that he could walk away, but Jamal didn't move.

Instead, he held my face between his hands. "Do you know how much I love you, Emily?"

"I know."

"I mean, really. Do you know that I truly love you?"

"I do."

Then he kissed me softly, a kiss that repeated his words. A kiss that told me that I had his heart. Right now, I wanted so badly to have my husband between my legs, but in my book, love always trumped sex. Even as deprived as I was feeling right now, I'd take his love over a romp in our bed any day.

"It's going to be all right," he said.

"What is?"

"Us. We're going to get through all of this. You with the kids and me with . . . my grief."

"I know that, Jamal," I said, trying to read between his words. There was so much more to what he was saying; my intuition told me so. But then I turned off my psychoanalysis button. I had to stop doing that.

He kissed me again, this time a quick peck, before he turned and left the room.

I eased down onto the bed, but kept my eyes on the bedroom door, hoping he'd come back. As I waited, my analysis button came back on. What had that exchange been about? What was Jamal trying to tell me?

Then I jumped up. I got it! This was Jamal's first time returning to the fire station. This would be the first time he'd be there without Chauncey. He had to be feeling overwhelmed with emotions.

I wished he'd told me that; I would've been able to talk him through it. But no, maybe it was better that he was working this out himself. My husband was strong. He would handle this.

Turning around, I faced the bed, with the tousled sheets and the duvet half-on, half-off the bed. I shook my head, making my way back to the bathroom. If Jamal wasn't going to be here, I might as well get back to the hospital. The quicker I could help LaTonya, the quicker I could come home.

For good.

27

Miriam

I looked at the caller ID and smiled with relief.

Jamal Taylor.

He'd left so quickly, right after Michellelee appeared, that I wasn't sure what was going to happen next. But it seemed I'd been worried for absolutely nothing.

I grabbed up the phone. "Hey!" I said, filled with a schoolgirlish glee.

"Hey, yourself!"

I froze.

Emily said, "How you doin'?"

It took a moment for me to find my voice. "Emily?"

"Uh . . . yeah, who did you think it was?"

"You. I thought it was you . . . I knew it was you," I said, stumbling over my words. "It's just that I haven't heard from you." I wobbled over to the couch and sat down since my legs had turned to mush.

"I've been away from home, working on a case. That's why I haven't been able to call and check on you."

"Oh . . . you haven't been home?"

"No, I've been at the Children's Hospital. Jamal didn't tell you?"

"Uh, no, I don't think so. Maybe he did, I can't remember."

"Well, that's where I've been for the last five days. Can you believe it?"

No, I couldn't. Was that the reason why Jamal had been here with me?

Emily said, "So, I came home for a couple of hours to hook up with my husband. It's been so long!"

Emily moaned and I groaned. Was she going to tell me about being intimate with Jamal? I closed my eyes and hoped that would shut off my ears.

She said, "But he had to go."

My eyes popped open. "Go where?"

"He got called into the fire station."

From the moment I'd heard Emily's voice, my heart had been beating so hard my chest actually ached. But now my heart stopped cold. "Oh, my God! Did he go back to work?"

"No! It'll still be a few weeks before he goes back. He needed to sign some papers and give a deposition or something like that."

My heart started beating again.

"But the real question is," Emily said, "how are you doing?"

"I'm okay, I'm getting better—I'm really working on learning how to live without Chauncey."

"I guess you are. Michellelee told me."

Oh God!

"So, you're seeing someone."

I thought the worst moment of this call was when I first picked up. But I was wrong. Hearing her voice didn't compare to her saying these words.

"So, tell me about him, White," Emily said.

"It's nothing, really."

"That's not what Michellelee said. She told me that things had already . . . gone pretty far with you two."

"No, no, it's not what it looks like. Really, it's nothing."

There was a long pause, then, "Miriam, did anything happen with this guy? I mean . . ."

If she kept talking I was going to die. "No, Emily, please don't try to analyze this. Nothing happened. It's just that it's not what it seems."

"Oh . . . kay."

"I don't want to talk about this."

"Okay, okay," she said, like she finally got my message. "I'm sorry. You know how I am. I only do it because I care, but I'll give you room and you can talk about it when you're ready."

"Thanks." Why did my voice sound like I was five years old?

"Anyway, I'm heading back to the hospital now."

"How long do you think you'll be there?" In the past, I would've asked Emily that question with interest as her friend. But now I'd asked that question with interest as her husband's lover.

She said, "Just a few more days. I expect to be home Monday or Tuesday. And then you, me, and Michellelee will have to get together."

"That sounds great," I said in a tone that sounded like I had just pleaded guilty to murder.

I should've been more careful because this was Emily. She asked, "Are you okay?"

"Yeah," I squeaked. "Just tired."

Another pause. Then, "I hear that," she said, as if she'd bought my excuse. "But soon, I'll be there to help you with whatever you need. Every day. You won't be able to get rid of me."

She laughed and I wanted to break down and cry.

She said, "Okay, girl, I'll check in with you over the weekend; can't wait to see you and the boys."

"Okay, that'll be good."

"I'm gonna think of something fun the six of us can do." Then she spoke quickly. "Okay, gotta go, girl. Love you!"

"Mean it," I barely got out.

The dial tone was a blessing. Emily had been killing me softly. With every word, I was dying just a little more.

The Worst Person in the World award belonged to me. Or maybe it was the Most Confused award, because from the bottom of my heart, I still loved Emily.

My tears were falling before I fell back onto the couch. I hadn't cried in so long, not since Jamal had practically moved in with me. But now I cried because no matter what was going to happen, this was going to end one day. And it would end badly.

I jumped when I felt the soft hand on my shoulder.

"Junior! Oh, my God," I said, still crying. "I didn't hear you come in."

He sat down next to me and put his arms around my shoulders. "Mom, are you thinking about Dad?"

I nodded because I didn't want to lie to my son out loud. As he hugged me, I held him back. What was I going to do? Lord, Lord, what was I going to do?

28

Emily

D r. Caster stood for a moment, studying the pictures pinned on the hospital wall. There had to be at least twenty-five pieces of paper that I had put around LaTonya's bed. Pictures that LaTonya had drawn of her and her parents, most of which didn't include her sister.

"You're a very pretty little girl," Dr. Caster said to LaTonya as he rolled one of the chairs closer to her bed.

"Thank you," she said, her voice sounding as small as she was.

I felt like LaTonya was about to take a final exam, but I wasn't concerned. She would pass. Not that this was a test. I could sign the papers to have LaTonya released, but Dr. Caster had extended a tremendous professional courtesy by letting LaTonya stay and I wanted him to be part of the process.

"So, you're feeling good this morning?" the doctor asked.

"Yes," LaTonya said softly.

Quickly, I glanced at LaTonya's parents standing by the door, holding hands as usual. Whatever they had to handle, they were going to handle it together. Just like me and Jamal.

"So," Dr. Caster's voice brought my attention back. "Doctor H tells me that you drew this picture." He lifted the colorful paper from the bedside table.

LaTonya nodded.

"This is really nice."

She nodded again.

"Tell me about the picture."

LaTonya looked, and I smiled. "Go ahead, sweetie."

She took the paper from Dr. Caster's hand. "This is a picture of me and my mommy and my daddy," she said, glancing up at her parents. "This is our house."

The doctor nodded. "Wow, that's a big house."

"Uh-huh. We live in a big house," she said softly.

Across the room, Mr. Miller chuckled, and I wanted to leap at that first sound of joy that I'd heard from him since we'd met. It made my heart happy.

"So, I see the grass and the cars and the streetlights," Dr. Caster said. "You're a good little artist."

The ends of her lips twitched, but that was it. As if there was something inside that just wouldn't let her smile.

Then he pointed to the top of the page. "What's this?"

"The sky, and a cloud."

"So, you're in front of the house and you're on the cloud, too?"

She shook her head and her voice got even softer. "I'm in front of the house. That's LaTrisha on the cloud."

"Oh, I thought that was you."

LaTonya said, "No, that's my sister. We're twins."

"Why is your sister on the cloud?"

LaTonya pressed her lips together and lowered her eyes. There was a moment of such silence that I could hear the second hand moving on my watch.

Then, "'Cause LaTrisha went to heaven to be with Jesus and Grandpa. And she's on the cloud 'cause she's an angel now."

"Wow! You have your own angel."

She nodded. "She's going to take care of us from heaven and I'm going to take care of Mommy and Daddy from down here."

For the first time, Dr. Caster had a genuine smile. That was good—I didn't want him to think that LaTonya had been coached in any way. All I'd done was counsel her. For the last seven days, we'd been drawing and talking and reading. Her responses were 100 percent LaTonya, though getting there hadn't been easy. Some of our sessions were so sad, I didn't think that LaTonya would ever stop crying. But the tears had slowly stopped and I was now convinced that LaTonya, though still quite sad about her sister, wouldn't be attempting any more trips to heaven.

"That's really good, LaTonya. So, are you sad about your sister?"

Her eyes moved from me to her parents before she nodded. "But Doctor H. said it's okay to be sad. And that one day, I'll be happy."

The doctor reached forward and patted her hand before he stood and pushed his chair back. "Okay, young lady, I'm going to talk to Doctor H. for a minute. You'll be okay here with your mom and dad, right?"

"Yes, and they'll be okay with me."

I smiled proudly as I followed the doctor from the room. We walked side by side, silently, and then inside his office, the doctor directed me toward the chair I'd sat in just a week ago.

"Well, either you're one great doctor or that was some kind of a miraculous recovery."

I smiled. "I'd like to think it was a little bit of both."

He shook his head. "Seven days ago, she was talking about committing suicide." I held up my hand and he rephrased. "She was talking about going to heaven. What changed?"

"This is what I do, Doctor Caster. I help children see their lives in a different way. Seven days ago, LaTonya thought she had to be with her sister. Now, she believes she has to stay here."

He shook his head. "Is this permanent?"

I shrugged. "I don't know. The only difference between LaTonya and other"—I paused, because I hated saying this word—"suicidal patients is that she's six. I would tend to believe her over an adult who knows what to say to be released."

"It's still quite a turnaround."

For a moment, I thought about telling the doctor that I may have had a little help. I thought about sharing the session where La-Tonya told me that God and her sister had come down from heaven and that God told her she had to stay with her parents.

But I could imagine the doctor's reaction; he'd think a child seeing God might be reason enough to put LaTonya into an institution. So I said nothing, though I knew with all my heart what LaTonya told me was the truth. I didn't know if she had a dream or a vision. Whatever it was, from that day, she'd changed, and that could only have been God.

"Well, Doctor Harrington, if you say that she's fine, do your report and I'll sign it."

I stood. "Thank you, Doctor Caster."

"So, what's your plan of action?"

"I'll put the whole plan in my report, but she'll stay under my care every day for the next month, and then I'll see where I go from there."

He nodded and walked me to the door. "Well, good luck, Doctor Harrington."

I waited until I was out of his view before I raised my arm and flicked my wrist. If I'd had a ball in my hand, it would've been nothing but net.

I strutted down the hall with confidence and happiness. LaTonya was going home, and I was, too.

Both my thumbs were raised high in the air when I walked back into LaTonya's room, and the Millers grinned before they hugged each other. There was still so much this young couple had to deal with, but their angels, LaTonya and LaTrisha, would see them through.

"There's just some paperwork that has to be filled out, but in a few hours, all three of you will be going home."

The Millers kissed and then kissed their daughter. After all this tragedy, I wanted to stand there and soak all of this in, but my cell phone buzzed and I tiptoed out of the room. Checking out the caller ID, I smiled.

"Hey, Michellelee. Perfect timing."

"Perfect for what?"

"I'm going home today."

"Oh, you're still at the hospital?"

"Yeah, but I'll be home in a few hours and back in my office tomorrow."

"Terrific, we have to get together now. But I was calling to see if you'd spoken to Miriam?"

"Not since last week; I called her right after I spoke to you. Why?"

"Well, you know I speak to her every day, but she hasn't answered her phone or called me back since I saw her on Saturday. She wasn't even in church on Sunday."

Right away, my thoughts went to the last time I'd spoken to Miriam and how she sounded, almost despondent.

"I haven't spoken to her since last week. And now—"

"What?" Michellelee asked me.

"She acted strange. I asked her about the guy you told me about and she became so flustered. At one point, I was worried that she was going to burst into tears."

"She was acting weird with me, too, but I figured it was because I'd caught her. I thought maybe I'd embarrassed her, but putting what I saw with what you heard . . ."

"Well, now I'm really worried. Have you been by her house?"

"No, but don't worry. I'll head there now."

"That's a long drive for you. You don't have to get to the studio?" I asked, wondering if I was the one who should try to find her since I lived closer.

"I do, but I'll just swing by her place, do a sister check, make sure she's good, then call you back."

"Okay, and tell her to call me."

"Will do. Talk to you later. Love you."

"Mean it."

When I hung up, I stood still for a moment, wondering about Miriam. I pressed the button to call her, but then Dr. Caster passed by and when he turned into LaTonya's room, I followed him.

Michellelee would check on Miriam for now, and once I left here, I'd be able to check on her every day.

As I entered LaTonya's room, I dumped my cell phone into my purse. It was time to get LaTonya home, so that I could move on with my life, too.

29

Miriam

I stared at the phone as if it were a rabid dog.

Ring!

I recognized the number, and even if I didn't, I could certainly read the name across the screen.

Ring!

Jamal Taylor.

This was the call that I'd been waiting for. All I wanted to do was snatch it up and hear his voice since I hadn't heard it for three days. Not since Michellelee had invaded our utopia and brought us crashing down to earth.

Ring!

Suppose it wasn't him, though. Last time his name came across my screen, it was Emily.

Ring!

But if it were Jamal and I let this phone ring one more time, I would miss him.

Grabbing the phone, I held my breath.

"Miriam."

I closed my eyes and just savored his voice. "Jamal!"

"How are you?"

"I'm good," I said, and I resisted adding, "now that you've called."

"I wanted to know . . . if you had any time today. I wanted, needed to talk to you."

"Okay," was all I said, even though I had so many questions: where have you been, why haven't you called, and what do you want to talk about?

He said, "The boys are in school."

His statement was really a question. "Yes."

"Okay, I'm not far away."

Then he was gone. Leaving me with nothing but questions and fear. I sat on the edge of the sofa, with my knees together and my hands clasped, feeling like I was frozen in time and space.

I'd been feeling this way since Jamal had left on Saturday. Since then, I hadn't done anything except take care of my children and breathe. I hadn't left the house, I hadn't answered the phone. I'd just stayed in bed mostly, watching the clock pass time and waiting for the right call to come.

Well, the call had come, but with the way Jamal sounded, with what he said, with what he didn't say . . .

"Oh, God," I whispered.

If I didn't stop, I'd be a madwoman by the time Jamal arrived. I jumped up. I needed to get out of these sweatpants and T-shirt. Maybe put on a dress or fix my hair. But then I sat back down. None of that would make a difference.

So I sat and waited. Listened to the clock tick and waited. Counted the number of cars that drove by and waited.

Then I heard Jamal's car. Not that it had any special sound. It was just that I knew.

Still, I didn't move. I waited for the single honk, his signal for me to open the garage so that our cars could change places. The honk that we'd been doing all last week. There was no honk.

I stood, closed my eyes, and wished that I could talk to God. But all I did was take a deep breath to steady myself. Then I hurried to the garage. I pushed the remote, the garage door lifted, and Jamal's car was where it normally was. But he was already out, walking toward me.

It was clear; he didn't have any plans to stay, and sadness began to rise in me. I wanted to cry already.

I managed to speak with an even voice. "Hey." I stepped aside, letting him come in through the garage door, and when he walked past me, I remembered the last time. He'd met me right in this spot and pulled me into his arms. But today his hands were deep in his pockets like they were on lockdown.

"How are you?" he asked me once I closed the door behind him.

I nodded. "I'm good." Again, I stopped without saying all that was on my heart.

He stood at one end of the living room and I was at the other.

"We can at least sit down, right?" I asked him.

He nodded, but when I sat on the couch, he sat across from me in the chair in front of the window.

That sent my emotions reeling, but I took charge and pressed down the fear, the regret, the rejection, and everything else that was bubbling inside.

He said, "I wanted to tell you how sorry I am—"

I didn't let him finish. "I told you before, there's nothing for you to be sorry about."

"There is. I created a complete mess."

"You didn't do it by yourself. I knew exactly what I was doing."

He shook his head. "But you were vulnerable."

"So were you."

He held up his hands. "Please, let me talk."

I nodded, then squeezed my knees together not only to stop them from shaking but also to squelch the desire that was building just by seeing Jamal, just by hearing him.

"I really do feel like I took advantage of you, and though I know it's no excuse, being with you made me miss Chauncey less. I've tried to really think about it, tried to understand it. All I can say is you filled that hole that was ripped into my heart the moment I dragged Chauncey out of that building."

I couldn't keep quiet anymore. "That's how I feel about you. You took away most of my sadness."

He shook his head. "But still, we shouldn't have been . . . doing what we were doing. I should've been the grown-up in the room."

I leaned back, surprised by his words, but then I relaxed when the ends of his lips twitched into a slight smile.

He explained, "What I mean is, I should've been the one who kept my head."

"I don't know why you're saying this when I wanted this as much, probably more than, you did," I said.

Jamal covered his face with his hands and breathed deeply. "This is a mess, you know. It's a mess because"—he looked up and stared at me so intensely—"I love Emily."

I tried not to flinch, even though if he had slashed my heart with a machete, I would've hurt less than the way I felt hearing those words.

Then he repeated it. "I love my wife."

Why did he keep saying that? Didn't he know how much he was hurting me? But then how could I be hurt? How could I be mad? Jamal was doing what he was supposed to do: loving his wife, and telling me the truth.

"I love my wife," he said, as if he needed to say it again, "but I don't know how to end this with you."

Suddenly, the slashes in my heart didn't feel so deep.

I said, "Remember when you told me that we didn't have to figure this out right now? Maybe we can take our time and let this work itself out."

"We are working this out," he said. "Right now. Because it's so wrong and because too many people could get hurt." He released a quick breath. "Michellelee told Emily you're seeing someone."

"I know. Emily called and asked me a lot of questions." When he stared at me, I shook my head. "I didn't say anything."

He nodded. His voice was strong when he said, "My wife can't be hurt, so this has to end." Then he spoke in a whisper when he added, "Now."

What I should've done was just stood up and agreed. Hugged Jamal and told him good-bye.

I just couldn't.

"But you're like a lifeline for me," I said, hating my words, hating my emotions, hating the fact that I'd become the begging other woman.

"I'm still going to be here, still be your friend, still help you. It's going to be just like it was, just like it's always been with us . . . before we became intimate." He paused as if he wanted me to really understand his next words. "It's the right thing to do."

"I know, I know," I cried.

I'd been a champion, holding my emotions back for the last three days. Pushing them down when Jamal walked through the door, knowing then that this was the end. Maybe that was why I lost it. My tears broke through and burst like a rushing river. My shoulders were heaving, my body was shaking; next, my nose would be running and snot would be coming.

Jamal stood and came to me. He reached his hand toward me and I took it. I didn't have enough energy to stand on my own, so he pulled me up and into his arms, letting me sob into his chest.

He held me and consoled me. I only stopped crying because I

got tired. I leaned away, and with the back of his hand he softly and slowly wiped away the residue of my tears.

Then, just like it always was, I don't know which came first—his lips or mine.

Our lips connected.

We kissed with passion.

Then the doorbell rang.

He pushed me away and I stumbled backward. "Were you expecting someone?"

"No! No!" Stepping across the room, I peeked through the drapes. "Oh, my God!" I whispered as if my voice could be heard outside. "It's Michellelee again."

"You weren't expecting her?"

"No! She should be at work. Oh God. I can't answer the door. She'll see you. Or you can go hide in my bedroom," I said, moving toward the hallway.

But he didn't follow me. "No," he said calmly. "My car is in the driveway."

"Oh God!" Every part of my body was trembling.

He held me by my shoulders, making me look at him. "It's perfectly normal for me to be here. To be checking on you."

The doorbell rang again.

"Oh God!" I repeated.

He said, "You have to get it together; you have to answer the door."

"Okay." Using the tips of my fingers, I wiped my face, hoping to erase any of the tear tracks Jamal had missed.

I took a couple of those deep yoga breaths as I moved toward the door, wishing once again that I was talking to God, because only He could save me from this. As I put my hand on the knob, I reached inside for the acting gift I'd been given and yanked open the door with sort of a smile.

"Hey, girl!" Michellelee said, hugging me before she bounced into the house. In the living room, she greeted Jamal the same way. "What's up?"

Jamal hugged her back. "How's it going, lady?"

I stood to the side, waiting for my cue to speak my next line.

When Jamal leaned away from Michellelee, there was total silence. My best friend looked at Jamal, then stared at me.

Oh, God. Could she see that I'd been crying?

She said, "I'm not interrupting anything, am I?"

"No!" Jamal and I spoke together, though his voice was much calmer than mine, as if he was the trained actor.

He continued, "I just came to check on Miriam and now I'm gonna turn her over to you."

I wanted to protest, tell them that I wasn't some kind of ball that could be volleyed between my friends. But at this point, it was best that I didn't say anything.

With just two steps, Jamal was in front of me, and then he hugged me. One of those Sunday church hugs that were exchanged between Sister So-and-So and Brother What-Not, where you were so far apart your arms barely reached around each other. He held me only for a second, nothing like the embrace we'd shared just a few minutes ago.

"Take care," he said to me. This good-bye was so different from the others. Because this time our good-bye had an audience, and this time I knew for sure that he wasn't coming back. To Michellelee, he said, "I'll check you later."

"Okay," my best friend and I said together.

I walked Jamal to the door. As if he needed to seal our final good-bye, he said, "I'll tell Emily that you're okay."

"Thank you," I said. I would've added more, but I didn't trust my voice and I certainly couldn't trust my emotions.

He walked out the door and I wanted to stand there and watch him until he drove away. But I felt the heat of Michellelee's stare.

I closed the door, closed my eyes, took a deep breath before I faced my friend. I couldn't even get a word out, though.

Michellelee marched right up to me and growled, "Are you sleeping with Jamal?"

My answer—I burst into tears.

"You are! Oh, my God!"

"No, no," I said, finally finding my voice. "I'm not sleeping with him." At least, that was the truth to me. I'd never been in bed with Jamal and fallen asleep.

"Well, what is that? I walk in here, your eyes are red, I ask you if you're sleeping with him—"

"I'm not sleeping with him!"

"Well, why did you start crying?"

"Because we were talking about Chauncey and that was in my head and—"

"Stop lying, Miriam!"

Her words slapped me into silence—at least for a moment.

She said, "I've known you half your life. Something's going on." She paused and held her hands to her head. "Oh, my God. Those were his clothes the other day."

"No!"

She looked at me and shook her head. "I don't believe you."

"Well, I don't know what to tell you."

"Try telling me the truth."

I pressed my lips together. The truth would never come from me.

Michellelee took a breath, stood straighter, and calmed her voice. "Miriam, please. You've got to tell me."

I didn't want to faint, so I sat down on the sofa and said nothing.

"What's going on between you and Jamal?"

"Nothing," I said, sounding weak even to my own ears. But I was going to stick to this story.

Michellelee was pacing, walking from one end of the living room to the other. "This is a disaster!"

"I'm not . . . sleeping . . . with him."

She stopped moving and looked down on me as if I was dumb. "There's a reason why all those Emmys are sitting in my office. I'm one of the best investigative reporters in the country. I know what I know, and I know . . . that you're having an affair with Jamal!" Her voice was rising again. "That's Emily's husband!"

I did it again, cried like someone was beating me. "I know who he is!"

"So you admit it!"

"No!"

Michellelee threw up her hands. "You know what?" She stomped over to the chair where she'd dropped her purse. Then she swung back around and glared at me with a stare that burned through to my soul. "So that I don't say anything *you'll* regret"—she paused for a moment—"I'm going to just walk out of here." Her steps were heavy, almost echoing through the house as she made her way to the door. But then she faced me again. "You know this is wrong. And you know that it's going to end. And when it ends, it's going to be bad. For everyone."

There was no need to say anything. She already knew the truth.

Then she added, "Jamal loves Emily," as if I didn't already know that. As if I didn't already feel like trash.

All I did was watch her walk out the door, and then I sat alone in the dead silence. She was right about everything and she knew it.

What was I going to do? I had no idea, but what scared me more than not having answers to my own questions was Michellelee. What was *she* going to do?

30

Emily

H oney, I'm home!"

Dropping my bag by the door, I stood with my arms open wide, waiting for Jamal to come rushing out of the bedroom or the kitchen or the bathroom. But after a few seconds of just standing there, I realized that I was alone.

I pulled my cell phone from my purse, but paused before I dialed his number. I hadn't called Jamal because I'd wanted this to be a surprise. And the surprise could still work, and be even better if I hurried.

Inside the bedroom, I tossed my suitcase onto the bed, then rushed into the bathroom. In less than two minutes, I stepped into the shower, turned it on full blast, then leaned against the wall and closed my eyes. My plan was to relax, but thoughts of the last three weeks played in my mind like a video. I hadn't had time to do my own grieving, and as a psychologist, I knew that I had to take time for that. Now that I was home, I'd be able to mourn Chauncey with Jamal and help my husband in the process.

Then the shower door opened and I shrieked.

"Oh, my God, you scared me!" I held my hand over my heart,

but in a second, the fear was gone. Now the fierce pounding in my chest had nothing to do with being afraid.

It was the chiseled chocolate body that stood in front of me that had my heart thumping.

My husband.

For a moment, all I did was stare and savor the perfection of him. His muscled chest, his six-pack abs, and all that wonderful territory below.

He was totally naked. He was all mine.

I wrapped my arms around him and kissed him from my soul. God, how I had missed this man. Lord, how I loved him.

As the shower's rain poured down on us, Jamal pressed me gently against the wall and I could feel how much he'd missed me and loved me, too. I wanted him to take me right then, but he was in no hurry. Our lips lingered, though it was getting harder for me to just kiss. Jamal teased me with his lips and with his fingers. I moaned, but what I really wanted to do was scream.

Finally, his tongue began to take a journey and I leaned back, soaking in the sensations. But I couldn't take it anymore. Patience had never been my virtue and it had been three weeks since I'd had this man. I wasn't going to wait any longer. Holding on to him, I wrapped my legs around his waist, letting him know with my cries that I was so ready.

I could have exploded right then, but Jamal slowed me down and made me savor every stroke, relish each sensation. But even though he tried to control the pace, not even a minute passed before I cried out, squeezing my eyes and every muscle in my body, trying to hold on to every second of this ecstasy.

When I opened my eyes, Jamal's beautiful brown eyes were right there looking at me.

"I am so happy to have you home," he said, speaking his first words.

I held him as tightly as I could. "You have no idea how happy I am to be here."

"Turn around," he whispered.

I grinned. Round two. I leaned in against the wall, but then I felt the loofah against my skin. Jamal massaged the sponge into my back and the fragrance of my aloe vera bath gel filled the air.

As much as I wanted my husband again, this felt so good. Like before, Jamal took his time, pouring the gel on my skin, then rubbing it in with the sponge. He covered every inch of me, from my ankles to my calves, then to my legs, back, and shoulders. He turned me around and kissed me as he spent extra time on all the parts that made me a woman.

I took the sponge from his hand and returned the favor. Now, I took my time, touching my husband in all the places and all the ways that I'd missed.

By the time we stepped out of the shower, my fingers were puckered, but I didn't care. He wrapped me in a towel, then wrapped one around his waist and we held hands as we walked into our bedroom.

Jamal let go of me for a moment, then dashed into his closet. "And these"—he came out holding a bouquet of roses—"are for you."

I took the vase and inhaled the fragrance. "Thank you, but how did you know I'd be home today?"

"You said you'd be home on Tuesday and then when you didn't call this morning, I figured you were going to try to surprise me."

I grinned. "Yeah, that's what I wanted to do."

"Well, I wanted to be here to greet you with these. And tell you that I love you. Today, tomorrow, the next day, and the next. I. Love. You." Taking the flowers from me, he placed the vase on the nightstand, Then he pulled me into his arms once again. "Do you know what I want to do?"

I took a quick look at the bed and he laughed.

"You gotta give me a moment, babe," he said. "What I want to do is go out. Go out and have a good time."

"Where?"

"I don't know. You wanna do Gladstones?"

I clapped. "That would be great." It had been a while since we'd gone to one of the best seafood restaurants in Malibu. It had been a while since we'd done so much. But it seemed like the week I'd been at the hospital with LaTonya had been good for Jamal. He was smiling, he seemed happy.

I jumped into my favorite jeans, added a white blouse, a navy blazer, and a red infinity scarf, and I was ready to go. When I stepped out of my dressing room, Jamal was wearing jeans and a navy blazer, too. We laughed; we were so in sync, the way we were supposed to be.

I grabbed my messenger bag, and just as I started to transfer what I needed from my purse, Jamal pulled my arm. "Wait, I want to get my license and a credit card. My wallet won't fit in this bag."

"You don't need any of that." He twirled me around. "You're with me. Big Poppa got you."

"Big Poppa?"

He nodded and grinned.

"I guess a lot has happened since I've been away."

His grin faded, but just as fast, I got it back when I said, "Well, if that's the case, let's go, Big Poppa."

All the way down in the elevator, we held hands as we chatted.

"I'll be back to regular office hours tomorrow," I told him.

"Now that you're back, I know I can live again," he said to me.

That just made me want to love him more. And even though the elevator doors had opened I kissed Jamal as if I couldn't get enough.

Inside the garage, we slid into his car, then Jamal steered with one hand and held my hand with his other. At the red light, he lifted my hand to his lips and planted a soft kiss.

"Do you know how much I love you?" he said.

I smiled. "You've given me some idea."

We rode in the quiet comfort of just being with each other. These were some of the best moments for me, knowing that without a word being exchanged, I was loved, completely.

We were just a few blocks from home when the Bluetooth system announced "Incoming call."

Glancing at the console screen, I said, "Oh, it's Miriam! And Michellelee has been trying to reach her!"

It took only a millisecond for me to press the button to connect the call, but before I could even say hello, Miriam's voice rang through the car. "Jamal!" she cried out. Her words came fast, as if she wasn't even breathing. "Michellee asked me if we were sleeping together and I didn't tell her anything. She asked if you were the one who was here the other day and I told her no, but she didn't believe me and I think she knows. She knows it was you and—"

Jamal snatched his hand away from mine and punched the button, disconnecting the call.

My mind tried to put the words I'd heard together as if they were pieces in a puzzle. Because that's how they sounded to me, a jumbled mess of nonsense.

"Oh, my God," I whispered.

"Emily."

Slowly, I turned to him and stared at the man I'd loved for all this time. We were so connected that he didn't have to speak. Just looking at him, I knew the truth.

"Emily," he said again. "Let me explain. I—"

I held up my hand. "Take me home."

"I have to tell you—"

"Take me home."

"You have to listen to me."

"Fine!" I screamed, pushing open the door even as the car was moving.

"Emily!" Jamal punched the brakes, making the car squeal. The car lunged forward and when it screeched to a stop, I jumped out and ran.

"Emily!"

I ran across one lane of traffic, hit the sidewalk, then ducked into an alley, knowing there was no way for Jamal to follow me. He couldn't leave his car in the middle of the street.

But even though I knew that Jamal wasn't behind me, I ran and ran until my chest ached, my throat burned, and my eyes were nothing but water. I didn't have any idea where I was, but I couldn't go on.

I was breathing hard when I leaned against a building and slid down until my butt hit the cold pavement. I had run away from Jamal, but no matter how fast or how far I'd gone, I couldn't outrun Miriam's voice.

My husband had been sleeping with my best friend!

If God Himself had come down from heaven and told me this, I would've thought this was a case of mistaken identity, because there was no way Jamal would've cheated on me. It was only because the words had come from Miriam that I knew it was the truth.

But how? Why? When? The questions swirled inside me. How long? Had this been going on before Chauncey died?

"Oh, my God!" was all I kept saying.

"Miss, are you all right?"

I looked up and into the eyes of a young man holding a bulging black plastic garbage bag and wearing a long white apron over his jeans.

"Are you all right?" he repeated.

I burst into tears, but through my sobs, I was able to tell him, "I'm fine."

"Are you sure? Do you want me to call somebody?"

"No," I sniffed. "I'm fine."

Who would he call anyway? My husband? My best friend? I couldn't even tell him to call my other best friend. Michellelee had betrayed me, too. Because if she'd known about Jamal and Miriam, she should have told me.

Then I remembered. The call from Michellelee. She was going to see Miriam, but she hadn't called me back. Probably because they were in cahoots.

My husband, my best friends—they had all betrayed me. All I wanted to do was sit here, but the young man would not leave me alone. So I pushed myself up, dusted myself off, and wobbled down the alley, not having any idea where I was going.

All I knew was that I was never going home.

31

Miriam

What happened?

I'd been holding my cell phone for the last hour, wondering what I should do. It had been more than an hour since I made the call. But I'd been cut off. Why?

When we were first disconnected, I was about to press Jamal's number to redial, but something stopped me. I had the feeling that my message had been received.

So, what happened?

I had only been trying to warn Jamal. After Michellelee left, I didn't know what to do. The questions overwhelmed me—should I call Michellelee, should I call Jamal, should I do nothing? But after weighing the options, I was sure that Michellelee was on her way straight to Emily, and I couldn't let Jamal be blindsided like that.

But now, I wasn't so sure I'd done the right thing.

I leaned back and curled up on the lounger, then closed my eyes. What was I going to do?

"Mom, why're you sitting in the dark?"

I raised my head and saw my oldest child, standing right outside my bedroom. The light from the hallway shone behind him, making him look angelic.

"Sweetheart, I didn't even realize it had gotten dark." I held out my arms and Junior stepped into the bedroom to join me on the lounger. When he sat down, I asked, "Where are your brothers?"

"Upstairs, they're playing video games."

"I need to check on them and make sure their homework is done."

"I checked all of that, Mom. And I cleaned up the kitchen, too."

Tears came to my eyes as I held my son's face in my hands. Before Chauncey had passed away, we'd almost had to bribe the boys to complete their chores. But now, Junior was stepping up, taking on more responsibility than I wanted him to. I motioned for him to lean back with me.

He laid his head on my shoulder. "Are you sitting in the dark 'cause you're sad?"

I waited for a moment before I answered, "Yes. A little."

"About Dad?"

This time, I didn't hesitate. "Yes."

"I'm sad about him, too. A lot."

My heart dropped an inch and I wrapped my arms around my son. "I know you are. But you do know that every day you'll be less and less sad, right?"

He nodded.

"And we're both going to be all right."

He shifted his head so that he could look up at me. "That's what I was going to tell you. We're going to be all right, Mom. 'Cause Uncle Jamal said he was going to make sure of it."

An image of Jamal, in this room, in my bed, naked, flashed through my mind. I answered my son only with a smile.

He said, "Did Uncle Jamal go back to work?"

"I'm not sure," was all I said, because I didn't want to have any kind of discussion about Jamal with Junior.

But my son went on, "Oh, I thought he did 'cause he hasn't been here. Is he coming tomorrow?"

Another image, of Jamal leaning over and kissing me. I had to swallow before I answered, "We'll see."

"I wanted to talk to him about going to Crenshaw High 'cause that's where he played basketball."

"Crenshaw's not in our district, but there are plenty of other schools that have great basketball teams."

"I knew you were going to say that." He sighed. "Well, anyway, we have our first basketball game in a couple of weeks and I really hope that Uncle Jamal will be there. So, do you think he'll come?" Junior repeated.

"I'll ask him."

"Or I'll ask him when he comes over tomorrow," Junior said, so sure Jamal was coming back.

I almost asked Junior if he wanted Emily to come, too. But I didn't. Because the world had shifted. Our secret was out and if Jamal came back to me, I was sure that none of us would see Emily again.

My son jumped up. "I'm going to check on Mikey and Stevie," he said, sounding like he was trying very hard to be the big brother.

"Okay. I'll be up there in a little while."

I watched Junior stride toward the door, but then he turned around, ran back, and hugged me with what I was sure was all of his might. "I love you, Mommy."

Mommy . . . it had been a long time since he'd called me that. "I love you, too, Junior."

He stood once again. "Mom, I don't want you to call me Junior anymore."

I frowned.

"I want everyone to call me Chauncey."

It was one of those Hallmark moments, and I nodded because I couldn't speak. As if he knew that he'd taken my breath away, he kissed my cheek and then walked toward the door.

As I watched him move away, my head and my heart swelled with even more love for my son. Chauncey, along with Mikey and Stevie, were the reasons I had to find a way to be whole again.

That thought brought Jamal's image back. Only this time, I saw him the way he left this morning, walking out like he might never come back.

I shuddered. I wanted to be whole, I needed to be whole, but could I do that without Jamal?

32

Emily

The sun had long ago begun its descent as I circled back and trudged down Ocean Avenue. I didn't realize how far I'd run until I decided to walk back. But now, all I wanted to do was get one of the rooms in this hotel, take off my boots, lay my head down, then wake up tomorrow, thankful that this had only been a nightmare.

My heels clicked against the marble floors of Shutters on the Beach, the exclusive hotel that was just blocks from our condo. The four-hundred-dollar-a-night price was certainly a lot, but I didn't care. I wanted to rest on the luxurious sheets and not think until morning.

At the front desk, the attendant smiled and welcomed me to the hotel.

"Do you have any rooms?"

She nodded. "All I'll need is your ID and a credit card."

I reached into my bag and froze. As the attendant waited for me, I recalled a long-ago lesson from my mother:

Whenever you go out, no matter who you're with, always have enough money for a phone call and a cab.

I'd always left home with my mother's advice and my own money in my pocket. I was never going to be stranded because of a man.

Only here I was, stranded. Because of a man who was my husband.

"I'm sorry," I said to the woman, then turned away and rushed back through the lobby.

With no ID, no money, and no credit cards, I had no choice.

The thought of going home and packing my things made me want to cry, but as I began walking toward our condo, I wondered: why was I thinking of leaving? I hadn't done anything. Jamal was the one who'd broken my heart and our home. He was the one who needed to go!

It was completely dark when I stumbled into the building. As I rode up in the elevator, I prayed that Jamal had done the right thing, the decent thing, though it was clear that there wasn't much decency in him. I just hoped that he'd packed a bag and left our home.

But when I stepped over the threshold, Jamal was right there, just a few feet from the door. His shoulders were slouched and the muscles in his face were slack, making him look exhausted and filled with sorrow.

I wanted to ask him why he was so sad. Why did he look so hurt? He should've been a happy man. He had two women.

"Emily."

I held up my hand as I stomped past him. He tried to block me, but he must've forgotten who I was, an all-star who'd broken through thousands of blocks and taken down plenty of players.

He stumbled backward as I pushed past him. It would've been a foul on any court, but I figured I had a million fouls to give.

While he was trying to stand upright, I marched into our bedroom, slamming the door. He was two seconds behind me.

"Em," he said when he busted in, "please, we have to talk."

I sat on the bed and kicked off my boots, doing my best to tuck my emotions deep inside. I didn't want to explode. I didn't want to give Jamal the satisfaction of seeing my pain.

He said, "You have to talk to me."

His words hit me like a right hook, and I spun my head toward him. "Are you kidding me? I *have* to talk to you?"

He replied, "What I should have said is that we *need* to talk."

My voice was still soft. "I don't *need* to do a damn thing with you."

"But we have to talk . . ."

"Talk about what? I know everything. Miriam said it all." I closed my eyes for a second. For all the hours since I'd heard that phone call, I'd fought hard not to think about Miriam. Because betrayal by one person I loved was more than I could handle. I wouldn't be able to breathe if I had to think about Jamal *and* Miriam.

"You don't know everything," he had the audacity to say.

"I know enough. I know what's important. I know that you and Miriam are . . ." I stopped. That was enough of the thought for me.

"We're not having an affair."

I stared silently, giving him time to take that back. When he didn't, I moved slowly toward him until I was right in his face. He didn't back away.

"So, what are you saying?" My voice was still no louder than a whisper. "Are you calling Miriam a liar?"

His chin fell just a bit. "I just want to sit down and explain what it was and how it happened."

I stepped back a little, and crossed my arms.

He said, "When you hear it all, I think you'll understand."

I tilted my head, then I busted out laughing. And it took me a while to stop because truly, that was funny. I would *understand*?

Jamal knew that my laughter wasn't from a good place, so he said something that took my breath away. "Emily, I love you."

He reached for me and I took two giant steps back. Not only because I didn't want him to touch me but because I was shocked by his words. I never expected to hear him declare his love for me ever again. But those words made me stumble, at least mentally.

"I love you," he repeated. "I really do. And I'm so, so sorry."

He sounded as if he meant what he was saying.

Good thing I knew the truth.

"You're a liar."

He pressed his lips together and I knew I'd scored. I was pleased by the damage those words had done and I hoped I had a few more weapons inside me.

"I'm not a fool," I continued. "There's no way you could have loved me and done this."

"This had nothing to do with you."

"And that right there is the problem. Because you being with another woman has everything to do with me. We took vows, Jamal, to be faithful."

I waited for him to jump in with some new lie, but he stayed quiet.

I continued, "We said that we would love each other forever."

"I do," he whispered. "I do love you."

"If you love me, then why do I hurt so much?" A sob rose from my throat, but I fought to keep it back. "Why am I feeling a pain that I've never felt before?"

"I'm so sorry."

I looked up toward the ceiling, hoping that if I blinked fast enough the tears would go away.

"Just get out."

"What?"

"I want you to get out of my life!"

"What do you mean?

"I mean, get the hell out."

✦

Jamal had thrown a grenade into my heart, and now he had to go. At first, I stayed sitting on the edge of the bed until Jamal came out of his closet with his suitcase, the small one that could be carried onto any plane. I wanted to tell him that everything he owned couldn't fit in that bag, but I said nothing.

He lifted it up, placed it beside me, then stood back as if he was waiting for me to say something, to stop him, maybe.

My answer: I simply stood and walked out of the room.

I hoped my move insulted him, hurt him, made him want to cry, since that's all I wanted to do.

I walked straight into the kitchen. Inside the freezer, I found exactly what I was looking for: the half gallon of butter pecan ice cream. I couldn't remember when we bought this. And when I took off the cover, the freezer burns let me know that it had been a while. But ice cream didn't spoil, did it?

I hoped not, because this was exactly what I needed. This ice cream was old, it was hard, and it would have to do.

I didn't even try to scoop out a couple of spoonfuls. I just put the entire carton into the microwave for ten seconds, then took a tablespoon, went back into the living room, clicked on the television, and curled up on the couch.

The television was already set to ESPN. The talking heads were debating about the Major League Baseball race to the finish. The Yankees were still number one, though those Baltimore Orioles refused to budge.

"J—" I yelled out, then stopped. This was something that I would have shared with Jamal on any other day. But I guess I'd almost forgotten. We wouldn't share these moments anymore.

Pressing the button, I turned the volume down, almost to Mute, and just watched. And just ate. Tablespoon after tablespoon. Until I was full. Then I ate until I was stuffed. Finally, I ate until the container was empty.

I heard Jamal's footsteps coming out of the bedroom and when he got to the living room entry, he stopped. The tears that were in his eyes matched the ones in mine. His heart was pleading with me to give him another chance. My heart told him that it would never be open to him again.

He stood there not moving, as if he planned to wait it out. Wait for me to talk to him. I turned back to the TV, picked up the remote, and pressed the volume up all the way, until the sports commentators' voices blasted through our apartment.

Jamal nodded, then picked up the bag. "Em, I'm only leaving because I think you need some space, but I will be back."

That's what he thought.

"You're going to hear me and we'll work this out."

He clearly had me confused with someone else.

He stood there for a bit longer. I guessed he was waiting for me to say something, do something. But finally, he caught the clue and turned to the door.

"Emily," he said softly.

I turned to him with a laser-sharp stare.

He said, "I'm sorry."

I said, "Good-bye."

I watched him twist the knob, grab the handle of his roller bag, and then he walked out the door and out of my life.

33

Emily

Why are your eyes red?" LaTonya asked the moment she sat down in one of the green children's chairs that I had around the low yellow table in my office.

Crouching down, I sat across from her. "Are they red?" was my answer, even though I knew the little girl was right.

She nodded. "Were you crying?"

"No," I said, telling her a lie. "I'm just tired."

"Oh." Then she lowered her head. "My eyes get red when I cry."

"Have you been crying?"

She didn't respond, just reached for the box of crayons and the pad of construction paper on the other end of the table. I sat back, watched her, and tried not to yawn. At least I'd told the truth about being tired. I was exhausted, but that's what being up all night would do. And exhaustion and tears always equaled crimson-red eyes in the morning.

It was amazing that someone's world could crash in just a moment. But then, I was sitting in front of a little girl who'd lost her sister in a second. So even with what I was going through, someone else always had it worse.

Still, it was hard not to feel as if I was the only one in the world who'd ever lived this nightmare. I was tortured by the question that had kept me up all night: how long had this been going on?

I'd searched my memory, trying to recall every moment over the years with Jamal, and all the time we'd spent with Miriam and Chauncey. I tried to remember every glance they'd exchanged, every word they'd spoken, every time they hugged.

And I remembered the day of Chauncey's funeral and my suspicions then.

But even when I'd stared at Miriam with her eyes closed and her arms around my husband, I never imagined the true fact, that they were *actually* sleeping together.

Since that day when Miriam had taken me and Michellelee into her bedroom and given us those bracelets, I'd turned off that sixth sense that I believed every women had. I turned mine off because, obviously, my sense had gone haywire.

I was so mad at myself. There had probably been signs and signals right in front of my face.

And all of that made me want to cry from anger and pain. But I was not going to cry. I was not going to break down.

"So," I said to LaTonya. "How're you feeling?"

"Fine," she said, though she didn't look up.

I sat back, wanting to let LaTonya draw as we talked. "How're your mom and dad?"

"Fine," she said, her attention on the roof that she was constructing on the house she'd drawn.

"So, did you do anything special when you got home from the hospital yesterday?"

She nodded, though she didn't take her eyes away from her picture. I studied her as she drew the windows and then colored in the curtains.

"What did you do?" I asked her, trying to pull out a longer response.

"I had ice cream," LaTonya said, making me think about all the ice cream I'd eaten. Another reason why I'd been up all night; my aching stomach matched my aching heart.

"So," I said, pausing because I wanted to see her reaction to my next question. "Are you looking forward to going back to school?"

She stopped drawing and hesitated. "Mommy said that I'm going to school on Monday," she said, sounding like tears weren't far away.

I nodded. "Aren't you happy?"

"No."

"Don't you want to see your teacher, Ms. Parker, again?"

"No."

"Why not?"

"I don't want to go to school by myself."

"What about going to school with your friends?"

She shook her head and said nothing.

I let her get back to concentrating on her drawing. Now that the house was finished, she sketched three figures in front, just like she'd done with the picture that was in Dr. Caster's file.

Though LaTonya no longer talked about joining her sister in heaven, I was still concerned. According to the Millers, LaTonya had always been the gregarious one, but I would never have been able to tell it. Since the fire, she'd become an introvert, taking on the personality of her sister.

I had never even seen her smile.

At first, my goal had been to save her life. Now I wanted to help her get her life back. Not exactly to where it used to be, but I had to help her find a new normal that included her laughing and playing and loving school again.

I pressed, "Don't you want to see your friends in school?"

"I don't want any friends."

I felt LaTonya's pain right now. I wasn't sure that there would ever be another woman in life I'd trust enough to call a friend.

But still I had to ask LaTonya, "Why don't you want any friends?"

She looked at me. "I just want LaTrisha."

"But you know . . ." I paused to see what LaTonya would say.

"LaTrisha's in heaven."

I waited for her to say more, but she said nothing. She'd put a period on that sentence, which was a good thing.

I moved away from the talk of school and looked down at her picture. "That's a big sun," I said.

"LaTrisha liked the sun."

"What about you?"

"I like the sun, too." Then she stopped and admired her work. "Can I take this home with me?"

"Of course."

"I want to put this on LaTrisha's side of our room."

"That sounds great."

I'd told the Millers to keep LaTrisha's bed in place and to let LaTonya talk about her sister as much as she wanted. My hope was to get LaTonya to the day when she was ready to live with just her sister's memory.

After fifty minutes, I turned her over to her parents, confirmed her appointment for tomorrow, and returned to my office, and in just minutes, loneliness descended upon me.

I'd felt it all along, from last night to this morning. From the moment that Jamal had walked out, loneliness had been hovering like a vulture, waiting to swoop down and come in for the kill.

The plan was for me to gather my purse and briefcase and head home. But for what? The vulture would be larger there, the pain would be greater. So I sat behind my desk, closed my eyes, and wondered about the days ahead.

My life was really going to be different now. I'd loved Jamal for so long, I could hardly remember the time before him. But now I'd once again be alone. I could handle that—at least, that's what I kept telling myself.

My cell phone vibrated on my desk and I didn't even have to reach for it to know that it was another call, or another message, or another text, from Jamal. He'd left so many messages last night that I'd had to clear out my voice mail this morning, though I hadn't listened to a single one.

Picking up my cell, I clicked on the text message icon and nine popped up from Jamal. The messages were all the same: I love you. I miss you. I'm so sorry.

I deleted them, then tossed my phone back onto my desk.

"It was never supposed to be like this," I said aloud.

All that was supposed to be waiting for me in life was happiness. That's what Jamal had promised, and not just with his words. From the moment we'd kissed on the beach's edge in Maui, my heart had been filled with joy, though it had come at such a high, high price. A high price that I'd been so willing to pay . . .

✦

August 29, 2003

It was just a little more than two years ago when Jamal had knocked me out with that kiss as we sat on those rocks in Maui. We had sat there and just kissed, soft kisses, gentle kisses, love kisses—what I would call, from that day forward, Jamal kisses.

The sun was long gone by the time we broke away. For at least an hour after that, I leaned back in Jamal's arms while we listened to the music of the ocean as the surf crashed on the rocks. It had been so dark when we'd finally decided to go inside that Jamal had to carry me down.

From that point on, we were Emily and Jamal, though we made no announcement. Not that any was necessary; it showed in the way we were.

At breakfast the next morning, while Jamal and Chauncey chatted at the waffle station, Miriam and I stood in front of the omelet chef.

"The last time I saw you, you and Jamal were like brother and sister. And now it looked like he was gonna cry when you walked away from him. What a difference a day makes."

My face was filled with my grin, but all I did was shrug.

"Oh, so you think you're gonna get away with not saying anything? You're gonna tell me something."

"A woman never kisses and tells."

"So there was a kiss!" Miriam exclaimed. "I knew it! I knew it!"

I laughed, but told her nothing more. Not that I had to. For the rest of the weekend, Jamal and I behaved like we were the ones on our honeymoon, and I would've cried when the weekend ended if Jamal and I weren't headed back to LA together. Back in the city, our lives and our love continued. I was in school, and Jamal was working a schedule as an EMT that was just as demanding.

No matter what, though, we spent as much time together as we could. Sometimes I took stacks of books to his apartment in Ladera Heights and studied while I lay across his lap. Or he'd come to my place and we'd rent movies.

Of course, like everything else, we had the same favorite movie.

Love Story.

It was no surprise that I loved that movie, but it was a little bit shocking that a guy would admit to it.

"Ryan O'Neal was no punk," Jamal explained to me. "And I want to love my woman the way he loved his. And you know what?" he asked, as he kissed my neck. "I already do."

Jamal's words, his kisses, his embraces, always made me swoon.

So now, two years into our relationship, it was time for the love of my life to meet the people who had loved me all my life. The only thing was, I had tricked Jamal, just a little. I hadn't told him the truth until we'd stepped off the plane at Jackson-Evers International Airport.

"Wait a minute! Your parents don't know we're coming?"

"Nope!" I said. "I wanted to surprise them."

"Em, in what country do you think it's a good idea to be walking into your house with a black dude without telling your parents first?"

"Oh, please," I said, waving my hand at Jamal's words. "My parents know all about you."

"Yeah?" He looked at me sideways.

This time I nodded, because I couldn't keep lying out loud. I felt bad not telling the whole truth, but I couldn't let him know that I was a little nervous about my parents, which is why they hadn't met him yet. They didn't know about Jamal, at least not in the important ways . . . like the fact that he was black. And I'd shortened his name to Jay whenever I referred to him.

I really had wanted to tell my parents everything about the man I loved, but I just wasn't sure about the way they would react. In their world, everyone had their place. Not that they were really prejudiced, at least not in the white-sheet, hood-wearing kind of way. If you asked them, they'd tell you they loved "the blacks." To them, Nellie, the woman who really raised me, was part of our family. And one of my father's favorite charities was the United Negro College Fund

because he felt everyone should have the chance for a college educa-
tion—just not at Ole Miss.

It was because of these beliefs that I knew a telephone call would
never do. The best way to present Jamal was face-to-face. Once my
parents met him, shook his hand, looked into his eyes, talked to him,
they would see what I saw—perfection personified. And then they
would love Jamal, too.

"So," Jamal began when he got behind the wheel of the rental
car that we picked up at the airport, "do you actually live in Jackson
or in some suburb?"

I shook my head. "No, we live in Jackson." When he looked at
me out of the corner of his eye, I added, "I mean, we don't live in
downtown, but we live in Jackson."

He grinned, took my hand, and kissed it. Then, with one hand,
he steered and I directed him to my childhood home.

Twenty-five minutes later, when we drove up to the double
wrought-iron gates, Jamal's eyes widened. "Whoa! Your house is
somewhere behind all of this?"

"Stop it." I hit his hand playfully, though I did know that the
grounds were grand. I keyed in the code that opened the gates and
then Jamal and I began the drive up the mile-long winding driveway.

"Where the hell are we?" Jamal asked.

"What?" I said, not wanting Jamal to think about this as any big
deal. "I told you that I grew up in a big house."

"Okay, but there are big houses and then there're plantations."
He paused. "This was once a plantation, wasn't it?"

I shrugged, as if I didn't know, as if I didn't care. I didn't care, but
I did know. I would never tell Jamal, but I knew my family's history
back for at least ten generations. This had been a major plantation,
and my male ancestors had fought hard in the Civil War to preserve
the institution that had made the Harringtons wealthy.

My family was a long way from that time, though. Those days had nothing to do with me and even less to do with Jamal.

By the time we parked the car in the circular driveway, Jamal was shaking his head. He looked up at my three-story home and I couldn't tell if he was impressed or intimidated.

"I don't have a good feeling," he mumbled as he pulled my suitcase out of the trunk.

I waited for him to get his bag, but he just stood there. "What are you doing? Get yours out, too," I said.

He shook his head. "Maybe I should stay at a hotel somewhere. I could even stay at my grandmother's house."

"Your grandmother's is over an hour away and you don't like your cousin, remember?" I told him, referring to a younger relative who was living in the home that Jamal now owned.

"Oh, yeah." He grinned and I breathed. At least he was only kidding.

I trotted up the steps ahead of Jamal and then used my key to let myself in.

"Surprise!" I said the moment I stepped into the rotunda.

Just a few seconds later, I heard soft steps clicking against the floor. "Miss Emily, is that you?" It was Nellie, dressed as always in her navy-and-white uniform, who rushed out first to greet me, and I wrapped my arms around the woman who was like a grandmother to me.

We had barely said our hellos when my mother sauntered in from the parlor. She walked slowly because a proper Southern lady never got caught up in excitement. But I could tell that my mother was happy to see me.

"Emily, what are you doing here?" Nellie stepped aside and now I was in my mother's arms. I had to bend over to get my hug from her; I'd clearly gotten my height from my father.

My mother said, "I'm so glad to see you, sweetheart. Why didn't you tell us that you were coming?" Her Southern drawl was so thick to me now that I'd been away from home for more than seven years.

"I wanted to surprise you," I said.

"What's all of this ruckus?"

I grinned as my father strolled down the circular staircase looking like the leading man in *Gone with the Wind Revisited*, with his smoking jacket and his pipe in his hand. "Daddy!" I met him at the bottom of the steps. I loved, loved, loved my mother. But everyone knew I was a daddy's girl. I kissed my father over and over on his cheek. "I'm so happy to see you."

That's when I heard the cough behind me. "Oh, my goodness." I turned to Jamal.

But before I could say anything, my mother said to Jamal, "Just leave her bags right there." And then, to my father, she said, "Honey, I don't have any spare change. Do you have a twenty or two you can give this nice young man? He's been so patient."

"Oh, no, Mom," I said, knowing that my face was probably fire-red. "He's not my driver." I took Jamal's hand. "This is Jamal."

My mother, father, and Nellie stood with blank stares.

My mother spoke first. "Jamal?"

"Yes, *Jamal*." I said his name as if they'd heard it before. "Jamal Taylor, the guy I've been seeing."

"Seeing him do what?" my mother drawled.

I swallowed. My mother was a bright woman, and she knew exactly what I meant. But in order to get past this awkwardness, I had to play her game. So I said, "The man I've been dating."

My parents' expressions did not change, and even Nellie stared at me like I had lost my mind.

After many long moments, my father turned and walked into the parlor. Without a word, he just walked away from me.

I looked at my mother and pleaded with my eyes for her to fix this. All she said was, "Emily, your father and I need to speak with you."

That was it? That was her save?

"Okay," I said and took Jamal's hand, though he didn't budge an inch when I tried to follow my parents.

When my mother saw that I was trying to pull Jamal with me, she added, "Privately." She turned to Nellie. "Can you take Emily's . . . guest into the kitchen? He may want something to drink. He does look a little parched."

"No!" I said. There was no way I was going to let my parents disrespect Jamal this way.

But Jamal spoke softly into my ear. "Go on," he encouraged me. "Talk to your parents. I'll go with Nellie."

"No," I whined. "You're supposed to be with me."

"I know. But go and talk to your folks. I'll be fine." He squeezed my hand before Nellie led him to the other side of the house.

My mother raised a single eyebrow, but I stomped past her and into the parlor. She followed me, then closed the sliding doors behind us. I wanted to tell her that wasn't a good idea because the steam that was rising out of me was enough to start a fire, and we might need to get away quickly.

My father stood with his elbow propped up on the mantel as if he was posing for *Architectural Digest*. When my mother sat on the floral-patterned sofa, my father motioned for me to do the same.

But I didn't move. I stood in place, folded my arms, tapped my foot, and glared at the people I'd loved my whole life. It was true, I didn't know what to expect. But I certainly didn't expect my parents to behave so rudely. I could not remember a time when I had to press down my emotions and work hard to be respectful. I'd never been angry with my parents, so this feeling was foreign to me.

But it was real. I was hurt. And I was pissed. Like I said, I didn't know what to expect when I brought Jamal home. But I can say that I didn't expect this.

"Sit down, Emily," my father said.

"No."

"I said, sit down."

"I'm fine where I am."

He glared at me and I glared right back. It probably would've been better to sit down and talk this out, but I couldn't be rational.

My father gave in first. He nodded, then turned forward so that his whole body faced me.

But before he could say a word, I jumped in. "What was that about? I bring a friend home and both of you treat him like I just met him and picked him up at the bus station or something."

I was growling, but my parents didn't seem to notice. "We didn't know you were coming home," my father said, softer this time. "We didn't know you were bringing a friend."

"I've brought friends before and you've never acted like this."

"But you've never brought home a colored boy before." It was my mother's Southern twang that made those words sound so dirty . . . so racist.

Tears came to my eyes, but not because I was hurt. I was just mad now. "And what does Jamal being . . . black have to do with anything?"

"Daughter, do not act like you have no idea what this is about," my father said, with the sternness back in his voice.

"I don't know what this is about," I said. "Because the thought of what it may be about makes me sick."

"Don't talk to your father that way." My mother's tone was as demure as the way she sat, so prim, so proper, with her ankles crossed and her hands folded in her lap.

"I can't help it because I can't believe what's happening," I said.

"Why not?" my mother questioned. She tilted her head as if she were trying to get a better look at me. "We had this talk before you left home."

"We didn't talk. You *told* me—"

"That the Bible says that everyone is to stay with their own kind," my mother said, repeating my grandmother's words.

I steamed.

My father jumped in. "This is exactly why I didn't want you to go to LA."

My mother drawled, "And don't forget that basketball thing." She shook her head. "I always knew that was a bad idea. For a girl to be playing sports." She shuddered.

My eyes opened wide. Really, I shouldn't have been so hard on my parents. I mean, didn't Miriam react the same way at first? And Jamal, too. He'd rejected me because of the color of my skin.

Miriam, Jamal, and I had worked it all out. It never should've been an issue with my parents. They should've just loved Jamal because I did.

My mother said, "Your friend can stay here tonight because it's late and we would never turn anyone away." She paused and glanced at my father. When he gave his permission with a nod, she added, "But tomorrow . . ."

Clearly, my method wasn't working, so I unfolded my arms and, with a deep breath, sat next to my mother.

"Please don't do this," I said. I looked from my mother to my father. "Let us stay here for the weekend so that you can get to know Jamal. Once you talk to him, you'll see that he's smart and he's funny and he's caring, and it won't matter if he's black."

"Being black or white *always* matters, Daughter," my father said.

"But, but . . . what about Nellie? She's black and she lives here, and she's here for all of the holidays and you always say she's like family."

"We pay her." Those simple words made me lean away from my mother. Then she made it clear to me. "Do you think she'd be here for anything if we didn't pay her? Do you think she would attend our parties and talk and laugh with us if she weren't getting a very good paycheck every two weeks?"

I wanted to tell my mother to take it back. Nellie was family. But I could only fight one battle at a time. "You've always trusted me," I said to both of my parents. "Trust me now."

My mother turned to my father and he shook his head. "We've told you what we're willing to do," she said. "But your friend is not welcome here for more than one night."

Jumping up, I said, "If you don't want him here, then you don't want me."

"Oh, Emily"—my mother waved her hand as if she was dismissing my words and my emotions—"don't be so dramatic. We're just being good parents, which means we have to guide you and direct you, and—"

"I'm twenty-five years old. You don't have to guide me or direct me or tell me who I should fall in love with."

It was as if I'd sent an electrical volt through the room. My father glared at me before he said, "You don't love him."

It was ridiculous that I even shaped my lips to answer him, but I did. "Yes, I do."

My father kept staring, while my mother looked like she wanted to cry.

"It won't last," he said.

"We're getting married," I threw back.

Now, those words were to just shock them, because Jamal and I hadn't talked about marriage. At least not in a serious way. We'd both said we wanted to spend our lives together, but Jamal insisted that I focus on my doctorate, and I had at least three more years for that.

I had no doubt, though, that we would be married. It was destiny to me.

"You can't do that!" My mother's accent was more pronounced now. It was always that way when she was upset. "Not in this family."

I jutted my chin forward and, without a word, dared her to say that to me again. When she said nothing, I turned to my father.

He nodded, then moved closer until he was standing over me. "We've put up with enough of this, Emily," he said, calling me by my name for the first time that I could remember. "We let you go to Los Angeles . . ."

He said that as if I'd just traveled to California to hang out for a few years rather than go to college and grad school.

"We let you play basketball," he continued. "And then we let you stay out there."

Let me? Was he really saying that?

My father kept on, "We've supported all of that nonsense—"

"Nonsense?"

As if I hadn't spoken, my father continued, "But we won't support this."

A part of me wanted to go through and argue all of his points, but I had to keep my focus. "Daddy, you raised me right. You know I'm smart and I make thoughtful decisions, and I don't do anything blindly."

"Clearly, that has changed," my father said without emotion.

"I don't know what to tell you," I said, my voice cracking for the first time.

He nodded a little. "You do what you have to do," he said. "But make sure you're thinking about the consequences."

"I am."

He paused for just a moment. "Then, we'll do what we have to do." He reached for my mother and she took his hand. Standing up, they both paused as if they were giving me a moment to change my mind.

I didn't budge, not physically, not mentally.

Then they walked out of the room. I sat there trembling, letting minutes pass by, not believing what had happened. Surprisingly, I didn't cry. Maybe because I was just too shocked to shed a tear . . .

✦

BUT I HAD cried many times through the days and months and years that followed. Jamal and I had left their home that night, though Jamal had insisted I stay. I'd told him that if he was leaving, I was going, too.

Jamal never asked me what my parents had said, but I figured Nellie had given him a good earful when she sat him down in the kitchen. She'd been a longtime employee of the Harringtons. She probably knew my parents better than I did.

I'd been sure that once my parents realized how serious I was, they would accept Jamal. They had to; I was their only child.

I was wrong.

When I returned to school the following week and was called into the Admin Office, I found out that my parents would no longer be paying tuition.

"So, you have to make other plans," the head of Admin told me.

I'd barely had time to process that before I found out my credit cards had been canceled, and then two weeks later, my landlord had knocked on my door telling me the rent was overdue.

I'd been devastated, and Jamal had tried to walk away so that I could save my relationship with my parents.

"I don't want to be the cause of you being estranged from your mother and father."

"But if I give in to them, who will I be? I love you, Jamal. Now, if you don't love me, then you can walk out that door. But if you stay, know that I'll never leave you."

He kissed me. "Then let's do this thing together, forever."

We had figured out our life, without my parents' money. And in fact, because of them, we'd married sooner, just four months later, over the Christmas holiday. A call to Pastor Ford, telling her what my parents had done and what we wanted to do. Then, with just six people in the sanctuary, we became husband and wife.

It was the best day of my life. And with the gift certificate from Pastor for a two-night stay at the Westin, it was the best night of my life, too.

Through the academic struggles, the financial struggles, the working struggles, we were so happy. We had each other and we had love. Unconditional love. A love that I'd never known. A love I thought I'd have forever.

But forever hadn't lasted very long. And now I didn't have anyone in my life who truly loved me.

I was alone. And alone was such a scary place to be.

34

MIRIAM

Before God had made me a wife, before He blessed me with my children, He had given me friends.

Friendship was not a relationship I ever wanted, and I definitely didn't need it. At least, not until I walked into the suite that I'd been assigned at USC.

I'd been so apprehensive when I found out that I had to have roommates. The full scholarship I received from Upward Bound paid my tuition, fed me, and gave me shelter, but that promise of a roof over my head didn't include having my own room.

I completely dreaded the prospect of having to live with two girls.

Until I met them.

In a letter, I'd been told their names: Emily Harrington, from Jackson, Mississippi; and Michelle Lee, from Omaha, Nebraska. The two of them were already in the townhouse when Chauncey drove me to the school, sitting in the middle of the floor, with their legs crossed and one of those supersize bags of barbecued potato chips between them. When I walked in, they were chatting and laughing like old friends.

Within minutes, though, I found out that this was just how Emily and Michellelee were, and they drew me into their circle, literally.

"We've been waiting for you," the white girl said as she jumped up to help me with my bags since Chauncey had gone to find a parking space. I figured she was Michelle, the one from Omaha.

But then the other one, who was gorgeous enough to be a model, said, "Hi, Miriam. I'm Michelle Lee. But that was my Midwest name; now that I'm in LA, my new name is Michellelee." She fanned out her hands in the air, as if she was setting her name in lights.

"Isn't that cool?" the white girl, who I now figured was Emily, said.

"Uh. Yeah, Michelle Lee."

"No! Michellelee, it's all one word," Michelle explained. "I figured that since I'm going to be famous one day, I need a single name. Something like . . . Oprah."

"Oh, okay," I said, knowing for sure that she was a little weird.

And the white girl said, "I'm Emily. Just Emily." She laughed as if she'd told a joke. And Michellelee laughed, too.

Both of these girls seemed kind of special in a they-might-have-to-be-committed-one-day sort of way. But they weren't lazy. Before Chauncey had the chance to park, they'd helped me drag my three bags into the first-floor bedroom that they'd left for me, and then we went out for pizza.

"Since Chauncey has a car, he can take us," Michellelee said, as if she was the boss of all of us.

"Yeah," Emily piped in. "And I'll pay for everything."

It was fine with Chauncey, so it was good for me. By the time we got back to our townhouse, we really were friends.

Michellelee made us laugh, Emily was so generous, and they both embraced Chauncey. We started off that day as strangers, but by that night we were friends, and before August turned the calendar to September, Emily and Michellelee were truly the sisters I'd never had.

Talk about having each other's back. They'd been by my side when I'd stumbled into the townhouse after the trauma of my first Statistics exam. When I received a D in Biology, Emily tutored me even though she'd only received a C. And it was because of Michellelee that I auditioned for the drama club, and after my performance in our first play, a rendition of *Fences*, she demanded that I change my major to theater arts.

We had cried together, laughed together, studied together, and made it through one of the best colleges in the country together. And our after-college life was just as connected. They were with me when I married, gave birth, and now, had been with me through Chauncey's death.

Always by my side, and I'd let them down, especially Emily.

I needed to fix everything, but I didn't know how. For the past three days, I'd just been walking through life, filling the hours with housework, breaking up sibling fights, watching TV with my children, and preparing four-course dinners that looked a lot like Thanksgiving.

But though I'd worked hard to fill my time, nothing filled the void left by not speaking to Jamal or Emily, or even Michellelee.

Fear had me working like a madwoman during the day and then that same fright kept my eyes open at night. I wasn't sure if I'd had five hours of sleep in the last seventy-two hours, and there was no way I'd survive another night without answers.

So, I did the only thing that I could. I called Michellelee.

"Hi," I said, sounding weak and scared even to my own ears. "It's Miriam."

"I know who it is," she said, sounding like she wasn't quite sure if she should've answered the phone.

I ignored her tone. "I really need to talk to you."

"Okay," she said. "You know how it is with us, speak."

"No," I said. "I need to do this in person."

"Well, I'm already at the studio, and with a full news day, I won't be able to come down there till after work and that might be pretty late tonight."

Inside, I groaned. It was only ten in the morning; I'd never make it through the rest of the day. "What if I come to you? Would you have just ten minutes to talk?"

It had to be my desperation that made her say, "Sure," without hesitation. Michellelee was in the middle of a hectic workday and she wasn't anywhere near happy with me. Yet she was going to make time. Sisters. A gift I didn't deserve.

"Okay, I'll be there in"—I glanced at the clock—"thirty minutes. And I promise it'll only be ten minutes."

Michellelee told me to meet her at the coffee shop around the corner from the studio, and before I hung up, I had already grabbed my purse. It wasn't until I was in the van that I realized I should've changed my clothes. These jeans and this T-shirt, my standard Mommy gear, made me grossly underdressed. But it would have to do. What I needed to learn was far more important than what I was wearing. So I hit the freeway, tuned the radio to KJLH, and tried to bust the speakers. I figured that if I gave myself a headache I wouldn't be able to focus on what was in my head.

Thirty-five minutes later, I swerved into the parking lot, then hurried inside to search for Michellelee. When I didn't see her, I ordered a green tea, then chose a table far away from the bustle of the front of the coffeehouse.

I wrapped my hands around the cup, soothed by the warmth. When another five minutes passed, I had a moment of doubt and wondered if my friend was going to show up. But just seconds after that thought, Michellelee glided into the shop.

It only took her a moment to spot me, then several minutes to make her way through the patrons who stopped to say hello, snap a picture, and one who asked for an autograph. I studied her as she made her way to me, trying to see signs, anything that would give me a hint.

By the time she made her way to the table, she'd used up almost five minutes of the ten that I promised her. She stood over me for a little while, then finally she leaned down and hugged me. "How you doing, girl?"

I nodded. "Thanks for seeing me. I didn't think you would after the last time."

She laid her hand over mine as she sat down. "Miriam, I was mad as hell, but we're friends, no matter what."

"Thanks for saying that," I said, though I wondered if those would be her sentiments if I told her the truth. Then I looked down at the tea in my hands. "Michellelee, did you . . . say anything?"

"About what?"

My eyes were still lowered, but I knew hers were on me.

"Did you say anything . . . about what you asked me the other day?"

"Was there anything to say?" She added, "Is there something going on with you and Jamal?"

Just like the last time, I burst into tears, making Michellelee lean back in her chair. When I looked up, I knew there was no longer the need to play this game of chicken.

As the tears rolled down my face, I said, "I don't know how it happened. I don't know . . ."

When she stood up, I thought she was so pissed that she was just leaving me there to cry. But she was back in a second, with a couple of napkins from the dispenser.

"Thank you," I mumbled as I wiped my face. "I am so sorry. You don't have any idea."

Michellelee shook her head slightly. "I don't understand how this could happen."

So I told her the story. Of how it started on that Saturday. Of how my tears had come first, and then our hug, and then I told her how we'd found ourselves in bed. I didn't leave out a single detail, though the way Michellelee finally held up her hands let me know that I may have given her too much information.

"Okay, I get it," she said. "It started with him comforting you."

"Yes, and me comforting him."

"And it ended in bed."

"It never should have, but yes."

"More than once?"

"What do you mean?"

"Did it happen more than once?"

Slowly, I nodded.

She groaned. "It would've been hard, but I could've understood once, but more—"

"It always happened for the same reason," I sniffed. "It was never planned, and now I don't know what to do."

"I can tell you what to do: stay away from Jamal!" she shouted. Then, when she saw people looking at us, she lowered her voice. "What you did was jacked up."

"I know, but it's over. That's what you walked in on Tuesday. Jamal was telling me we couldn't see each other anymore." I paused and added, "And I agreed." That last part was a little lie. I mean, I did agree with Jamal in my head. I just didn't agree with him in my heart. "And I haven't heard from Jamal since, but I'm really scared 'cause I haven't heard from Emily either. Have you spoken to them?"

She shook her head. "No, I've been so busy with the election and the arsonist's trial. And frankly, I didn't want to see either of them until I decided what I was going to do."

"Well, thank you so much for not telling Emily, but I still feel like something's wrong." Then I spoke my greatest fear. "Michellelee, suppose Emily knows. Suppose she found out some way?"

Michellelee bobbed her head up and down, slowly, as if she were pondering my words. "That would be tough, but we're not going to go there yet. Let me find out what's going on before you start having a nervous breakdown."

"Okay."

"I'll give Em a call and see if she knows anything."

"Okay."

"And then, if she does, we'll figure it out, but if she doesn't, I'm not going to say anything."

I'd been prepared to get down on my knees right here and beg Michellelee to keep quiet. Then she said, "I'm not doing that for you. I'm doing that for Emily. Because I'm not trying to blow up her marriage . . ."

The way she let her words trail off made it sound as if Michellelee thought that's what I was trying to do. But I wasn't . . .

She said, "Now, Miriam . . . are you sure—"

I didn't even let her finish. "Yes, yes, yes! It's over."

"Good!" She gave a quick glance at her watch. "I'm sorry, but I've got to get back."

"Oh, I know, go. I just appreciate you meeting me."

"Wish it could've been longer." She stood. "But I promise I'm going to find out what's going on." She hooked her purse strap onto her shoulder and added, "I don't know how we're going to do it, but we'll find a way to be all right. We have to."

All I did was nod, because I didn't want to tell Michellelee how ridiculous it was for her to think that Emily would consider me anything but an enemy after this. If Emily knew or if she ever found out, I'd be lucky to escape with my life.

I was just about to get up, but Michellelee held out her hand, stopping me. Instead, she leaned over and gave me another hug. "Love you," she said.

"Mean it," I whispered back, because right about now, I wasn't sure that I deserved her love.

Then Michellelee sailed through the crowd again, stopping every few steps, leaving exactly the way she came in.

I sat alone for quite a long time, thinking. Could it be possible that even if Emily did find out, she could find forgiveness in her heart for me?

I didn't dare wish, I didn't dare hope. I just closed my eyes. But as much as I tried, I still couldn't pray.

35

Emily

The October breeze wrapped around me while the sand tickled my toes. It was chilly, but I strolled on the edge of the Pacific, taking in the sounds of Saturday in Santa Monica. I couldn't remember the last time I'd had an afternoon like this. It almost felt like a day off, though I had worked this morning. One client, just LaTonya.

Once that appointment ended at ten, I had to deal with my own life, and I'd come home. It didn't take me long to realize I couldn't spend another moment in that condo, staring at the antique-white walls. So I'd trudged outside to enjoy the afternoon in a way that Jamal and I loved, walking along the beach.

I blew out a long breath. Did every thought have to be about Jamal? Couldn't I think of one thing that was just about me? I hadn't always been in a couple, though it felt that way. Especially in the last four days.

Reaching into the pocket of my sweatpants, I pulled out my phone and clicked on the message icon. There were over twenty, though not one was from Jamal. I didn't know why that made me feel bad. He'd stopped calling, but he hadn't stopped texting.

He texted me about everything.

He texted to let me know where he was staying: *I'm at the Westin, Em. Remember? I love you and I'm so sorry.* As if mentioning where we spent our honeymoon was supposed to affect me.

He texted me about what he was doing: *I'm just sitting here, thinking of you. I love you and I'm so sorry.*

And now his latest text: *Em, sweetheart, I'll be in church tomorrow and I hope you'll be there. I love you and I'm so sorry.*

I shook my head. Now he wanted to go to church? Well, thanks for the warning because if he was going to be there, I wasn't.

Then I checked my visual voice mail. I had two messages from Pastor, and five from Michellelee. Funny, I hadn't heard from Michellelee since Tuesday when she was worried about Miriam. But since last night, she hadn't stopped calling. I deleted all the voice mails without listening to any and then stuffed the phone back into my pocket.

If Pastor was calling me so much, that meant Jamal was calling her. So if she was talking to him, she didn't need to talk to me. And Michellelee . . . I couldn't yet wrap my brain around Jamal's betrayal. So I didn't have extra room for what Miriam had done, or for Michellelee, because if she was really my friend, she should have told me what was going on.

Ugh! Now I was back in that ugly place and I needed to get away from this agony. But how? Go back to my apartment? No, I'd only cry there.

I was only a block away from my condo when I climbed up the sandy hill, slipped on my sneakers, and then sat on a bench facing the ocean. Stuffing my hands into my pockets, I gazed at the afternoon surf. The wind was really brisk, and on any other ordinary day I would have rushed to the warmth of my apartment. But my life no longer had ordinary days.

It was time to make some decisions so that I could move forward.

At least the biggest decision was made. I hadn't talked to Jamal, but no details of his affair would make me change my mind. I didn't care if Jamal had been cheating on me for one week, one month, one year, or the entire time that we'd been married. It didn't matter if he'd cheated with only Miriam or if he had a stable full of women who'd done his bidding. The only thing that mattered was that Jamal had cheated. And cheating put a period on our marriage.

The wind swooped down from over the ocean and wrapped around me, making me jump up and scurry across Ocean Boulevard. I rubbed my hands together to warm up a bit, then turned in to the courtyard of my building. I was digging into my purse for my keys, with my eyes down, when I bumped into someone.

"Excuse me," I said.

"That's okay, I have about eight other toes. I'll get along just fine with those."

Michellelee laughed, and I smiled, until I remembered.

"What're you doing here?" I asked without saying hello.

Her forehead crinkled. "You got a problem?"

"No problems. I just asked a question." And then I asked her again, "What're you doing here?"

"I'm here to see you. And why would you ask me that anyway? Or has it been so long since you've seen me that you've forgotten you love me?"

"Oh, I love you?" My eyebrows shot to the top of my forehead, the way my mother's always did when she disapproved of something. "Yeah, that's right. I love you probably about as much as you love me."

I pushed past her, and really, I wanted to say so much more. But the concierge was looking at us with curious eyes. Of course, he knew me, and he knew Michellelee. Not only was she there often, but she and Miriam had "no-call" privileges. They could come up to our condo without being announced.

So I said nothing else. When Michellelee followed me into the elevator, I didn't push her out, even though that's what I wanted to do.

"Do you want to tell me what's going on?" Michellelee asked.

I just stared at the elevator doors.

"You know you're acting like a child, right?"

I wanted to punch her in her face. I was acting like a child? After what she'd done to me? After what Miriam and Jamal had done? Every single one of them should've been happy that I *hadn't* behaved like a child.

She said, "This is not the Emily I know."

She was right about that. The Emily she'd known was gone. Her body had been pulled under by the tsunami of tears she'd shed since she'd found out the truth about her life.

When the elevator doors parted, I stomped off the elevator and Michellelee followed me inside and tossed her bag onto the sofa before she posted her hands on her hips. "What is your problem?" she asked, like she had a right to demand an answer from me.

"You want to know," I exploded. "My problem is you. My problem is having a friend who doesn't have my back."

"What are you talking about?" she asked, though now her words were softer and her hands slipped down to her side.

"Jamal and Miriam."

I watched her swallow.

"Yeah, I thought so. You know, don't you? Jamal. And. Miriam."

"Emily—"

"You knew they were having an affair and you didn't tell me."

She held up her hand. "Now wait a minute. It was not my place—"

"Oh, yes it was! If you were my friend, it was your place to tell me."

"Let me finish, Emily! It was not my place to tell you something that I wasn't sure about."

"So you suspected that they were together? When you told me that she was seeing someone, you suspected that it was Jamal?"

"Oh, come on, Emily," she said, throwing up her hands. "I suspected it was Jamal, but I was going to keep the secret from you, so I was only going to tell you half of it? How much sense does that make?"

Okay, she had a point.

"So," Michellelee said, "maybe now you can shut your mouth and listen."

I really didn't want to hear it, but I was trapped in my home with a woman who I knew wasn't going to leave until she had her say. So to get it over with, I bounced down onto the sofa, folded my arms, crossed my legs, and pouted. But I kept my mouth shut the way she'd asked.

"Thank. You." Michellelee took a breath. "I did not know. When I called you and told you that Miriam had a new man, I had no idea. I didn't suspect a thing until I went over to Miriam's house on Tuesday. Remember when we talked and I told you I was going over there because I hadn't heard from her?"

I didn't acknowledge her question.

Michellelee continued, "Anyway, I walked in and Jamal was there and Miriam looked like she'd been crying and there was this energy . . ."

She stopped when I inhaled deeply.

Then she said, "Everything in my head started clicking and when Jamal left, I asked Miriam if anything was going on and she said no."

"And you believed her?"

"No, I didn't. And I didn't know what I was going to do, but I wasn't going to come to you with just my suspicion. What kind of mess would that have started?"

"Turns out that your instincts were right."

"I just found that out, Emily. Just yesterday, I found out that what I suspected was true."

I unfolded my arms and legs.

"Miriam called me, 'cause she hadn't heard from you and she hadn't heard from Jamal."

I'd wondered if Jamal had left me and gone straight to Miriam.

"She said she called Jamal on Tuesday and got disconnected . . ." Michellelee paused and I could see the dots connecting in her mind. "You heard her call, huh?"

I nodded. "We were in Jamal's car and his phone rang. I saw it was Miriam, and I connected the call without thinking."

"And Miriam talked without thinking," Michellelee said.

"Yup, it was on Jamal's Bluetooth and I heard about their affair in surround sound."

Michellelee looked at me for a long moment, then sat down. "Honey, I'm really sorry about all of this."

I pressed my face into my hands. "I never thought I'd be in this situation. My best friend and my husband. This sounds like one of those cheap paperback novels, right?"

"Yeah, so, what's going on? What does Jamal say?"

"All he ever says is 'I love you.'"

She shrugged a little. "That's a good place to start."

"Really, that's the end for me. I don't need to talk to him, I don't need to hear a word he has to say."

"So he's not staying here?" She took a quick look around as if she was looking for some sign of my soon-to-be ex.

"No, I haven't seen him or talked to him since Tuesday. Not since I heard Miriam . . ." I squeezed my eyes shut, hoping to block out the sound of her voice.

"So, you haven't heard his side?"

My eyes popped open. "His side? There's no side. I'm one of those women who has an issue with my husband having an affair with my best friend."

"From what I understand from Miriam, it wasn't an ordinary affair."

I let those words settle in. "No ordinary affair, huh? I didn't know there were ordinary and unordinary affairs."

"Well, before I talked to Miriam yesterday, I would've agreed. But after listening to her, I gotta tell you, I'm mad as hell at her, but there's a little part of me, that . . ." She paused. "Now don't get upset, but I can see how it happened."

"What? What did Miriam say?"

Before I had even finished asking her, Michellelee was shaking her head. "No. You're not going to hear this from me. Not second-hand. You need to talk to Jamal." I rolled my eyes. "And you need to talk to Miriam," she had the nerve to add.

I laughed out loud at that one. "You really think I will ever be in a room with that woman again?"

"I hope so, because I'm telling you, it didn't go down the way you think. This isn't what it looks like, it isn't what it feels like."

"You're going to have to explain that to me."

"I can't."

"So, you're still keeping secrets."

"You know that's not what I'm doing. It's just not my place to tell you. You have to hear it from Jamal. You can't make decisions without knowing anything."

"I know enough."

"You don't know squat. All you know is one end of a short phone call."

I leaned back on the couch and once again assumed the position: crossed my arms, crossed my legs, and glared at her.

She shook her head. "Fine." She grabbed her purse and stood. "When you're ready to talk and ready to listen, call me, and I'll be right here."

I didn't say a word as she stomped toward the door. But then she turned back. "You need to fix this. You need to work this out with everyone."

"Are you kidding me? I'm the only one in this crazy foursome who didn't do anything."

"And you're the only one among us who is trained to understand people and trauma and tragedy." She paused as if she wanted her words to hang in the air. "Work it out, Emily. If there is anyone who can, it's you."

And then she walked out of my door, leaving me seething in the truth.

36

MIRIAM

I had been waiting and waiting and waiting. It had only been a little more than twenty-four hours, though it felt like twenty-four days.

Finally, I saw it. Michellelee's number on my caller ID. I grabbed the phone before it even had a chance to finish the first ring.

"Hi," I said with a cheer in my voice that I didn't feel.

"Hey, girl. Listen, if you can find someone to stay with the boys, let's get together tomorrow after church. We can do brunch."

Well, first of all, I wasn't going to church. And secondly, I couldn't possibly wait to hear if Michellelee had spoken to Emily.

"Uh, I'm not going to church," I said.

"Oh . . . kay." She asked, "Does this have anything to do with what's going on?"

Yes, that was one issue, the other being I still didn't see any purpose in going to church. But all I said was, "No, I have something to do." I crossed my fingers the way I used to when I was little. Even though I didn't feel close to the Lord right now, it wasn't like I wanted to take any chances. And lying about anything that had to do with God couldn't be a good thing. "Did you talk to Emily?" I asked, needing to get to the point.

"Yeah, I did. I'm just leaving her place now. But I was really thinking that we should talk in person and I'm on my way to meet up with Craig, so I can't come over to you."

"That's okay," I said. "And anyway . . . Please don't make me wait, Michellelee. I have to know. I can't eat, I can't sleep . . ."

"Okay, okay, I get it." She breathed. "You're right, she knows."

The phone slipped right out of my hands. "Oh, my God! Oh, my God! Oh, my God!" I said as I picked it up. "Does she hate me?"

"Yeah, that pretty much sums it up."

"Oh, God!" I stumbled over to my bed, not able to stand any longer.

"But it's only because she's really hurt," Michellelee explained.

"I'm just so sorry." I really was, but there was this other side of me. The other side that pushed me to ask the next question. "So, what's going on with Emily and Jamal?"

I had to ask, because I couldn't imagine Emily ever forgiving Jamal. Faithfulness was important to her, just like it was to me. At least before I became unfaithful.

"Well, it's not good right now," Michellelee said. "He's not there with her."

"Where is he?"

"Miriam, I'm not going to talk to you about this. Just like I told Emily, it's not my place. What's going on between the two of them needs to stay between the two of them."

"Of course," I said, though the wheels in my head were churning so fast it was hard for me to keep up with my own thoughts. "I was just asking."

"Yeah, I know. But I really believe that with the right amount of time, the right amount of space, and lots of prayer, they can work this out."

No, they can't! I shouted in my mind. Michellelee knew that about Emily, too. How many conversations had we had where we all said we would never stay with a man who cheated?

Michellelee said, "She gave up a lot to be with him. She's not going to let this break them apart."

If the circumstances were different, I would've asked Michellelee if she wanted to take a bet on that.

She continued, "And Jamal is not going to let her go."

He wasn't going to have a choice, but of course I kept my mouth shut.

She kept on, "Like I said, Emily is really hurt, but her heart will soften. She'll open up to Jamal, and maybe even to you."

Now, that was never going to happen. Even if Emily could stand seeing me, there was no way I could face her. I couldn't imagine the day when I'd be able to look into her eyes.

"Well, I don't know if she'll ever talk to me again, but I really hope that she and Jamal will get back together."

There was a pause, and then Michellelee said, "Do you mean that?"

Oh, my God! Had Michellelee heard something in my voice?

"Yes, I mean it," I said in a tone that let Michellelee know I was insulted by her question. "I don't want Emily hurt." Now, that was the truth. "And I really feel bad for the part I had in all of this," I added, meaning every word.

"Good, because like I said, this can be worked out, but the thing is, you and Jamal can never, and I mean never, make that mistake again."

"I know."

"I'm serious, Miriam." Michellelee spoke to me as if I was a child. "Whatever chemistry the two of you had needs to burn out."

"I know that. I get it. It's out!"

"Because—"

"You don't have to say it again! I feel bad enough."

Michellelee said, "Okay, I know. I'm sorry. Just pray for them."

"Okay, well, I know you have to get going." I was so ready to hang up. "Thanks for letting me know."

"I'll check on you in a couple of days."

I was pacing before I even clicked off the phone, already thinking about the next call. Michellelee had told me to pray, but as I stared at my cell, the only words I could gather were, "Please, God."

Then I pressed the contact number for Jamal. It rang, and went to voice mail.

"Jamal, this is Miriam. Please call me."

I hung up and pressed his number again. What I'd just learned had given me newfound courage. I knew Emily. This was the end of their relationship for her.

And her end could be my beginning. Was anything wrong with that?

So I called him again. And again. And I left him another message. And then another. I called him until I lost count. I called him until he finally answered.

"Miriam, is everything okay?"

The only other person who had given me this much joy just by the sound of his voice was Chauncey. I smiled for the first time in days.

"Yes, I'm calling because I'm concerned about you."

He paused, and I wondered if he was sorry he'd answered. He said, "There's nothing to be concerned about."

"I just found out that Emily knows."

Another pause, then, "She was in the car with me when you called . . . the other day."

So that's what happened! "Oh, God. I just wanted to warn you. I'm so sorry, Jamal."

"I know. But like I said before, this isn't your fault."

I took a breath and inhaled more audacity. "I understand that you're not home."

He didn't respond.

"Well"—I took another deep breath—"you're more than welcome to stay here, with me. And the boys."

There was nothing but silence on his end of the phone, and on mine, too. Except for the thundering beat of my heart.

Finally, he said, "No. I'm fine where I am."

Where are you? I wanted to ask, though I was pretty sure I knew the answer to that.

I said, "Just know that you can stay here." I added, "You're welcome here."

More silence.

"Thank you," he said. "Look, Miriam, I've got to go."

"Okay, but would you mind if I called you? Just to check on you."

"There's no need for that."

He was trying to shut me down, but it wasn't going to happen. "Yes, there is. Because you need someone now. Just like how you were there for me, I want to be here for you. Remember, a soft place to land. Remember?" I asked, hoping that he'd recall how he felt when he was with me.

"Yes."

Was that a smile in his voice?

"Well, your soft place is here," I told him.

"All right."

I had the feeling he was agreeing so that he could hang up. But that didn't matter. He would think about my words, and he would come to me.

Jamal hung up first and I held on to the connection for a little while longer. In my head, this was so, so, so wrong. But my heart was winning.

I crawled onto my bed and laid my head where Jamal had laid his not so long ago. I imagined the day when he would be back. Because now, I was absolutely sure that Jamal would be back.

All I had to do was see him again, and once we were together, that thing that always happened between us would happen again.

Tears came to my eyes, but I couldn't say it was only because I was sad. "I'm sorry." I sent those words into the atmosphere. "I'm really sorry."

But I had to do what I had to do.

37

Emily

Thirty hours. All I'd heard for the last thirty hours was Michelle-lee's voice in my head.

It wasn't an ordinary affair.

I punched my pillow, then nudged my head into the crevice, but after just seconds, I turned over again.

It wasn't an ordinary affair.

What did that mean? Not that it made any difference, because an affair by any other name still made me walk out the door.

I rolled over, thinking that resting on my back would work. But after a few minutes, I flipped onto my stomach.

It wasn't an ordinary affair.

Pushing myself up, I leaned against the headboard. Going to bed early was supposed to help. I was exhausted since I hadn't slept at all last night. But tonight was just like last night. Another sleepless night that I couldn't afford.

It wasn't an ordinary affair.

I tossed back the duvet and scooted out of the bed. The T-shirt I was wearing would have to do; I only slipped on leggings so that my legs wouldn't be bare. I grabbed my wallet, my cell, then my trench coat, and in less than five minutes, I was in my car.

Maybe if I had some answers, I could get some sleep.

I drove without thinking, turning the radio to KJLH, but when the Sunday-night guest pastor started talking about the rate of divorce among Christians, I pressed the power button, making the car silent.

I sped onto the 405 and in the light traffic, I exited in less than twenty minutes. Then, a turn onto Century and not a minute later, I hardly slowed down as I swung my car into the driveway of the Westin.

My car was still running when I marched past the valet.

"How long will you be?" the attendant asked.

"Not long. The keys are in the ignition," I shouted over my shoulder, still moving.

Inside the lobby, I kept marching, knowing exactly where to go. After spending our honeymoon here, we came for weekend retreats. Even though it was just a few miles from home, this hotel was special to us . . . at least it had been special, until now.

An elevator was already open; thank God I didn't have to wait. Jamal was only on the third floor; thank Him again, the ride up wasn't long. And he was in Room 301; more praises, I didn't have to walk far.

Because at any of those points, I could've changed my mind.

I raised my hand and hesitated for only a moment before I banged on his door. I banged like I was the FBI. I banged like I wanted to kick the door in and then kick him.

"What the hell?"

I heard Jamal before I saw him, before he swung the door open and stared at me with wide eyes.

"Em . . ."

With just one long stride, I was in his room and in his face. And with both hands, I shoved him. He stumbled back.

"Emily!" He held his hands high as if he was surrendering, or maybe he didn't want to take the chance of shoving me back.

This hadn't been my plan. Actually, I didn't have one when I'd left home. I'd just wanted answers. But seeing him made my rage rise and I shoved him again.

"Emily!"

I shoved him again and again, until he hit the bed and fell back. I sprung on top of him, straddled him, and noticed for the first time that he wore only a T-shirt and gym shorts. I tore at his shorts, roughly yanking them from his body.

His eyes were wide and wild, probably just like mine.

I moved quickly, not giving him time to react. In not too many moments after, I was naked, too, at least the bottom half of me. I didn't know what happened to my clothes. All I knew was that I had to climb on top.

"Ahhhh," he cried out the moment we connected.

I was silent.

I moved fast and I moved furiously, riding him like he was a prized possession. He tried to maneuver, tried to shift, but I wouldn't let him. He leaned up and tried to pull me down, as if he wanted to kiss me. But I stayed upright, keeping my lips a mile away from his.

Jamal could hardly keep up with me. My breathing became shallow; I couldn't get enough air. Sensations overwhelmed me like never before. The tingling began in my toes and spread through every inch of me. I felt like a hostage to the pleasure.

It didn't take long.

Probably sixty seconds for him, and Jamal's moans filled the room.

Probably sixty-one seconds for me, and I screamed from my soul.

We collapsed, but I rolled right off my husband. In the past, I would have stayed in that moment, on top of him, still connected and enjoying the afterburn. But tonight, I'd just had some of the best sex of my life and I couldn't wait to get up and get out.

I made my way to the bathroom, slammed the door behind me, and leaned against the wall. I inhaled a couple of deep, deep breaths until I gathered myself, then grabbed a washcloth. I washed without looking in the mirror, as if I was ashamed of the way I'd just behaved. These weren't the actions of a proper Southern girl. This was more like the rage of a scorned wife.

The rage was still burning inside me when I came out of the bathroom. Jamal was sitting on the edge of the bed and my eyes bored through him as I stomped across the room. I snatched my leggings from the floor and slid into them.

"Emily!" He reached out and when I backed away, he frowned as if that was the last reaction he expected.

I stood, doing my best to press down my fury. Then I said, "I have two questions."

He nodded. "Anything. Ask me anything, because I want to explain everything."

I gave him a chance to stew a bit in the silence before I said, "Does any of this have to do with me being white?"

"What?" he asked, as if I'd spoken in another language.

I repeated my question.

"No," he said, jumping up from the bed. "Why would you ever think that?"

"Because you had a problem when we first met."

"That was years ago."

"Or because Miriam had a problem and my parents had a problem and Nellie had a problem and black women we pass on the street have a problem, and white men who see us together have a problem—"

"Their problem, never ours. For all these years, I have loved you. Just you, because you're you."

As if I didn't hear him, I added, "Or maybe because me being white is the only reason I could come up with for you breaking my heart." I bit my bottom lip to stop it from trembling. "Because you were supposed to love me."

At first, it looked like Jamal didn't have an answer. He took a step forward, I took a step back. He said, "I do, Emily. I really love you."

I shook my head, not because I didn't believe him, but because I didn't want to.

"The second question."

He swallowed, but nodded.

I asked, "How many times?"

"What?"

I didn't repeat my question, knowing he'd heard me. I hoped that my stare burned right through him, and after a second, he turned away. "Emily," he whispered.

"That's not an answer."

He hesitated for a moment. "Why do you want to know?"

"Because one time means one thing. And many times means many things."

When he lowered his eyes again, he'd answered without speaking. Michellelee had been wrong. This *had* been an ordinary affair.

Jamal still hadn't said anything, but I wasn't going to let him get away with that. I wanted him to tell me, to say it out loud, and then watch the pain travel from my heart to the rest of me.

I waited. When he said nothing, I asked, "Did it start before Chauncey passed away?"

"No!" he exclaimed. "It was after his funeral. It was only a few times."

I swallowed. "But . . . it was more than once."

He nodded.

Why hadn't he told me it was just one time? He was a cheater, didn't that make him a liar, too? A lie might have saved us. That truth had truly just destroyed us.

I'd heard enough. Actually, I'd heard too much. This meeting hadn't changed my mind, it just hurt my heart.

Taking another quick glance around, I found my trench coat dumped by the door, though I didn't remember dropping it. Before I could reach it, Jamal lifted my coat and folded it over his arm.

"I want you to stay."

"Why?"

"Because we haven't talked."

I snatched my coat from him. "We've talked enough," I said.

"But I thought you came over here to—"

"To what?"

"To work this out." He glanced at the bed.

"Oh, don't get confused. That was nothing but ex sex."

"What?"

"The moment you got in bed with Miriam, I became your ex. I only came over here to make sure, but I'm going to see Carl Bell tomorrow and, hopefully, he'll be able to get us divorced as quickly as we got married."

I reached for the door, but Jamal tried to block me.

"No!" he shouted.

I shoved him again, the way I'd shoved him before. This time, I meant it. He fell against the wall, and I flung the door open. Running into the hall, I looked from one end to the other. There was no way I could take the elevator. Jamal would be right behind me.

Dashing to the Exit sign, I grabbed the doorknob to the stairwell, then I looked over my shoulder.

Just like I thought, there was Jamal.

38

Miriam

I stopped at the edge of the hotel's driveway, turned off the lights, then cut the engine.

Sitting at least two hundred feet from the front door, I asked myself again, what was I doing here? This was so not me, yet here I was.

The clock was ticking toward midnight, but the Westin felt alive with a kind of a midday energy.

Since I was down at the far end of the hotel, with my headlights off, no one noticed me. That worked; I didn't want anyone coming over, asking questions I couldn't answer.

Last night, when I'd put this plan together, it'd made sense. It hadn't been hard to figure out where Jamal was staying. And I'd confirmed that with one phone call. I'd asked for him, was connected, but hung up when he answered.

Then I put everything else in place. I'd called the sitter and even practiced what I would say to Jamal when I told him that I was in his hotel. I figured he'd be shocked, but he'd come down, and in some quiet corner of the lobby, I'd tell him how I felt, convince him it was right, and that maybe this was even our destiny.

It was all worked out in my head, but not totally in my heart, because of Emily. But what was I supposed to do? Especially now that Emily had kicked Jamal out, was I supposed to walk away? If I found a million dollars on the street, I wouldn't just step over it because the money wasn't mine to begin with.

It made complete sense.

At least, it had last night.

But now it wasn't so clear as I sat in the dark. Now my arguments only felt weak, pathetic, and a whole lot desperate.

I sighed. I couldn't sit here any longer debating with myself. I'd already wasted so much time. On the way over, I'd stopped at Starbucks and then I got this incredible urge to go to the movies alone, though I couldn't tell you what I saw.

Now my time had run out; either I had to do what I came to do, or I had to go home.

Turning on my headlights, I revved up the engine, shifted to drive, and just as I eased my foot off the brake, two people ran out of the hotel, stopping in the spotlight that shone from my headlights.

A man. A woman.

Jamal. Emily.

My eyes and mouth opened wide in horror, though I wasn't the only one. The people who stood in front of the hotel, waiting for their cars or sliding out of cabs, stepped to the side, not wanting to get involved.

It played like a silent movie in front of me. Emily's face was drenched with tears, and Jamal was crying, too. She yanked away from his grasp, he pulled her back into his arms.

I'd been frozen in place at first, but then I shut off the lights and the ignition, then scooted down in the seat. I kept my eyes right above the steering wheel so that I could still see it all.

An attendant walked over and gestured with his hands as if he was asking if everything was okay. Emily and Jamal nodded together and waved the man away. Then Jamal gently pulled Emily to the corner. Now they were partially hidden by a large shrub. Emily's back was to me, but I could see Jamal.

Jamal cradled Emily's face, and I watched as he begged her with his heart. She shook her head, and my heart pounded.

Her objections didn't stop him. Jamal pleaded with everything inside of him, with a love that I'd only seen once. He begged with a love in his eyes that I could see even in the dark. A love that I'd only seen . . . from Chauncey.

That was when my first tear fell.

Jamal wrapped his arms around Emily and led her into the hotel.

I didn't let a second pass before I turned on the ignition. But I didn't turn on the lights and I didn't shift the gear into drive. Instead, I backed the van out, an illegal move that was in line with everything I'd done recently.

I waited until I was a block away from the hotel before I turned on the lights. And then I aimed my car toward home. Slowly. I had to drive slow; what else could I do when my tears had turned me into a blind woman?

What I'd just seen was now a loop that ran over and over in my mind. Clearly, I needed to change my plans. But before I could think, I had to cry.

39

Emily

Yo!"

I sniffed. "Hey, Red," I said into my cell.

"Where I need to be at?" Michellelee said.

Even though tears were still seeping from my eyes, I chuckled. Michellelee, the so articulate, so polished anchorwoman who used the King's English all the time, cracked me up when she went into her version of what she called Ebonics. "What do you mean?" I asked her.

"You're calling me after midnight . . ."

Quickly, I scanned the dashboard. Dang!

Michellelee continued, "And you're crying. So, where I need to be at?"

I laughed out loud this time. "I'm sorry. I didn't realize it was so late and I was trying not to cry. I just needed my friend."

"Where are you?"

"In my car."

"What's going down?"

"Nothing, really."

"Please don't make me ask twenty questions. It's too damn late for that. Just come over to my place," Michellelee said.

"I don't really want to bother you."

"Girl, please."

"Is Craig there?" I asked,

"Yeah, but you don't have to worry about him 'cause I already gave him some, so he's knocked out. He won't wake up till morning, when it's time to get some more."

Only Michellelee could keep me laughing when all I wanted to do was cry.

She said, "So come over here. How long will it take you?"

"About three minutes," I said, looking up at the twenty-story tower where Michellelee lived. "I'm right downstairs."

"Heifer, get up here!"

She hung up on me and I wiped away the tears that were left over and slid out of my car. I'd found a premium space right in front of her building, which was something that didn't happen in the middle of the night. Especially not a Sunday night.

When I stepped into the building, the concierge motioned for me to go right up and I figured Michellelee had already called down.

I may have had the condo on the beach, but Michellelee's eighteenth-floor apartment in the Wilshire high-rise paid homage to all that was fabulous about Los Angeles. The panoramic views of the Hollywood Hills were postcard perfect, even on the foggiest of days. And the Hollywood sign reminded me just how special this city was.

Though it was after midnight, Michellelee greeted me in full makeup, with her weave flowing down her back. If she wanted to, she could have gone straight from her bed to the studio. The thing was, she always went to bed like this when Craig was in town. It was a lesson from her grandmother, who told her that you needed to look your best at all times in case your husband woke up in the middle of the night and wanted to have sex.

When Michellelee had first told me and Miriam this when we

were at USC, we'd cracked up. But when I realized that Michellelee truly practiced this going-to-bed-looking-like-a-princess, I'd laughed harder. At any other time, I would have made some joke about her looking like a star at midnight. But I didn't have a joke in me tonight.

Michellelee's greeting was a hug, and I held on to her tightly. When she put her forefinger to her lips, I nodded, then I kicked off my shoes and we tiptoed across the pure white plush carpet.

Everything about Michellelee was over the top, and her apartment was no different. The guest bedroom, with its four-poster mahogany bed and gold-brocade drapes, had the feel that royalty would be arriving soon.

She flicked on the soft light, closed the door behind us, then flopped onto the bed. She patted a space next to her and I crawled onto the alpaca fur bedspread.

"So, what's up?" my friend said, without any ceremony.

"I saw Jamal tonight."

"Really?" When I nodded, she asked, "Did he come home?"

"No, I went to him. I couldn't sleep, I had so many questions, so I went to get some answers."

"Good! Finally. You talked to him."

"Not really, not much."

"What happened?"

I stayed silent, and that was all Michellelee needed. She busted out laughing. "Good," she said once her laughter had diminished to just a chuckle. "Sex is always a great place to start."

I gave her a sideways glance before I turned to her window. "I'm filing for divorce."

"What?" She sat straight up, as if my words were shocking.

I nodded. "I can't do it. It's not in me to stay."

"I can't believe this. So Jamal is going along with this?"

I shrugged. "What can he do? He saw tonight that he really

can't stop me." I told Michellelee the whole story. How I'd run out of Jamal's room and down the staircase, the whole time hearing his footsteps behind me. He caught me in the lobby, but I'd broken away from his grasp. Jamal had been determined, though, and he came after me. And I'd had to live my drama in front of a whole bunch of strangers, something a good Southern girl should never do.

I continued, "He just kept telling me that he was sorry and that he loved me. He said he could fix this."

"That's what I'm talking about."

I shook my head. "If Craig cheated on you, you would be out. I know you, Michellelee. You would leave."

"That's what all women say." She waved her hand. "But here's the thing. No one ever knows what they'll do until it happens to them. And if you take a situation like this. This is so—"

"Sad," I finished for her. "But there's no way I can give Jamal a pass once he committed adultery with my best friend."

"Can we let the record show that Jamal slept with Miriam."

"What do you mean?"

"Whenever you talk about this, that's where your focus is."

"Well, that's what happened."

"Can you change your focus just a little? To you and Jamal? I mean, I'm no psychologist"—she paused and I smirked—"but at some point, in order to heal, you have to get past the beginning and at least move to the middle before you get to the end."

"No," I said, shaking my head. "I don't need the middle. The end is good enough for me."

"I don't know how you can divorce Jamal without making any effort. What about counseling? Or at least a cooling-off period."

"What part of 'I'm getting a divorce' don't you understand? I will never be one of those women who allows herself to be walked over by a man."

"Whoa. Not sure that's what's going on here."

"That's what it feels like. And don't tell me that's not how it feels. You don't have my heart."

"No, I'm not invalidating your feelings. I'm just saying that you shouldn't make decisions when you're in such an emotional place."

"There's no need to delay the inevitable."

"I think the reason you won't give yourself time is that you know Jamal will get to you and you might change your mind."

"Look!"

"Okay," she said, throwing up her hands. "Well, I'm your girl and I'll always support you."

"I know that."

"Even when you're wrong."

I shook my head.

"And can I say one more thing?"

"No."

Michellelee ignored me. "You and Jamal have been married a long time, and you gave up a lot to be together."

I nodded. "That's why it never should've happened."

"I agree, but that's why you can't let it fall apart."

Shaking my head, I said, "Don't make it sound like it's my fault. This is all Jamal. Remember?"

"Yeah, I remember, 'cause you ain't neva gonna let anyone forget. And yes, what Jamal did was pretty bad. Foul, really. Probably the worst thing he's ever done in his life."

I studied Michellelee's face, knowing there was some kind of punchline coming.

She said, "But I don't think anyone is as bad as the worst thing they've ever done. No one should be defined that way."

"I would think you'd be on my side."

"I am, Em. That's why I'm saying all this. I've known Jamal for a long time, too, and I know his heart. And you know it, too; you've just forgotten because you're hurt."

I leaned back on the pillows and Michellelee did the same thing on her side of the bed.

"You really surprise me," I said to her. "I really thought you'd be leading the charge to divorce court."

She shook her head. "Girl, some women are good for telling another woman to leave her man. First of all, those women are usually man-less, and if they do have a man, they ain't got a clue. You'll never hear me say some foolishness like that, 'cause unless I'm sleeping under that couple's bed, I don't know everything. I only know what I've been told."

Some time went by and then Michellelee said, "You can lie here and find all kinds of reasons to leave. But it takes the same effort to come up with reasons to stay."

"You know you're getting on my nerves, right?" I told her.

"That must mean I'm making progress."

"You're not. You're just wasting syllables. I already told you, this is the end. Game over, and I don't want to talk about this anymore."

After a couple of wonderful, quiet minutes, Michellelee said, "Can I ask you just one more thing?"

"No."

"You hardly mention Miriam."

My feet began to shake and I knew that soon that tremble would rise all up in me. "Can't talk about her, because I don't want to think about death."

Michellelee laughed, but then her laugh turned to a giggle, then a chuckle, and then nothing. She tilted her head, looking at me as if she wasn't so sure if I'd been kidding. "That's a joke, right?"

"No."

"Yes, it is."

"Okay, whatever you say." I closed my eyes, letting Michellelee know our conversation was over. But I could feel her eyes on me, wondering. Then she lay down beside me.

Now I felt bad. She was worried, and she'd stay with me all night, probably not even closing her eyes. She'd probably check my purse in the morning, making sure that I didn't leave with a butcher knife or two.

Still, though, I snuggled under the softness of the fur blanket. It was too bad for Michellelee, because I could already tell this was going to be some of the best sleep I'd had in many nights.

40

MIRIAM

I called Michellelee, asking for one simple favor.

"I need you to set up one of our lunches. With you, me . . . and Emily. Can you do it?"

In the silent seconds that followed, I could hear Michellelee's surprise. Then she said, "Are you sure that's a good idea?"

Closing my eyes, I took a deep breath and remembered the scene that had taken place in front of me on Sunday night. I had to do what I had to do. "It's a great idea. Emily and I have to have it out . . ."

"Have it out?"

"I mean"—I stayed calm even though I could hear Michellelee breathing heavily—"Em and I need to really talk. Even you said that," I reminded her.

"Yeah, but I talked to her, and I'm thinking that you might need to wait a couple of weeks or years. A decade might even work better."

I hoped Michellelee meant that as a joke, though I wasn't sure. "Look, I've been thinking a lot about what you said . . . about us being sisters," I said.

"Yeah."

"You were right. No matter what."

"Which makes your betrayal even worse," Michellelee reminded me.

"I know that. But we're going to have to do this one day, and doing it now is better for her and for me."

"Do you have some kind of death wish?"

"That's not funny, Michellelee."

"Okay, I'm sorry. But meeting with Emily right now is kinda like that."

"Look, I know Em wants to move forward." At least, that was my hope. I continued, "And in order to move forward, sometimes you've got to take care of stuff in your past."

"That's what I'm saying," Michellelee exclaimed. "The stuff that went down with you and Jamal may not be far enough in the past. So like I said, wait a decade, or now that I think about it, a century might even be better."

I filled my cheeks with air, then blew out a long breath.

I guessed Michellelee could hear my frustration. She said, "Look, I'm not really kidding. Emily is one pissed-off white chick."

"That's why we need to do this," I said. "Letting time sit between us won't help. So we need to do this and we can both move on."

She paused for so long, I thought we'd gotten disconnected. "You sound like you're the psychologist."

"I just know what I know."

More hesitation. "Oh . . . kay. What're you thinking? One of our morning breakfasts?"

Even though she couldn't see me, I shook my head. "No, 'cause we're gonna need you there, and whenever we get together during the week, you're called away. So, what about Saturday?"

"Yeah, that's a good move, 'cause I'm gonna need to be there to keep her off you."

Again, I thought it was a joke, but I wasn't sure.

"One other thing," I said. "Don't tell Emily that I'm gonna be there."

She sucked her teeth. "What? You want to blindside her?"

"I'm not going to blindside her or do anything else. But do you think she's really going to show up if she knows I'll be there?"

After a moment, Michellelee agreed. She hung up with promises to call me right back. And just when I'd put the chicken in the oven for my sons' dinner, she called.

"We're on for Saturday, but be ready, Miriam . . ."

"You didn't tell her?"

"No."

I thanked Michellelee for that and then told her that I was looking forward to Saturday, even though I wasn't.

For the next three days, as I went about my life, I thought about my children, and I thought about Jamal. I thought about him over and over.

And when I wasn't thinking about him, I thought about what I was going to say to his wife.

41

Emily

My instinct was to say no when Michellelee called inviting me to lunch. But then she went into her spiel about how I needed to get out from those four walls in my house, and how I really needed a friend.

All of that was true, but it was her last point that moved me.

When I made the left onto Via Marina, I pushed thoughts of my troubled marriage out of my mind. For just an hour, I would be free. Free in a way I hadn't been in the eleven days since I'd found out about Jamal and Miriam.

Miriam!

Every time she came into my consciousness, I pressed her down—I could only deal with one rage at a time. And since Jamal was the one always in my face—or trying to be—I had to annihilate him first.

I stepped quickly into the restaurant, but then I slowed down and salivated at the dozens of cheesecake slices that put inches on my hips just by looking. There were at least six that I could've ordered as my entrée, and I was trying to make my decision when the hostess greeted me.

"Oh, sorry," I said. "That's just my favorite sight."

She laughed. "I understand. Do you know how hard it is to work here?"

"I'm meeting someone," I told her. "Michellelee."

"She's already here," the hostess gushed.

I smiled as the hostess talked about my friend as if she were a major star. Michellelee could run for office if she wanted to.

We stepped past table after table, moving toward the back. Finally I spotted my friend, all the way in the corner. I guessed this was one of those days where Michellelee wanted more privacy, because most of the time, she was in the center of the room—to see and be seen.

"Hey, girl." She stood as she hugged me.

I held her just as tight. "Hey, yourself," I said. It had been too long since we'd gotten out together like this.

I was just about to dump my bag in the chair across from hers, but there was already a purse there. My first thought was that the bag belonged to Michellelee, but then I saw the Louis Vuitton that she always carried was on the table.

I measured the situation, adding it all up, and just as I was about to come to my own conclusion, I heard the voice behind me.

"Hi, Emily."

I swung around, and she was just lucky that my hand hadn't been balled up into a fist, because I would have made contact and knocked her out. I glared at Miriam, but then I turned the heat of my stare onto Michellelee.

"I thought this was going to be just the two of us."

Michellelee put her hand on her chest, feigning innocence. "I never said that."

"You didn't tell me that she was coming."

"You didn't ask."

There had to be steam coming out of my ears. Once again, I was learning that Michellelee couldn't be trusted.

Michellelee said, "Em, you guys need to talk."

"You know what she did to me."

Behind me, Miriam put in her two cents. "That's why we need to talk."

Once again, I whipped around, and this time, my finger was right in her face. "You don't get to say a word," I growled. "Not a single word."

She stood there quietly, though she didn't look the least bit intimidated. I was impressed. I wouldn't ever want to be the mistress in the path of a scorned wife.

Back at Michellelee, I said, "I can't believe you did this."

"I did it because it needed to be done."

I swung my purse over my shoulder, missing Miriam's jaw by two inches. "I'm getting out of here."

Michellelee grabbed my arm, and then dipped her head slightly as if she were trying to hide. "Can you do me a favor?" Her eyes darted to the tables around us, then she whispered, "I'm a big celebrity, so can you not make a scene? I mean, I don't want to see this on TMZ." Her lips hardly moved when she said, "Just sit your narrow behind down and hear her out."

I didn't budge, and shot Michellelee a look that was meant to kill. But that didn't seem to mean a thing to her.

She kept on, "Just listen and after that, if you want to walk out, then it's on you. But give her at least a couple of minutes. Do it for the sake of us once being sisters."

"Oh, yeah, I forgot"—I turned and shot daggers at Miriam—"it must've been that thing she did with my husband that made me forget about our sister thing."

"I agree," Michellelee said. "What Miriam did was a low-down, dirty move."

If I hadn't been in the middle of a fight, I would have busted out laughing at the shocked hurt on Miriam's face. Good!

Well, now that Miriam was exactly where I wanted her, I snapped, "Fine!" Actually, I wanted to see if Michellelee had any more jabs to throw at our friend. I flopped down into the chair, crossed my arms, and bored my eyes into Miriam.

Michellelee had been sitting across from me, but she moved her bag and slid her chair closer. She scooted so close, she was almost in my lap. I guessed she wanted to be near enough to stop me from throwing punches.

That was a smart move.

As we sat without saying a word, the waitress tiptoed over, as if she had watched from the sidelines and wasn't quite sure she wanted to be the one to serve us. The young woman whispered, "Do you want to place your drink orders?"

"Just water for me," I mumbled without taking my eyes off Miriam.

At first, neither Miriam nor Michellelee said anything, until the waitress cleared her throat.

Then Michellelee said, "Bring three waters and we'll order in a minute," and waved the young girl away.

More silent seconds, and then Miriam laid her hands flat on the table as if she wanted me to see that she was unarmed. Then she looked me straight in my eyes. She had a strong confidence that I'd never seen. Had being with Jamal given her that? That thought made me nauseated.

Miriam said, "Really, there's not a lot for me to say except that I'm very, very sorry."

She paused as if she was giving me a turn to speak. But Miriam needed to understand that this was going to be her monologue and not our dialogue.

After a few seconds, she continued, "The reason I asked Michelle-lee to arrange this . . ."

I squinted at Michellelee once again, wanting to smack her, but I had to handle one fight at a time.

"I really wanted to tell you I'm sorry," Miriam said again. "But I also wanted to get together because I wanted to explain other things to you."

"Like what? The details? You want to tell me exactly what you and Jamal did? You want me to know the exact dates and times and positions?" I shook my head. "I don't need to know anything else. I know enough."

"Well, you don't know that this had nothing to do with love."

"Oh, I know that. I know my husband doesn't love you."

Two points! Miriam didn't flinch, but she blinked. Hard. And rapidly for a couple of moments. I'd hurt her with words. That's all I had. Just words. And I hoped those words caused her half the pain that she'd caused me.

But then she kept on as if I hadn't spoken. "This wasn't about love, this was about loss." She let those words settle. "When Chauncey died, I needed someone to talk to."

"Oh, that's a good reason." My voice was thick with sarcasm. "You're blaming this on me not being there for you."

"I'm not blaming you, but you weren't there," she said, seemingly unfazed by my attitude. "You need to understand that even if you'd been there every day, this would've happened anyway."

Okay, those two points I'd scored a minute ago needed to be taken off the board. Because those points couldn't compare to the ten points she'd just scored with those few words.

"I'm telling you the truth," Miriam said. "I owe you that."

She waited for me to nod or say something, but I didn't move.

"I needed someone to talk to—I mean really talk to. I knew that

I could talk to Michellelee, and even with you working, I knew that you would've listened to me all night if I had called.

"But the thing was, I couldn't talk to you"—Miriam shook her head—"not the way I could talk to Jamal. I could talk to Jamal about Chauncey in a way that I couldn't with anyone else. No one knew my husband like Jamal and when we talked, I felt as if Chauncey was right there with me. I didn't feel so much loss when Jamal was around."

She paused as if she wanted me to say something; I said nothing.

Miriam said, "Being intimate was never our intent."

I didn't want to flinch, but I did.

She continued, "It began when I started crying one day and Jamal was comforting me and it happened."

My plan was to let this be her soliloquy, but I couldn't help it. "You know, I've heard that before. That *this* just happens. That clothes *just* fell off, and people didn't know *what* hit them. So let's just say it went down . . . just . . . like . . . that." I placed my arms on the table and leaned forward, so close to Miriam that I could smell the mint-scented fragrance of her toothpaste.

"So how does it happen *again*, Miriam? How do you fall into bed with your best friend's husband *again*? Were you crying *again*? And he came to your rescue *again*?"

She looked down for a moment. "There was never a time when it was planned." Now she glanced up. "But it was always wanted. Jamal got me through the days so that I could sleep at night."

Okay, I was beginning to hate myself. Because she was telling the truth, and her truth did nothing except hurt me.

Miriam went on, "I'm not justifying anything. I'm explaining because I think you should know."

"Why?"

"Because I know you. If we never had this meeting, you would definitely leave Jamal."

It made me livid that she knew me so well. Better than Michelle-lee, apparently.

She said, "But now hearing me, you and Jamal have a chance. And you need that chance because he loves you."

I smirked.

"Now, you're gonna have to think about what I've said. And you're gonna come to understand that it was horrible, it was a mistake, it shouldn't have happened, but there was a reason."

I crossed my arms once again and stared at her so hard that she finally had to look away.

Miriam waited for a moment. "That's it. It was never about sex, it wasn't even about lust, it certainly wasn't about"—her voice got softer—"love. Like I said, it had everything to do with loss."

I dropped my arms. "So you've had your say now, Miriam. And you know what?" I paused because there was no way I was going to cry in front of her. "I still want to choke the life out of you and my husband. I still hurt."

"I will always be sorry for that," she said softly.

The waitress came back asking if we were ready to order. The stare I gave her made her scurry away.

When we were alone, I asked, "So, you went through all of this just to say that? You could have just called me."

"You wouldn't have taken my calls."

She was right about that.

"Plus," she continued, "you deserved to look into my eyes and see that I was telling the truth."

"So now I know your truth; what do you want from me?"

She nodded slowly, as if she'd been expecting that question. "Right now, forgiveness would be as good as gold."

"Forgiveness?" I grabbed my purse, swung it onto my shoulder, and looked straight into her eyes. "You want forgiveness? Well, let me tell you what I want. I want to know why you pretended to be my friend, yet all these years you've hated me."

"What?"

"You've always hated that I was with Jamal."

Her eyes got as big as silver dollars. "That's not true!"

"You hated that he married a white woman. You hated that he married me."

"No!" Miriam shot a look at Michellelee as if she was some kind of life preserver, but I kept my eyes on her.

"Well, I guess you made sure that this turned out the way you always wanted. You made sure that Jamal ended up with the black girl."

"Emily . . ." Michellelee said.

That was good. That meant that I'd gone too far. That meant that Miriam was probably good and hurt.

So all I had to do now was finish. "Think about that when you're wondering whether or not I forgive you," I said to her, then sat there for a bit longer, just until I saw the tears come to her eyes. Then I kicked back my chair and stomped out of my favorite restaurant, not even taking a second peek at the cheesecakes as I strode quickly to the exit.

42

Emily

I was steaming as I revved up the engine and shot out of the restaurant parking lot. There was never going to be another day in my life when I would speak to Miriam Williams. Or Michelle . . . Lee . . . for that matter. "Michelle Lee," I said, purposely calling her by the name that her mother had given her. I wished that I was standing in front of her face right now, so that I could call her that and piss her off.

I screamed, and the sound echoed through the car. Surely there had never been a time when I'd been filled with such fury.

I wasn't even sure what made me angrier, Michellelee setting me up, or Miriam having the audacity to ask me to forgive her. How in the world could she think that I would ever forgive her?

It was never about sex.

I gritted my teeth.

It wasn't even lust.

I punched my hand against the steering wheel.

It certainly wasn't about love.

"Get out of my head," I screamed, and then pressed the button to activate the Bluetooth. "Call Carl Bell," I said. And after a couple of seconds, my call was answered by the receptionist, who checked to see if my attorney was available.

I was seething as I waited, my anger in the deep breaths I was taking.

"Emily, how are you?"

"Have you spoken to Jamal?" I said, hating that I sounded rude, but I needed to get to the point.

"I spoke to Jamal and he was going to have someone call me, but I haven't heard anything."

"When did you speak to him?"

"A few days ago. I was going to give him some time to get back to me."

"He doesn't need time. This divorce isn't complicated."

"Well, you do have property and other assets."

"So, how long will this take?"

"I told you, about six months, once we get going."

"Can you do me a favor and call Jamal? I need to get this done."

"I can." He paused. "Are you sure you don't want to call him yourself?"

"I'm sure," I said.

By the time I hung up, I was pulling into the garage. I'd never been so grateful to find a parking spot right away.

I didn't even calm down when I got up to our condo. I flung my purse onto the sofa, then marched into the kitchen in search of ice cream. But I hadn't replaced the last carton and I wished Häagen-Dazs delivered. Flopping down onto the couch, I was so mad at myself for falling for Michellelee's play. So mad that I'd sat there and listened. So mad that Miriam's words were still in my head.

It wasn't about sex.

"I don't care," I yelled out. "An affair is an affair."

When the bell rang, I frowned, but I jumped up at the same

time. I was grateful for whoever stood on the other side of that door. Anything to break up this conversation with myself.

I swung the door open, and then stood in shock. I'd expected it to be one of my neighbors, or one of the concierges with a package, since no one had called up ahead.

"This is not my day."

Jamal frowned.

"What're you doing here?" I certainly didn't feel like seeing the other half of the Miriam-and-Jamal couple. Then I squinted. "Did Miriam call you?"

"I haven't talked to her. I'm not going to talk to her."

"Then what are you doing here?" I repeated.

He motioned that he wanted to come inside, but I didn't move.

"Okay"—he shrugged—"we can have this conversation right here."

I rolled my eyes and stepped aside.

When I closed the door behind him, he said, "You seem upset."

"You think?"

He held up his hands. "I'm not here to cause trouble."

I didn't move from the door because my plan was to open it up, very soon, so that he could find his way out.

He said, "Your attorney called me the other day." When I said nothing, he continued. "I'm not going to cooperate, Emily. Not until we really talk."

I shook my head.

"Just listen to me and if you still want to do this, then I'll have to let you go. Even though it'll kill me, I'll let you go. But not before we talk."

"No." There was a whole lot more I was going to say, but then the doorbell stopped me. What was this? My patience was hanging by a thin string, and I yanked the door open with a full scowl on my face. "What?"

"What?" Pastor Ford smiled. "That's not a great greeting, honey." My pastor hugged me before she glided into our apartment.

"Pastor," I said, softly closing the door, then facing her. How had she gotten past the concierge?

But then when I took in the sight in front of me—Pastor Ford and Jamal, standing shoulder to shoulder—I realized it had been Jamal. He'd told them to let her up, and again the rage began to rise in me. I'd been set up. Again! Twice in one day.

"So," Pastor Ford said, "do you guys have some time now?"

I folded my arms. "For what?"

"Uh . . . Pastor, I haven't talked to Emily. I just got here."

"That's fine," Pastor Ford said, taking charge. "We'll all talk. You do have some time now, Emily, don't you?" She didn't wait for me to answer; she just sat down on the sofa.

Jamal sat next to her, but I didn't move. I stood there, steaming and huffing.

"Emily," the pastor said so sweetly, "are you going to join us?"

If it had been anyone else coming into my home and telling me what to do, I would have just thrown them out. Better yet, I wouldn't have let them in.

But this was Pastor Ford. No way was I going to do that to one of God's apostles.

Still, I wanted her to know that I didn't appreciate being blindsided like this. So I took my time, almost dragging my feet as I walked across the room. I was glad, actually, that Jamal had sat next to our pastor. That meant that I could sit alone, in the chair catty-corner from them.

As soon as I sat, though, I felt like it was me against the world.

"I left you a few messages, Emily. Did you get them?"

"Uh . . ." I coughed. "I did. But I've been really busy."

"I know that. You've done a great job, especially with LaTonya. The Millers are grateful."

"I'm glad."

"So, how are you?" she asked.

I shrugged. There was no reason for all of these niceties. I knew why she was there. We just needed to get to the point! "I guess Jamal talked to you."

"He did."

"He told you we're getting a divorce."

She shook her head. "No, he didn't tell me that part," she said, as if Jamal wasn't sitting right next to her. "He told me that you wanted a divorce, but he was going to do everything to fight it."

When I looked at Jamal, I wondered if he could see just how upset I was at all of this, especially bringing Pastor Ford into our battle.

"So, do you want to talk about it?" she asked.

No was what I said in my head. Aloud, I told Pastor Ford what I'd been telling everyone else. "There's nothing to talk about."

"I think there is."

"Well, if we have to talk, let's talk about Jamal sleeping with my best friend."

"That's a good place to start."

That wasn't the response I expected. Not from Pastor and not even from Jamal, who nodded as if that was what he wanted to talk about, too.

Then Pastor Ford said, "Emily, I hate to say it, but I saw this coming."

Those words blew my heart into a million shattered pieces.

I stared at the woman I loved so much, the woman who had stood by me and Jamal when my own parents had not, who had encouraged me when I was in school, and who taught me so much about the Lord. I wasn't quite sure where they came from, but I burst into tears.

Jamal jumped up and knelt in front of me. "Emily."

I knew he wanted to comfort me, but I didn't want that from him. Right now, I wouldn't even have taken comfort from my pastor. I just wanted them to go, leave me alone.

My hands covered my face when I felt Pastor Ford come over and sit on the arm of the chair and hold me, even though I didn't want to be touched.

As I sobbed, Pastor Ford said, "I'm sorry, Emily, but that's the truth. I saw it, and I hinted, but I never spoke to you directly. But with the time that Jamal and Miriam were spending together, with their grief, with their relationship to Chauncey, and with you being so busy . . ."

"What . . . was . . . I . . . supposed to do?" I asked, sniffing back my tears.

"Make sure you hear what I'm saying. I saw this coming, but it was not your fault. This is totally on Jamal and Miriam. Now, I've been working with Jamal. He came to me. And even though Miriam's been dodging me, just like you"—she paused—"I'm going to talk to her, too. All three of you need counseling."

"Together?" I was horrified. Surely I'd been tortured enough.

"No, no. Not together. You and Jamal. I should've been spending more time with Miriam myself, and I will. But you and Jamal, we'll do your counseling together."

Wasn't anyone listening to me? I wanted a divorce! No counseling, just a decree that said I was no longer married. But Pastor Ford was speaking as if counseling was a fait accompli.

I sniffed again, and this time Jamal jumped up. Just seconds later, he was back with a tissue and I only took it because I didn't want to keep using my hands.

Once I'd cleaned up, I said, "All I want is a divorce."

Now she was the one who knelt in front of me. "Why are you

trying so hard to run away from this? Why won't you even talk or just listen? What are you afraid of?"

I pressed my lips together, trying to push back my cries. "I can't figure out why everyone is running to Jamal's side. No one seems to get how I feel."

"Oh, I do," Pastor said. "I understand. He violated your vows and your trust."

"Yes!"

"And now, you're very hurt."

"Yes!"

"And you want to hurt him as much as he's hurt you."

"Yes!"

"So you feel the best way to get back at him, the best way to hurt him, is to divorce him because he will really hurt then."

"Yes . . ." I said, though not as emphatically as the last times. Because this time, my agreement didn't sound quite right.

"You don't want to divorce Jamal because you no longer want to be married. You want to divorce him because that's the only way you can hurt him. That's the only way you know how to make him pay. But, Emily, divorce is the ultimate price. If you're divorcing him for that reason, it's going to cost you, too."

She waited for me to say something, but all I did was wipe my nose.

"Do you know how many men and women realize this *afterward*? They realize this when it's already done, and it's too late.

"I was there at the beginning with the two of you, I've been there with you all this time, and if there is one thing I know it's that Jamal loves you."

"I do," my husband said softly.

"And I know you love him. That's the reason why you're so hurt. So are you willing to throw away love for payback?"

I bit the corner of my lip, trying to transfer the pain that Pastor was dredging up with her words. "But . . . how do I know that he won't do it again?"

"You don't."

That was the wrong answer.

"I won't, Emily," Jamal said. "I'll never do it again."

I could hardly look at him. "That's what you promised in our wedding vows, and that's what you promised every day since."

"I know. And all I can say now is that what happened didn't have anything to do with us. It was all about me."

"But you're a part of us. And you can't say 'it was all about me,' and leave me out of the equation."

Pastor Ford returned to the sofa, and now Jamal moved over to where she'd been. "I mean, there was nothing that you did wrong, there was nothing that you could've done. I was searching for a way not to hurt so much and—"

"I wasn't home. But when I came home, you should have talked to me. I tried to talk to you."

"I know." He shook his head. "And I'm just so sorry."

He'd said that so many times, though I never tired of hearing it. Truly, I believed that he was sorry, and he wasn't just sorry that he'd been caught. I believed that he was sorry that he'd slept with Miriam. But I didn't believe that he wouldn't do it again. That was the problem. And that was why our marriage had to end.

When I didn't say anything, Pastor said, "Emily, I've worked with lots of couples. And while there are many who never recover from infidelity, you would be surprised at the number who do. Because when couples find a way to put everything they're feeling into words, trust can be restored, marriages can be healed. Especially a marriage where God has truly brought two together for a purpose. He wants His purpose fulfilled, and I've seen marriages thrive when the husband and wife truly want to stay together."

It sounded so good, so professional, so spiritual. And yet it didn't do a damn thing for my heart. So I just sat there, staring at the tissues I held.

Pastor Ford said, "It's probably a good idea for us to leave; we can start your first sessions on Monday."

Who said I'd agreed to counseling?

"Let's talk about it and set the time after church tomorrow."

Who said I was going to church?

I didn't ask those questions, though, as Pastor hugged me and then Jamal kissed me on my forehead.

When the door closed behind them, I was so glad. I just wished that they'd taken the sadness I felt with them.

43

MIRIAM

I was thankful that Michellelee had stayed with me. Thankful that she hadn't left me just sitting in that restaurant by myself, crying. We'd ordered lunch, though both of us ended up taking most of our entrées home. Not only did we not have much of an appetite, we didn't have much conversation.

Michellelee just kept saying, "I told you."

And I just kept crying.

Finally, I dried my tears, we hugged each other, said good-bye, and I drove away in my van. There was one thing left that I had to do.

As I maneuvered through the Saturday afternoon traffic, I reminded myself that even though my heart was bleeding, I'd done the right thing. If I'd never said a word, Emily would have never gone back to Jamal. I was sure of that. She had to hear the story from the other woman. She had to hear that Jamal didn't pursue me. She had to hear that there were no emotions on either of our parts. She had to believe that there was no love, just loss.

That's just how my friend was.

If they got back together, I had just saved their marriage. Not that I was sure she would even go back. But there was one thing that

I was sure of: Jamal would never come back to me.

It was the look in his eyes the other night outside the hotel. He looked at Emily the way Chauncey looked at me. It was the kind of love that was reserved for just one person.

Jamal would never be mine. His heart would always belong to Emily.

So I'd done my part. I'd been truthful, even when she'd cut me with her words. I'd spoken from my heart and told her everything . . . well, almost everything.

There were some things that a best friend didn't need to know.

I swerved quickly onto Prairie, then took another turn, another block, and I was where I was supposed to be.

I sat in front of the church for a few minutes, just staring at this building. I'd been a member of Hope Chapel since I was twelve years old, one of the few good things that came out of being in foster care. Back in those days, Pastor Ford came to the group home where I was living and had Bible study with the kids. When I told her that I wanted to go to church, she made sure I had a ride every Sunday.

Pastor Ford had been an integral part of my life for longer than any woman. Until I met Emily and Michellelee, she and Mama Cee were the only women who had ever loved me. That's why I was going to have to do something about the dozens of messages she'd left me.

Turning off the ignition, I stepped out of the car, hurried across the street, but then slowed my steps as I approached the front of the building. Even though it was Saturday, the church would be open, but the question was, would the sanctuary be free?

Not that it mattered. Pastor said the altar was always open, no matter what was going on around it.

Walking up the steps, I peered inside. There was nothing but quiet.

My steps were silent as I moved across the green carpet, and I stopped only to place my purse on the first chair in the first row. Then I approached the altar.

I bowed my head before I bent down onto my knees. I shifted until I was comfortable, then I said, "I'm so sorry, God. Please forgive me." I stayed there for just a couple of seconds and then I rose.

I'd prayed what I meant and I meant what I prayed. So much had happened and I was asking God for forgiveness for it all. I wasn't one of those people who believed that the longer the prayer, the more God heard. I was absolutely sure that God believed in Twitter prayers—quality, not quantity. So? I always kept it short, kept it simple. God knew I loved Him and that I was already saved. He knew that I was sorry for how I'd tossed Him aside, and sorry for what I'd done to Emily. The moment I asked, I had the Lord's forgiveness. Thank God, His forgiveness was always instant. Now, with His grace, one day I might have Emily's forgiveness, too.

I took just a few steps away before I turned back. But this time, I just bowed my head, 'cause all this getting up and down was hard on my knees. I closed my eyes and said, "One more thing, Lord. Please soften Emily's heart. Not toward me, but toward Jamal." I waited another second to see if anything else came to my mind. Nothing did, so I opened my eyes.

That was my sincere prayer, but I didn't have a lot of hope. I loved Emily, but she was stubborn and I wasn't so sure that she knew how to forgive. She'd suffered from so much unforgiveness. After almost nine years, her parents continued to exclude her from their lives; they still hadn't forgiven her for marrying Jamal. She hadn't been forgiven, so I didn't think she knew how to do it.

If this was any other time, place, or circumstance, I would've made my best friend sit and listen while I broke it down and made it clear for her. But I'd never get the chance to be close like that to her again. I wasn't a fool; I knew our friendship was over.

With that thought, new tears came to my eyes. Another death. This one hurt just as much, in a different kind of way. This time, the death was my fault. I was the one who'd set our friendship on fire. And today Emily had tried, convicted, and sentenced me to life without her. I had to live with that, because even forgiven sins had consequences.

I took a last glance at the altar. And all I had to say this time was, "Amen."

44

Emily

I didn't know how I was going to keep ducking and dodging my pastor, but I was gonna try. Hiding out from her had worked well enough yesterday; there wasn't much chasing she could do on Sunday.

But then as soon as I got to the office and checked my e-mail, there was a message from Pastor, sent at around five in the morning: *I'll see you in counseling at 7:30 tonight.*

First of all, who got up at five already sending e-mails, and why did my pastor think that she could run my life?

I sent my own e-mail: *Sorry, Pastor. Right now, my life is just too busy. I won't be attending counseling.* I wanted to add *not now, not ever*, but if I'd done that, Pastor Ford would have shown up at my door again.

My prayer now was that she'd be too busy with her own schedule, and wouldn't even think about me for at least six months. And by then . . .

But my pastor would never give up, and neither would Jamal. Of course, he'd called last night and this morning. But in the weeks that we'd been separated, I'd gotten used to ignoring him.

Jamal was easy; Pastor was my problem. She would insist on

counseling. And I couldn't give in because once I sat in that room with her, I'd be broken.

Pastor had only been in our apartment for ten minutes on Saturday and the breakdown had already started.

Her words, joined together with Miriam's, were getting to me. Last night, their words had chased me in my dreams . . .

It was never about sex . . . it had everything to do with loss . . .

You don't want a divorce because you no longer want to be with Jamal. You want a divorce because you want to hurt him . . .

Those words and so many others planted themselves in my head, taunting, haunting, until I'd given up trying to sleep. Then I'd resorted to my new pastime. In the kitchen, I'd pulled out the gallon of ice cream I'd bought after Pastor and Jamal left. And from three to four to five in the morning, I just ate, and with the TV on mute, I watched *Love Story* over and over.

So now, I was tired, pissed, bloated, and hiding from my pastor.

I was relieved when I heard the knock on my door and my receptionist walked in holding LaTonya's hand. She was my fourth and final client of the day.

No matter what I was going through, this little girl made me smile, because I had such hope for her.

"How are you, LaTonya?"

She shrugged.

My receptionist said, "So, I'm gonna get going. You're still okay with me leaving early?"

"Oh, definitely. I'll see you tomorrow," I said as I followed LaTonya to the table.

Like always, my plan was to sit across from the little girl and talk to her while she drew, but she didn't reach for the construction paper and crayons. "You don't want to draw?"

She shook her head.

"What do you want to do?"

She lowered her eyes. "I wanna go home."

"You don't want to even talk to me today?

Again, she shook her head.

"Why not?"

It took her a few seconds to say, "'Cause LaTrisha can't talk, so I don't want to talk either."

I nodded, wanting her to think that I understood, though I didn't. I had already contacted another psychologist in San Diego. Dr. Phillips had done studies analyzing twins who'd suffered the loss of their sibling, and he assured me that this was all part of the grieving process.

"She knows she can't go to her sister, so this is her way of keeping her sister here," he'd said.

It made sense, but with each session, it seemed like LaTonya was getting worse, and I didn't want her to fall into any kind of depression.

"Well, what about if you and I talk to LaTrisha together?"

She looked up, and at first, her eyes brightened. But then I could see her skepticism, even in her six-year-old eyes.

I walked to the shelf filled with toys and grabbed the black Raggedy Ann doll. "Do you wanna play a game?" I asked.

LaTonya just looked at me as I handed her the doll.

"Can we pretend that this is LaTrisha?" I asked.

"LaTrisha didn't look like this," LaTonya said. "She looked like me."

"I know, but it's just a game, right?"

Another moment, another shrug, "I guess."

"So if you were talking to LaTrisha, what would you say?"

She looked at the doll, then me, before she turned back to the doll. Then she said, "I'd ask her if she was going to school."

"Okay, ask her."

She looked down at the doll.

"Go ahead, just pretend she's LaTrisha."

After a moment, she said, "Are you going to school?"

"Yes," I answered.

I shocked her, for just a moment. But then she asked, "Do you like school?"

"Yes," I spoke for LaTrisha again. "It's a cool school."

The tips of LaTonya's lips twitched and I prayed that she would smile. She didn't, but she seemed to like our game. She asked her sister all kinds of questions, many about heaven. And I answered every single one, as best as I could.

LaTonya still hadn't smiled, but she had talked. More than she had in any session. When our fifty minutes were up, I reached for the doll, but LaTonya hugged the doll to her chest.

"Can I take her home?"

My objective had been to get her to open up, to talk more, but I didn't want her to get used to talking just to a doll. But then I said, "Sure. But only if you promise to bring her back tomorrow, okay?"

She nodded, and when the ends of her lips turned up, like a smile wasn't far away, I knew I'd made the right decision.

"Okay, let's go see your parents." I held her hand like I always did, but the moment I opened the door, she broke away and took off running.

I blinked a couple of times, trying to make sense of the scene in front of me. LaTonya had run right into Jamal.

"What are you doing here?" I asked at the same time that he was saying "Whoa!" to LaTonya.

The Millers stood up and Mrs. Miller rushed to her daughter. "LaTonya, what are you doing?"

"He's the man I saw when I talked to LaTrisha."

"What?" the Millers and I said at the same time.

"He was with LaTrisha," she said with certainty. "And then he carried me."

It must've been the way her parents and I stared at her that made LaTonya say, "I'm sorry."

"No, it's okay." Jamal held up his hand to Mrs. Miller, then knelt down in front of the girl. "What's your name?"

"LaTonya."

"Well, it's nice to meet you," he said. "I'm Doctor H.'s husband."

"You are?"

She looked up at me and I nodded. Because what else was I going to do? Explain affairs to her? Discuss divorce?

"And you know what?" Jamal asked LaTonya.

She shook her head.

"These"—he glanced up at me before he looked back down—"are for you."

He held out a bouquet of flowers and LaTonya grabbed them. Then she did something that I'd never seen.

LaTonya smiled.

And reached out her arms and hugged him.

I wanted to call foul! Really a technical foul. Because Jamal came here and was using this child to get to me. Using her to remind me that he had a heart. A great heart. A loving heart. Because children always knew.

But I wasn't going to be fooled.

"Tell Mr. Harrington thank you," Mrs. Miller said.

I opened my mouth to correct her, but Jamal held up his hand, stopping me.

"It was nice to meet you," the Millers told my husband before Mr. Miller took the flowers from his daughter.

Then Mrs. Miller held LaTonya's hand and led their daughter from my office.

Before she got to the door, LaTonya turned around. Still holding on to the doll, she waved and then gave me another smile. A smile that made me grin.

She walked out the door with her parents and I faced Jamal. I was still smiling when I looked at him. But then I remembered all that he'd done and my grin faded.

Turning around, I stomped into my office. "What're you doing here?"

He followed me inside. "Pastor said you sent her an e-mail about counseling."

"That's correct," I said, keeping my back to him. I picked up my bag and stuffed two folders inside. My plan had been to work here for another hour or two or four. I didn't want to go home, but if Jamal was going to be here, then even my empty house would be a better place. "There's no point to counseling. I've been trying to tell you that, but you're not listening, you're not understanding."

"I understand that you're hurt."

I pivoted, and now, I was facing him. That was my first mistake. Because what I should have done was just slap him, then walk out of the office.

"Hurt? You think that's what I am? If that's what you think, then you don't understand anything!" I shouted. "Because hurt doesn't even begin to describe what I've been through. Hurt is when you drop a bowling ball on your toe.

"What you've done to me . . . that's not hurt. What you've done to me . . . that word hasn't been created." I got close enough to point my finger in his face. "There's nothing to describe all the agony, all the crying, and wondering what I did wrong. Wondering if it happened because I wasn't good enough, I didn't satisfy you enough. Wondering what it was like for you . . ."

That was my second mistake. Because for all this time, I'd fought hard to keep that picture out of my mind. I never let myself imagine Miriam in bed with my husband. Because if I did, I'd lose it.

So I'd kept that picture at bay.

Until now.

But now they were in my mind. Together. Snapshots flashing. Of Miriam and Jamal. Hugging. Kissing. And the photo of them together in bed . . .

"Oh, God!" I pressed my hand against my stomach because I could feel the bile rising in me. "Oh, God!"

My knees began to shake, and by the time the first tear came, my body had collapsed. But before I could wither all the way down, Jamal caught me and gently lowered me to the floor.

Screaming, I squeezed my eyes. I had to get that image out of my mind. But it wouldn't go away. The louder I screamed, the bolder the image. And the tighter Jamal held me.

I curled up, bringing my knees to my chest, trying to find some way to cover my aching heart. Because it *was* aching. But no matter what I did, the pain wouldn't leave.

I cried as if I hadn't been crying yesterday, and the day before that, and the day before that. I cried as if this pain were new, even though it felt so old.

My sobs were choking me, but I had to push the words out. "How could you do this to me?"

I didn't think it was possible, but Jamal held me tighter. "I'm so sorry," he sobbed with me. "I'm so, so sorry."

Every last tear that was in me was released, and soon there were no more.

There was silence now, at least inside the office. Through the window, the sounds of the city came through: the hum of car engines, the honking of horns, and in the distance a siren that faded in just a minute.

Still, I stayed in Jamal's arms. Though he had brought me this pain, his embrace was taking every bit of it away.

More minutes. Another hour. And really, I could've stayed there one more day. But I had to get up sometime. I shifted, and Jamal's eyes were on me. And there were his tears.

Now, I cried again, for a different reason. I cried because I'd been broken.

And I was glad about it.

45

MIRIAM

November 16, 2012

This didn't look anything like the house that we'd lived in the last eight years. This didn't look anything like the place where I loved my husband, loved my children, loved my life.

I sat on the bottom step of the staircase, taking in the stacks of some brown, some white U-Haul boxes and the sheet-covered furniture. Our life had been dismantled, first by Chauncey's death, and now by my hands, along with Michellelee and a few church members who'd helped me pack.

But even though everything had been taken apart, the life we'd lived in this house was still whole. So I took these moments to soak up all the memories, all the passing years. From the day Chauncey had lifted me and my eight-month-pregnant belly up and stumbled as he carried me over the threshold, to when we brought home every single one of our sons for the first time. We'd celebrated birthdays, anniversaries, first days of school. We'd rejoiced at graduations from kindergarten and elementary school. We'd had some sickness and a whole lot of health.

This house had been full of life and filled with love.

It was probably a good thing that my phone rang or I would've sat there all day in the comfort of remembering. When I checked the caller ID screen, I smiled.

"Hi, Junior!"

"Mom!"

"I'm sorry . . . hi, Chauncey."

I could hear the smile in his voice when he asked, "What're you doing?"

"Just waiting for the movers. They should be here any minute."

"Everything is packed up?"

"Yes. I'm ready to go. What're you guys doing?"

"We just finished eating breakfast and Uncle Charlie is gonna take us to school. Will you be here when we come home?"

"No, I'm not getting into Phoenix until about eight tonight."

"Okay. I'll wait up for you," Junior said.

"Me, too!" I heard Mikey shout out.

"I'm gonna stay up, too," Stevie piped in.

"Who's that in the background?" I asked, pretending not to know.

"It's me, Mom. Stevie."

"And Mikey."

"I put the phone on speaker so that you can hear all of us," Junior said, taking charge.

"Oh my goodness. You all sound so grown-up. I don't think I'm going to recognize you when I get there."

My youngest boys giggled. "It's only been a week, Mom," Mikey said. "You'll recognize us."

"Whew! Okay, that's good."

Mikey asked, "Mom, can we go to the airport with Uncle Charlie to pick you up?"

"You have to ask your uncle and Grandmama Cee."

"Okay," Mikey said. "Grandmama Cee lets us do everything!"

I rolled my eyes, but I couldn't help but smile. The greatest gift

I could've given to Mama Cee was having her grandchildren in Arizona with her. And to hear her tell it, I was part of that gift, too.

Finally making the decision to definitely move to Phoenix had been a present for me. A new life away from old memories.

The sound of a slamming car door made me say, "Boys, the movers are here."

"Okay, Mom," Chauncey said. "We'll see you tonight."

"I can't wait," I said. "I love you guys."

"We love you, too, Mom," they sang together.

I hung up, but held the cell phone to my chest. Those were my three reasons for moving on, and I was happy that they were doing so well.

Their excitement had surprised me on the afternoon I'd met with Emily, then came home and told them that I'd finally decided to move and that we were going to do it now. Even Junior, who'd just made the basketball team, thought Phoenix was going to be great 'cause he'd be a star there. As I called Mama Cee and made plans, my children's enthusiasm had been contagious. I was almost as happy as they were.

Almost.

The knock on the door stopped my thoughts. "It's open," I said, turning toward the living room. I surveyed the boxes, wondering where the movers should begin. When I heard the footsteps behind me, I said, "I think it'll be best to start in here."

And then, he said, "Miriam."

I froze, but only for a second before I swung around. My heart started doing one of those teenage things, beating so rapidly, my breath was taken away. I didn't know if it was because I'd already been visiting the past, but I started remembering everything about Jamal: the first time I saw him when Chauncey introduced me to his best friend at a Christmas dinner. And then the last time I saw him, when he stood in front of the Westin fighting for his love.

My most vivid memory, though, was the last time I'd seen him up close like this. The last time we'd kissed. Only God knew what would've happened if Michellelee hadn't shown up.

He held up his hands. "Don't worry. Emily knows that I'm here."

I shook my head. "I wasn't worried. I'm never worried . . . when I'm with you." Jamal shifted from one foot to the other as if my words made him uncomfortable. So I said, "How are you?" hoping to get our conversation to a place where Jamal wanted to be.

"I've been good," he said, relaxing once again. "But the question is, how are you? And the boys?"

"We're good." I paused and glanced around the living room quickly. "You're probably a little surprised . . . we're moving. I'd been thinking about it for quite some time, but finally just decided to do it."

"I'm not surprised at all. Michellelee told Emily, and I speak to Mama Cee every week."

"I didn't know that, but I'm glad. Mama Cee loves you."

"Yeah, she still feels like family, you know?"

I nodded. "I understand that. She's the only mother I've known."

"I'm glad you're going to be there with them. They'll look out for you and the boys."

I wondered if his happiness had anything to do with the fact that I'd be far away from his life.

He must've read my mind. "I'm sorry we won't be seeing you as much . . . now that you're moving."

I chuckled a little bit. "I have a feeling even if I were staying, we wouldn't be around each other too much."

He gave me a small smile. "You're right about that." He paused. "Miriam, I wanted to thank you for talking to Emily. She told me that you explained . . . what this was. And I appreciate that."

"I told her the truth. And I appreciated her listening and not even once taking a swing at me." When Jamal shifted again, I realized my humor wasn't hitting the mark this morning. I added, "I don't know if I would've been as gracious."

"Yeah, she's been amazing. She's really trying to handle this."

I had to swallow, because right there in front of my face, I could see the love that he had for his wife. It was like he was washed in it. "So . . . you guys . . . are back together?"

"We're working toward that."

I wanted to know what that meant, but I didn't dare ask. I didn't even ask Michellelee whenever we talked. It was an unspoken rule— Jamal and Emily were never to be discussed.

He said, "It hasn't been easy, but we're working it out. We're in counseling."

"I'm glad," I said. "Because you and Emily . . ." I paused and shook my head as I remembered all those years ago when she'd barged into my room talking about this man. We were only nineteen and she'd known then. "You and Emily were meant to be."

"Thanks for saying that."

Then silence stood between us. We stared, we looked away, we shifted, then turned back to each other.

Finally, he said, "Well, I should be going so you can get moving."

"Yeah."

His eyes were back on mine again. "Have a wonderful trip. Have a wonderful life, Miriam."

My lips began to tremble, so all I did was nod.

"We're going to be in touch with you, and the boys. Junior's still our godson."

Now I could speak. "He wants to be called Chauncey now."

"Yeah," Jamal replied. "I talked to him last week when they first got to Phoenix."

"Oh, they didn't mention that. Well, thank you. I want him, and Mikey and Stevie, to be in touch with you . . . and Emily."

"We're going to find a way to be there for them. We're going to work it out so that we can be there for you, too."

"Thank you," I said. That was all that would come out because my throat was starting to ache, as if a big cry was coming on. But I wouldn't cry. At least not in front of him.

"So," he said.

"So," I said.

Then we stood there in the most awkward moment of my life. How were we supposed to say good-bye?

Jamal took a step forward and I did, too. He wrapped his arms around me and I held him. When he didn't back away, I closed my eyes and held on tighter. I hardly breathed because I didn't want anything to interfere with me locking every inch of Jamal Taylor into my memory. I wanted every second of this moment inside my mind.

We held our embrace and I began praying. Praying about what would happen next. What I wanted to happen—Jamal leaning back, Jamal smiling, and Jamal kissing me for one last time.

Time began moving like I imagined. Jamal leaned back, smiled. But then he simply walked away.

I stood in the center of my living room, watching him, willing him to come back.

But he just kept going and when he got to the door he didn't even turn around.

That was when I realized that I was standing in the exact spot where we'd had our last kiss. If I'd known that was the last kiss, I wouldn't have let it end. I would've kissed him straight into eternity.

It wasn't until I heard his car door slam that I whispered the words that I'd wanted him to know. "I love you, Jamal Taylor. I don't know if I always have, but I do know that I always will."

46

Emily

December 15, 2012

I rolled over, so I could hold up my hand in the December morning light and appreciate this new gift on my finger. Even though I held my hand steady, the kaleidoscope of colors from the diamond ricocheted from the ring to the walls, creating a rainbow in our bedroom.

Turning back over, I was surprised when I was met by the open eyes of my husband.

"Good morning." I smiled.

Jamal pulled me into his arms. "This is more than a good morning. It's the best morning that God has ever created."

Gently, I kissed his lips. "Welcome home, Mr. Taylor."

"I am so happy to be here, Doctor Harrington-Taylor." He grinned. "So, I saw you checking out the ring to see if it's real."

I laughed. "Not at all, though you know I've checked out the color, clarity, cut, and carat."

He laughed.

"But even if it wasn't the perfect diamond," I said, "this is one of those situations where the sentiment is what matters." I held up my hand again. The light didn't hit the diamond at the right angle this time, so the colors stayed on the stone. But it was still amazingly beautiful.

I said, "You know you didn't have to buy me this, right?"

"Okay, well then"—gently, he pulled at my finger—"let me take it back."

I snatched my hand away from him. "If you want to live to see your next birthday . . ."

We laughed together before I settled back into his arms. It had been a long way to here, though some might say that ten weeks wasn't that long at all. But for me and Jamal Taylor? It was an eternity.

My husband had described it best in our first counseling sessions. "Not being with Emily is like being held captive in some corner of hell," he said.

It had been exactly that way for me, though at the time, I didn't tell Jamal or Pastor Ford. I'd wanted them both to believe that I was fine and that I was hardly suffering without my husband. But if the walls in my bedroom could have talked, they would have told the truth.

We were back together, though, all because of Jamal. Because my husband never gave up or gave in. Before counseling and during counseling, his faith was in me and our marriage. And now we were here.

Another beginning.

In our first counseling session, I'd told Jamal that I wasn't ready to live with him. I was willing to go to counseling, but I wanted to be separated.

That didn't make him happy, but Pastor Ford suggested that we use our time apart to date each other.

"Keep it open and easy," she'd said.

I took that to mean that we could keep the sex out of it, which was fine by me. I didn't want to connect with Jamal in that way. Not with Miriam still dead-center in my thoughts.

So Jamal and I met for walks on the beach, coffee at Star-bucks. We had brunch at the Cheesecake Factory and hooked up for drinks at the Martini Bar. One day, we pretended that we were tourists and checked out the Hollywood Walk of Fame and Grau-man's Chinese Theatre. We hiked together, biked together, jogged together.

We became friends all over again, just like we'd done the first time. Every day, my heart swelled with love, leaving little room for unforgiveness, even though there were days when I wanted to hold on to that. But I couldn't. Love nudged the grudge aside.

That's why I'd decided to cook dinner last night. We'd been eat-ing out and I wanted us to have more space to talk. We were a long way from getting back together. At least, that's what I thought.

Maybe subconsciously, I'd wanted something to happen. But in the best of my dreams, I didn't think it was going to be something like this . . .

✦

I dIdN'T kNOW why I was so nervous. It wasn't like Jamal had never been here. We'd shared years of happiness inside these walls. And the shrimp creole that I'd made was one of his favorite dishes. So why did this feel like a first date with a stranger?

Before I had a chance to reflect any more, the doorbell rang. Even though Jamal had his key, he was respectful of the boundaries we'd set.

"Hey, you," he said when I opened the door and he greeted me with a bouquet.

"Hey, yourself," I replied, taking the flowers. "And thank you." Turning away from him, I added, "Dinner's almost ready," and I headed toward the kitchen to get a vase. "I made one of your favorites." Looking over my shoulder, I expected to see Jamal following right behind me.

But he was still by the door. Only he wasn't standing. He was bending down; at least, that's what I thought at first. Actually, he was down on one knee.

I was just about to ask him what he was doing when he said, "Emily, I have always loved you. From that first moment, when you opened the door for Chauncey, our hearts connected. And like we always say, it took us a little while to find each other, but we did. And I've been so happy."

He paused, and I hoped that he didn't expect me to say anything. I had lost all ability to think, so speaking wasn't possible.

"I've always been happy, Emily. You have to know that. I have loved you and our life together and if I could, I would pay any price to take back—"

I didn't let him finish. I knelt down in front of him and looked him in his eyes. "I know you would, Jamal. I really know that now."

Without taking his eyes from me, he reached into his pocket and held up this glistening thing. At first, that was all it was to me, until he took my hand and slid off the ring I was wearing. Then he slipped the new diamond onto my finger.

I had to suck in a big gulp of air to keep breathing.

He said, "Will you do me the honor—"

"Yes!" I exclaimed.

But he shook his head. "I need to finish this. I need to say it all."

"Okay," I said, through the lump in my throat.

He cleared his throat, took a breath, and exhaled the words slowly. "Will you do me the honor of showing me what true love is? Showing me what can happen when a man falls down and truly repents. Showing me a heart of forgiveness. Would you do me the honor of allowing me into your life and your love once again?"

When he stopped, I didn't say anything and he frowned.

I said, "I just wanted to make sure you were finished this time."

"I am. So . . ." Then he swallowed, as if he was now concerned about my answer.

Was this man kidding? After all we'd been through? All the painful counseling? Learning that while what had happened was all Jamal, there were so many things I could've done better, like not expecting my husband to be like Superman? Yes, Jamal was strong, but there was nothing wrong with weakness at times, and there had to be room for that. That was the greatest lesson that I'd learned from Pastor.

I was so looking forward to getting to the good part—the next eight, and another eight, and another eight, and another eight years of a wonderful marriage.

"Yes!" I shouted, and threw my arms around him.

And while we were on our knees, we kissed. A kiss that felt so spiritual, maybe because we were on our knees . . .

We didn't have dinner last night. At least we didn't have the kind of nourishment that added inches to the hips. Instead, we burned so much off that I'd be able to eat anything I wanted for a week.

"So," Jamal began, breaking into my thoughts, "last night you said you'd be my wife."

"Of course I did."

"So, that means—" He jumped up and out of bed so fast, he startled me. And standing there in all his naked glory, he said, "There's going to be a wedding."

"What?" I sat up, pulling the sheet over me.

He sprinted into his closet and came out with a garment bag. "Now, I haven't seen this," he said. "Pastor Ford and Michellelee took care of it, but this right here"—he grinned—"is your dress."

"What?"

He turned around and dashed back into the closet. "Everything I need is in this garment bag and this bag here," he said, holding up his duffel bag.

"Jamal, what are you talking about?"

This time, he kissed me before he ran away.

None of this was computing, and just when I was about to zip open the garment bag, he jumped out of his closet, dressed in a jogging suit. Moving quickly, he grabbed his garment bag, duffel bag, gave me another kiss, and said, "I'll see you in a little while, babe."

He turned and dashed out of the room, leaving me sitting there. But I didn't have to wait long before I heard his footsteps coming back toward our bedroom.

Only it wasn't Jamal. It was Michellelee.

"What in the world?"

Michellelee put her hands on her hips. "What're you still doing in bed?" Before I could ask what she was doing in my apartment, she said, "Now that your man is gone, what are you still doing in bed?"

"Will you tell me what's going on?"

"Didn't your man tell you? There's going to be a wedding today."

It had to be my blank stare that made her sigh.

"Didn't he ask you to marry him again?"

"Yes, but . . ."

"Well, you're getting married again . . . today."

"Huh?" I knew I sounded like a dummy, since I felt like one.

"Silly girl, you don't even know what today is." She shook her head. "Today, nine years ago, you married Jamal Taylor, and you're going to do it again. Now, will you get your happy behind up so that I can get the bride ready?"

Slowly, I smiled, and it all became clear to me.

I got it. Finally, I really, really got it.

✦

IT WAS JUST like the first time—well, almost. There were two fewer people in attendance. But my joy was exactly the way it was in 2003 when we'd come to Pastor Ford and told her that we were getting married in a week.

As I stood at the altar, holding hands with my husband and grinning like we were sixteen-year-olds, I couldn't believe that Jamal had done all this. For the last month, he'd worked with Pastor and Michellelee. Apparently, he'd been sure that I'd say yes.

Pastor Ford said, "Well now, finally, we can begin."

Everyone chuckled and I had to laugh, too. I was supposed to be here an hour ago, but I'd been a bit late. That hadn't been my fault, though. After all, I'd found out twenty minutes after I'd awakened that I was getting married. Was I supposed to just get up and get going?

First, I had to have my own celebration, Michellelee and I. At least thirty minutes passed before we finally stopped jumping around and admiring my ring. Only then were we able to get down to the business of becoming beautiful.

Pastor Ford said, "I love officiating over weddings, bringing the love of two together. But even more than that, I really love presiding over the renewal of vows. Because this means that the commitment is still there. This means that if you had the chance to do it all again, you would. And, you are."

Behind us, Michellelee sniffed.

She was standing in as the best woman for both me and Jamal. He didn't want to replace Chauncey and I . . . well.

"So, it gives me the greatest honor to stand here with Emily and Jamal, and say that with everything that has gone on in your nine years of marriage, through any sickness, and all the health, through the riches—and, blessedly, there hasn't been too much that you can consider poor—through it all, what the two of you are saying today is that you still love and honor each other."

I hoped no one had seen the deep breath I'd just taken. In counseling, I'd come to understand that even in the middle of his transgression, Jamal still loved me. I got that part, but it wasn't until this morning, maybe not even until this moment, that I understood that Jamal still honored me, too. His transgression didn't diminish that.

Now, if he did it again . . .

Pastor Ford interrupted my short reverie. "So, it means a lot to me to stand here as these two proclaim their love once again for each other. Emily"—she paused and turned to me—"and Jamal, I know you haven't had time to write anything, but I think that's a good thing. It's about what's on your hearts anyway, so why don't you talk to each other, for just a few minutes. Tell each other what you think, what you feel, and why you love." She glanced at my husband. "So, Jamal?"

I was thankful that Pastor hadn't started with me because I didn't know what I was going to say.

Jamal took my hands, but when he looked into my eyes, I wasn't so sure that his going first was the right move. Because the love that was in his eyes was sure to take me out.

He cleared his throat. "Emily." Just the way he said my name made my knees turn into jelly. "When I decided that we were going to stand here and do this again, I wanted to come up with something profound, something that would truly let you know what you mean to me. But even though I've had weeks to think about this, weeks to go through the dictionary, weeks to search the Internet, I couldn't find anything, because I discovered that words aren't sufficient. Words alone would never do. So, I will start with the words, I love you. I love you so much that my heart pounds a little harder when I think of you and it grows a little more every time I look at you."

I knew it—Jamal was trying to make me faint.

"Those are the words, and after the words will come my actions. And I promise you"—he stopped and then repeated, "I promise you," as if he wanted to make sure that I heard him—"that I will spend every minute of every hour, every hour of every day, every day of every week, every week of every month, and then year, after year, after year, telling you and showing you how much you are loved, honored, and a blessing to me."

When he paused, Pastor said, "That was beautiful."

But Jamal held up his hand. "Pastor, there is one thing I want to add."

She nodded. "Go ahead. For love like this, I got all day."

He said, "When I first told Pastor that we were going to do this, I told her what I wanted to say. She"—he paused and looked at Pastor Ford—"didn't think we had to talk about this, but I want this to be part of the renewing of our vows." He took a deep breath. "I didn't get it right the first time, Emily. God help me and I'm so sorry, but I didn't get it right. When we stood here before, I thought I was going to, and I tried to, but I didn't. But this time, I know that I will. Because this time, I'm going to get on my knees every day and ask God to deliver me from anything that doesn't prove my love for you. So this is a promise and a vow that I'm kissing up to God." He cradled my face in the palm of his hands. "Emily Harrington-Taylor . . . I love you."

Then he kissed me, pressed his lips against mine, and then parted my lips gently with his tongue.

Pastor Ford cleared her throat. "Uh . . . uh . . ."

We leaned back and looked at her as if we were surprised that she was there. Then we busted out laughing.

"I'm sorry, Pastor," we said together, and that made us laugh even harder.

"Well, I'm just saying that the kiss is usually saved for the end, but after that, I don't know if there is anything else that anyone needs to say."

"I haven't had my chance," I said, raising my hand. "And I promise it will be short."

The pastor motioned for me to proceed.

"Jamal Taylor . . . I love you. And I will love you for the next fifty years, and the fifty after that, and the fifty after that. I told you from the beginning we were meant to be." Then I did what he'd done to me; I held his face between my hands and gazed into his eyes. "I. Love. You."

And I kissed him the way he'd kissed me.

When we broke apart, Jamal hugged me. I closed my eyes and held him as Pastor Ford and Michellelee clapped so loud, it sounded like there were fifty people in the sanctuary.

I held Jamal because I didn't want to let go. Not ever. I was still holding on to Jamal when I opened my eyes.

And that was when I saw her.

Miriam.

At the back, in the corner of the church.

Our eyes locked, and for a moment we just stared. It had only been two months since I'd seen her, but she looked so different. Her hair was out of her signature bun, flowing free, touching her shoulders and making the white streak more visible. And she'd lost weight, just a little. It all looked so good on her.

After a while, her lips spread into a smile that matched the one on my lips. She pressed her hands together, with the tips of her fingers curled and her thumbs creating the peak of a heart.

And then she held the heart she'd formed with her fingers close to her chest. She mouthed, "Love you."

It took me a moment, but then I mouthed back, "Mean it."

I blinked and she was gone.

That quickly. As if she'd been a figment of my imagination.

With a breath, I broke our embrace and then hugged Michelle-lee. When I stepped back, I looked at the door one last time.

There was no way that Miriam would ever be a part of my life the way she'd been. But I was really glad that she'd come, even if it was just for ten seconds. Michellelee had probably told her, and I'd thank her for that later. Seeing Miriam helped me to know that now I was whole, I was complete. I guess it was true—forgiveness was really good for the soul.

The end . . .

So, that's my story. Well, like I said in the beginning, this is not my story alone. This is the story of me and Emily, and now that you know how it went down, I have to ask, would you or wouldn't you? Is there any situation where you would ever get involved with your best friend's husband?

But wait!

Before you say that would never happen, before you say something like, "I'd never be as low-down as that chick," make sure you've cried while you walked two weeks in my shoes. Don't answer that question unless you've found yourself deep inside the gulf of grief. Because grief, if given the chance, will wrap itself around you and squeeze, making you lose all sense of up and down, black and white, right and wrong. Grief will hold you hostage and make you pay the ransom with your soul.

That's what happened to me. Except Jamal came to my rescue. He pulled me up and out and then held me, until he didn't hold me anymore. The challenge was, I wasn't ready to let him go. And the truth is, I still want him now. That's why I had to move away. I truly love that man.

I know, I know. This has got to sound crazy. You're probably ask-ing how could I possibly love Jamal Taylor when I loved Chauncey Williams? And you might even be saying that with the way I acted, I never loved Chauncey.

But I did. I loved my husband with all my heart. He'd come into my life and loved me when there was not another soul on Earth who did. He'd given my life purpose, he'd helped me achieve my dreams.

He'd rescued me, and my love for Chauncey was a complete and grateful love where I couldn't do enough to return it. My plan had been to spend all the days of my life loving Chauncey back, and then praying that I was pouring a tenth of the love he'd given me into him.

But my love for Jamal was different. It was a grown-up love that came to me when I knew who I was. Jamal's love came to me when I was feeling good about the person I'd become. His love came to me when I already had a life. And that's why that love was so wonderful.

So, while Chauncey always, from that first day, had my heart, Jamal had captured my soul.

And you know what? Some of you may say that I probably loved Jamal all along. Maybe you're right. I don't know. I can tell you that I never felt anything except friendship for him, but who knows? Maybe this is a case study that belongs in some Psych 101 class. Maybe stu-dents need to analyze how Chauncey's love for me blocked my love for Jamal. Like I said, who knows?

What I can tell is that my love for Jamal was the right kind of love. It was just a shame that I'd found the right love with the wrong man.

At least I know that I have the capacity to love this way, and my prayer is that I will have a Jamal kind of love again in my life. Not that I expect that to really happen. How could one woman get two blessings in one lifetime? That really is too much to ask.

So if I never find this kind of love again, it's fine with me. I'm only in my midthirties, but I've already been showered with more love than most women will experience in their lifetimes.

Now I ask again, would you or wouldn't you? That, for sure, is the question. But I want to admonish you—make sure you never say never.

A Note from

Victoria Christopher Murray

Never Say Never is my fourteenth adult novel, and is actually based upon truth. Not the truth of my life, but something I heard about years ago. After 9/11, there was a phenomenon that was happening so much, it was written about in several newspapers and even became a *Law & Order* episode: firemen were leaving their wives for their best friends' widows. It was so interesting that I wanted to explore it—with a couple of VCM twists, of course. So *Never Say Never* is the result of that exploration, and Emily and Miriam are now two of my all-time favorite characters. No, I don't think there will be a sequel. Their stories are complete, I believe. They just became my favorites because I could actually see this happening and understand the who, what, where, and why of this situation. This novel truly made me ask, what would I do? What would I do if I was Miriam? What would I do if I was Emily? Those questions have stayed with me, and my prayer is that I could say, "Never," but who knows?

So, I hope you enjoyed reading *Never Say Never* as much as I enjoyed writing it. I often tell readers and new writers that the final product of my novels is a major team effort. My stories would never be good without the people who are committed to helping me become better, and for so many years, I've been blessed with the best team at Touchstone. First, I have to thank Heather Lazare, who always asks the questions that help me take my novels up a notch. We're two for two, Heather. And then Shida Carr—I could never thank you enough. You have been my publicist for eight years, and I truly believe that no one would know VCM without you. Thank you for every city, every interview, every ad, everything! To everyone else at Touchstone, from Editorial to Marketing, thank you for the years of cheering, encouraging, and just being in my corner.

In every part of my career, I've been blessed to have the best. And when Liza Dawson became my agent, that track record continued for me. Thank you, Liza, for making me feel like I'm the only client you have and for caring about me and my career beyond the next contract. With you, I know I have someone who cares about me for the long haul. It means so much that you believe in my writing. And you, too, Judith Engracia! Every time I call, you make me smile, and I know that I have no greater cheerleader. Thank YOU!

But even with the greatest of teams, none of this would matter if I didn't have the amazing support of the readers. What can I say? All I have is, "Wow!" From my friends on Facebook and Twitter, to everyone who decides to share their time with me when I'm out on tour, there would be no stories without you! Thank you for reading, thank you for spreading the news about my novels, and thank YOU for your encouragement. I write so that I can breathe, and I'm glad that I'm still breathing!

A special thank you to four people who gave me some "behind-the-scenes" knowledge so that I could make this novel more authentic. To one of my best friends, Monique Jewell Anderson, who helped me talk through this story. To my niece, Deundra Christopher, you gave me more insight about firefighters than you probably know. My Facebook friend, Angela Hardiman Hammond, I would never have been able to write the story of LaTonya without you. Thank you so much for taking the time to explain some of the basics to me. I had another Facebook friend who helped with the firefighters' story from the management side. I searched and searched through my messages and I could not find this young woman. But I really thank her, too.

Okay, I think that's it. I hope I didn't forget anyone. If I did, you know it has nothing to do with my heart, but more to do with these things that happen to a woman of a certain age. Now, on to the next book . . .

Never Say Never

After a devastating fire kills Miriam's firefighter husband, Chauncey, and leaves the surrounding community in shock, Miriam is not sure how she will ever be able to move on with her life. Left with three young sons, Miriam relies on her two best friends—Emily and Michellelee—and Emily's husband, Jamal, for support. But as she grieves, Miriam begins to develop a strong connection to Jamal. When the two spend more time together mourning the loss of Chauncey, they find themselves in the midst of a passionate affair born of their mutual sadness. *Never Say Never* tells the story of love, friendship, and betrayal, and ultimately asks, Can real love find a way to forgive?

For Discussion

1. *Never Say Never* begins in Miriam's voice, framing the story that follows as an explanation for her affair with Jamal. On page 2, she asks the reader, "Would you or wouldn't you?" Answer Miriam's question with your group members, weighing both Miriam's and Emily's sides.

2. Revisit the moment when Miriam must tell her sons that their father is dead, beginning on page 22. What role does Jamal play in this scene?

3. On page 43, Emily says, "I had to save Miriam from as much pain as I could. I had to make sure that she would get through, and know that every day, in every way, Jamal and I would be there for her." Discuss this quote, and try to decide whom you see as the victim in this story—Miriam or Emily?

4. Discuss the role of race in the novel. What is Miriam's initial reaction to Emily's interest in Jamal? What makes Miriam change her mind about the couple? Look back to pages 54–55.

5. "I didn't know why I felt a bit annoyed when he mentioned Emily. I mean, she was the one who was my friend. It was because of her that Jamal was even here with me so much" (page 107). Do you think that Miriam was out of line in wanting to spend so much time with Jamal? At one moment, did she cross the line from grieving widow to adulteress?

6. How would you characterize Jamal? Do you like him? Can you defend his action in any sense? How so?

7. How does the fire stand as a metaphor for all the problems presented in the novel? Consider the way fire moves quickly, is hot, and destroys everything in its path. If you had to name one character in the novel who is similar to the fire, who would it be? Why?

8. At the end of the novel, Pastor Ford hints to Emily that she could see the affair coming, that circumstances were ripe for Jamal to look for love and comfort outside of his marriage. Think back to the moment that Jamal, Emily, and Miriam were supposed to go out to lunch. If Emily had not had to go to the hospital to be with LaTonya, do you think the affair would have continued? Is it fair to blame Emily, in part, for the actions of Jamal and Miriam? Why or why not?

9. Many of the characters believe that if Miriam and Jamal had slept together only once, it would have been forgivable; repeated action was the real betrayal. Discuss with your group members. Can you come to a consensus on the ethics of this implication?

10. What role does faith play in the novel? Do you think that Jamal and Emily could have saved their marriage without Pastor Ford and faith?

11. In many ways, Michellelee is caught in the middle of the fight between her two best friends. She is the one who first discovered that Jamal and Miriam were sleeping together, and she is the one who forces reconciliation in the diner. She says to Miriam,

"I don't know how we're going to do it, but we'll find a way to be all right. We have to." (page 287). Do you think Michellelee is the voice of reason in the novel? If you had been Michelle-lee, would you have told Emily about your suspicions? Do you think Michellelee made the right choice in staying out of the fight?

12. Is forgiveness for those you love—even if it is not deserved—a theme of the novel? If not, what would you name as the theme of the novel? Why?

13. Discuss the ending of *Never Say Never*. Do you think that Emily and Jamal are going to make it as a couple? Why or why not?

A Conversation with Victoria Christopher Murray

You have received countless awards for your novels. Many reviews praise you; in particular, the *Clarion-Ledger* in Jackson, Mississippi, called your "vividness of faith . . . inspirational." What is your goal when writing?

I feel blessed that many see my writing as inspirational even though that's not my initial intent when I write. I know that, as a writer, I'm an entertainer, and that's what I set out to do first. But I always tell people that I am a Christian, and no matter what I do, my faith goes with me. I'm always glad when my faith "shows up" in my writing. If that can inspire someone, that's even better.

Who is your favorite character in *Never Say Never* and why? Do you relate to one of the women more than the others?

This book turned out to be one of my favorite books of all time because I haven't written too many non–African American characters. So writing Emily was a wonderful experience for me. I wanted to stay as true to her character as I could, and I had a lot of help with that from my editor. Emily is probably my favorite, but only by a little—because I find all of these characters just so interesting. I find Emily and Jamal's love amazing, and that was fun to write, because I can remember years ago when I was . . . "challenged" by interracial relationships. But then Miriam was wonderful to write because she was the victim . . . at first. And even I don't know when that changed. So . . . I know I didn't really answer the question. I loved them all.

Do you hope to break any stereotypes with this novel?

I'm not sure that I wanted to break stereotypes, but I did want to challenge us as women. I know many of my friends (and me!) for many years had issues when we saw black men with white women. (I'm just being honest!) And so in this book Emily is white, but she is the wife. As readers we usually cheer for the wife (except in the TV show *Scandal!*) I wanted to see if my readers would still cheer for Emily, or if the color of her skin made a difference. I cannot wait to get on the road and find out!

Why did you decide to tell this story from both Miriam's and Emily's points of view? In what ways does presenting both sides of the story change the course of the novel?

Telling both sides of the story is a no-brainer in this case. In this story, two sides had to be told. The story would have been incomplete with only Miriam's or Emily's voice.

At the end of *Never Say Never,* **you mention this real-life phenomenon that occurred after 9/11 where many firefighters were leaving their wives for their best friends' widows. Can you talk more about these events, what surprising discoveries you may have made in your research, and why you felt called to write about this phenomenon?**

I work out a lot of my issues through my writing. LOL! Seriously, when I read about something or hear about something, I wonder about it and then write about it so I can discover, What would I do? Everything I learned in the research of the fire departments' "dirty little secret," you read in the novel. The greatest thing I learned, however, was that before I wrote this book, I looked down on those husbands and widows who destroyed the wife's life. But after writing this book, all I can say is . . . never say never!

Do you agree that forgiveness, even when it is not deserved, is the theme of this novel? Why or why not?

First of all, I always think forgiveness is deserved. Because forgiveness is not about the other person. Forgiveness is for you—so the anguish won't grow on your heart. You deserve to have peace, and that's why forgiveness is always deserved. Now, is it the theme of this novel? Hmm . . . not sure about that. Before I started writing this novel, I had no idea where it was going to go. I was glad that Emily forgave Jamal . . . and Miriam. I was also glad that Emily realized she would never have the same relationship with Miriam. And Miriam realized that, too. Because you can forgive, but it's just a little more difficult to forget. . . .

As a writer, who are your influences? Where do you go to get inspired?

I'm inspired by the fact that I write full-time for a living, and I've developed wonderful relationships with food and shelter. I love eating and sleeping in a home, so I write because this is my job. I just happen to have a job that I love, that's my passion. I think I'm most influenced by pop culture, things that are going on in the world. I read a lot of books, watch a lot of movies; spend a lot of time studying people in airports, in parks, at the gym—wondering, What's their story? I can turn a man and a woman kissing at Starbucks into a four-hundred-page novel!

Do you think that Emily and Jamal's marriage will survive and that Miriam will learn to live without the two loves of her life? Can we rest assured that everyone in the novel will live as happily ever after as can be expected?

I'm not so sure I believe in happily ever after. *If* these were real people (and they're not, LOL!) I would hope that they would find happiness. Of course life is a road that is covered with speed bumps, but I think they will all find their way to where they're supposed to be.

Did writing this novel teach you any lessons? What lesson do you hope readers will take away from this story?

The greatest lesson *ever* . . . "never say never" is no longer just a cliché for me. It's real!

What is your next project? Can we expect to hear any more about Emily, Michellelee, and Miriam in future novels?

I think, I hope, I pray that this is the end for Emily, Michellelee, and Miriam. My next project does bring back characters that many are familiar with. I'm working on a sequel to *The Ex Files* called *Forever an Ex*. I was inspired to do this because *The Ex Files* has been optioned to become a movie, and the producer was saying that they love those characters so much that if there was more to their story, they may be able to even do a series. So I'm just giving them what they want! :-)

Enhance Your Book Club

1. Throughout *Never Say Never*, Emily refers to her favorite movie to watch with Jamal: *Love Story*. Have a movie night with your reading group and rent this classic 1970 film. Discuss the ways in which the film mirrors Emily and Jamal's relationship. Why do you think the couple loved this movie so much?

2. After a tragedy, some people react in ways that are often bizarre and shocking, while other people manage stress and grief more traditionally, such as turning to faith and organized religion or spending more time with a loved one. Have a "share" night in which your group members share the ways in which they deal with grief in their own lives. Do you reach out to others, or do you keep to yourself? Do you express your emotions through writing, exercise, or art, or do you prefer to sleep through the pain? Decide which character you resemble most in the way you handle grief and stress. Are you like Miriam and Jamal, who need comfort; or more like Emily, who needed to bury herself in her job?

3. Many of Victoria Christopher Murray's books are entertaining and instructive, making them the perfect choice for a book club selection. Have your book club read *Destiny's Divas*; *The Deal, the Dance, and the Devil*; or *Too Little, Too Late*. Afterward, consider how these books are similar to *Never Say Never*. What common themes can be found woven into all of Victoria Christopher Murray's novels?